black

ANGELINA J. STEFFORT

black

WINGS BOOK 2

Black

In This Series:
White
Black
Gray
Spark: Adam's Story
Fire: Adam's Story
Ashes: Adam's Story
Crash: A Wings Prequel

First published 2017

Copyright © by Angelina J. Steffort 2017

All characters and events in this publication, other than those clearly in the public domain, are fictitious and any resemblance to real persons, living or dead, is purely coincidental.

All rights reserved.

No part of this publication may be reproduced, stored in a retrieval system, or transmitted, in any form or by any means, without prior permission in writing of the publisher, nor be otherwise circulated in any form of binding or cover other than that in which it is published and without a similar condition including this condition being imposed on the subsequent purchaser.

Print: ISBN 978-3950441826
Ebook: ASIN B0774H9KJG

Cover by Fantastical Ink
Typeset int EB Garamond

MK
www.ajsteffort.com

"I love good and pleasure, I hate evil and pain, I want to be happy and I am not mistaken in believing, that people, angels and even demons have those same inclinations."

--Nicolas Malebranche

Prologue

JADEN

What are nineteen years compared to the eternity of a millennium? I asked myself as I looked at her tormented face. She seemed older than she was when comprehension was written all heavy on her features like that.

I felt her pain in my own body. It was almost unbearable. How did this fragile form stand that all-consuming ache?

I had felt many fosterlings' pain. Too many times I had suffered with them. It was my duty as their guardian angel. It was a burden. It made me feel incomplete—human. I hated to be bound to feel with them—I couldn't live without it; it was my destiny. As long as I would live, I was going to suffer over and over again.

But this girl was different. I hated that I was willingly suffering with her. I would suffer *for* her now if that was possible. She wasn't mine to look after, not anymore. Still, I couldn't help caring about her—more than was good for one ancient supernatural such as me.

Her mouth twitched as she rolled over to one side. I sat still, motionless, glad that she had finally fallen asleep. I wanted to give her as much time to rest, to escape, as possible. I owed her that.

My hand lay on hers. The contact they made comforted me. It made it feel more real that she was still there. When I had seen her crouching on the roof, I thought that I had lost her, that she was going to disappear into the darkness like her angel.

She hadn't. Instead, she was lying here with me, pale and breakable.

"Adam," her weak whisper touched my ears. "Adam... Adam," over and over again.

He wasn't the one to suffer with her, the one to be here, anytime, to look after her. He was dead. And still, it was his name that was escaping her lips, not mine...

It wasn't just an eternity of suffering; it was an eternity of inequity, too.

I squeezed her hand softly one last time before I left her to her fate and took off to follow my other duties...

1.
Trauma

CLAIRE

The room looked the same as always, except for the feathers, which were floating midair. They were a shiny white but they looked soft and strong at the same time.

I lifted my eyes to the ceiling, half-expecting to find strings holding the feathers in place. Instead of strings and a ceiling, I found cloudless, blue skies. A light breeze was playing with my hair, drawing strands of it upward, letting them float like Medusa's snaky curls. The feathers hung motionless. They seemed to not be affected by the soft stream of air at all.

Above me, a shadow circled in the sky. It had a human shape with two large wings spreading left and right from his shoulders.

"Adam," I called to the shadow. "How can you stay up in the air when the feathers of your wings are down here?"

I watched him circle for a while before he answered.

"Yes—" He looked down at his wings. "I suppose you— are right," he simply said, and then, without further warning, he plunged from the sky, crashing to the ground with an earsplitting thud.

"Adam!" I knelt down beside him, cautiously, on the wooden floor of my room. He was hunched under the window, the shine of a million stars lighting the space around him.

"Are you alright, Adam?"

With a feeling of utter terror creeping through my body, I took in the sight. His wings weren't the same as I remembered them. Instead of white feathers covering the surface, there was thin air filling the gaps between forks of pale bone...

I woke up with a scream stuck in my throat. I had stopped letting the screams escape after a few days, but the dreams kept returning, and there was nothing I could do about it. Even if I could, nothing would change—he would still be gone forever, rotting in a coffin somewhere beneath the cold ground.

Get a grip, I told myself, although I knew it wouldn't help. I shook out of the quilt and reluctantly got to my feet. The floor was filled with shadows drawing dark lines and shapes across the room, starting under the window. Through the glass, I could see countless stars in the dark winter sky. Half-expecting to find Adam hunching on the floor beneath, my gaze shot back down even though I knew what I would see there. Nothing but bare wood.

The horrors of the former weeks crushed down on me with full weight, filling my head with images—images I'd rather lock up in the darkest corner of my mind. Images of a perfect creature being smashed by the force of evil. Images of Adam being killed by demons.

The fact that I'd been in love with a man who had turned out to be an angel was growing more irrelevant by the hour, and so was the fact that he had been killed. The only fact relevant now was that he had been killed because of me, to protect me, that it was entirely my fault that he was dead. And he had taken a piece of my soul with him because I was the one who had made him spread his wings for the very first time—I was his catalyst, his mark. Our souls had been interlinked, twined forever—or as long as both of us lived. The moment one of us died, the other would suffer forever with the pain of the loss—or go insane.

I wondered if I would be able to recognize insanity when it hit me. It surely felt like I already arrived there. Hardly an hour passed without my mind brimming with images of Adam. Every moment, waking or sleeping, he was there, filling my thoughts.

No matter how many times my sister Sophie and her boyfriend Ian had tried to talk to me and make me feel better, it seemed I was resistant to any type of better. All I knew was the constant dark cloud obscuring my vision and my feelings, the ache inside my heart that felt like someone was wrapping it up with barbed wire, the desperate wish to evade this feeling of utter inchoateness for even a fraction of a second.

I turned on the spot and, without bothering to switch a light on, made my way out of the room and down the hall to the bathroom. The door swung open willingly under the pressure of my fingers. Behind it, darkness stretched. I found the darkness welcome, a perfect match for my inner being. My hands searched the room for the basin and twisted the handle of the tap for cold water.

The melodic sound of cool liquid trickling from metal to ceramic ceased the continuous flow of thoughts and calmed my mind for a moment. I held my hands out to wet them then pressed the palms to my face. I barely felt them. My body was still numb with the shock of the past events. So I sat down on the edge of the bathtub and decided to just stay there and listen.

The water reminded me of Adam. I could almost hear the pattering of the rain on that day we'd sat in Noel's coffee shop. The barbed wire tore through my heart afresh as images of the two of us were stealing their way into my mind—Adam and me, sitting inside, talking, kissing, while outside tons of water pouring from the sky were covering the ground with a ruffled film of wet.

Unable to stand the sound—and the memories it brought up—I got back to my feet after a minute or two and turned off the tap with a groan. I sank to the floor in shame and pain and buried my face in my hands, not wanting to believe that, once again, I was destroyed and adrift. After I had lost my parents in a car accident a few years ago, I had never wanted to see myself grieve like that over anything again. I had been determined to be strong and live my life with my sister, who was my only living relative. But all of the quiet of my small but well-structured existence had been whirled around by the most beautiful creature I had ever seen. Adam. I had fallen in love with an angel who had brought me back to life, given me a reason to smile and be happy again, and had made me more confident and courageous than I had ever thought I could be.

And here I was—back to mourning, back to pain—torn and broken like I had never been before. I heard my quiet sobs reflecting off the bathroom walls as I tried to stifle them in my forearms. Still, sobs continued to shake me until another sound mixed with them: footsteps coming from the corridor.

"Claire?" It was my sister's voice.

The door swung open, and I lifted my head to look at her as she entered the room.

"What's the matter, Claire?" Sophie's voice was cautious as she crouched beside me without touching. I could sense how frightened and uncertain she was about how to handle this little drama in the middle of the night, and I loved her for trying, not just now but ever since that awful phone call to tell her Adam was dead.

We both knew that I wasn't stable right now. I hadn't been in a while. I was happy enough to live through the seemingly endless days and cold and dark nights. Sophie didn't ask too many questions. Instead, she acknowledged my loss as a valid reason for my tormented mood, and I was grateful. I couldn't stand another minute, explaining why I was feeling like my heart had been ripped from my chest—the true reason would never be spoken between us. Sophie couldn't know the truth about Adam, and that left me helpless and alone in my misery.

"Can't sleep," I lied without hesitation. I didn't want her to know that I was still being haunted by the ghosts of the tragedy. I wanted to appear stable to the rest of the world. It helped me stay coherent, at least, for a while, when I acted like everything was fine; but usually, my mind didn't let me trick myself into believing that was the case for too long. After a very short phase of numbness, the pain returned—always. How I wished it wouldn't.

"Come on," Sophie held out her hand for me and waited for me to take it. "I'll make you hot milk with honey."

She smiled at me with this far too motherly expression in her eyes.

"Honestly, Sophie," I said as I ignored her hand and scrambled to my feet on my own. "You don't have to do this."

"But I want to," she said as we both walked barefoot downstairs.

"You've dreamed of him again, haven't you?" Sophie asked carefully, not taking her eyes off the mug of milk as she poured.

It didn't take a word to let her know she was right—my silence gave away more than I intended.

"It will stop," she placed the mug in the microwave. "It will stop. You'll be better soon."

The door of the microwave was startlingly loud as it snapped shut under Sophie's hand.

"—like with mom and dad, remember? You'll be better."

I snorted in reply.

"I know you think you won't—but you will. You'll see. In a few weeks or months..."

"Pfft," I dismissed her assurances with a disdainful puff of breath.

"Or years or decades," I finished her sentence sarcastically. "—how about maybe *never*?"

Sophie watched me for a few seconds. The ringing sound of the microwave announcing that the milk was ready made us both turn our heads. She fetched the mug out from behind the glass door and spooned in some honey.

Immediately, I was sorry when she merely pressed her lips together and handed me the mug.

"Drink," she commanded gently, "you'll be able to sleep."

I took the mug from her hands and carried it up to my room. I heard her climbing the stairs behind me.

"Thanks," I said over my shoulder, putting remorse in my voice and closing the door quietly behind me. I switched on the light and turned to my bed.

Clang! The mug hit the floor where it shattered to pieces, soaking the pair of jeans that lay beside my desk with milk.

I had stared at the bed for only a few seconds before I heard Sophie's knock on my door.

"Are you alright, Claire?" Her voice sounded through the wood.

"Yes, I'm fine," I said, trying to keep my voice casual. "Just bumped my knee."

"Sure?"

I turned back and opened the door only a few inches, blocking the view of my room from her.

"I'm fine. I don't know about the bed frame, though." I forced a smile.

Would she buy that? She smiled back at me with relief.

"Good night then," Sophie said.

"Yeah, good night," I repeated, the tone of my voice climbing up nervously.

Sophie turned and walked back to her room. I didn't move until I heard the click of her bedroom door, and then I whirled around furiously to face the bed.

"Sorry," Jaden said before I could open my mouth to speak. "I didn't mean to startle you."

I eyed the beautiful creature sitting on my bed for a while. His incredibly golden hair shifted a little as he tilted his head apologetically.

Disarmed, I could only sigh. Jaden, my guardian angel. He deserved an outburst from me, I thought.

After doing everything to keep me alive after Adam's death, Jaden had eventually left me to myself. I had been expecting him to stay with me to ease my pain and help me through the darkest days of my life. To reassure me that all of the supernatural forces I had felt with Adam coming into my life had not completely abandoned me after his death.

Instead, he had disappeared, leaving me to figure it all out on my own—how to get up every morning from unrefreshing sleep, how to go to school and come home again, how to keep my friends as friends, and how to not be a burden to my sister. How to want to go on living in the torture chamber of my life after Adam.

I was basically alone now, all dependent on my self-motivation and ability to take good care of myself—an ability I appeared to have lost long ago, in another, unreal-seeming time that was only a hazy memory of happiness to me.

We looked at each other for a few seconds while I could feel my anger returning and, with it, the desire to chastise him.

"So, where have you been?" I whispered, grimacing the words as if I was screaming them at him, and choosing to overlook the reality that I didn't know the first thing about how angels worked. Or, for that matter, why. Which meant it was a stupid question.

After the countless times he had turned up out of thin air beside me, I shouldn't be surprised he had done so yet again.

Jaden was my age today, a choice he usually made when we appeared together in public. In truth, he was nearly a thousand years old and could assume any age he pleased. I had seen him appear as a seventy-year-old man and a seven-year-old boy. His twenty-year-old self looked dazzling. In the back of my mind, I wondered why he had chosen that appearance tonight since there was no one else around.

"I was unable to get in contact for a while," Jaden said softly.

"Okay," I responded sourly and bent down to mop up the spilled milk with a towel. "Do I get to know why?"

I wasn't going to let him off the hook with just that.

"Claire, it's complicated." Jaden tried to excuse his absence.

"Try me," I challenged. "I think I can keep up."

And suddenly, irrationally, my tears began to flow. I was overwhelmed by feelings of loneliness and emptiness. Adam was gone, and Jaden seemed to be playing games about whether he was in or out of my life. I was caught half-in and half-out of a world of the supernatural with no one I could share that with. I had decided that Chris, Adam's father and an angel himself, was off-limits to me as I didn't want to bother him while he dealt with his own grief. Almost certainly, I would be hunted to the death by Adam's killers, and there was nothing I could do about it. Even Jaden would not be able to save me, assuming Jaden would even be there. I had never felt weaker or more alone. I was crushed beneath a weight I didn't understand and couldn't fight off.

I closed my eyes to prevent more liquid from escaping past them.

"Don't cry, Claire." Jaden's voice whispered beside my ear. His hand curled around my neck and pulled my head against his shoulder.

My eyes flew open reflexively. He must have teleported from the bed to my chair the second I had closed my eyes. Without a doubt, he had read my emotions—a mixture of being positively angry with him for leaving me alone, my grief for Adam, and the all-consuming fear of what was going to become of me, combined with constant pain flaring in my insides like flames licking my body, soul, and psyche.

"Shhh—" Jaden pulled me tight to him. "I'm here. No need to worry now."

I dug my fingers into his shoulders to prove to myself that he wasn't a hallucination—I didn't trust myself with anything these days. If it wasn't for the constant pain, I would sometimes be a hundred percent sure it had been a dream; but it hadn't, and Jaden being here with me was living proof.

My guardian angel cradled me in his arms and hummed to me soothingly. He didn't complain about my fingers clawing him. I felt more tears wet my face and soak his shirt. The way he held me comforted me a little. It took away the anger, the fear—but not the pain. The pain was too intangible to ease it with a physical touch. It was too real in every fiber of myself.

"I'm glad you're back," I sobbed into his shirt. I was sure he felt the relief that was flowing through me that very second. "Will you stay for a while?"

"I'm not sure how long I can."

I felt his body stiffen as he felt my disappointment.

"But, I'm here now. Don't worry for the moment. I'll stay as long as I possibly can."

For some reason, his words didn't convince me I wouldn't be alone within minutes again.

I tore away, out of his embrace, and tried to catch his gaze.

"What's kept you away?"

Jaden's eyes turned to the ceiling. They were unnaturally golden in the artificial light that was brightening my room in this very early hour of the day.

"Do you think you can pop up in my life, keep me from killing myself, and then vanish like nothing happened—" I accused.

"There is hardly anything I *can* do." Jaden's voice was cold and controlled, the usual softness in his eyes gone. He took a step away from me and leaned against my desk where he froze into a statue.

"What do you mean, *can do*?"

Happy as I had been to have him back a second ago, he was strongly irritating me now.

"As I said—complicated." The dissatisfying answer shot from his unmoving lips in an unmelodious flow.

I turned so I faced him fully.

"As *I* said—I can keep up." I pointed a finger at him and touched the fingertip to his chest. "Shoot!"

Jaden's eyes wandered off again, searching the room for something—I imagined it could be the right words—before they locked on mine.

"You don't want to know everything—believe me."

I coughed at his words. "I think *I* very well know what I want and what I don't." The way he looked at me made me feel like a misbehaving little child.

"Believe me—knowing that I wasn't there is enough information. You don't necessarily need to know where I have been and what has kept me." The words seemed a little bit more like an excuse than an explanation. The way he was rolling his gaze across the walls while he talked to me gave me a vague idea of how bad the truth might be.

"Just tell me you weren't held by the demons," I stressed. An image of Jaden's body, bent under the force of Volpert's power, shot up in my head. I could almost hear him scream in pain as my imagination played me a vivid movie of my worst fears.

The fear was certainly plain on my face. I could tell by the way Jaden darted toward me and cupped my face in his hand.

"No," he said, almost toneless.

I felt my psyche snapping again. Tears were blurring my vision, making my lashes stick together in blond clusters around the rims of my eyes.

"Don't you worry about me," he said with a smile that looked almost natural. "I can take good care of myself."

I nodded halfheartedly.

"You should go back to sleep." Jaden took my arm and led me to the bed with gentle force. "You've got school tomorrow."

I let him press me down and tuck me under the blanket. He sat down beside me and took one of my hands into his.

"Cry if you need to," he said. "It's okay. Nothing is going to be better if you don't."

"It hurts, Jaden—so much I'm not sure I'm able to live through this for much longer." It felt so good not having to hide anything. With Jaden, I could be myself, whether I wanted to or not.

"I know—" he squeezed my hand and smiled wryly. "I am feeling whatever you feel—right now, it's almost unbearable."

I rolled my head to the side as Jaden reached out to touch my cheek. He stroked it once. "You're so much stronger than you give yourself credit for."

A second later, he had vanished from my bed, and the switch of the light clicked the room into darkness. Another second, and Jaden's weight reappeared beside me. He had teleported over to the switch and back.

A soft golden glow was hovering over me—Jaden's eyes. They were staring at me out of the darkness.

"Time to sleep."

Jaden's hand pressed down on mine, and I felt myself drifting into blackness. The last thought I could form was the wish that I would finally wake up from this nightmare. Then everything went dark.

The alarm clock tore me from the first restful hours I'd had in weeks. I knew I had to get up, find some clothes, and get presentable for school, but my eyelids were too heavy right now to lift them. I liked Saturdays and Sundays better. On the weekends, I wasn't forced to go outside and be around people—something that had been exhausting me lately. I lay there, listening to the alarm, for a short while—a minute, maybe less—before I reluctantly lifted my hand to mute the noise. On the way from under the blanket to my bedside table, my hand bumped into something warm and hard. My eyes fluttered open in surprise.

"Good morning, Claire," Jaden greeted me from unexpectedly close by. My hand was lying against his chest where it had hit it. He was resting on his side on the edge of my bed, propped on his elbow, his head in his hand. "Wait a second."

He turned around in a swift movement and silenced the alarm. Then he turned back and eyed me critically.

"You don't look rested at all—though you looked like you did rest in the last couple of hours. Your eyes were closed and your breathing even, at least."

"I had a dreamless sleep." I sat up and shook out of the blanket. "That's good, I suppose." But seeing Jaden meant I hadn't dreamed the last weeks. It meant that everything was real. And that was how I still felt. Empty and aching.

I left Jaden lying on my bed and got to my feet to hurry through the morning routine. I didn't even look at the clothes I was pulling out of the closet. I didn't care whether the colors matched; I just slipped into them, trying to keep a grip on myself as long as possible. If I had to go to school today, I didn't want to make a fool of myself, sobbing through the lessons—again. I just wanted to vanish for a while, become invisible to the world. This was why I had done only the most necessary things during the past weeks and spent most of my free time at home in my room. I felt a little safer there than elsewhere.

"Should I take you?" Jaden stood beside me and watched me tie my shoelaces with a worried expression on his young face.

I shot him an ambivalent frown. I didn't want to be alone outside, but I didn't want to attract attention either, and I definitely would when Jaden was with me. He was quite a looker, and simply everybody would notice us entering the school grounds together. I also feared the endless stream of questions my friend Amber would throw at me the moment we would be alone. Jaden would be her type—tall, beautiful, mysterious. I didn't want her to be put in any danger because of the people I was being surrounded with.

"Er—no, thank you."

"Sure?" He ran his hand through strands of golden hair, which were dancing on his forehead as he looked down at me. "I was headed in that direction anyway—I could drive you."

I examined my shoes for a second, buying time before I got to my feet.

"Maybe if you drop me off far enough from the entrance so nobody asks questions—"

"Sure—" He opened the front door for me.

I half-expected Nigel, my cat, to be waiting outside, looking at me with big yellow eyes, but he was gone. Demons had killed him to hurt me, to give me a sign that they could get to me anywhere, anytime. I had understood, and I still felt like they might pop up any second, aiming for me this time. But in reality, outside, everything was exactly like it should be at the end of a cold February. The sun was still hiding behind thick clouds, and the dim light told me that winter wouldn't be over for a while.

Sophie's car was already gone. I figured she was at the campus early, for some reason. I hadn't heard her get up and leave the house. On the end of the driveway, a very elegant slate-colored car was parked under a leafless tree.

"Since when do you own a car?" I asked, surprised as he led the way to the gray vehicle. "I thought you travel by teleporting."

"Usually I do, but right now, I'm in need of a presentable, human way of locomotion." His eyes glimmered mysteriously as he quickly looked at the handle of the shiny gray door.

He got into the car and waited for me to climb in on the passenger side.

"Do you like it?" he asked in an unusually insecure voice.

"It's a nice ride." I had a quick look at the interior. "A bit flashy, maybe."

Jaden started the engine, and we rolled off toward Aurora High School. I watched the houses fly by outside. A knot was forming in my stomach, big enough to fill my entire torso. The pain in my heart was throbbing constantly. I was glad I had at least managed to have seemingly normal conversations with everyone at school. My fellow students would think I was depressed or sad, but they wouldn't know I was in continuous pain. Only Jaden would know. And he didn't comment on it all of the time. He very well knew there was hardly anything he could do about how I felt. All he could do was stay with me and suffer with me. And it was a lot more than I would ever expect anyone to do for me. Nobody should suffer like that. It was inhuman.

"Just drop me off here." I pointed at a driveway a few streets from the school buildings.

Jaden pulled in and let me get out of the car.

"Thanks for dropping me off—and thank you for staying with me last night. In fact, it was a lot more restful than all the other nights since—" I swallowed and let my chin sink down.

Jaden nodded, understanding without me finishing the sentence.

"You're welcome."

"When will you come back?" I asked through the open door. My hand clamped the handle fiercely as if I could hold the car in place with only my grip.

"We will meet sooner than you expect." He winked at me.

Hesitantly, my fingers detached from the cold metal. The door fell shut with a noise that said very *expensive car*, and Jaden half-opened the passenger window.

"Take care," he said through the gap and then rolled off into the morning traffic of Aurora.

My eyes followed the gray car until they couldn't make it out in the stream of vehicles.

It was a raw morning, and the sidewalks were damp. After a minute of walking, I reached the parking lot. It was full of students who were all heading toward the main building. I quietly filed in between people I didn't know and made my way down the hall toward the classroom. I knew that my chances of staying unnoticed were infinitesimally small. Somehow though, I hoped that Amber, Lydia, and Greg, my best friends, would realize I wasn't in the mood to be social. I honestly wished they wouldn't mind me staying the passive element of our clique. All I wanted was to be, to exist—I couldn't handle more. Existing and not feeling was my biggest desire. Since I couldn't escape the barbed wire tearing through my heart and what was left of my soul, all I could do was live through another day, tormented by memories and ashamed that my emotions were so obvious on my face. Having my friends around me would give me a somewhat secure space to exist.

I stepped through the classroom door, my books clamped tightly to my chest as if to shield myself from the looks I knew would be coming my way. I was used to heads turning in my direction. It happened every day. People thought they knew the story, and they did, to a degree. They knew the official story I had given out. My boyfriend had committed suicide one night at a party. What else they thought they knew, I couldn't tell. We'd had a fight? He had been high? He had been mentally unstable all along and showed up suddenly at our school because he needed to get away from where people knew his history? And certainly, there was speculation about my role in his death. I was either a fool to fall so hard for a guy with no provable past, or I was an awful person, capable of ruining a nice guy's life. Some people's eyes told me it was my fault Adam had felt an irresistible death wish. The way they looked at me didn't leave any doubts. For a week or so, I had wondered what they might be thinking, but then I figured out that needing to know was just one more weight on my heart, and I was better off blocking it out.

I pretended not to notice the secretive whispering behind my back. I didn't care anymore who it was or what they said. Nothing they thought or shared was of any concern to me anymore. Getting through the days was all that mattered. I didn't pay attention to the way they looked away, blushing when I caught them staring or whispering.

I sat in the back row all the time now, invisible to my classmates—which was what I wanted to be. And I was grateful that my teachers, at least for the moment, left me alone. It was a good place to hide from their gazes during classes. Most of the teachers didn't bother to ask me anything—they knew I wouldn't have an answer for them, no matter what the question would be.

Sophie had insisted on me going back to school a few days after the funeral. She said it would be the best way to get my life back. She had pried on me for a while, monitoring me closely for signs of an eating disorder like after our parents' deaths, knowing that could derail my life all by itself. But I went to school every day, and I ate reasonably well, and I could hold a sensible conversation, so that gave her hope that things would work out okay eventually. I said nothing to her about any recovery I expected to make. She had no idea Adam's death wasn't as simple as it seemed and that the indescribable fear, suffering, and horror I had experienced went far, far beyond the tragic loss of a friend and the ending of a teenage romance. What the loss of Adam and his violent death had done to me was irreparable.

As I reached the back of the classroom, Lydia joined me at a table.

"Hey, Claire," she smiled at me, kind and warm like the person she was.

I gave her what messed up curved line my mouth remembered a smile to feel like in return. From the way it felt on my face, I was positive that it looked like a distorted grimace.

"How was your weekend?" Amber joined us. She took a seat in the row before us and turned around in her chair to talk to us.

"Not so good."

I knew, without looking, that Lydia was rolling her eyes.

"Richard and I had a fight—again."

Richard was the younger brother of Ian, Sophie's boyfriend. Lydia and Richard had met at our house at one of Sophie's college parties and clicked immediately. They made a cute couple. Although lately, it seemed the course of true love was not running smoothly. I had a hard time staying interested in their boring little squabbles. Instead of trying, I stared out the window and scanned the parking lot, searching for a distraction. It was only feeling a new energy in the room that brought me back. Students were shifting in their chairs, and there was a wave of nudging, giggling, and whispering.

"—and will finish this last year of school at Aurora High. Please give him a warm welcome," Ms. Fields finished, and there was a smattering of applause while a couple of the more outgoing boys aired their social savvy by saying *welcome* and *glad to meet you.*

I would have looked up front to see what the commotion was about, except that at that very second, a private little lightning bolt immobilized me. From my seat, I could see a car in the parking lot that somehow stood out in the humdrum line of student vehicles. It was a very nice car. It was slate-colored. And a little flashy.

2.
Shadow

My eyes snapped to the front of the class. A pair of awesomely golden eyes stared back at me.

"I hope you'll like it here, Mr. Ableton," Ms. Fields said to him. "There is a free seat in the second row. Just on the left, over there." She pointed at a table near Greg. I hadn't noticed him come in and sit down there, just as I hadn't noticed our new *student* enter the classroom.

"Thank you, Ms. Fields." The sound of his voice was soothing even when he didn't talk to me.

I watched him walk over to where the teacher had directed him. His movements were smooth and elegant—worthy of an immortal. He wore jeans and an ordinary, black, long-sleeved shirt. The clothes were hiding his majestic posture in usualness.

Not a girl in the room wasn't looking at him, those slim hips and broad shoulders sliding gracefully into his seat and that impossibly golden hair. Even Ms. Fields' eyes followed him with curiosity.

Before he glided into his seat, Jaden turned toward me for a second. I saw a slight glow in his eyes, though it could have been the reflection of the light. I didn't trust my senses these days.

Once Jaden was seated, Ms. Fields returned to normal and began to talk about an upcoming test—she was determined to teach us something useful. It was clear none of the girls were likely to grasp anything just then.

"Geez," I muttered and earned a dirty look from Amber, who was obviously fascinated.

If any of them knew what he was—

I imagined Jaden telling them his true age or changing his appearance to that of a sixty-year-old man—then they wouldn't be that excited.

I got through the first class of the day by spending my time building various scenarios of what Jaden's story would be. Would it be a standard *my-parents-moved-so-I-had-no-choice*-story or a scary *I-really-did-bad-stuff-at-another-school-and-they-strongly-suggested-a-change-of-scenery-would-be-good-for-all-concerned*-story—I was looking forward to what he had made up.

I wished I could read minds so I would know what Jaden was up to. It was very likely that he had chosen to play the student in order to keep a closer eye on me during the days, and I didn't know if I liked the idea or not. Another, but unlikely intention, could be a wish to feel human—but this would be too much of a coincidence.

The bell tore me from my thoughts. I hadn't copied one of the calculations from the blackboard to my notebook. Instead, I had scribbled meaningless patterns. I didn't even look at them as I put the notebook away into my bag.

"Biology next," Lydia told me, sounding impatient.

"What's up?" I quizzed, studying her face.

"You don't look too happy," I told her.

"I was just wondering what they all want with him—" She nodded to the scene across the room. Jaden was literally trapped at his desk, surrounded by students, mostly the girls and especially Amber, who was perched on his table and playing with a strand of her black hair while flashing a fabulous smile.

Jaden seemed somewhat lost between the bunch of girls fighting for his attention. I could only guess what was going on inside him right now. If he felt every single thing they were feeling, he might become overwhelmed within seconds—but then, Jaden was an old angel and could probably handle it. Most likely, he had experienced situations like these before.

"Like we couldn't guess what's going on," I said sarcastically. I slung my bag over my shoulder. "Let's get going. If we're fast, we might snatch a seat in the back of the biology class."

Lydia nodded, and we headed out of the room into the corridor. Jaden didn't look up as we hurried past him. I interpreted it as a sign he preferred pretending like we didn't know each other.

"Wait a second!" Greg joined us a few steps outside the door. "Can you believe it? This guy sets foot into our school, and within seconds, all the chicks are freaking out."

"I don't know what they see in him—" I said, trying to sound casual and disinterested. But I felt a little off-balance, suddenly awake to Jaden's remarkable beauty that shone so brilliantly when compared to the ordinary boys at Aurora High.

Until now, I had never fully appreciated how beautiful he was. I had always had other things on my mind when he had been around. Pain and guilt and fear. I had never looked at him that way. For me, he had been the one who had taken care of me when I had most needed it, even when I hadn't known I needed him—age or looks hadn't played a role in our relationship. I had seen him as a young boy as well as an old man. There was hardly any way I could see him as the normal teenager he pretended to be.

"Yeah," Greg nodded. "He's *just* a new student, for heaven's sake. Nobody paid attention to us on our first school day here."

"I remember something different," I disagreed.

"That's because you joined when we'd been having classes together for a year or two. You were the new mysterious girl."

"I wasn't." I chewed my fingernails while we were walking down the corridor to the biology class. I remembered my first day here too well. I had been all alone at first, but it hadn't taken long until people had started showing interest in me. I had spent most of the breaks in the bathroom, hiding from people, unable to feel comfortable in crowds like these. Greg, Lydia, and Amber had been the only people being kind to me. They hadn't been nosy. They had just helped me find my classrooms and sat with me during lunch breaks, letting me eat in silence, telling me a bit about themselves, the school, the town. I hadn't felt the pressure to tell them everything. They had just let me be who I was. It hadn't taken long for me to feel comfortable in Aurora, and they were the reason why I had been able to blend in so well, so fast.

"It's just unfair he gets all the attention—" Greg went on complaining.

"Oh, come on, Greg," I said, perhaps a little too brusquely if I was supposed to be disinterested in the new boy. "Suck it up! They'll do that 'till he decides on one of them, and the rest of them will sulk and go back to doing whatever they've done before."

I could already imagine how Jaden would eventually fall for one of them—some of the girls in my year were very pretty—and then abandon his primal plan—whatever it was. I just hoped he wouldn't be in biology. The feeling of constant observation was something I honestly didn't appreciate. I hoped Jaden knew.

As we turned around the corner and walked in, the classroom was empty. I chose a seat in the back corner of the room and settled there. Lydia and Greg sat down beside me.

"You look better today," Lydia commented.

"Probably because I slept at least a few hours," I answered darkly.

"Probably," Lydia commented, not pressing any deeper into the topic. She knew that I didn't talk about Adam. The usual pain tore through my body with the barbed wire cutting through my heart as Adam's name sprang to mind. This topic was an absolute no-go, and she completely respected that all of the time.

The plan had been to get to biology early enough to find seats in the back, and it worked all too well.

We had five minutes to kill before the room began to fill up, and I occupied myself by staring uncomprehendingly at the writing on the blackboard. Amber was the last to arrive. Amber and Jaden, actually. I couldn't quite tell if Jaden had fallen for her charms yet, but it was plain that Amber had fallen for his. She sparkled and shone as she nabbed two chairs next to each other at the front and turned the full light of her lovely eyes on him, not taking any notice of us sitting in the back.

For a second or two, my stomach twisted. It was a pang of jealousy. Jaden hadn't even looked at me, not to mention talked to me. Maybe his showing up at school didn't have anything to do with keeping an eye on me. Maybe he really just wanted to experience high school again—had he been in high school before? I was positive he knew everything he needed for a university diploma and more; but had he, in all of his years of existence, ever attended school?

I watched them for a while until Mr. Jackson, the biology teacher, claimed our attention. It took less than a minute before my thoughts wandered off once more and I began replaying Adam's death in my head. I remembered the roof as clearly as if I was standing there right now. The sound of the gravel being stepped on by heavy shoes was vividly present in my ears. I could almost feel the cold night air, and then I saw Adam being hit by the ray of silver light shooting from the demons' hands, Adam falling backward off the roof, spreading his wings, looking at me with his beautiful green eyes—

I took a deep breath. How could it be that even if I didn't want to think of him, my mind knew little more to ponder about than him? It was self-destructive, the way he kept springing to my thoughts. Everything reminded me of him, even the most ordinary things like a water faucet or a coffee cup or a flower; like the red rose I had thrown onto his coffin before the wet earth had swallowed him forever at the funeral.

A tear ran down my cheek before I could get a grip on myself. I quickly dried it with the sleeve of my shirt. I was surprised as I took in the color of the shirt. It was light blue. How on earth had I ended up wearing a light blue shirt when everything inside me was bleeding. I felt more like black or gray at least. Making a mental note to start caring about what I put on in the mornings, I forced my attention back to the classroom.

Mr. Jackson was talking about DNA and RNA and how the body was able to reproduce its own chromosomes. Only some of the students were paying attention. I tried to but found myself unable to keep track for longer than a few minutes.

Amber was copying notes into her book. I watched her hair moving on her shoulder as she kept writing. She seemed concentrated on what she was doing—unlike Jaden. He had turned his head to the side. His eyes were directed at the back of the class—at me. A big question mark was displaying on his face. He didn't lower his gaze as I caught him staring at me. I felt myself blush and looked out of the window, hoping to hide my embarrassment, and then instantly remembered that Jaden felt whatever I was feeling anyway.

It wasn't too long before the bell saved me for the second time this day. I got to my feet and grabbed my things before I headed for the lockers where I swapped my books for my gym uniform.

PE was the one class I looked forward to these days. It distracted me, kept me physically busy. All of my thoughts, the pain, and my fear rested for a little while when I could run several laps or climb ropes. The way coach Laney expected us to give everything forced me to remain focused on my muscles, my breathing, and my pulse. Everything else was forced to retreat into the background.

Amber joined me as I ran my laps much too fast for warm-up.

"The new guy is so hot," she told me between several rhythmical breaths.

I didn't look at her but sped up a little instead.

"He's gorgeous, and I walked him to biology in the morning. He's really nice." She slowed the talking, trying to keep pace with me.

"You don't know him, do you?" I threw at her, critically.

"And you do?" she replied coolly.

"Nope," I breathed, well aware that sooner or later, our paths would cross during classes and we eventually would have to talk. I honestly hoped nobody would notice that Jaden and I were quite familiar.

"Well—I'm going to sit with him at lunch today." She sounded almost proud. "And guess what—he asked." With a wide grin, she pulled me off the field toward a small bench at the side of the gym. "I think he's good-looking and nice and interested."

The way she was smiling told me that she really thought Jaden could be her new boyfriend sometime soon. *Overenthusiastic as always*, I thought to myself.

"It's just—" I was searching for the right words to caution but not discourage her. "—just take it slowly. You don't know him and you don't know what he thinks about you—I mean—it's always likely a boy thinks you're pretty, or hot—but you've seen this guy for the first time in your life today. Don't fall in love with the idealistic first impression you got." I tried to give her an encouraging smile, wondering what it would look like. "You don't know what secrets he might have. Just be careful."

"Of course I will. I won't find myself some weirdo who turns out to have psychiatric issues—I'm not stupid," she said into the space between us.

That hurt. I knew that Amber had never been able to completely like Adam, even when she had thought him to be a *hot guy*. She had told me more than once that he wasn't good for me. Obviously, she was convinced that he'd had issues, given that he had killed himself; but what did she know about the truth—

"Oh my God," the look on Amber's face changed completely within a fraction of a second. "I'm so sorry. I didn't mean—"

"It's alright." I didn't want to hear whatever she was about to say. Being reminded of Adam that way was bad enough. It was almost unbearable to act like it was true that he had committed suicide when he had actually died at the hand of evil, protecting me from harm.

I got back to my feet and filed in with the others, leaving Amber behind. I knew that I was being complicated and over-sensitive and easily irritated, but I couldn't help it. Whatever effort I made to be the friend they had known, I failed, over and over again. I also failed to be the person I had become through my love for Adam. That part of me, full of joy and happiness, was gone. It seemed as if the part of my soul that had died had been this part—the part Adam had touched with his warmth and his gentle nature. I was just a shadow of the person I used to be—

Unwilling to think about it in any more detail, I shook my head and concentrated on the rhythm of my feet making contact with the floor.

I still hadn't calmed down by the time gym was over. I showered and changed as quickly as I could, folding my uniform neatly into the gym locker. Lydia was waiting for me at the door with her head tilted to one side, examining me with her big eyes.

"Hungry?" she asked as I walked toward her and she turned in the door to join me on the way to the cafeteria.

"Yes," I nodded at her, and we hurried off.

When we were climbing the stairs to the main corridor, I saw Amber and Jaden turn the corner to the cafeteria in front of us.

"Do you think she knows what she's doing?" I asked Lydia peevishly and was pleased to see her frown in response. We both watched them melt into the lunchroom crowd.

"I hope so."

We followed them and lined up with the other students. Today's lunch was broccoli soup, cheeseburger, and yogurt for dessert. The soup looked like an inedible green slime. I skipped soup and ordered the burger and dessert right away. Then I looked for a small, free table so Lydia and I could sit alone and I wouldn't have to act like a cheerful version of me.

"Have you done your essays for English and literature?" Lydia asked with an epic eye-roll.

I shook my head and bit into the burger. It wasn't very tasty, but it was huge, and the vegetables inside at least looked fresh.

"It's annoying. I mean—we barely have time to work on our other subjects, let alone find free time to enjoy life!"

"What life?" Greg asked as he joined us at our table.

"Greg's right," Lydia went on complaining. "What free time? Ms. Watts literally buries us with homework."

Ouch! Instantly scenes of the funeral flashed through my head without me being able to stop them.

"—pay attention to what you're saying—" I heard Greg whisper to Lydia beside me.

I didn't care. I was caught in my memory, in my own head. I looked away and pretended I hadn't heard either of them.

As my gaze crossed the room, my eyes were locked mid-path by a pair of golden ones. They were almost liquid with warmth and full of sympathy.

I need you, I thought at Jaden. *I need to get out of here. I can't stand another minute pretending to be fine. I am* not *fine.* It hurt to admit it to myself. Luckily, Jaden wouldn't hear my thoughts—just feel how miserable I was.

I sank into the depth of his eyes, longing for a minute or two without pain and incompleteness.

"Claire?" A voice beside me tore me from my thoughts. "Are you going to eat your yogurt?"

"No," I answered absentmindedly.

"Sure?" the voice asked.

I looked down onto my tray. The burger was half-eaten and had gone cold, and the yogurt sat untouched. My stomach felt full—full of food, of ache, of knives.

"Go ahead, Greg." I shoved the bowl toward him. "You can have it."

Without a second look, I turned to fall back into Jaden's gaze; but he had turned back to Amber and was seemingly listening to whatever stories she was telling him. He looked so out of place—the way he sat, the way he moved, his irresistible smile that engulfed you completely but still seemed a million miles away. He had watched over our foolish human race for more than nine hundred years. He had saved countless lives and killed demons. He was no ordinary teenager, and to someone looking attentively, wouldn't it show? I wondered how long it would be before my classmates started noticing, started wondering, started talking.

I sighed and lifted my tray in one hand, my bag in the other, and got to my feet.

"See you around," I said to Greg and Lydia before I left the cafeteria.

Halfway through the door, Ms. Weaver called me from the corridor.

"Miss Gabriel, can I have a word?"

The way her eyebrows knit together as she asked me made me feel like I didn't want to have to talk to her.

"Actually, I'm in a hurry—" I tried.

"Oh—I'll be quick." She gestured me to an empty classroom, and I felt obliged to follow her.

I entered the room behind her. The woman was near forty and somewhat pretty for her age. I inevitably remembered what Adam had told me about her—that she preferred women to men. I grinned—I had no problem having a lesbian teacher.

Ms. Weaver turned and sat down on the teacher's desk.

"Please, sit down," she gestured at a desk in the first row.

I did as I was told. The longer the scene took, the more insecure I was feeling. Had I done something wrong? To be honest, I couldn't remember most of the things I had done at school lately. I had been so distracted and caught up in the messed-up situation of mine that I had hardly taken any notice of what had been going on around me.

Miss Weaver threw me a serious look before she started talking. "I'm worried, Claire. You did so well at the end of last semester, but it seems like all of your newly-gained excitement for history has died."

I coughed unintentionally.

"I know you've had hard times—traumatic things happened in your life—but unless you take things into your own hands, you won't get better." Her eyes bore into mine, merciless. "I gave you almost a month to get back on your feet. It's time for you to wake up and accept what happened. You need to start working again, pay attention in classes, study, homework—"

I was having an out-of-body experience. Whatever had happened, it was none of her business.

"I don't want to tell you what to do or not to do, Claire, but if you keep going like this—I don't think I'll be able to give you a passing grade."

"We haven't even had a test this semester," I protested, waking up to the meaning of what she was trying to tell me.

"You think so?" Ms. Weaver's eyes were more serious than ever. "We did. You just didn't take any notice."

"What?—When?"

I was shocked. How could I miss such a thing?

"A week ago." She shook her head. "It was one of the lessons you decided too much for you. You stood up and left the room without a word."

I remembered something like that darkly. I had done that several times—whenever I had preferred not to cry in public. *Damn!*

"Sorry," I tried.

"No need to be sorry," Ms. Weaver told me. "I know how hard it is to lose the people you love—especially when you're young and think there will never be anyone you could love as much as the one you lost..."

She glanced away uncomfortably, giving her thoughts distance, "—but believe me, there's always a way to overcome it."

Her head snapped back to me, her face back to normal. "Just promise you'll put some effort into history in the next days. We have another exam next week, and I don't want to see you fail. Your future is too precious to just throw it away like that—because of things you had no influence on."

She gave me an understanding smile. "It's not your fault he jumped off that roof."

I swallowed down the tears, which were about to press their way out. "—anything else?"

"No." She shook her head. "Go ahead."

"Thank you," I said, using all my strength to stay appropriate, although my voice was thick and quavery. I wanted to say just the opposite. I was furious and unstrung. I had to get out of there before I lost it.

I bolted gracelessly from the desk and charged into the corridor. I didn't remember deciding to hide in the bathroom, but seconds later, I was flinging the old red door open with such force it bounced noisily against the wall behind it and forced me to step in quickly to avoid the rebound.

The bathroom was empty.

I took a deep breath and looked into the mirror. I hardly recognized the girl staring back at me. Her face was a grimace of anger and pain. Unable to stand the vision of my face, I turned around and paced the small room several times.

It seemed like my period of grace was over. People were expecting me to pay attention and to behave normally again.

A few weeks were all they had given me. A few weeks to grieve, to mourn. A few weeks to dwell in self-pity. It made me want to cry out loud or hit something with my fists.

None of them *knew* the truth. None of them had the right to tell me to move on. None of them had a clue about what was going on inside me—how it felt to live with only half your soul. I was drowning in people's misinterpretation of my behavior.

Full of frustration and despair, I punched the door of the nearest cubicle.

"Ouch!" I cried aloud.

I looked down to see my knuckles starting to bleed. Red liquid was escaping from small cuts in my skin.

"Oh, damn it—Jaden," I whispered. "Where are you?"

I felt utterly helpless just knowing that he was nearby, that he could heal me with just a touch of his hand, and he was the one person who would understand the pain in my soul.

I had to pull myself together and go back to class. One deep breath and another and another, and I was ready—well, not ready at all to be honest, but as ready as I would get.

Before I opened the door—gently this time—I rinsed my fingers at the sink, patting them more or less dry with a paper towel, then hustled out.

The corridor was empty, and I realized with a sinking feeling that I must be late. Sure enough, class had begun.

"Sorry I'm late," I mumbled an apology to Ms. Watts as I scanned the room for an empty desk. There was just one. In the second row—right in front of Jaden.

As I headed for the table, I noticed Amber sitting beside him. She was leaning a little too close for my taste. I gave her what should have become a half-smile, but I was positive my mouth hadn't managed to curve the right way. She winked at me, radiating with joy.

"When Ms. Gabriel has finally settled down somewhere, I would appreciate being able to continue with my lecture," Ms. Watts said blackly.

"I said I was sorry, didn't I?" I whispered to myself and hurried into the chair, dropping my bag to the floor beside me.

"Homework, Ms. Gabriel." Ms. Watts had followed me to my table and was holding out her hand.

I wished for the floor to open and swallow me.

"I'm sorry, I forgot it," I said tonelessly.

"Well, that's too bad, isn't it?" She turned around and marched off to the teacher's desk where she wrote down something in her book. Then she stretched up and started talking about a book we apparently were supposed to have read, and I definitely hadn't.

I lived through the English lesson, petrified by Ms. Weaver's speech and Ms. Watts's sudden harshness. I had to change something in the way I was handling my everyday life. I had to become more attentive and at least do as much work as was necessary to not stand out in a negative way. I wanted to be invisible, and this included being invisible to teachers as well. If it took studying with Greg for history and reading books and writing essays for English and literature and whatever things it was for other subjects, I would gladly do them—anything was better than being exposed like that. I was too much the center of attention already, just because I was unable to control my stupid tears.

I was surprised by how much faster the lesson seemed to pass when I paid a little attention. The day was over in no time, which was something good for once. I walked home with Lydia. She had gotten used to my silence. Since she had started out with Richard, she had changed into a way more communicative person than she had been. I liked it. She kept talking, and I listened without any pressure to answer. She didn't talk gossip. All she said was relevant somehow. It was ordinary things about her family, about school; sometimes she complained about Richard. I didn't mind most of the time, as long as she didn't expect me to offer some good advice.

Today I had something I wanted to tell her.

"Lyd," I interrupted the flow of her words. "I've got a question."

"Sure—ask," she encouraged me, surprised that I was pulling information.

"I know I've been a bad friend in the past month—"

"No, you have your reasons—I don't mind," she quickly undermined my explanations.

"Yes, but I'm really not worth anything right now. I want to thank you for being so patient and kind with me."

She just smiled at me without a further word.

"And I wanted to ask whether you could help me catch up at school a little."

I knew that it was too much to ask, but I needed help. I couldn't do it all by myself, considering there were subjects I had already had problems keeping track of when I had been all happy and motivated.

"No problem," Lydia said, and her smile stretched across her face.

"Thanks, Lyd!" I really considered myself lucky to have friends like her. "You don't need to help me with everything—I will talk to Greg about history, and Amber for—I guess Amber's occupied at the moment..."

Lydia grinned. "Guess so. I talked to Jaden after you left the cafeteria. Amber introduced us. He seems fairly nice."

She had no idea how right she was about nice. He was beautiful and good. But a human who grew too close to him would be in danger. I had experienced myself what it meant to be with an angel, what demons would do to drive an angel insane, what they did to make an angel's human suffer—

"I hope she's careful, still."

We had reached Lydia's house. She took a step toward me and slung her arm around me in a cautious hug.

"See you tomorrow," she said and squeezed me for a second.

"See you, and—thanks."

She let go and turned to walk away but then stopped and looked back at me. "I'm glad you've decided to return to normal life. You've been so far away in the past few weeks; I sometimes wasn't sure you were still there." She half-smiled, hope flashing in her eyes. "I missed my friend."

I didn't know what to answer. Before I could think of something fitting, she had turned and vanished through the front door of the Porters' house.

Hopefully, she was right. Would I find a way to return to normality—ever?

I started walking down the street toward my house. I had just turned the corner when I heard the low thrum of a powerful engine and the whisper of tires. A car was deliberately pulling up alongside me. I turned as casually as I could, and my heart jumped. The car was a bit flashy. And it was gray.

3.
Effort

"Fancy a ride home?" Jaden asked through the open window.

I was surprised to see him talking to me after a day of ignoring me at school.

"Thanks, but no thanks," I was only a few streets away from my house, and walking in the cold air made my head clear a little. I continued walking. Some part of me felt strangely satisfied that he had to roll beside me to be able to keep talking to me. I hadn't realized I had been angry at him for not talking to me at school—for not telling me that he was going to be at school in the first place.

"Okay," he lifted one hand from the steering wheel and waved at me without enthusiasm before he closed the window and accelerated around the next corner.

I at once regretted being rude. Sure, it had been an awful day. First Jaden, without warning or explanation, had appeared at my high school as an enrolled student and—

who would believe it—had exactly the same schedule as I did. Then he acted weird by staring at me when no one was looking but ignoring me when others could notice. Then two of my teachers had made it crystal-clear that I was failing and I had better do something about it immediately. Stress and exhaustion were dominating my feelings.

Jaden was the one person I could trust with everything, and I considered him my friend. He was probably the only person who truly understood my situation. Maybe I should have given him a chance to explain.

Trying to not think at all, I hurried my steps past the comfortable little houses on my street. Thinning patches of snow still stood where the ground received no winter sun. The houses were warm islands in the still frosty winter landscape. I thrust my hands into my pockets for warmth and shifted my backpack which was extra-full because now I knew I had to really hit the books. My breath expelled as white fog before my face.

When I turned into our driveway, I found Jaden's car sitting there as if it had never moved this morning. And there he was, pacing my porch, the uncertain look on his face showing that he'd been waiting for me.

"What are you doing here?" I blurted out. "For that matter, what were you doing in school?" It was churlish and disrespectful of me to start in on him like that. After all, he was my guardian angel. But my social resources were entirely depleted.

"I'll be gone in a minute," he promised. "I just needed to know what happened today. You were really upset—I could feel it—but I couldn't understand it."

"A second may be all you have," I advised. "If Sophie comes home and finds you here, how am I going to explain it? She probably knows you were here this morning, too."

"Just tell me what's wrong, Claire," he said.

"It seems like the officially accepted time for mourning is over," I told him sarcastically.

"I don't understand," he said, his face instantly changing to a questioning expression.

I eyed him for a brief moment. After a day of seeing him at school, it was so easy to forget that Jaden wasn't a normal boy.

"It's everything," I complained. "*You* showing up like that, and then I didn't know what to do or how to act. And school, having two teachers back-to-back put the hammer down on me for my grades. I can barely make it through a normal day, but this was horrible.

"The teachers must have had a meeting about me or something. What do they call that, a staffing? And they agreed to try to get me to put things behind me, but I don't think I can do that. I don't think I can—*move on*. And I don't think I can be the student they want me to be, anyway. And with you in every classroom every day, for some reason, that makes it all worse."

I stepped past Jaden, unlocked the front door, and walked inside.

"I'll be back in five minutes—okay?" Jaden called after me and closed the front door from outside. A second or two later, the engine of a car sprang to life, and the sound moved away down the street and around the corner.

Where the hell was he going now?

My room was like I had left it that morning. I placed my bag on the desk then picked up the milky jeans from the floor and carried them to the washing machine. A pile of dirty clothes was waiting to be washed, so I stuffed it into the washer and switched it on. I stayed, hunched on the floor, and watched the pile of clothes blur into a multicolored whirl behind the glass of the machine's door.

Sophie wasn't home yet. If she had been at the campus today, she would arrive any minute. It wouldn't be wise if she took any notice of Jaden turning up. I didn't want her to even know that he existed. It would be way safer for her, keeping her in the dark.

It wasn't even five minutes later when Jaden popped up beside me. I half-fell into the washing machine, jumping with surprise.

"How did you know I wasn't in my room?" I asked him critically.

"I always know where you are," he plainly said, not showing any kind of emotion. "It's my job."

I really didn't want to hear that. It was bad enough that he always knew how I felt when he was around me—which meant *now*, too.

"It's really your job?" I was skeptical. "How exactly does it work? Who's your boss?"

"One of the archangels—Michael. I don't know if you've heard about him—" he answered casually.

"Michael? Like *Michael*-Michael?" I asked disbelievingly.

Jaden nodded and took a step toward me.

"Let's take this conversation to your room. I don't feel comfortable here when your sister might show up any second."

"I thought he was only a figure in the Bible—" I ignored his request.

He stretched out one hand and placed it on my shoulder. I instantly lost track of time and space, and the solid ground vanished from under my feet. Then I felt like I was being pulled through cold water, and finally, my feet hit the floor in my room.

I looked around. Jaden was standing right in front of me, his hand still on my shoulder.

"Could you at least warn me *before* you do this again?" I growled. "I could have easily *walked* here—"

"Oh," was Jaden's answer. He instantly removed his hand from me and took a step back toward the window. His eyes lingered on the floor for a few seconds.

I turned and walked over to sit down on the chair at my desk beside the closed door.

"I'm sorry," he said. "I'm just so used to doing this—you know, protecting people. In life-threatening situations, I never ask if I can teleport someone—"

"This is not a life-threatening situation, is it?" I snapped at him.

"I know." Jaden leaned against the windowsill and eyed me, guarded. "I'm still not good at being human," he said, his face suddenly sad. "I used to be worse, but at least now, I look like a human when I move and sound like a human when I talk."

I looked at him from the other side of the room. "Just promise you'll ask me next time before you teleport me through the house—or elsewhere," I said, not really able to take in the meaning of what he was saying.

"I will do my best," he said solemnly.

"Good. And now, tell me more about your *job* and about why the hell you decided to become a student at Aurora

High," I demanded. If I had to have him around every day at school, I might as well know why.

"Yes," he glanced sideways out the window. "I will—later. Sophie is coming." And without another word, he was gone.

"Hey," I started to protest the second he vanished from my windowsill, but he didn't hear me—or didn't react to it. Anyway, he remained gone.

The front door made a noise that revealed that it was being opened. Sophie.

I decided to go downstairs and greet my older sister so she wouldn't surprise me in my room later when Jaden was back.

"Hi," I called as I was on my way down the stairs.

"Hi, little sister," Sophie greeted me from the kitchen. "Have a nice day?"

"Mhm..." I lied. I didn't want to pull her into the trouble of my life more than necessary. She had already become too much of a caring parent substitute for me. "How was yours?"

"Great," she beamed. "I got the results of an exam—I got an A," she couldn't hold back the good news.

"That's great," I faked enthusiasm. Actually, I was happy for Sophie, but right now, I didn't have it in me to be the gleeful celebrating companion.

"I know," she couldn't stop grinning.

"And there's another thing," she said happily.

"That is—" I waited for her to tell me what she wanted to get out.

"I can finish my internship in Indianapolis," her voice became guarded. "They said I could start in early March if I want to. And I need to stay for three months." She rushed the words out as if trying to make bad news sound good by spilling it quickly.

Sophie had been in Indianapolis for her internship when Adam had died—I felt my heart twist—and she had come back to be there for me as soon as she had heard what had happened. I was so grateful for what she had done, and I was the last person to want to stand in her way when it came to her dreams; and, becoming a doctor was her dream. She needed to go to Indianapolis.

"I could tell them that it's impossible right now—that I could come later this year. Autumn or winter—" she started, but I interrupted her, ignoring the guilt in her voice.

"I think it's brilliant that they give you this second chance that soon." I forced my lips to curl upward. "Go, Sophie. I can take care of myself."

Sophie smiled at me with an almost motherly expression on her face. "I'll be here another two weeks before I have to leave. If there is anything I can do for you—"

"Thank you." It sounded too cold, but it didn't bother my sister.

"I'm going to have dinner with Ian at a nice restaurant somewhere later tonight to celebrate the exam result. Would you like to join us?"

"Hmm—do you mind if I stay home? I'm…tired and, yeah—I just don't feel like celebrating right now." I gave Sophie most of the truth so she wouldn't insist. A fact I didn't tell her was that I was grateful that the house would be empty in the evening and Jaden would be able to stay with me for a while without me getting paranoid that my sister might hear us talk.

"Of course you aren't. I'm sorry, Claire." Sophie tilted her head, wearing an expression full of pity on her face. "Stay home…I don't mind."

"Thanks." I went over to open the cupboard and took out a glass. Then I filled it with water and looked at the tiny bubbles of oxygen swirling through it, making the usually transparent liquid look more milky. I waited until it had cleared up completely before I took a hesitant sip.

"I'll be upstairs then," I said into the silence and started walking, carrying my glass with me.

"Okay," Sophie said as I passed her by on my way to the stairs.

"Have fun." I turned and gave her the semblance of a half-smile before I walked back up to my room, closed the door behind me, and sat down on the edge of my bed, my head full of thoughts and my heart full of ache.

In my room, I pulled out my phone. I didn't know when Jaden would be back, and I had no intention of spending the time sitting around, waiting. Instead, I dialed Greg's number and held the phone to my ear.

"Hey, Greg," I shot as he answered unexpectedly fast.

"What's up?" he asked, cheery.

"I could use your help," I admitted, half-thinking it had been a bad idea to call him. How did I know he wouldn't get upset if I asked a favor from him after all that had happened? We'd had some differences earlier this year. It was the time when I had needed some distraction after Adam had decided that it was best for us not to be together. The date Greg and I had gone on had been a complete disaster, and I had ended up kidnapped by demons. Greg had confessed his feelings for me, and our friendship had gone through some tough ups and downs since.

I grimaced an ironic laugh. After all that had happened since that date, one could truly believe that Adam had been right to try staying away from me. He might still be alive if he had. I felt a pang of guilt for being so selfish that I hadn't cared enough about his safety to let him go.

"Hello?" Greg's voice tore me from my thoughts. "Is there anyone out there?"

"Umm…sorry, I was distracted." I tried to disguise the truth.

"So, what does my favorite depressed girl need?" He didn't sound upset at all. On the contrary, he was delighted.

"Greg—would you mind helping me with history once more?" I spit it out and felt better the moment the words had left my mouth.

"Look who's back," Greg chanted. "I thought you would stay all passive and inattentive until you ended up repeating another year of school…" His voice was light and joking, but I knew that he meant what he was saying.

"I do my best to prevent this from happening," I joked back in only a vague semblance of his merriness—if anything, it sounded nonchalant at the best.

Greg's laugh came from the other end of the line. I had the growing feeling that he wasn't taking me seriously.

"Come on, Greg, are you going to help me or not?" I asked desperately. I still wasn't stable. Every tiny wave of emotion could break me down and I felt it coming right now.

"Sure I will," he answered. He didn't sound as lighthearted now. It was as if he could finally sense the severity of the situation.

"Thank you, Greg!" Relief spread through my brain.

"When do we start?" he asked, his voice back to delighted.

"Tomorrow after school—that is if you have time."

"Sure I have. For you—any time."

"Great! Thanks again—and—see you tomorrow."

"Okay," Greg said. "See you."

I hung up and put the phone aside.

The week had hardly begun, and I was already proud of myself for taking some action. I put all the effort I could in building a stronger facade, in hiding my pain and my loneliness, in fighting against the horror of my angel being gone. If I was to continue bleeding inside—I had already attempted everything to stop the flow of blood from my inner wounds—I had to become a perfect actor. I had to seem perfectly healed and back to life so nobody would pity me and try to talk with me about Adam. I simply couldn't stand anyone saying his name. No one had any right to talk about him, to try to comfort me and help me get back on my feet, because no one knew anything about him and how dreadfully his life had been ended.

The doorbell interrupted my brooding. I shuddered and suppressed an audible reaction to the wave of pain rolling through me.

Sophie's footsteps were passing my door on their way downstairs.

"I'm leaving!" she called as she hurried past with her shoes clunking on the wooden steps in rapid intervals.

"Okay! Bye!" I called back, wondering if she heard my weakened voice. Weakened by the wire tearing through me over and over again.

It was less than a minute when I heard Ian's deep voice cheering for Sophie's success on her exam. Her girlish laughter rang through my window from outside as they left the house. A car's engine sprang to life—definitely not Sophie's—and then after a few seconds, the sound became more distant.

I lay back on my bed and closed my eyes, hoping to shut the world out for once...

Adam's face was close—too close for such a pale, dead thing. Not close enough for something so unbelievably beautiful. He looked fragile with his skin stretching over his bones like a too-tight silky layer. His long black lashes framed his motionless lids as they blocked the world's most meaningful eyes from my vision. His body was cold. Still. Light wind ruffled his hair, making black strands dance over his forehead.

He was lying on the ground, except there was no real ground. It was more like we were floating on a colorless grid in the middle of nowhere. When I looked up, I could see branches of a greening tree from the corner of my eye. I could smell spring in the air. Birds were singing somewhere up in the tree I couldn't fully make out. I felt soft grass where I was kneeling beside Adam. But as I looked down, no grass was growing. Below, the grid was the only thing that stretched in every direction.

"Adam," I spoke into the undefinable space. It swallowed my voice. I didn't even hear the words myself.

A drop of crystal-clear liquid appeared on his cheek. I looked up to see where it had come from, but there was nothing but blue sky above me. As I looked back down, another drop appeared on his cheek. It slowly slid down the side of his cheekbone and vanished into his hair.

It took me a second to understand that the liquid was dripping down from my own cheek. I was crying, I realized, and those were my tears on his perfect face.

"Open your eyes, Adam!" I called helplessly. The words were audible this time but so muffled that I could hardly understand them.

Adam didn't move when I gingerly touched his face with my fingers. His skin was cold. There was no response. I used my thumbs to tenderly sweep away the tears even as they continued to fall from my eyes.

The next moment, his body began drifting away from me, deeper into the grid, while I remained motionless, suspended between the green spring above and the gray nothingness below.

Desperate not to lose this contact, I called his name and reached out to pull him back, but I couldn't get a hold of him. Every time my fingers tried to close around his arm, his shoulder, his neck, my hands closed around thin air.

He drifted farther and farther as I screamed for him, panicking, to no avail.

"I need you!" I wailed, but it was a desperate plea with no hope in it.

I helplessly watched him float out of sight. All I could do was wait until he would be gone.

Just before he vanished from my view completely, his eyelids suddenly tore open. Their light green bore into mine for a fraction of a second before he vanished into the grid, and I felt my own eyes fly open. My alarm clock said 8 p.m. I had been asleep for an hour.

I steadied myself with a deep breath. My lungs expanded unwillingly as I forced the air down. I closed my eyes for a second to calm myself and then got to my feet. I headed for the bathroom. A hot shower was what—if anything—could help a little.

As I reached out to open the door of my room, I stopped in my tracks. My hands were wet. I shook my head sharply. This was impossible.

Shaking my head at what sprang to my mind, I ran into the bathroom and thrust my face into the mirror.

No tears. I smelled my hands and gently touched them. No odor, no texture. It seemed completely foolish, but I touched my tongue to my hands. Salty, as I had been afraid it would be. Sweat, I told myself, wanting to believe it and too shaken by the lifelike dream to contemplate anything else.

Salt burned on my tongue like a reminder. I rinsed the taste from my mouth and gave up on the shower in favor of returning to bed and pulling up the quilt.

It wasn't a minute before Jaden appeared at the end of my bed. He wore an expression of obvious worry.

"What's wrong?" he asked from across the bed.

I nestled deeper under the quilt like it would protect me from him knowing my emotions. Even though his ability came in handy at times, being transparent wasn't exactly appeasing.

"Am *I* making you uncomfortable?" he asked.

I didn't share with him that he had guessed right. Instead, I scooted up so I could lean back against the headboard and closed my eyes.

"Had a weird dream," I told him without reopening my eyes.

"Tell me all about it," he encouraged. I felt him slide further up toward me. When I reopened my eyes, he was sitting close, leaning his weight on one muscular arm, his gaze curious and worried.

"Don't want to talk about it right now," I said unenthusiastically and pulled my knees up a little.

Jaden exhaled in frustration, and his lips tightened with disapproval.

"I don't know why we have to keep talking about this," I said, looking away from him pointedly. "I'm only going to tell you, for the hundredth time, how much I miss him, how much it hurts, how I don't see how I'll get through this."

I felt tears threatening to fall. I didn't give them a chance to even touch my cheeks. Control was the most important thing. That and becoming sociable again.

"You're hurting so much, and I only want to help," Jaden said softly. He was the comforting guardian angel again, finding the perfect tone, but he didn't change his position, and he was definitely leaning in toward me.

I exhaled, letting go of all the sorrow as much as I could—almost not at all—and forced myself to take charge of the moment.

"You were telling me why you decided to go to school," I said, reminding both of us of our former conversation.

He backed away an inch, somewhat reluctant.

"Of course." His tone gave a glimpse of how hesitant he was to share the information.

I directed my eyes at him and remained silent, waiting for him to speak. We sat there for a while, looking at each other; I was happy that he didn't force me to tell him more about that dream, and he...I couldn't really tell what was going on inside him. His face was too much a mask of controlled politeness.

Eventually, he clenched his jaw, something I had never seen him do before, and lowered his gaze to the floor before speaking. He seemed to have reached a decision.

"First of all, I am honestly sorry for not telling you that I was going to school." He kept his eyes on the floor beside my bed, the way an ashamed child would. "I just didn't want people to know we know each other. I want to blend in like any *normal* new student would.

"Any connection to you would have endangered my cover. Any connection to anyone would have," he explained in a voice that sounded more like he was confessing a crime.

I watched him, not knowing what to expect. I basically never did. Jaden was a mystery. An angel, ancient and full of surprises.

"I was very grateful you didn't give any sign that you knew me today at school. It was like you knew you shouldn't—" He turned toward me, looking me straight in the eye. "Did you?"

I shrugged. "Umm—I guessed…since you didn't talk to me or give any sign of knowing me, I thought it would be best not to react to you at all—more than a *normal* student would to a new one."

"Well, you guessed right." His lips twitched a tiny little bit at the corners. A sign of approval.

"So I got at least one thing right today," I sighed.

Jaden grinned for a second. "Yes."

I waited for him to go on talking while my mind took me back to scenes of Jaden talking to Amber. The strange jealous feeling, the uneasiness when I thought about him knowing how I felt even if he wasn't with me…

"I decided to go back to school because I thought it was time to keep a better eye on you. When you're at home, I can easily pop up beside you when you're in danger. Nobody would notice. But when you are at school, there is no way I can teleport to you unnoticed. There will always be people around you. If the demons decide to get you there, I'd rather be near you in an unremarkable way so nobody would really take any special notice."

I felt a surge of happiness that somehow felt wrong to me. It was true, then. He was doing this for me, not for Amber or anyone.

I knew he could feel my emotions, so to cover my feelings, I rushed the conversation.

"The demons haven't lifted as much as a toe to come after me so far. They haven't attacked at school before—" I waited a second for the pain to pass. "—so why would they now?"

Jaden's forehead creased a little as he listened to me.

"I just think it's good to be near you…in case something happens." He looked back down at the floor.

"*Is* something going to happen, Jaden?" I tilted my head and leaned imperceptibly toward him to emphasize the importance of my question.

"Of course not," he answered just a bit too quickly. I didn't believe him and knew he would sense my feelings.

I straightened my back against the headboard of my bed again and looked at the ceiling.

"You have been to school before?" I asked innocently.

"Why would you think that?" he answered my question with a question of his own.

"You said *back to school*."

He flinched ever so slightly.

"When?"

I watched his chest rise and fall with deep breaths, counting four of them before he spoke.

"Long ago…"

Silence hung heavy in the air.

"When?" I asked quietly, determined to get him to tell me as much as I could while he was in this strange mood.

"Another time. Another story. Another person." Jaden's eyes darkened. He was gazing into the distance, and the features of his young face grew ancient with sorrow.

I studied him—golden-haired, golden-eyed, and leaning close— my protector, an ancient angel, and a beautiful young man. I wondered what he was seeing.

After a minute, he returned to the present, and his eyes refocused on me. He shook his head the tiniest bit, and his face returned to being polite and friendly. A mask.

"Just something I had thought I should experience once… It turned out it wasn't what I had expected." He added a smile. It didn't look convincing.

I eyed him, pondering whether or not to press the topic, and decided not to, for something in his eyes told me that was all I would get—*for now.*

"It's nice you're looking out for me," I said lightly to change the topic.

"It's my job," he answered, still with the same expression.

"Seems like most of the students are thrilled to have you in class," I dragged the conversation on. "Especially the girls." I couldn't help rolling my eyes."

"They're all very friendly, helpful," he said formally.

"That's not what I mean," I said, poking a playful finger into the arm he was using to prop himself upright in my bed. The muscle felt as solid as it looked.

"What?" he grinned, flattered and suddenly boyish.

"Don't tell me you haven't noticed they are lining up just to talk to you."

"They aren't," he objected.

"Yes, they are." I countered with feminine conviction. "And Amber's the lucky one you picked from the group."

"What?" He looked positively confused.

"All the girls would have given anything to sit with you at lunch...or in classes. But you chose Amber," I explained to him like I was explaining to a child that fire is hot or water is wet.

He laughed out loud.

"You think I'm interested in Amber?" He was still grinning, making me wonder if boy angels had male egos like their human counterparts.

"Yes, I do," I admitted, a little ashamed that the thought of it was irritating me. "Well, she is obviously interested in you," I added in a voice that I intended to sound nonchalant.

"Oh—" his grin faded. "That's not what I wanted. I hope I didn't make her think I am."

"You're not?"

"Not at all." He shook his head like a dog shaking water from its fur.

"Why spend almost all the time at school with her then?" I asked, not understanding.

"I chose Amber because she is one of your best friends. I think she will introduce us very soon—only a matter of time." He smiled proudly.

"Oh." I didn't know of something better to say.

I was sure this was going to turn out to be a bad idea. Amber was en route to falling in love with the *handsome new guy*, and she would be mad at me if he spent more time with me than with her after she introduced us. Bad, bad, bad. I already had enough problems.

"I am not interested in her," Jaden repeated.

"But she's the prettiest girl at Aurora High—"

"Maybe," he said with a grin that was between provocative and mocking. "Anyway, try to be around her as much as possible in the following days so we'll have to officially meet." What was that expression he wore now? Smugness? He did seem pretty pleased with himself.

"Fine," I said as nonchalantly as I could muster. "But we aren't going to become a couple, are we?"

As soon as the words were out of my mouth, I blushed and regretted them. All too easily, I saw in my mind's eye Jaden embracing me in a school hallway while jealous girls sailed by in disapproval. And what would Amber say?

Jaden shifted his gaze to the window.

"I don't think becoming a couple will be necessary," he said with a hint of that angelic stiffness that sometimes characterized his speech.

"Great," I said and hoped he couldn't hear the ambivalence I was feeling. My mind had placed Adam in the picture instead of Jaden. In my daydream, Adam was now holding me in his arms. I could almost feel his hands on the small of my back. And then my heart hurt again, a pulsating lump throbbing inside me.

Jaden stroked my cheek lightly.

"I think it's best if you go to sleep," he told me. I couldn't read his face; it was set.

"Maybe," I answered, willing the pain in my chest to stop without success. I carefully moved away from his touch and slid from the bed.

I pulled out my nightie and headed for the bathroom without looking back.

4.
Visit

As always, the information I could extract from the conversations with Jaden wasn't half as satisfying as I'd hoped. I'd been filled in on his plan to *socially* meet me at school, so nobody would be suspicious of our friendship. Other than that, I knew particularly nothing. What he had told me about the demons possibly coming to get me sometime soon was vague. It hadn't even scratched the surface of what he knew. I had learned to notice when he wasn't telling me everything he knew.

I was watching Greg, who was sitting across the table with his head bent over an open book. How could I concentrate with everything crashing down around me? I started to worry if it had been a good idea to study with Greg. I wasn't sure I would be able to concentrate long enough to even have a chance at memorizing any of the important things. I doubted it.

"...the Admiral's name was..." Greg asked in a tone like it was the billion-dollar question. He looked up when I didn't answer.

"I don't know—don't remember," I scowled at him.

I felt like an ungrateful git. *I* had asked him for help, not the other way around. Now I was sitting here, lethargic—a complete waste of time and space.

"Come on, Claire, you already got that," he encouraged me with a boyish grin.

Fortunately, Greg had a cheerful nature. I could name days in my life I had wanted to kick him for his usual happy mood and days I had envied him for the ability to stay cheerful when the world seemed to crash down around him. I needed bits of his happiness lately.

I swallowed my thoughts and worries and returned my attention to my willing teacher.

"Sorry, Greg," I pulled up one corner of my mouth a little—not even a half-smile but as close as I could get these days. "Can you repeat that?" I asked and expected him to laugh at my lack of memory. He didn't. He just smiled and began to tell me the same story he had already told me.

I fought hard to keep track, but I was sure I wouldn't be able to remember half of it by the end of the hour. The living room's interior held much more fascination. I marveled at the flaws in the furniture. I had never examined the table's painting so thoroughly; it was amazing how the many little scratches that had occurred over the years decorated the gray surface in unorganized patterns.

I concentrated as hard as I could, intending to make today worth my effort and his time. In what seemed to be no time at all, the hour had nearly passed. I leaned back and yawned behind my book.

"I think you're cooked for today," Greg commented.

"Think so, too," I agreed, stretching my arms. "Thanks so much, Greg."

"Let's see if it helped before you start the hallelujahs," he joked, and my lip twitched at the corner. It was as much a smile as anyone could get out of me.

"Okay."

We got to our feet simultaneously, and I started cleaning the table while Greg moved to the hall and put on his shoes. He poked his head in through the door after a minute.

"See you tomorrow, Claire," he called and I hurried over to hug him goodbye.

"See you." I slung my arms around his neck quickly and let go even quicker. *Don't give him the wrong impression*, I reprimanded myself.

I waved after him as I closed the door behind him. It had been a long, long evening after a longer afternoon after an even longer morning; but I had lived through it. I had paid attention in class as I had promised myself, and it had worked most of the time. I had been able to pretend to care about what the teachers had to say, and I had been able to pretend I was no longer suffering. I had finally managed to look normal—no matter how agonizing the pain in my chest was.

I had tried to stay with Amber most of the time like Jaden had asked me to, but after a while, I had needed Lydia's quiet personality and stuck with her for lunch. Greg had kept us company, too. To go with Jaden's plan, I would have to learn even more self-control.

Exhausted and tired by the activities of the day, I went to bed and fell into a dreamless sleep. I slept through the whole night without waking up and reopened my eyes to the stinging noise of the alarm clock. I felt relatively good—considering my situation—and went through my usual morning ritual with surprising enthusiasm. I even checked my clothes before I put them on. Matching colors today. Gray jeans, purple blouse, and a grayish-beige vest. I pulled my hair up in a ponytail and checked my reflection in the mirror. I looked decent—better than I had in weeks.

Sophie rushed past me on my way downstairs.

"Good morning, and goodbye!" she called as she shoved me aside and squeezed past at the bottom of the stairs.

"Running late?" I called after her and hurried to catch up with her at the front door.

"Surprisingly, yes." She grimaced as she knelt to put on her shoes.

"Because you're never late," I said, sarcasm heavy in my voice.

She flashed me a wonderfully bright Sophie-smile. One of the smiles that said "Shut up and get lost!" while making you think she had just said *I love you*. I bit my lip and concentrated on my shoelaces.

"See you," Sophie said before she got to her feet and rushed out of the house. I put on my jacket and picked up my bag then headed for my car.

On my drive to school, I spotted Jaden's car in the mirror. After I picked up Lydia, he was suddenly right behind me. I wondered where he had come from. Did he have a house or a flat nearby? I earned myself angry honks when I continued gazing into space through the green traffic light, thinking where Jaden might be when not with me or at school.

"Okay, okay...no stress!" I called at no one specific and hit the gas violently. As I glanced into the rear view mirror, I glimpsed Jaden grinning in amusement. Surely he had heard me and he had sensed my blast of feelings. A new one—anger—after weeks of pain.

"Do you think it's gonna rain tonight?" Lydia asked cautiously, obviously taken aback by my outburst.

I shook my head at her question a little too wildly and took a quick glance up at the sky. A few gray clouds floated in the brightening overhead. "I don't know." My voice sounded annoyed, and that was how I felt. I tried to concentrate on the road, but the car in the mirror made me nervous somehow. I didn't understand myself. Maybe Jaden would.

"Richard and I have plans to go for a nice long walk with his parents tonight," Lydia enlightened me. I didn't care. I just wanted to reach school and hit Jaden's head with something solid for honking at me. I was surprised by the violence of my thoughts.

"Sounds nice," I commented. My voice was contained again, and I had no intentions of letting my control slip now. I didn't want Lydia to ask questions.

I pulled into the parking lot and saw Jaden do the same.

"Over there," Lydia directed me to a free spot near the entrance of the west building of the school. She didn't take any notice as the car, which had followed us since shortly after she had gotten into my car, parked two vehicles from mine. We got out of the car together, and I locked it before we turned toward the entrance.

"Hey there," I heard a voice call from somewhere nearby. I turned around instinctively and saw Greg hurrying toward us from the next row of parked cars.

I felt my heart lighten that it was just him. I tucked my bag and books into one arm and waved at him with my free hand.

"How are you today?" he asked, smiling. "Still tired?"

I shook my head. "No, I slept really well, actually." I told him disbelievingly.

"Phew..." he whistled out the air in fake astonishment. "Who would have guessed that?"

I hit his arm with my fingers, and Lydia stared at us like we came from outer space.

"Can you believe it?" Greg continued, half-whispering to Lydia, conspiring. "This girl," he pointed at me, "*sleeps*."

"Sure she does," Lydia said dryly and shook her head at him. "Don't you?"

Lydia led the way to the history class. I felt my stomach growing nervously nauseous as I thought of the number of things I should have remembered but surely hadn't.

"Don't worry," Greg whispered from the seat beside me when Mrs. Weaver entered the classroom.

Amber was late today. She came in a few minutes after the teacher, apologizing for the delay. Jaden sat at the front of the room in the first row. I noticed Amber's eyes flashing straight in his direction the moment she entered the room. The chairs beside him were already occupied. Amber's lips tightened for a second, and then she walked to the back of the room where she sat down in the seat next to Lydia. From the way she sat stiffly through the whole lesson, I could tell that she was annoyed. She didn't like seeing Jaden with other girls. It was his third day at Aurora High, and Amber was already possessive like a dragon on a heap of jewels.

I wondered what she would be like when she found out that Jaden didn't care for her at all—at least not in the way she did for him. What would she think if she found out he did for me? Would it be the end of our friendship? I forced my eyes back to the blackboard and started memorizing names and dates that were written there.

The morning went too quickly to talk much to anyone. I sped from class to class, constantly running behind without a real reason. Maybe I was doing it subconsciously because I was afraid of the conversation that would surely come. Every time I saw Amber or Jaden, I slowed my pace to fall behind. Whenever I saw both of them together, I felt an echo of nausea and hurried to the next bathroom to get out of their way.

"What's up with you today?" Lydia asked as I grabbed her sleeve and pulled her into the bathroom with me when we walked down the hallway to the cafeteria. "You're—different."

She didn't sound upset, just worried; so I decided to give her some of the truth.

"I'm trying to start leading a normal life again."

"By hiding in bathrooms?" Lydia asked, looking like she was positive I had lost my mind.

"I'm not *hiding*," I lied.

"Yes, you are," Lydia confronted me. She had become more of a self-confident, determined person since she had been with Richard. I hadn't noticed before, but I could see it now. I hadn't been very perceptive since—

My heart became heavier than it had felt the whole day. A web of barbed wire was cutting into it, and I remembered that I had more than one reason to hide.

"Okay...I am," I admitted and instantly regretted it as she asked me why. What should I tell her? Obviously, not the truth—that was out of the question. "I want to wait 'till most of the people are gone from the cafeteria. I don't feel like sitting in a crowd too much today." The pain in my chest would surely be visible in my face, and this had to make my answer plausible to her.

As I had expected, Lydia's face was full of pity. "You still miss him, don't you?" It wasn't a question. "I believe that it's hard and that it hurts, but you can't exclude yourself from life any longer. You have to go back to normal patterns, Claire. Life goes on; with or without you. And I'd rather it was *with*."

She took a step toward me and put her arm around my shoulders. "Your friends need you. Greg and Amber—well, maybe not Amber, she's currently so busy crushing on that new guy that she doesn't see anything else—" Lydia laughed and shook her head briefly, "—but I need you."

I let myself lean against her for a while, slinging my arms around her.

"It will be okay," she hummed and patted my head.

I didn't cry. All of my tears were safely locked away for now, but I felt that I needed her and my other friends because that was the only thing left of Adam. Their memory of him. It didn't take more than a few seconds for me to make the connection that besides me and my friends, there were other people whose memories of Adam (another sharp cut of pain in my chest) were at least as strong as mine—I had to visit the Gallagers.

"Thank you, Lyd," I said and pulled away. What I really meant was, *thank you for helping me get the idea of visiting Chris, Jenna, and Ben Gallager, Adam's family.*

Suddenly, I felt the urge to make the day pass even faster. I wanted to rush to the cafeteria and make time speed up by watching the crowd. I didn't care anymore whom I'd meet. All I cared about was to be somewhere I had been happy, to see the people who had shared a life with the man I had loved—still loved insanely, irrationally, self-destructively.

"Anytime." Lydia smiled at me, and we left the bathroom and headed for the cafeteria.

We were lucky not to run into Amber and Jaden. I spotted them leaving the cafeteria the moment we sat down with our trays at a round table in the far corner of the room. Greg found us after I had finished my soup. He had Sam with him, and they were talking animatedly about soccer in Europe. He was telling Sam about how terrible the teams were in the small country his grandparents came from, the one with the mountains, the names of which I didn't know.

"...You can't imagine how absolutely lame they are. I think there's no more than nine or ten teams in the league..." Greg blabbered, and I concentrated on the vegetables on my plate.

I was grateful that the afternoon went as fast as the morning. It was almost like no time had passed at all when I was back at home, fumbling my cell phone out of my pocket, and dialing a number I hadn't thought I would dial ever again.

"Hey, Jenna," I croaked as she answered the phone. "It's Claire."

A long silence filled the air, and then Jenna's voice reappeared at my ear.

"Claire, dear," she almost cried. "It's been so long since we heard from you...We thought you might be—" she fell silent abruptly for a second. "How are you?"

"I'm fine," I said casually, trying not to start crying. "Jenna," I wanted it out before my emotions went awry. "Do you think I could come visit you tonight?"

Another short pause from her side.

"If you'd like to. I would love to see you—and I'm sure Chris would, too." Her voice became heavy and sad at the last few words.

"Is he still—suffering?" I couldn't name it better.

"Of course he is after everything he's been through. But I'd like to tell you in person, not on the phone if you don't mind. There are some things—"

"I'll be right there. I'll just put on my shoes, and I'm on my way," I said, already jamming a foot into a sneaker.

"Good," Jenna said in a low voice. "Don't hurry too much. We don't want you to get hurt on your way, do we?"

"Don't worry. See you in a minute," I said and hung up, already stowing my phone back into my pocket. My freed hands raced to help my feet into my shoes, and before I could start thinking about what I was doing, I was sitting in my car.

Instead of immediately starting the engine, I dialed another number.

"Hi, Mr. Baker," I called into the phone. "I just wanted to tell you that I could work tomorrow afternoon if you need me."

The old man was happy to hear my voice and told me he needed me, that he was looking forward to seeing me the next day.

Proud of myself for leading my life back onto the rails, I turned the key in the ignition. The pain in my chest was for once bearable—for a few seconds.

The engine came to life, and I steered the car out of the driveway, down the street, and through the city, a direction I hadn't taken in a while.

The winding road to the Gallagers' estate had never seemed so long, and I was glad when the big house finally appeared in view. Some of the nervousness I had felt this morning returned to my stomach, and I shook my shoulders to get rid of the upcoming hysteria. There was no need to be afraid. Nothing was going to happen, or so I hoped.

I took the steps to the door in a flash and rang the doorbell, feeling both excitement and dread. The door opened immediately.

Ben was standing there, so tall and trim in a dark blue pea jacket with his car keys in his hand. Clearly, he was not there to answer my ring but was heading out. As he registered my presence, his expression changed from preoccupied to hostile. I shrank back an inch or two and opened my mouth to speak, but I must have looked like a fish in a fishbowl because nothing came out. My cheeks flamed before I found a few words.

"Sorry—Hi, Ben." Sorry? Why should I be sorry? It wasn't wrong of me to visit the Gallagers, was it?

My heart dropped in my chest. Adam's younger brother had never liked me. Right now, it seemed like *not liked* was a bit of an understatement. Ben hated me, but I didn't know why.

I simply could not understand that cold, wordless glare rooting me to the spot as he turned to sidestep around me as if I were something repulsive. He said nothing but launched himself off the steps. I stayed immobile, still facing the open door but not seeing it, only listening to the crunch of gravel under his feet then the sound of his car engine and wheels as he shot down the driveway. Ben. He wanted me gone, I was sure of it.

"Miss Gabriel?"

I snapped to attention and saw that Geoffrey, the Gallagers' butler, was right in front of me, his face polite as always.

"It's good to see you again, Miss Gabriel. Please, come in."

I watched him pull the door open wider as if to show that I was still welcome at this house.

Yeah, right, I thought as a flash of Ben's hateful face reminded me of the opposite.

Maybe Geoffrey was glad to see me, but at least one member of this family couldn't stand the sight of me.

"Mrs. Gallager is expecting you in the living room." I offered a weak smile and a nod at Geoffrey, such a kind man, who was gesturing for me to come in.

Strings of hesitation were trying to hold me back as I stepped over the threshold into the old house. Was I really welcome? Ben certainly didn't feel that way. Maybe they all were just waiting for me to get over Adam and get out of their lives. And only Ben was honest enough to convey that. Despite this awful thought, I somehow found the will to step into the hall. I took in the familiar sight... The marble stair on the right wound upward into the balcony that was carried by four massive columns. The artfully decorated walls were still standing in the same places, cutting the entrance hall into an impressive room. I shrank a few inches just looking up at the ceiling.

I realized I had stopped again and Geoffrey was still politely standing there as chilly evening air filtered in, unable to close the beautifully carved door until I moved.

I knew I had to do something, either turn and run or go forward. So, I took a deep breath and stepped toward the living room.

The door was open, and I slowly moved one foot after another until I could see Jenna sitting on the beige brocade sofa across the room. She held a white china cup in her hand and was about to lift it to her mouth when she noticed me standing in the doorway.

"Come in, Claire," she said in her warm and friendly manner as she got to her feet.

I walked toward her, my heart hopping in place, and tried a smile—as usual, without success.

Jenna met me in the middle of the room.

"Hi," I croaked with my throat tightened by the irony of the moment. Jenna was wearing a blue cotton dress. The one she had worn when Adam first introduced me to his family. It looked lovely on her, even now with the memory of her dead son clinging to the sight.

Jenna pulled me into a tight hug. I felt a stab in my chest as I heard her sob into my hair. I put my arms around her and tried to comfort her with quiet pats on her shoulder. I felt worse at the thought that it was my fault that she was still mourning for her stepson, and I felt miserable when I painfully remembered how he had died for me. Worst of all—Jenna didn't even know. She still thought it had been suicide.

I pulled away after a minute, full of guilt, knowing that I wouldn't be able to hold back my own tears much longer.

Jenna kept one arm on my shoulder and led me to the sofa where she sat down while I let myself fall into one of the beige sofa-chairs.

"Would you like some tea?" she asked me, gesturing at a china teapot in the middle of the coffee table. It was sitting on a silver tray with a fresh cup and a plate of cookies.

I nodded. At least, the tea would give me something to do with my hands. Jenna took the pot and poured some of the hot liquid into the cup, handing it to me before taking her own cup back into her hands.

"How are you?" she asked with a faint smile on her lips. It was an echo of the warm smiles I had seen her offer.

I looked into the teacup, trying to find an answer to her question there, but I already knew what I was going to say.

"Fine, I think," I told her, not looking up. I was positive that she would see the lie in my eyes if I did. "How is Chris?" I asked in return, trying to get the topic as far away from what *I* felt as possible. "You said you wanted to talk about him ..."

"Yes, we need to talk." Jenna shifted uncomfortably and glanced at the open door to the entrance hall.

"Where is he?" I asked, following her gaze but finding nothing but the yawning emptiness of the entrance hall. "Is he alright?"

"Sure he is—as good as he can be in this difficult situation."

"Is he here?" The way she was talking about him started to make me anxious about him.

"He is," she said with a meaningful look in her eyes.

"Can I talk to him?" I asked, honestly worried now.

Jenna got to her feet, her cup still in her hands. "Follow me," she said and started walking back toward the entrance hall. "And take your cup, too. This might take a while."

I did as she told me, mystified by her words. Jenna led me to the room at the other side of the entrance hall. The room was as big as the other one, but it looked completely different. A hearth fire was burning cosily to the left, and comfortable armchairs were arranged around it with a couch.

A small table was standing between them. It was overflowing with books and notes. Chris was sitting in the chair farthest from the door. His eyes were staring into the fire; his face was expressionless. Nothing but the fire lightened up the huge room, and it was steadily getting darker outside.

"Chris," Jenna closed the door behind us and walked to stand beside her husband. She put her hand on his shoulder, and his head snapped up, his eyes locking on hers. "I've got a visitor for you."

Chris turned his head slowly until his eyes found me in the twilight. I felt them burn on my face as he stared at me for a few seconds.

"Hello, Chris," I said, not knowing what to expect, and took a step toward him. Jenna nodded encouragingly and took her husband's hand.

"She's come to see how you're doing," she told him with a kind tone.

"Has she?" Chris suddenly asked. His voice sounded broken. It held all the suffering that was written in the lines on his face and even more; invisible pain was sounding in his words.

"How are you, Chris?" I asked him and took another few steps toward him until I stood close enough to touch him.

Suddenly, he jumped to his feet and pulled me into his arms with such force that I could barely breathe. "They're gone," he whined into my ear.

"I know, he's not coming back," I said a little surprised, my arms outstretched, not knowing what to do. Helplessly, I glanced over Chris's shoulder at Jenna, who was lifting her hands defensively and grimaced apologetically.

"Not *he*," Chris said a little harsh. "*They!*" He pulled me closer, clinging to me like a drowning man would to a piece of wood.

"What do you mean—they?" I asked utterly confused.

"My wings."

I stared at Jenna, mouth gaping, eyes wide open. She didn't even flinch at his words.

"But I thought you said she didn't know," I whispered to Chris, well aware that Jenna would hear me.

Chris pulled away and looked at my face while he talked. "She knows everything."

I felt my eyes jump between Chris and Jenna hysterically as I took in what he had just said. Jenna knowing everything meant Jenna knowing that it had been my fault that her stepson had died. It meant Jenna knowing about Chris's secret, and it also meant that she would know that there was a chance, her second son, Ben, could be taken from her one day for similar reasons. My body went stiff with fear from the fury I was expecting to rain down on me any second. Internally, I cringed away from Chris's hands as he held me at length and shook my shoulders in the hope to trigger a response in my stone-like body.

"I think she's in shock," his voice touched my ear from a distance. From the way I was feeling, I thought I might agree with him.

"Let's give her a minute." This time, it was Jenna's voice. She walked over to stand beside Chris. "It's alright," she said. "Everything is going to be fine."

"Fine?" I finally spluttered out. "How are things supposed to be *fine*?" I unfroze from the place I was standing and launched myself into the nearest armchair. I had no idea where they came from, but crazy thoughts were whirling wildly in my head. I felt desperate and responsible for these good people. I felt I had to warn them, protect them. "She's in danger, Chris," I half-shouted at him. "Don't you understand?"

His face was calm and still carried the burning expression it had before.

"They are going to come for her. Maybe not today or tomorrow, but sooner or later, they are going to take her away from you." Plain hysteria made my mind go blank again. If they were going to come for her, they might stop by to get me as well. And what about Ben—

"You have to hide somewhere, Jenna. And take Ben with you." I could clearly feel the desperation in my words. I was fearing for their lives as much as for my own, and I wished there was a way to protect them. Worst of all, I already guessed that there would be neither a place for us to hide nor their willingness to hide at all. I could see it in their eyes; their decision had already been made, and it obviously wasn't my call to tell them what to do. I was the reason their first son was dead. I wouldn't put any trust in myself if I were them—how could they after all that had happened?

"Claire, calm down," Jenna told me. She didn't sound angry.

"Why didn't you tell me?" I demanded, my voice shaking with a mixture of emotions. "Why didn't you tell me that you knew?" I repeated.

"We were about to call you any day now." Jenna sat down on the armrest of my chair and put one hand on my shoulder.

"We wanted to give you some time," Chris said, and his face looked a little smoother, less pained, more focused, as he talked to me. "We knew that you would suffer almost as much as I do. All we wanted was for you to be stable enough. We knew it was about time to talk to you, but we were hoping you would call yourself—as you did, luckily.

"I know I should have called—checked on you," I mumbled, embarrassed that I hadn't taken care of my angel's family.

"It's fine," Chris interrupted me. "We could have called, too. But we didn't, hoping that you would be ready soon. You needed the time to get over the worst."

"How long have you known?" I turned to Jenna, beginning to feel a little confused. "What did he tell you?"

Jenna gave me a motherly smile and stroked over my hair lightly.

"I've known from the beginning. Of course I knew. How couldn't I?" Jenna smiled at Chris, and he grinned back at her. It broke through his tormented expression like a ray of sunlight through the cloud bank. They smiled at each other for a while, making me feel like they had forgotten I was there.

"Chris told me that he was an angel in the very beginning," Jenna said, still smiling. Her smile became even wider.

I remembered how Chris had told me about Adam's birth, about what had happened there.

I cleared my throat cautiously, and their gazes became a little less distant.

Her eyes lingered on my face, scrutinizing it for a moment. "When Adam showed the first signs, we were so worried."

"I'm sorry," I tried to wrap my head around what Jenna had said. "I don't understand—"

Jenna and Chris both turned their eyes on me.

"You both knew," I gasped. "Why wasn't it dangerous for you to know?" I was confused. Everyone had made such a fuss about how it would have been best if I had never known about Adam...

Jenna laughed. How could she laugh about something like that? Adam was dead. Being an angel hadn't helped him at all. I felt like tearing her smile from her lips with my nails.

"Claire, you mustn't be angry with me," she said, the smile fading. "I am grieving for Adam. You know I loved him like he was my own child. I miss him, and I always will." The words sounded honest.

"Then why—" I didn't get to word my question. Jenna was answering it the moment the first words had left my mouth.

She reached behind her back with her hands and I heard a sound like a zipper being opened. The next second, Jenna was framed by feathery shapes on both sides of her shoulders. Her eyes were glowing a light brown, a color very similar to the one I had seen in Jaden's eyes.

5.
Family

I was sitting in the Gallagers' living room, the hearth fire warming my side, and reassessing the situation. Jenna had made her wings disappear when I had managed to close my mouth after a minute of gaping at her. Chris had stood beside her, perfectly calm, marveling at her like a boy. Now the two of them were sitting opposite me in two chairs, their eyes on my face, a little nervous. I had panicked and almost knocked my chair over as I had shifted it back half a yard, hysteria filling me.

I still didn't feel comfortable with opening my mouth to speak, though I had millions of questions I wanted to throw at them. How had they been able to keep me in the dark? How was it possible neither of them had ever suspected the other for what they were? How had Jenna been able to carry a child? Was it normal for angels? Did Ben know? What did this mean for me? Would I be in less danger? Or in more? What about Jaden? Could I tell him? Did he already know?

My stomach growled with tension. I looked up, half-expecting Jenna and Chris to react to the sound, but they stayed where they were. Chris's blue eyes were alive, scanning my face carefully, and Jenna wore an apologetic expression. Both perfectly patient, waiting until I was ready.

I inhaled deeply and shifted in my chair. I felt oddly out of place in this all-magical set of people. The air filled my lungs, and my mind slowly began to grasp what that meant.

"Jenna," I rasped. My voice didn't sound like it belonged to me at all.

"Yes, honey?" She was on her feet and standing right in front of me in no time. I couldn't even blink, it happened so fast. The backrest of my chair forbade my shrinking too far away from her too-quick movement.

"Sorry," her eyes searched my face for signs of new hysteria. As they didn't find any, she reached out her hand to touch my head; a comforting gesture. "I didn't mean to startle you."

I just shook my head. "You didn't," I lied.

Jenna smiled at my feeble attempt. Naturally, she was seeing right through me.

"When I came here today, I didn't expect anything like this," I said, my voice still not really under full control.

"Do you understand now—why we waited to tell you?" Chris asked from where he was sitting.

"But I'm not stable at all." I was still feeling the wires tearing through my insides, my heart screaming for mercy, and my mind unable to shut out the images of my beloved Adam.

"You are stronger than you think, Claire." It was Jenna again. "You are an amazing girl—the way you handle all the loss and the pain."

I thought about what she was saying for a while.

"Does Ben know?" I asked.

Chris shook his head.

"We want to protect him as long as we can." Jenna's voice was dark. "He might never transform if there is no catalyst. Who knows?"

"It would be best for him." Chris agreed.

I nodded weakly. Then a question sprang to my mind, and it rushed out through my lips before I could hold it back.

"How old are you, Jenna?" The words flowed on their own. I bit my tongue the second they were out, but it was too late anyway.

She gave me a warm smile. "Forty-two—right now."

"And your real age?" The number she had named obviously wasn't her true age.

Another smile, a little girlish this time.

"I'm older than this house."

I sucked in a breath, and my eyes widened with surprise. That wasn't what I'd been expecting, but somehow, it seemed odd that she would express her age in terms of the house. I tried to remember what Adam had told me. Lenard Mansion, built by William Lenard in the late nineteenth century.

"So, William Lenard was not your great grandfather—?"

"He was my brother," Jenna said dryly. "I was born in eighteen-seventy-eight as Jane Louise Lenard. My oldest brother, Charles, was seven years older than me. He was a good man. He always took care of me and my other brother, William.

Jenna's eyes grew distant, and even Chris's face hardened a little as she continued talking.

"Charles and I had a lot in common. He had a love for arts and for knowledge. He read hundreds of books. He always cared for the poorer and less-blessed in this world.

"William, on the other hand, was a greedy man. He already was as a boy—nothing of any value was safe from his greedy little fingers. He was a year younger than me. Our parents died when we were young—I was only fifteen." my heart sank with sadness as I realized the fate of the woman standing in front of me was so similar to mine. "And Charles was left to look after us. He had to bring in the money and it was only a matter of time until William began to claim all of it.

"We couldn't live off what our parents had left us for long, so William presented the idea to go away, to start some place entirely new. Charles and I found it a good idea to get away from the memories, from the problems in the country—it was hard times then—and so we left Europe and found ourselves on a ship to America." She smiled without humor.

"After weeks on the ship, we set foot on the new land. Charles found us a place to live. He was an educated man and had no problem finding a job in a bank. He earned enough for us to live on. William worked too, but just a little, living mainly on Charles' money.

"It wasn't more than a year later when Charles became ill. We had several doctors checking on him, but nobody found any reason for his sickness. He became weaker and weaker within days, and after little more than a month, he died, leaving William and me behind. It was hard times then. We ran out of money quickly, and I tried to find a job, but as a woman, nobody would hire me anywhere. And William—he had plans of his own."

Jenna shook her head slowly, her eyes far away in the memory.

"After a few years of living on whatever money William provided—I still think most of it came from criminal activities; he was much too lazy for honest work—William thought it was time I brought in some money of my own. I was young then, pretty. Eighteen. William invited me to a restaurant one evening. It was a fancy place. Too expensive for us, but he insisted he wanted to take me there that night. We met several people there, and two men had dinner with us, Frank Linberg and Albert Gracy. Both of them rich businessmen. Frank was a kind man around fifty. He reminded me a little of our father—with his gray wavy hair and the dimple in his chin. Albert, on the other hand, was younger. Thirty-two. He was the only son and heir of an entrepreneurship in New York, where we were living.

"It was only after dinner, at home, when William introduced me to his plans to marry me to Albert Gracy. The deal was already made, or so he told me. I would become Albert's wife, and William would get a monthly payment and a flat in the nicest district in New York. He would get rid of me. That was what he was after all along. Money and nobody he had to share it with."

I watched Jenna turn to the window. She had me caught up in her story. I didn't worry about anything right now; I was too amazed by what she had to tell.

"I had no choice. William would have kicked me out onto the streets that day if I hadn't agreed. Charles would have never let that happen had he still been alive.

"It was less than a month before the wedding took place. I became Missus Albert Hugh Gracy. William was only too pleased when Albert announced that he wanted to move further into the country to build some new business, as he called it. So we moved, and that was when Lenard Mansion was built."

I didn't dare to interrupt, but I was glad Chris did. It seemed like he didn't know all of the story himself.

"Why is it called Lenard Mansion when it was Albert Gracy who built it? Why not Gracy Mansion?" Chris asked curiously. He seemed as caught up in the story as I was.

Jenna smiled bitterly. "Be patient. I'll tell you in a minute." And then she continued.

"Albert was very successful. He became even wealthier within years. In the beginning, he took me out to parties a lot. He needed me as his accessory. He acted the perfect gentleman there, but at home, he wasn't. I was unhappy at the parties, and I was afraid to come home with him after them, for he would be drunk, and when he was drunk, he didn't care when he hurt me.

"After a while, I was alone at home most of the time with our servants. He lost interest like a child with some toy, and I was grateful that he did. That meant I didn't see him that often, and I didn't have to think of excuses for my black eyes or bruised lips." Jenna's face hardened. "He wanted an heir, and when it became apparent we could not have children, he blamed me, and the beatings began. I wrote to William to come and get me, that it was unbearable.

"William neither answered the letter, nor did he come to my aid. It was thirty-seven years of bruises and pain when justice found me. I was grateful he had stopped thinking of me as a woman long before that night. After one of his parties where he had probably been drinking with some of the young girls he used to keep around, he came home completely drunk, acting loud and noisy, and waking up the entire house. I remember Carla, our kitchen-servant, standing in the entrance hall in her nightgown. I was standing on the top of the stairs, afraid it might be burglars.

"When he saw me standing there, he yelled at me as usual. He stumbled up the stairs, shouting about what a useless whore I was and how he would kill me if he hadn't promised my brother not to. He grabbed me around the waist and…" Her voice trailed off.

"What happened?" My whisper was loud after the silence. Jenna turned around and pressed her lips into a thin line, her soft brown eyes hard as stone.

"It was the last time he ever hurt me. Carla hurried up and tried to pull me away. Albert just lost his balance. You know the staircase. Straight down. Twenty-two steps. He was dead before he hit the hall. It was the happiest day of my life. I was finally free of the constant fear and the regular pain my husband inflicted on me. It was the night I spread wings for the first time. Nobody was with me. Nobody triggered my abilities. I don't have to carry the burden you call a *mark*. And after what I've learned since then, I'm endlessly thankful I don't."

Silence filled the room for a while. Chris stood brooding in one corner of the room. I hadn't noticed him walking over there.

"What happened to your brother?" I asked, unable to restrain myself.

"As Albert and I had no children, I was the sole heir, or so I thought at first. William turned up a short time after

Albert's death to claim half of my inheritance, and it was legal. Albert had put it down in his last will.

"When William came back, he brought a young woman with him—Greta. She was half my age. She was his wife. We became friends after some time of living together. She was very unhappy with my brother, and I couldn't blame her. He wasn't violent, but she didn't love him, and with my half of the inheritance, I could afford to buy a small house in the east of the country where I had Greta visit me as often as possible.

"William died some ten years later, leaving his possessions to his wife, and we moved back in together. By then, I had managed to get in control of my powers, and I had learned how to age and re-age. I could confide in Greta with my secret and moved in as her twelve-year-old niece, and as Greta's surname was Lenard, the house just remained Lenard Mansion. End of the story." She smiled with the last words. It was a warm expression.

I sat there, having soaked up her every word. How could I never have noticed how much there was to this woman—more than anyone would have expected? She was such an old soul. All of the bad things that had happened in her life hadn't made her bitter.

It took some time for us all to return to the present. We spoke long and urgently about our new understanding of each other, and it was with reluctance that I finally said I had school the next day and needed to go home. We still had so much to talk about.

"Will you come back tomorrow?" Chris asked at the door. His face showed traces of the burning expression I had seen earlier this evening.

"Sure I will." I hugged him goodbye. "I want to know everything, and we will find a solution for your problem."

"My wings—" he exhaled the words, almost inaudibly.

I nodded. "Good night."

On my way back home, I had much to think about. Too much to process so quickly. But most importantly, I knew now that although it was my fault Adam was dead, I was still wanted at his parents' home, and this made me feel like a tiny part of my inner wounds were starting to heal. It gave me hope.

When I pulled the car into the driveway, light greeted me from inside of the kitchen window. The back of Sophie's head was visible as I walked from the car to the front door.

Hoping that she wouldn't have been worried, I unlocked the front door and let myself in.

"I'm back!" I called as I slipped out of my shoes and my jacket.

She was sitting in the kitchen with Ian, both of them laughing at some joke I had missed.

"Where were you?" Sophie asked between two laughs. I was glad she hadn't checked the time, yet.

"Over at the Gallagers'." I made it sound casual, like it was nothing special to do, hanging out there.

"How come?" Her voice was guarded now. I could tell from the way the words hung in the air that she expected a good answer. She didn't trust my mask of stability.

I closed my eyes for a second, hoping to put on a believable face when I opened them again.

"I wanted to see Jenna and Chris. I hadn't seen them in weeks."

Sophie eyed me suspiciously.

"I wondered how they were doing." That was almost the truth.

It seemed like Sophie was satisfied with my answer. She turned back to Ian, and they returned to the conversation I had interrupted.

On my way upstairs, I felt the pressure of the day crushing down on me. I had handled most of the situations reasonably well; I had even had a real conversation with my friend. I had found the courage to finally see the Gallagers, and it could have been worse.

I got ready for bed and crept under the quilt. My body felt heavy and limp as I stretched out my limbs on the soft mattress. My heart was bleeding. The entire day, I had been able to cover the pain of it with sensations of all kinds, always keeping the constant torment at a low level, but I had felt it all the same. Maybe today, I had just made a first step toward not reacting to the continuous ache anymore. But did that make me stronger or weaker?

The next day, Thursday, I was sitting in the cafeteria with Lydia. I had picked a table in the corner farthest from the entrance, hoping I would be mostly invisible there, and we were sitting in silence with our lunch and little interest in the conversations going on around us. I was deep in thought, with a slice of pizza paused halfway to my mouth, when I heard familiar voices alarmingly close by.

"No," I moaned at my plate. "No, no, no. Not today."

Slowly, I set down the slice. I didn't need to look. It was Amber and Jaden. Even though my voice wasn't more than a whisper, Lydia shot me a curious look. I merely frowned at my pizza and dropped my head. If I could only conjure an invisible force shield that would keep them away—but, of course, I couldn't. In reality, I could not have been more apparent to everyone and there they were, standing at our table and smiling broadly.

Regretfully letting go of the thought that with a few seconds warning I could have grabbed my books and bolted, leaving Lydia to deal with it all, I simply raised my head and forced a smile.

"Hey, guys," Amber said—too loud for my taste and a bit shrill. "This is Jaden, our new student."

As if I didn't know.

"Hello, Jaden," Lydia's tone was polite and friendly. I managed a neutral nod.

"Jaden, these are my friends, Lydia and Claire," Amber trumpeted. Golden light seemed to swirl in the air as Jaden's hair fell forward with his nod and brilliant smile. I saw Lydia's eyes widen involuntarily.

"Mind if we join you?" Amber was working this moment pretty hard, and I wondered if it really was too late to grab my books and go. I disguised my upcoming eye roll with a blink and quickly looked back at my pizza.

"Everywhere else is full," Jaden said helpfully with a tiny glint of amusement as he looked at me. Lydia responded by taking her book bag off a vacant chair and setting it on the floor.

"Please," she gestured an invitation aimed more at Jaden, I thought, than Amber. I couldn't blame her. He was amazing. They sat down, Amber making sure to take the chair next to me, putting Jaden across the table.

"Jaden's from Washington D.C. and is going to spend his final year of school here in Aurora." Amber was practically chirping with delight.

"Oh, really, Washington," I acknowledged, smiling a little in spite of myself. Probably Jaden knew Washington inside out and could be convincing as anything if there were questions.

"What made you move from the capital to this, well, whatever it is at the back of beyond?" Lydia asked with what seemed like honest interest, although little enthusiasm for Aurora.

"Didn't have a choice," Jaden said, "My father got a new job. But Aurora seems like a pretty nice place." His eyes flickered toward me for a microsecond, not long enough to alarm Amber. I admired how smoothly he told his story.

"His father's a lawyer…" Amber took over to tell Jaden's story. It seemed a little like she wanted to show us how very well she had gotten to know the new guy in the past few days. I stopped listening after a while, watching her body language instead. The big word *claim* was written in her eyes, and I saw it from the way she looked at him from the corner of her eyes. In her imagination, she was already planning their wedding.

I saw it coming that she would hate me, blame me when Jaden wasn't interested in her. If Jaden was watching out for me, his attention would inevitably focus on me, and unable to provide her the real reason, Amber would make up her own version of the story. She was going to get hurt, and it was going to be my fault.

"Claire?" a voice tore me from my horrifying visions. It was familiar. Jaden.

"Sorry, what?" I looked at him, and he locked his eyes on mine, not letting my gaze escape his.

"Amber just told me about your problems with history," he said.

"Did she?" I replied coldly. "Thank you, Amber," I muttered at her without being able to take my eyes off Jaden.

"Hey, I didn't know this was a secret," Amber defended herself.

"If you need any help," Jaden continued as if Amber hadn't spoken at all, "I'd be honored to lend you a hand."

My eyes were sinking into his, falling deep into the light brown of his irises. A minute ago, I had wanted him to stay away, to leave me alone to deal with my problems my way. Now, I felt the heat of his nearness, and I wanted him to stay with me forever. I wanted the people around us to vanish and time to stop. I felt oddly at home with him. All of my sorrows had suddenly disappeared—all but that bleeding heart of mine. I took a deep breath and kept falling deeper into his gaze.

Amber cleared her throat a little too violently to sound natural. I jumped in my seat, and the connection between Jaden and me was gone.

"Thank you, but I have somebody who helps me," I croaked, knowing that Amber would throttle me if I accepted Jaden's offer. My gaze lowered back to my plate, and I lifted the rest of my pizza to my mouth and took a big bite, indicating that I was finished with talking.

"Oh," Jaden's disappointed voice was almost swallowed by the noise of the crowd around us.

Amber turned toward him and pulled his attention back to her with detailed questions about his life in Washington. Lydia shot me another inquisitive look, and this time, I just shook my head at her and continued eating.

On my way from school to the library, I had a little time to think about everything that had happened lately. Jenna being an angel. Chris not being able to spread wings. Jaden becoming a student. Amber crushing on Jaden. The strange feeling I'd had as I had exchanged gazes with Jaden.

Mr. Baker, my boss at the public library, was already waiting for me as I hurried from my car into the building.

"You're late," he told me with a cranky expression on his wrinkled face.

"Sorry, Mr. Baker." I dropped my bag behind the counter and got to work. A box of new books was waiting to be numbered and registered in the system, and some people were strolling through the rows of shelves.

I used to work at the public library most Thursdays, but I hadn't in the past few weeks for reasons I'd rather not have had. It felt strange to be back here. It felt almost like everything was back to normal, and I was reminded of the Claire I had been six months ago. But that girl didn't exist any more than the reason that had made her change in so many ways. I took a deep breath and started to take books from the box, register them, and carry them to their designated places on the shelves.

It was an ordinary afternoon at the library. Between books and customers, there always were minutes left in which I could ponder my situation.

"Excuse me, Miss." A bald man around the age of fifty said in a tenor voice. I looked up from the counter to see what he needed.

"I'd like to borrow these." He handed me two books. One was some novel by a French author I didn't know, and the other was 'A Compendium of Seashells' by Anthony Shriner.

I took the books from his hands, scanned them into the system as lent, then handed them back to the man.

"Thank you," the man said in a kind tone as he took the books from my hands and let them sink into a bag made of sand-colored fabric.

"You are welcome," I said and pursed my lips while I waited for him to leave.

As I watched him straighten the handles of the bag, I took a closer look at his appearance. His clothes reminded me a bit of a mad professor—a scientist, maybe. Cord trousers in a muddy brown collar and a woolen pullover under a beige trench coat. His belly was round, and he wasn't much taller than I was. I made a mental note to ask him what the 'Compendium of Seashells' was about. Was it a novel or scientific literature? I was curious.

"Goodbye," the bald man said and turned to leave.

"Thanks and goodbye," I said in return and watched him walk to the door in small, shuffling steps. He seemed a bit lost, and I wondered if he was going to make it to the door without stumbling over his own feet.

He did make it. A few seconds later, he was squeezing out through the door he was holding half-open with his free hand. I shook my head over the odd man and returned to a completely different thought. How was I going to help Chris? I had seen it in his eyes the day before that he was hurting, that he needed help, but I had no idea what I could do.

My fingers drummed on the wood of the counter absentmindedly as my thoughts ran laps in my head, trying to find some point where I could be of use to Chris. To help him in any form, I needed information. There were only some things I knew about his situation, but I was pretty sure that I knew the most important things. He was traumatized just like I was, only it was a lot worse for him—he had lost his mark, I had just lost my angel. Then there was the shock about Jenna being an angel, too. I didn't know exactly how he had taken this news in the first place. There was also the danger this meant for his second son, Ben.

And then it hit me like a club on the head. The last time I had held 'A Compendium of Seashells' in my hands, it had been alongside another book. The one without a name and author. The one from which I had learned the basics about angels and demons.

"Thank you so much, Anthony Shriner," I whispered to myself and darted from behind the counter to the shelf I had put it last. The library was empty, so I didn't have to conceal my intended destination behind detours, making it look as if I picked the book randomly. I simply grabbed it from the shelf and launched myself into the chair behind the counter where I opened it and started browsing through the pages.

I ran through passages I had already read last time, searching for something having to do with wings. It wasn't until the last chapter that I found something that sounded similar to what I was looking for.

The Loss of the Heavenly Gifts, I read the chapter title.

I let my eyes speed over the page, searching for keywords like *wings*, *disappear*, or *gift*, and found a small passage talking about angels that cannot return to heaven for their *means of rising up into the skies* won't show anymore. I sank into the text, hungry for any information I could get. Another passage told about *creatures of shadow and thunder* who used the *sons of God*'s fosterlings to torture them and deprive them of their gifts.

"Anything interesting in there?"

I jumped and snapped the book shut. Internally, I was

tensed for a fight.

Mr. Baker peered over the counter, his eyes looking slightly magnified behind his glasses.

My hand clamped the book tightly as I let it drop to my side casually and turned a little so the book wouldn't be visible to the old man. I smoothed my expression, hoping that he hadn't seen which book I was trying to hide from him.

"Not really," I lied. "I think I'm gonna put it back on the shelf." I glanced at the clock on the wall—quarter to six. It was almost time to close.

I turned back to Mr. Baker, pressing the book to my stomach, then slowly started walking in the general direction of the bookshelves.

"Do you like fantasy stories?" he said, his voice a perfectly kind melody. It was a different voice from the cranky rush of words he normally used with me. It was creepy.

I stopped, a bit surprised by his tone and his question, and instantly wanted to hit myself on the head with the book for doing so. Reacting to his question like this meant he had hit some nerve. Deciding I had already reacted to his question, it would be least suspicious to turn around and answer as if nothing was going on. I moved in a small half-circle, hiding the book as much as I could under my arms, folding them across my stomach in front of it.

He looked at me, still standing in the same place. His expression was calm and friendly. Maybe I was just being paranoid and his question had nothing to do with the book.

"I haven't read many," I answered truthfully, shrugged, and began to turn back toward the shelves. As I took my first step, Mr. Baker spoke once more.

"Interested in the local myths?" His voice was too intrigued for it to be by accident.

I stopped with my body half-averted from the gray-haired librarian. My eyes lingered on the shelf I so desperately wanted to go to—out of sight—and put the book back. I felt Mr. Baker's eyes on my back as his question hung heavy in the room. My intuition told me that he wouldn't leave it at that if I ignored him now, so I opened my mouth and answered with a question.

"Is there anything to be interested in?"

6.
Myths

I pronounced the words very carefully, putting a lot of effort into making it sound casual, nonchalant. The second they were out, I was positive I hadn't fooled him.

The silence following my question made the air in the room become tangibly thick with tension.

I stood frozen, waiting, counting the seconds in my head. When I reached thirty and still, no answer came, I gave a muted sigh and finished my turn to face him.

Mr. Baker was still leaning against the counter like a minute ago. His eyes were fixed on me the same way they had been before I turned away.

"I think it's time we talk," he no more than whispered.

My mouth fell open without my permission. From the way he smiled at me, bemused, I must have made quite a curious picture.

"But first, let's close. I don't think we'll have much use for more audience." He eyed me for another second as I stood, still and unresponsive, and then turned around and walked over to the entrance door. His hand dipped into the pocket of his coat and, after some searching, extracted a keychain. It held a bunch of old-fashioned metal keys and one modern keycard.

"Ah...there it is." He grabbed the card and shook the keychain once, gazing into the distance as he listened to the sound of metal on metal ringing into the silence of the room. "You know, girl, closing is always the best part of the work in the library. It means that it's time to read."

I watched the old man, tensed and ready to leap out of the way if he turned out to be an enemy. Right now, I wasn't sure whom I could trust to be what they pretended to be. A quick glance at the clock told me that it was already past six. I should be on my way to Jenna and Chris. They were expecting me. At least, I would be missed if I didn't show up. But would they come searching for me? Would it be too late?

The metallic *click* of the bolts snapping into place in the lock quickly brought my eyes back to Mr. Baker. He was already shuffling back toward the counter in seemingly uncoordinated steps, and he was gesturing for me to do the same.

"Please, come sit with me," he said warmly.

When I didn't move, he gave me a disapproving look. "You've never been afraid of me before, girl." A friendly smile followed his words, and he looked the same as he ever did, just kinder—the cranky mask was gone completely. *Why not?* I asked myself and cautiously set one foot before the other until I was only a few steps away from the counter.

Mr. Baker sank himself into one wooden chair behind the counter. "There's another one free."

After another set of seconds, I decided that if he had wanted, Mr. Baker would have had plenty of opportunities to hurt me or kill me, so I pushed myself toward the old man and sat down on the second chair in the small space behind the counter. We wouldn't be visible from outside the library. If he planned to slaughter me, nobody would see it. Probably nobody would hear me scream either. It was still winter, and the evenings were frosty enough to keep most of the population of Aurora inside their neat little homes after dark.

My hands were still holding the book close to my stomach. I felt them shake even as they were tightly folded over the book.

"Well then, Claire," he chuckled, and the skin around his eyes went all wrinkly as his eyes twinkled boyishly—an expression I had never before seen on his face. I felt stupid as I sat stiffly in my chair, awaiting the catastrophe to come. But it didn't.

Instead, Mr. Baker straightened up a little. He leaned forward and shook out of his coat, which he let fall over the back of the chair, then he leaned back, resting his hands in his lap and opening his mouth to speak.

"Long time ago—I think I was only six or seven years old—my father told me a story his father had told him once."

Mr. Baker smiled as he was talking and his eyes looked back into the past of his life.

"It's a story I want to tell you today—the story of Aurora. Not the official story. The myth that has almost died by now. Very few of the people living here know this story, and after tonight, you are going to be one of them."

As his voice became that of a storyteller and his face stayed the calm, friendly one I had gotten to know so well in my first months in Aurora, my distress lessened a little, and my spine managed to relax itself in my chair. My hands didn't move from the book, though.

"Imagine the place we are sitting right now as a huge field along the banks of Fox River. There are no cars, no streets, no houses. Occasionally, bands of Indians make seasonal camps along the river or build small villages, but the land is mostly the thick woods to the east, stretching all the way back to the Atlantic, and to the west, the prairie that seems limitless and only ends in the shadow of the Rocky Mountains."

Despite my preoccupation, I grasped his picture. The river I crossed over so thoughtlessly every day must have seemed like a dividing line between two different worlds back then. Before I could dive deeper into that image, Mr. Baker was going on.

"Nearly two hundred years ago, European settlers were on the march to conquer the continent, but some stopped here when they saw the good river we have and the incredibly rich soil. They were farmers; they had animals with them—horses, oxen, sheep. They cut down trees to build their cabins and barns; they plowed the soil and planted wheat and corn. Their life was hard, but there was plenty of land, and they were glad to work.

"Soon, they needed grain mills and saw mills, which they built along the river for power. They needed blacksmiths and wagon-makers and carpenters; they needed general stores and churches. More settlers came, and the dirt trails that led from the farms to the settlement on the river became streets. The settlement became a town, and the population grew quickly."

He paused and pushed his glasses up on his nose, breaking the spell of his story.

I glanced at the elaborate old tall case clock that stood nearby. It was one of the library's greatest treasures—more than a century old and still telling time perfectly. Right now, it was telling me I was going to be late to the Gallagers. I felt a renewed urgency to get going, and his story so far was nothing more than basic history, what you could learn online or at the history museum. I had problems that weren't going to be solved by Aurora history. Or so I thought.

"Okay," I said, trying to be polite. "Although, actually, I've heard most of this before." Then, not wanting to hurt his feelings, I added, "It's very interesting, though."

Mr. Baker sighed, the patient teacher waiting for the slow pupil to understand.

"Claire, this history has everything to do with that book you are hiding under your arms right now."

I groaned inwardly because obviously, this conversation was far from over, but still, I wanted to hear about the book, so I tried to relax and not check the time. I didn't need to, anyway, because just then, the clock spoke for itself by softly chiming the quarter-hour.

"We are getting to the book," he assured me with a smile.

"I know the book you are holding. I know what's written in there and, more than that, I know the story that made people write this book, and I know why it is still standing in this library."

My eyes searched his face for a sign of a trap but found nothing but kindness and honesty. Although staying on the alert, I loosened my grip on the book ever so slightly and left it leaning against my stomach.

"What does that mean, that you *know*?" I asked cautiously. My eyes hurt from keeping them open for too long without blinking, not wanting to miss any change in Mr. Baker's expression and body language.

"About the angels." He laughed as he spoke. "What did you think?" It wasn't a real question.

I sucked in a gulp of air and choked it back out again. Had I heard correctly? Had he said *angels*?

He smiled at my reaction. "I see you are surprised. I expected you to be. But you have to let me tell you the rest of the Aurora story because we are almost to the angel part."

I nodded, glad to divert attention away from myself and back to the book. I forced my breathing down to normal. I didn't know exactly how much of a secret the existence of angels was, but I knew that there couldn't be too many believers or the book in my lap would have become a bestseller.

"Where did I stop—" He scratched his chin absently and then began again. "Ah, yes—Aurora is growing. The railroad comes in the 1850s and not just for transportation. The location in Aurora is perfect for building locomotives and train cars. Suddenly, thousands of laborers are needed for manufacturing jobs of all kinds. They come from all over Europe and build their houses and churches above the downtown so they can walk to work. Along the river, bridges spring up; factories are built; sidewalks connect elegant buildings of three and four stories. You young people know them as apartments and trendy restaurants, but once, the heart of a city beat there."

His reference to the present day broke the spell again, and I shifted in my chair, sneaking another look at the clock. He followed my gaze with a patient smile and drew me right back into the story with his next words.

"Around the same time, a series of ominous deaths started.

The first to die is John Andrews Jr., son of a prominent factory owner, who is found dead by his sister in the family home. There are no signs of violence or illness. They bury John Junior, and his father, John Andrews Senior, kills himself a few weeks later—hangs himself.

"Only a short while after that, a young woman, not older than you are, Claire, is found on the streets, her body lifeless. Again, no signs of external violence, neither was she ill. There are no wounds or other signs of an accident either.

"People know that the boy and the girl couldn't have simply dropped dead. It just wasn't likely. But as there is no sign of poison found—

"Just a month later...two other bodies. Again, no trace of violence, poison, sickness. The deaths are a mystery to the police. People start to become afraid. Theories fly about the wicked murderer who doesn't leave traces. Townspeople look suspiciously at any newcomer. Some even revive the Indian legend of Devil's Cave, which, many years earlier, people thought was the riverbank hideout of a renegade Pottawatomie warrior."

I listened to him, hanging on his words like a child at story time. I didn't know where this tale was going to end, and I wasn't even sure I wanted to know, but I was hooked.

"Eventually, there was a murder with a witness. The beautiful daughter of a bookkeeper at the rail yards is found dead on a downtown street by a young man. He says he was on his way home when he heard a noise around the corner.

When he got there, he saw a human shape, which looked as if it might have had wings. He says he couldn't be sure because it was dark and it might have been the shadows, but he could be sure about one thing. The creature was floating in the air, a foot above the ground. And the girl was lying on the street in front of it—too far away for it to touch her. As he sprinted to help her, the creature disappeared just like that." He snapped his fingers. "Word about the winged creature spread faster than you could imagine. After less than a day, the entire town speaks of a creature that stalks the night, waiting in the shadows to kill its victims without a touch.

"Then, for a while, nothing happens, no deaths. Just the panicking inhabitants of Aurora and their superstition—or that's what most of the people would think when they heard this story. But not you, Claire, you know better than to think of superstition." He gave me a look that felt like he was x-raying me. It made me shift with discomfort.

"Then, when, after a month, another body is found, the body of a child. The local priest is the first to call for a search. He wants to find this *demon* that kills people without even having to touch them or point a weapon at them. A mob of people follows his call, all angry and driven by the feeling of helplessness against such a force of the devil. They trust the priest to lead them to the creature. They think, as a man of God, he must have the best chances of fighting and defeating the evil.

"In just a few days, they find him. A posse, headed up by the priest and the bookkeeper, are roaming the town when they discover a human form crouching over a body on the street. People report that he had huge white wings and his eyes were glowing bright blue. He was an awe-inspiring sight, but fear is very powerful. They must save their town, and without hesitation, the bookkeeper pulls a pistol out of his waistband and shoots. Now, the bookkeeper is a hero, and the townspeople, unwilling to think about any aspect of the strange situation other than that they are safe again, return to their lives."

The melodious chime of the old clock interrupted briefly. Half-past six. Getting late. But I wasn't ready to leave.

"They just killed him?"

His eyes snapped back to me as I spoke. "Yes."

I shook my head disbelievingly.

"The killings didn't stop, though. On the contrary, they became more regular. Dead bodies were found almost every week. This made the bookkeeper think. He tried to find a pattern. Age, gender, profession of the victims, or hair color, skin color… He found nothing. Not until, one day, a man came to his office. He asked for a word. When he was alone with the bookkeeper, he showed him his wings. It was the first personal contact between human and angel that is known of in this region.

"Of course, the bookkeeper needed some time to fully understand what was going on. The angel said he was a guardian angel, that he knew the bookkeeper was going to be the next victim, that he shouldn't wander the streets alone these days until everything calmed down a little. He also told the bookkeeper that the only reason he was showing himself to him was that he needed to know that the winged creatures were the good ones, not the enemy. One angel killed was bad enough."

I felt my mouth fall slowly open.

"Fortunately, the bookkeeper believed the angel. He brought the priest in on the secret, and together, the three worked to entrap the creature of darkness.

The plan was good, and the angel was powerful. And so, a demon, without the citizenry knowing anything, was killed in Aurora. But only one—the other one got away."

"There were two?" I half-whispered.

Mr. Baker nodded, seemingly pleased with my reaction. "Yes, the first one was a short, dark-haired man. He was killed almost immediately. But the second one—blond with shoulder-length hair—before he got away, he promised to keep returning until he eliminated each and every single part of the bookkeeper's family."

The gray-haired man fell silent. He looked at me over the rim of his glasses.

I stared back. "What happened then? Did he get all of them?"

"That's where the story ends. Nobody knows exactly what happened to the bookkeeper's family. But what is definite is that the bookkeeper was the first to write in the book you're holding."

I looked down and saw that my fingers had curled back around the back of the book.

"It's the crest of his ancestors on the first page, and if any of his progeny still exists, they could perhaps be identified by the crest."

I opened the book and looked at the first page. The ornate crest looked back at me, showing a tree, a sword, and a flame, gracefully surrounded by elaborate scroll work.

"Why would this book just be standing on a shelf in the public library?" I asked earnestly. "Shouldn't it be safe in a rare books archive or something?"

"Usually, nobody comes looking for it." He gave me a significant look. "But that's mostly because nobody knows about it. If anyone does, though, I want them to find it."

"But it doesn't have a title… How is anyone supposed to go looking for something without a title, and how are they supposed to find it here—even if they know it exists?" The questions just bubbled from my mouth with uncontrollable interest.

They made Mr. Baker chuckle.

"Of course, you are right," he said. "Still—" He tilted his head toward me and raised his eyebrows to signify the mystery of it. "There are some who found it despite all the reasons it ought to be hard to find."

I remembered the list of names I had read in the system last time I had held the ominous book in my hands. Riley Watson, Maureen McKensy, Adam Gallager. I shuddered involuntarily. How had Adam known about the book and where to look for it? I postponed finding an answer to this question and continued asking Mr. Baker the ones he might be able to answer.

"Where did you get the book from?" My words had an accusing note. I didn't like it, but I couldn't help myself; they came out as they wished—I was beyond self-control. All I wanted was to draw the information from this man. I wanted to understand his part in the story, and I wanted to know how many people actually knew about the mystic world they were living in.

"A friend of mine handed it to me eight years ago. He was ill, and he had only a few months to live. I visited him every day until his very last one. Every time I saw him, he told me another part of the story I just told you, and much, much more. He knew the contents of the book by heart. He wrote some of them himself. And he got it from his aunt." He frowned at the book in my hands. "Seems like this little thing has gone through many hands before it picked you to read it."

"Picked me?" I wasn't sure I wanted an answer to this, but the words were out all the same.

"I'm so glad I have finally found one," Mr. Baker said, almost solemn. He gazed at me with awe and flashed me a smile, exposing all of his teeth, that said *pride*.

I stared at him, uncomprehending, while he looked back at me with the same gleeful expression.

"Sorry, found what?" I pressed him.

He just continued to look at me as if I hadn't spoken, almost in a trance.

The old clock ticked gently, slicing the minutes of silence into sixty countable intervals of eternity. It was patiently overseeing this moment as it had overseen many human moments before. I wanted to be the clock, unmoving and discrete, just a witness to history and not a part of it. But I wasn't just an agreeable bystander. I was involved, and now Mr. Baker seemed to be implying something more.

"I don't know what you mean, Mr. Baker," I said, looking the white-haired man in the eye.

His gaze never changed, but he said, almost dreamily, "I've been dying to meet one since the day my friend Walter told me about them. And now I find out I've had one right under my nose. Thank you, Claire."

I felt a stab of panic. I had to stop this train of thought.

"I'm really sorry, Mr. Baker, but I still don't get it," I told him, even though I knew this wasn't going to be enough. His expression changed to a brilliant smile.

"You are the first angel I have ever met," he said, his eyes lit up with joy.

My heart stopped. No! He could not possibly have just said that.

Mr. Baker smiled at me, solemn and respectful. "Don't worry. Your secret is safe."

"I'm really sorry to disappoint you—" My head spun for a second before I could think straight again. What on earth made him think I was an angel?

He began to grin. "You don't have to deny it to me," he said. "I already know. Walt told me that there wouldn't be many people to come looking for the book, and those few who did would be angels or part-angels. He had the book for thirty-seven years, and every single person who asked him for it turned out to be angel or part-angel. I know what you are."

I stared at him, not knowing how to break the man's heart.

"Look, Mr. Baker, I've found this book by accident. It was just because it lay on the counter with several others last year when I came to work."

He didn't stop grinning. It made me feel like whatever I was going to say, it wouldn't change his mind.

"I browsed through it because there was neither title nor author. I thought it was some fantasy story," I lied and felt my cheeks grow hot while I spoke.

"Why did you take it today?" he asked like he was catching a criminal red-handed.

Damn! I didn't have a plausible answer to that.

"Believe it or not, Mr. Baker, I'm no angel. I never have been, nor will I ever be." As I fired these words at him, like the bookkeeper shooting at the wrong celestial creature, I heard the clock chime the three-quarter hour. It was a spur to get me out of there and this terrible misunderstanding and into the embrace of the Gallagers, who alone understood it all.

"It's really like I said—I found the book by accident, and it's more or less an accident that I'm browsing through it again today." I cautioned myself to use a milder tone this time.

"If you aren't an angel, are you a believer?" He no longer looked transformed with happiness, but there was hope on his face.

It really looked like I could trust him. He had been so delighted at the thought of meeting a real angel that I couldn't bring myself to fear him wanting to harm them. But I also knew that I couldn't speak entirely open with him.

"I am," I said, "and I have my reasons."

He looked at me, intrigued.

"I really would love to go on talking to you. I'd like to know what else you know about angels and demons, and I'd love to help fit some parts into the puzzle where I can—if I can."

Mr. Baker's eyes became wider as I spoke.

"Will you tell me where your knowledge comes from?" he asked.

I shrugged and got to my feet. "I can't promise anything. May I borrow this for tonight?" I asked, holding up the book we had been talking about.

"You know, I always liked you, Claire. You remind me a lot of my daughter." His face seemed more wrinkled as he looked down, his eyes sad, for a second. "Sure, you can have it. Just don't lose it. It's valuable." He winked at me. "Go ahead—good night."

"You know, I really *am* going to talk to you about this some other time. I promise," I said as I was already setting one foot after the other.

He lifted a hand to wave goodbye, half-nodding, and I was on my way, leaving the old man to his thoughts.

I hadn't lied this time. I was going to talk to him about angels again. I really was. I wanted to know whatever he knew in as much detail as possible. Maybe it could help me keep the Gallagers and myself safe; but first I needed to know what was safe to tell Mr. Baker, and I wanted to talk about it with Adam's family first.

I searched my pocket for my keys as soon as I was outside the building. The cold evening air made my teeth chatter, and I tightened my jacket around my chest to keep it out. I unlocked my car and jumped into the seat quickly so I could shut the door behind me. I threw my bag into the backseat over my shoulder and started the engine. It took a minute for the heater to kick in as I was driving slowly down the street, heading for the Gallagers. The warmth helped me recover from the rigid wind outside, but I wasn't remotely past the shock of my conversation with Mr. Baker.

"Seems like I'll be needing to keep an even better eye on you," a voice said from beside me.

I hit the brake instinctively. A car behind me honked violently as it pulled out from behind my frozen car, and the driver showed me rude gestures as he rolled past me.

"Keep driving," the voice commanded, "you wouldn't want to make any more enemies as you already have a horde of demons after you, would you?"

I looked over to the passenger seat and found, as I expected, Jaden's handsome appearance next to me.

"How many times do I have to tell you? Don't. Do. That." I gestured at him with both my open hands. "You are going to give me a heart attack one day."

"Sorry," said Jaden meekly, "It's so easy to forget to act human with you around. Oh, and keep driving."

"Why are you here?" I asked as I steered the car back into traffic, earning myself another set of angry honks.

"It's been a *long* afternoon," he said, his eyes searching the darkness outside the passenger window.

My heart was still thrumming inside my chest from the shock. As if the conversation with Mr. Baker hadn't been enough, now Jaden had to test my nerves, too. I turned down the heater, feeling the adrenaline doing its job faster than any heater in the world could have.

"Did you know Mr. Baker knows all about angels?" I threw at him before he could start with anything else.

Jaden remained quiet and continued looking out the window.

"He saw me reading this book in the library today…" I told him about the old book and how I had found it, and I had to laugh as I got to the point where Mr. Baker had thought I was an angel.

"I hope he's not too disappointed," Jaden said without any sign of amusement.

"I told him, I am willing to share with him what I know about angels, though, I can't think of a logical reason why I should know anything—ordinary human that I am. I'm going to have to make up another story. Great," I grimaced into the mirror, feeling the discomfort creeping up in my body as I thought of the next time I would have to talk to Mr. Baker.

Jaden's head snapped in my direction, his eyes a luminous gold. "How can you say you're ordinary?" he asked, his voice full of suppressed anger.

"Because I am." I stared at the road in front of me in a way that made it clear I wouldn't discuss this with Jaden. We had reached the Gallagers' driveway and were rolling up the curved road to the house.

"I think it's time for you to leave," I said to him in the last turn before the house, "I don't want anybody to notice you vanish… You never know who's looking out of the windows." I thought of Ben with a pang of sympathy. He was the one part of the family who still had to learn everything about what his parents were and what he was.

"Oh, I'm not going to *vanish*," he said just a little too loud to not sound aggressive.

"What do you mean?" I asked, not willing to accept another surprise today.

"I'm coming with you."

Jaden leaned back in the seat and folded his arms across his chest. I watched him from the corner of my eye, dreading that he was being serious.

"They don't know what you are, do they?" I asked, trying to get a clear grasp on the situation I was about to find myself in.

"Nope," he breathed at me, "but it's about time we officially met. The tighter the network of good supernaturals around you, the better." I heard him chuckle in the dark beside me.

He seemed so much like a boy when he looked the way he did now—a student, my age. It was hard to bear in mind that he was almost a millennium old.

"Get ready for a surprise then," I told him, and his chuckle stopped dead in his throat.

"What?" he asked, somewhat panicked I guessed from the sound of his voice.

I had to involuntarily laugh at his reaction.

"Nothing too bad." I clapped his shoulder with my right hand and stopped the car in front of the Gallagers' house. We got out of the vehicle together and walked over to the front door, all the time his eyes resting on my face. I faced the massive door so I wouldn't have to look back at him.

Jaden rang the bell as soon as we reached the door. Chris opened it and gave us a half-worried, half-surprised look as he saw the two of us standing there.

"Good evening, Mr. Gallager," Jaden said in perfect politeness, "I'm Jaden, I'm Claire's guardian angel. Claire was so kind as to bring me with her tonight. I've been wanting to talk to you for a while, but I figured it was best to wait until a proper occasion—such as tonight." His words came out in a continuous flow, almost like a speech. It sounded odd coming from such a young mouth, considering his looks.

Chris stared at Jaden, somewhat perplexed, and then at me, a big question mark in his tired eyes.

"Sorry, Chris," I said guiltily and then quickly hugged him for a greeting. "I didn't invite him. He more or less forced himself on us tonight," I whispered into Chris's ear while hugging him, "but he's okay, though. I'd rather he's on our side than on theirs." I was well-aware Jaden would hear all of the things I said, and it was good he did. He should know how intimidating he could be for me when he was so unpredictable.

"Well then, Jaden," Chris said with a sigh and interest lighting up his sunken eyes when I let go of him. "Please, come in."

7.
Pact

Jenna was sitting by the hearth fire in the big living room. She was twisting a strand of reddish-brown hair in one hand, the other hand resting in her lap, fingers curled around a small black box.

"I'm so glad to see you here, Claire," Jenna said when we appeared in the doorway. "We were beginning to think *they* may have gotten to you." Her worried face looked old in the fire light.

"Sorry," I said quickly and walked across the room to sit down beside her. She released the strand of hair from her fingers, and before I could even blink, her hand was holding mine.

"Don't be. I'm just glad you're okay." She smiled at me with a face that had changed to motherly warm.

"Our Claire here has gotten herself into an extraordinarily interesting chat with the local librarian," Jaden said, and he walked toward us with slow steps.

It was a strange start, and I wondered why Jaden had chosen to be so bold. A thousand years of guarding humans had certainly given him much confidence, but I didn't see why boldness was called for now.

I felt Jenna's hand tremble around mine for a second, all the warmth wiped from her expression and her eyes cold.

"Who's he?" she asked, alarmed. She looked like she was preparing to jump at him if necessary.

"He claims to be Claire's guardian angel," Chris, who was still standing at the door, said cautiously. I wondered if that was because he doubted Jaden's words or because he wanted to protect Jaden by trying to not set his wife off. I couldn't tell, but from the way Jenna and Jaden were tensing, I could tell they were preparing to fight rather than to talk.

Before either of them could act, I interrupted.

"It's true," I said in a voice more stable than I had believed it would be, getting to my feet and taking a step toward Jaden, placing myself between the two of them. "He has saved my life so many times—" It wasn't a good explanation, but it made Jenna concentrate on me rather than on my guardian angel.

"You've even talked to him on the phone, remember?" I stared into Jenna's eyes intensely, trying to persuade her to believe me. "The day Adam died and you called me on my cell phone to tell me. It was Jaden who picked up the phone then. He was with me, keeping me from killing myself."

Memories of those first hours after Adam's death flickered through my head, and hot pain spread through my body. It was happening again, I realized helplessly. The room began to rock around me, and my vision went blurry, everything just smears of orange firelight and brown wood. For a second, I felt unbearable agony, and then it seemed like everything was flowing from me; all strength was leaving my limbs, and I lost control over my body. I felt lightheaded, and then my mind showed me a glimpse of the man I'd been missing for so long, his green eyes gleaming in his pale face, before I swayed and gravity sucked me down, bringing dense blackness with it.

The room was still orange from the firelight when I reopened my eyes. I tried to lift my head to get a better view. Something restrained me. It was warm and strong. I was too weak to fight it.

"Adam?" I asked in a voice that didn't sound like mine. Speaking the one word used up most of the strength I felt I had left. I inhaled slowly, hoping to stop the room from spinning before my eyes.

"I think she's coming around," a female voice said somewhere near my head.

In a second, a face popped up in my vision. I didn't recognize it in the blurriness.

"Claire?" a male voice said my name.

I tried hard to remember what had happened. The library, I had been at the library; then I had driven to the Gallagers with Jaden. Jaden. I blinked and slowly shook my head at the unwillingness of my system to react normally to its surroundings.

"Claire, can you hear me?"

I gave a tiny nod. My body felt like lead, like almost all my energy had been drained from it.

"Okay, put her down on the sofa," the male voice commanded.

"I'm not putting her anywhere until she's fine again," another voice resonated close to my ear.

"Do you think it's comfortable for her that way?" the first voice snapped. It was Chris.

Light footsteps moved across the room. Maybe Jenna. Then I felt everything swirl once more, for a second, before I felt something soft under my legs and back. My shoulder rested against a warm, breathing chest.

"Jaden—" I said, hoping I was guessing right, "don't be stupid. I'm fine," but I ended with a little gasp of breath as I began to shiver.

The chattering of my teeth didn't help me sound convincing either.

"I'm not being stupid," I heard him chuckle above me.

My vision cleared, and I could see normally again. I made out Chris sitting in an armchair close by and Jenna standing beside my head, bending down to feel my forehead with her hand.

"She's cold as ice," Jenna said, her voice all worried. "Do you mind if I warm her up?" The question seemed to be directed at Jaden, for he tensed under my back, and his arms pulled me tighter to his chest.

I coughed under the pressure of his grasp.

"Sorry," he said to me and loosened his arms immediately.

I knew he could do it—warm me up. He had done so before, in the forest, not so far back in the past. But I wished he would let Jenna do it because it was obvious that there still was tension in the air between them and if he let Jenna help;

it might ease things a little. Did he already know she was an angel, too?

"You could bring a blanket," Jaden said stiffly.

"That's not what I meant," Jenna replied, and her voice sounded slightly amused.

"Then what did you mean?" he sounded somewhat annoyed. I shivered.

Jenna's hand made better contact with the skin on my forehead as she pressed her full palm against it, and I saw her eyes begin to gleam in a chestnut brown. Heat streamed through my body from where her hand touched my forehead, warming up every inch of me.

"Thank you," I whispered, relaxing against the sensation while Jaden's body tensed even more.

"You know, I remember you," Jenna said, obviously to Jaden again, "from before the telephone call. Seventh of June 1955. You almost looked the same—a bit younger maybe."

Jaden shifted under my back.

"It was the year I moved away from Aurora. I was an old woman then—everybody thought I had died." Irony was thick in Jenna's voice. Her usually motherly face looked dark with sarcasm. "Me—dead. As if that was possible."

"You two've met before?" I interrupted but didn't get an answer. I quietly wondered what had happened to make Jenna react so weirdly. Jaden was a good person—at least, that was the way I had gotten to know him. Good.

Chris, who had remained silent for a while, now shifted back into my line of vision. Seeing his slightly wrinkled face made it hard to believe that he was only the second youngest in this room.

"I'm sorry, Jenna, but you must have me mixed up with someone," Jaden said. The muscles in his thighs were hard under my spine. It made my back arch up uncomfortably.

Jenna sat down in the armchair beside us. I couldn't see her face anymore, but I could hear her voice from behind my head.

"No, no, no. I can remember it clearly. The day I decided it was time to leave town. You had a terrible row with Agnes. I saw you on the Downer bridge. You both were shouting, and she was in tears."

"Agnes, who? What are you talking about?" Jaden demanded with a note of panic.

"Agnes Hall," Jenna said as if it was the most obvious thing in the world and I sat upright in a flash.

"Agnes Hall?" I interrupted again. This time, nobody ignored me.

Both Jaden and Jenna started at my sudden movement and eyed me curiously. Jenna's brown eyes were wide.

"You know about Agnes Hall?" she asked.

Jaden reached out a hand and pulled me back into his lap with a haul so strong it made me cough.

"I know about an Agnes Hall whose father died when she was sixteen and who adopted her stepfather's name when her mother married again." My voice was low, and my story flowed smoothly. It was a story I had heard often from my grandmother. "It was 1956, and Agnes Hall became Agnes Gabriel."

I could feel Jaden's chest move as he gave a sigh of resignation. "Yes, her," he said, very quietly. "Your grandmother."

In my mind's eye, I saw a picture Gran had shown me of herself, a bright-eyed girl of seventeen with long black hair, holding a huge bouquet of pale blossoms in her slim arms. She was wearing a full-skirted dress in a floral print and smiling at the camera. She was not so much pretty as she was refined and graceful, I had thought. But there was a grace about her, even in this motionless memory of a black and white picture, that would make her stand out in any company.

Jaden had been tenderly curling my hair through his fingers, and now with sudden decisiveness, he pulled me in and kissed my forehead.

"Tell them everything you know—and about Mr. Baker's story, too," he said when his lips left my skin. I looked up, trying to catch a glimpse of the expression on his face. "I have to leave."

He lifted me up as he got to his feet in a quick movement and placed me on the sofa where he had sat a second before.

"Leave? Why?"

He gave me a tender look of gleaming gold before he vanished. "Sorry."

The word hung heavy in the air long after he had disappeared.

Chris walking over to Jenna, pulling her into an armchair with him, made me unfreeze. I hated how Jaden always seemed to have an agenda that he wouldn't share with me. He would appear and be wonderful, and then, with no indication of regret or affection, he would depart. More than ready, it seemed, to forget about me.

It was something he had mastered perfectly, and I was the one to stay behind, breakable and lost. I needed him. Did he not understand that? His seemingly random appearing and disappearing used to annoy me. Today was the first time I felt hurt.

It was probably a good rule that guardian angels were not supposed to reveal themselves to their fosterlings. If he had obeyed that one rule, there would have been fewer misunderstandings—also, I would be dead—

"What did he mean, tell us everything?" Chris said, tearing me from my thoughts. Jenna, sitting on his lap, looked at me with suspicious eyes.

"He isn't exactly dangerous, is he?" Jenna asked with a tense voice. Her eyes were tightening slightly as I sat up and leaned against the back of the sofa with one shoulder so I could have a better look at them.

"Not exactly, not to us," I murmured, my thoughts running laps in my head, trying to catch up with Jaden's reasons.

Both Jenna and Chris shot me a doubtful glance, which would have made me laugh out loud if I hadn't forgotten how to feel amused. That part of me was gone; buried somewhere in the wet earth of Aurora Cemetery alongside their son. I felt a jolt of pain running through my insides and closed my eyes for a second to steady myself.

"Are you alright, dear?" Jenna's voice came from too close beside me. When I opened my eyes, she was standing right next to me in front of the sofa. She must have teleported there. She acted like a worried mother as she bent down to feel my forehead with her hand once more.

"Temperature seems normal," she said to Chris.

"I'm f... fine," I croaked. I felt incapacitated, defenseless, like a puppet in its strings.

"There's no need to pretend with us," Chris said with a hard smile deforming his pale lips. The firelight threw shadows across his face that made it look bizarre. "You know, we feel everything you feel, and what you feel is not so different from what I feel."

I nodded, more to myself, and straightened my chest, breathing evenly. Of course it wasn't.

"I'm sorry," I apologized as if it would do any good, "I'm really trying to conceal my feelings and hide these moments of weakness that keep happening. If I don't, people are afraid to be around me. Everything is easier if I just pretend."

Chris nodded. I understood he was doing the same. Both of us were fighting the same horror in our lives, and both of us were failing over and over again. It had such power over him that he had lost his ability to use his wings. For a moment, a wave of pity washed over me. He was wrong. It wasn't similar, the way he felt, to how I was feeling; it was far worse. Adam had been his mark and his son, and he had lost both.

Jenna had sat down beside me and put her arm around my shoulders. She was comforting me, not in the way Jaden would have; she was doing it in a way a mother would comfort her daughter. I leaned toward her for a moment, savoring the feeling I had so long missed in my life. It wasn't the same as it had been with my mom, but it was close enough to feel at home for a while.

"So, Jaden wants me to tell you everything," I started, my voice muffled by the way I was leaning my head against Jenna's shoulder. I was positive he had his reasons to want them to know everything, and Jaden had never misled me, so I found it best to trust him and obey his wish. I started at the beginning; how I had found out about Adam's abilities, the book at the library. Chris and Jenna listened to me intently and never interrupted. They sensed how hard it was for me to speak about Adam. Chris already knew parts of the story, but he listened to it like it was the first time he heard about it. He soaked up all the information I offered, and I wondered if, to them, Adam's existence already felt like a fairy tale the way it did to me.

It wasn't until I told Mr. Baker's story about Aurora that they started asking questions. They wanted every detail of what the old man had said. I recalled everything as perfectly as I was able to and fed them the details willingly.

The whole time I was speaking, I was feeling how bizarre it all was. Me, plain little Claire Gabriel, sitting by the fire in a grand house, discussing history and supernatural beings with angels as if I did it every day. I half-expected it to be a dream, but it felt too real to be just that. I felt the heat radiating from the fireplace, Jenna's shoulder under my cheek, Chris's gaze on my face.

I lowered my gaze as I reached the end of the story. Silence had spread in the room, the only source of sound the crackling fire, all three of us sunken into deep thoughts of our own.

"What was she like?" I broke the silence, my voice barely more than a whisper.

Chris eyed me for a moment.

"Who?" he asked quietly.

I felt my head swim for a second as the profoundness of the words spoken tonight crushed down on my mind.

"My Gran." I slowly sat up and stretched my spine. It cracked somewhere in the small of my back.

I had to wait for a few minutes before either of them moved. The supernatural couple, both their beautiful faces stern.

"She was an extraordinary girl," Jenna finally said. The way her voice sounded let me know that she wouldn't say more right now, but even this simple sentence made my heart jump for a second. Of course she was—she had to be. I had known her as an old woman. She had lived alone—never married my father's father. She had always told me that they'd had one single night together and nothing more, but that had been enough that she knew she would never fall in love with another man. She stayed alone rather than marry out of fear of growing old unaccompanied. I had tried many times to imagine the courage she needed to face the attitudes of the times and the strength she must have had to raise her son alone and on her own. I wished I could be like her—standing tall in the face of everything life had thrown at her. I hoped she'd thought I'd made a good granddaughter.

We sat in silence for a while, all of us back to our own thoughts. It was unusual that the Gallagers' house was so quiet. It made me wonder why neither Geoffrey nor Ben had interrupted our conversation. Of course, it was fortunate they hadn't but still strange.

"What's the matter?" Chris asked me, clearly sensing my feelings.

"Where is everyone else?" I voiced my question.

"Geoffrey has a day off, and Ben," he lowered his gaze and turned around to watch the flames licking the insides of the fireplace, "he's gone out."

I heard Jenna sigh almost inaudibly beside me.

"She's always so scared—ever since we lost Adam—she almost didn't let Ben set a foot outside the house alone in the beginning," Chris explained the sound.

I understood. I would be scared, too. If I had children, I would probably be the worst mom in the world because I would be so overprotective, knowing what kind of dangers were waiting out there.

"Shh," Jenna hushed him, "we really have worse problems than my worries right now. Ben is no target for *them*, at least you keep telling me. It's *you* we have to worry about. If you don't get back your wings, your strength, you might be easier prey than even Claire."

I had always taken Jenna for a gentle nature; right now she seemed more like an officer, prioritizing measures to prevent a catastrophe. But I had to agree. None of the demons had ever had any contact with Ben. If we were lucky, they didn't even know he existed. But they knew about Chris, and they didn't like the way he had kept them from finding him for years, suppressing his angel-powers, never spreading wings, leading a normal life. If they somehow found out that he was as defenseless as I was, they might come for him any second.

I straightened up a little, eying Chris carefully. His face showed fear and pain, both fighting to claim the full space in his features.

"Jenna's right, Chris. We need to find out what's wrong with your wings, and you need your powers back. You're an easy target without them, and it's only a matter of time before the demons come after you." *As they will come after you*, a voice in my head added, reminding me painfully that Chris wasn't the only one I should worry about. *Maybe they will*, I countered the voice, *but I have Jaden who takes good care of me. He's basically guarding me around the clock. And he is ancient—powerful.*

The voice didn't argue.

On Chris's face, fear was winning the fight. He looked from me to Jenna and back again.

"I know you are right—and I don't like it." He grimaced as he admitted the magnitude of the problem. Then his eyes finally stayed locked on Jenna's. "But I'm not alone."

Jenna smiled warmly, her eyes melting into his, showing nothing but her love.

"Right," I interrupted their silent exchange, "but Jenna's not *that* strong. She might be older than you, but still, her angel existence is roughly one-hundred-and-fifty years old." I watched Jenna shift her weight, her eyes still on Chris's. Her violinist hands were folded across her chest, one of them rubbing her upper arm. She didn't look powerful nor dangerous. She looked like an ordinary woman, like an artist—nothing like supernatural.

"She can't protect you. If they come for her, she'll be lucky if she can protect herself. Alone, she is helpless; we all are. If we don't stick together, they can tear each one of us apart— some of us with more effort," my eyes remained on Jenna's lovely face, "some of us easier." Both Jenna and Chris looked at me. They knew I was speaking of myself. They could tell by the panic in my voice.

My breath had accelerated, and my heart was thumping madly against my ribs. Helpless—that's what I was.

Jenna had moved toward me slowly. She was putting her arms around me, pulling me against her like a mother would a child that had a nightmare.

"Shhh—" She rocked me back and forth. "I promise that I will be there for you if you need me. And Chris will, too." I felt Chris's hand on my head, and the tears I had been holding back ran down my cheeks, wetting Jenna's blouse.

"You're not alone. As long as the three of us are standing, we are going to fight against the darkness." It was neither Jenna nor Chris's voice.

"Jaden," I sobbed and broke out of Jenna's arms to rush into his. My frustration and disappointment over his behavior earlier vanished into thin air, replaced by a tidal wave of gratitude. He was back, and for the moment, that was all that mattered. I could ask him later where he had gone.

"And you, too, Chris and Jenna," Jaden said past my head, "you can count on my help, too."

"So that's it then," Chris said when I wound myself back out of Jaden's arms and stood beside him. "The three of us against the evil." He held out his hand to Jaden.

"The three of us." Jaden took it, and they looked into each other's eyes before they turned to Jenna, who placed her hands into theirs.

"The three of us," she said with fierce determination.

Chris smiled at the others and said, "I know I'm not much of a fighter right now, but as soon as I get my powers back, I'm going to kick those demons' asses."

I had never heard him speak like that. And for the first time since Adam's death, I saw something similar to hope flaring in his eyes.

"Wait," I half-shrieked as I took in that their little pact was based on the number of three. "I'm going to help, too."

"No way!" It was Jaden. He looked worried just by the thought of me putting myself in danger on a demon hunt.

"Yes way," I interrupted his thoughts, not wanting him to come to a conclusion. "I have as much reason to hunt them as you have." Images of Adam's smiling face flashed through my head, leaving me aching and empty. "I know I don't stand a chance if I try to hurt them—but I can do some research, and I can try to find out as much as possible about their weaknesses."

None of them looked too happy with my speech. Jenna's eyebrows were pulling together over the bridge of her nose, building a fine line of worry on her face. Chris mirrored my emptiness and my determination, but he hesitated to agree with me.

Jaden shook his head, almost angry. He didn't like the idea—I saw it in his eyes. It would mean more danger for me.

"Four of us," I said matter-of-factly and folded my arms across my chest. This was my life, too.

8.
Difficult

"What do you think you're doing?" Jaden's voice followed me into the car when I climbed in on the driver's side. "You... can't." He was nearly speechless with disapproval and distress, yanking open the car door and throwing himself into the passenger seat. He flexed his hands in front of his chest in a gesture that screamed *out of words*.

I ignored him. At least, I had been able to convince Jenna and Chris that it was the right thing for me to do—to help where I could until I could be sure that all the people I loved were safe.

Sophie, I thought. She was all of my family that was left. She was everything to me now that the man I loved had been taken from me forcefully. And she was already packing her bags to leave for Indianapolis. I would be on my own in no time. Which meant a lot of time for *research* on the one hand; on the other hand, nobody would miss me when the demons came for me. I swallowed the lump that was building in my throat. I knew that it was only a matter of time; and the longer the peaceful no-show of the evil side of this war lasted, the more suspicious it grew for me. I wanted to be prepared, I wanted to be a little less vulnerable—physically and emotionally. I needed something like armor to protect me from what was coming... a shield.

I quickly started the engine, determined to act, not talk. It sprang to life and set into motion the second I pushed down the gas pedal.

My anxiety over the safety of those I loved, not to mention my own safety, must have shown on my face because Jaden calmed down quickly and changed his tactics.

"Don't worry." He patted my arm. "I'll be there when you need me."

I *grmpf*ed and concentrated on the road. This was another thing I wasn't going to discuss with him. Relying on him just made me feel more vulnerable. I made a mental list of what I needed to do to take charge of my situation. Protect myself against the demons. Help Chris get his wings back. And of course, I needed to know everything Mr. Baker could tell me about demons. I needed—

"When's the last time you've eaten?" Jaden asked, interrupting me mid-thought.

"What?"

The road was almost empty. It was late. I hadn't noticed how late it was, and my stomach responded to Jaden's question like it had a mind of its own.

"Let's find a place to eat," he suggested. His voice was back to all friendly and controlled. There was no hint of his distress left in his tone, and from the corner of my eye, I saw that his face was relaxed.

"Looks like Bobby's is open," he announced, pointing through the windshield. "How about it?"

I pulled into the nearly empty lot, parking where the light from the windows fell most brightly.

Jaden's change of mood made me feel better. I needed his support these days, not his disapproval.

I climbed out of the car and waited for Jaden to do the same. After a few seconds, I bent down to take a look inside the vehicle. He wasn't there. The car was empty.

"Jaden?" I asked into the darkness, fear creeping up my neck. Where had he gone?

After a few seconds, I asked again, "Jaden? Where are you?"

"Right here," a voice beside my ear said.

I jumped and almost fell into the car as I leaned forward in reflex.

Two hands caught me by the shoulders and pulled me back. They turned my body around with a little too much force to be comfortable.

"Sorry."

I stared into Jaden's golden eyes.

"You scared me," I complained, out of breath. My heart was thumping at top speed.

Under the pair of golden eyes, Jaden flashed me a boyish grin.

"Don't do that again." I swatted his arm with the flat of my hand and grinned triumphantly when he reacted with an exclamation. Although, in truth, I doubted how much he had even felt my blow. I was pretty sure it took much, much more to make an impression on him. I shook my head in annoyance—what a child he could be.

"Let's go," I commanded, enjoying the chance to boss him around even if it was just over when to enter a restaurant, and marched ahead. Jaden opened the door for me, and I stepped in with my guardian angel close at my heels.

When we entered the restaurant, a cloud of voices and the sound of cutlery on china mixed with laughter greeted us. Jaden walked ahead. He crossed the room in quick strides, aiming for a table at the back.

"Take a seat, please," he said, politely pulling a chair out, and waited for me to settle down on the uncomfortable-looking piece of wood.

"Thanks." I walked around the table and sank down onto the chair. It felt strange to be with Jaden in such a public place. He was there at school, every day, but there we officially didn't know each other any more than he did the other students. There, we were just classmates and nothing more. Now we were—what exactly were we?

I was his fosterling. He was my guardian angel. He had become someone I could trust, somebody who was there for me. He had healed my wounds and taken away my pain. Images of the disaster in the demon's villa last year flashed through my mind. He had let the enemy capture him to be able to protect me, to be there for me. He had endured pain and humiliation just for me. He was more than just an angel. He was my friend.

My eyes wandered across the table until they found Jaden's face on the other side. He was already studying the menu, just another late-night customer with food on his mind. A pang of affection ran through my body.

"What can I get for you?" The voice of the waitress interrupted my thoughts. I looked up at her blankly.

Behind a pretty face and a mane of reddish-blond hair, I saw a sign saying "Burger of the Day plus soft drink".

"I'll have the burger of the day, please," I shot, surprised by the speed of my decision.

"To drink?" the pretty face asked in an unnerved tone.

"Nothing," I shook my head to the side and looked at her more closely.

"Sure?" Strands of reddish hair bounced from her shoulder as she cocked her head with an unbelieving expression like I had just said no to the jackpot.

I felt myself blush and gave her a quick nod before I looked back down, examining the tablecloth with unwarranted interest.

"Got it," the waitress sighed. "And for you?" she addressed Jaden in the same manner.

"The same as the lady, if you please," he said with a slight snicker.

"Okay," she said between her teeth which were exposed in a bizarre friendly grin. She turned on her heels in a somewhat elegant spin and disappeared behind a corner.

"What's wrong with her?" I asked into the red and white pattern of the tablecloth, not really expecting an answer.

"Pregnant," he said quietly but without hesitation. "And her boyfriend's on drugs."

I looked up, half-expecting him to show me a victorious grin that would tell me that it was a joke; but there was no grin on his face. Not the hint of a smile decorated his lips.

I leaned forward to get closer to his face. "Are you serious?" I wasn't sure if I wanted an answer to that.

A tiny nod confirmed my worries.

"How do you know?" I asked before I could think.

Jaden leaned back in his chair and smiled at me with white teeth. He seemed to be enjoying this. "Already forgotten who I am?" he challenged me with an indulgent grin and a twinkle in his eye.

"You're my—" I began, but then his eyes flickered around the room, and I broke mid-sentence and lowered my voice. "You're my guardian angel."

"Correct," he answered, equally hushed, "but I'm more than that." He eyed me for a second like he was waiting for the theatrical tension to build up. I waited for him to speak, watching his lips.

"I'm an angel."

Okay, I already knew that. I rolled my eyes.

"Don't do that," said Jaden with a forbidding look on his face. "I'm a real angel." He said it as if he was sharing something top secret with me.

"And Chris and Jenna are what?" I asked, a bit confused.

"Half-breeds," said Jaden in a whisper.

"Which is a bad thing?" I asked, somewhat disturbed by the way he said it.

"No." His answer was curt.

"What then?" I folded my arms across my chest and leaned back, fixing him with my eyes.

Jaden looked back at me. His golden eyes looked flat in the slightly orange light in the restaurant. He picked up a piece of bread from the basket that was standing in the middle of the table, separating the flat surface into two halves—his own and mine.

"Nothing," was all he said and took a hearty bite, keeping his eyes locked on mine.

I watched his jaws move rhythmically. I had never taken Jaden for someone who cared about what people were, where they came from. I had always thought that he was someone who judged people by what they did, not who their parents were.

After a moment, I dropped my eyes. I felt bad. What if he hadn't meant it the way I had understood? What if he really just meant half-breed as a sort of description of a creature's roots. Like a mixture of races. Nothing good, nothing bad. Just a statement.

"Oh, come on," Jaden said, and I looked up uncertainly.

I wasn't sure if he sounded angry or amused. It was something in between, and I neither felt like being shouted at nor like being laughed at.

When my head was completely lifted, I noticed the waitress slouching toward us with two heavily laden plates in her hands. My eyes snapped to her stomach. She had a small round belly that was too pronounced to be part of her slender form. My eyes fluttered from her to Jaden, to her, and back to Jaden.

The guardian angel nodded a tiny little bit, and I almost coughed at my own stupidity.

Of course she was pregnant. It was obvious. I just hadn't noticed before.

"Here you go," the girl said without enthusiasm as she set down the plates on each side of the basket. She didn't sound like her mood had improved at all.

"Thanks," I said, but my eyes were back on her belly until she turned around and vanished behind the corner again.

"Don't think I'm stupid," I told Jaden.

He gave me an innocent look.

"You saw her belly." My eyes bore into his accusingly.

Jaden withstood my gaze for a minute before he shrugged. "Sure I saw it."

I felt myself grow a few inches by the victory of seeing through him.

"But the belly didn't show the part about the boyfriend." He leaned over his burger, picked up a fork and knife, and started eating.

"Maybe he isn't," I suggested, and instead of just grabbing my burger, I mirrored his movements, picking up my cutlery as well and slicing up the burger that sat on a mountain of fries on a plain white plate.

"Be sure, he is." Jaden swallowed his mouthful of burger and replaced the vanished food with a fork full of fries.

"How can you know that?" I asked again, expecting a better answer than before. I even paused eating to listen to his answer.

"I already told you... I'm an angel. I know things."

I stared at him until his movements slowed and finally stopped.

"What now?" he asked, somewhere between amused and irritated.

"Don't tell me you can read minds," I dreaded the worst. "Because if you can, I swear to God, I'll..."

"Don't swear to someone you don't know," he interrupted me with cold eyes.

I swallowed the rest of the sentence and looked at him, feeling guilty.

"No," he sighed and let a half-smile flash across his face as he took in my expression, "I can't read minds—fortunately.

The mess of feelings in this room is enough to drive anyone crazy. I don't feel any need to know what they think exactly."

Jaden started to eat again while I watched him.

"I can assume a little better than the part-angels can. Call it intuition. I know almost exactly why somebody feels the way they do without asking."

Once more, I was amazed by what this heavenly species could do, and once more, I felt transparent, like I was nothing more than a glass bottle filled with reasons and motives, all visible to this thousand-year-old man across the table.

We finished the meal in silence and left an extra-large tip sticking out under the breadbasket. I had to admit that half a cow and a ton of French fries could make a hungry girl feel better even if the dinner conversation had been exceedingly unusual.

There was a cold, steady breeze blowing as we walked out into the darkness and climbed into my car. Spring was not imminent. I shivered just a little and decided to ask Jaden one more question.

"When do you think they will attack?" I asked while I was steering the vehicle out of the lot and back onto the street.

"They?" Jaden asked, surprised.

"The demons," I whispered and instantly wondered why—we were alone in the car.

"Don't know," he answered with a lightheartedness I hadn't expected to hear in combination with this topic.

"I'm still afraid," I admitted. He would know anyway.

His low snort and then a hushed chuckle as an answer made me wonder what he was thinking. Was he trying to downplay everything so I wouldn't put myself in danger?

"I'm going to talk to Mr. Baker on the weekend. I have to find out what else he knows," I returned to the discussion earlier this evening. "I think maybe he could help a little."

I was positive that Mr. Baker knew a lot of things that could help us, and I wanted to know every single one of them. I had a strong feeling that his knowledge might be essential one day. *One day soon*, the voice in my head corrected me.

I hurried down the corridor to the classroom the next day. I was late to school again. Jaden had left the minute I turned off my car the night before, promising to be there for me if I needed him. I had felt safe enough to take a quick shower, but once in bed, sleep refused to come. It had taken hours of tossing and turning for my body to finally shut down, and when it did, the dreams had come. Adam had been in them, bringing with him the awful, aching pain in my chest. The last dream had left me hot and drenched in sweat, my heart pounding as if I had just run a marathon. It hadn't been a nightmare.

"Over here," I heard Lydia call me from nearby. She waved at me and gestured at a free chair beside hers.

"Thanks," I whispered and sat down the moment the teacher entered the classroom.

Lydia already had her books open in front of her. I searched my bag for my books and came up empty. I hadn't packed the right things for the day. Instead, I had taken another shower right after I had rolled out of bed in the morning.

Sweat was building up on my neck when I just thought of the dream. I blushed and bent down, pretending to put down my bag so I could hide my face.

I could feel Adam's hands gliding down my neck, my back, my jaw, my throat, my chest, my thighs...

A loud cough brought me back to reality. My hand was lying on my neck, my fingers in my hair where Adam's hands had been only a few hours before. With a start, I snatched my hand away and looked surreptitiously around the classroom to see who might have noticed.

No one. Everyone was paying attention to the lecture. With one exception. With the tiniest nod and the biggest grin, Jaden let me know he had been enjoying my minute almost as much as I had.

Dang, I thought and hid my face behind my hands. Jaden always knew how I felt—always. So he had known last night. I felt myself die from embarrassment and shifted lower into my chair. The earth beneath me didn't open a hole and swallow me like I was hoping. It remained rock-solid beneath my feet for the rest of the morning.

"Steamy night?" Jaden asked mischievously when he caught up with me in the corridor after class. His golden eyes twinkled.

"Ummm—" was all I could get to leave my mouth. I felt my face turn pink and looked around for Lydia, who had to be somewhere near.

"Lydia," I half-shouted when I spotted her ahead in the corridor. I hurried on and left Jaden standing where he was. I simply had no idea what to tell him. I had never had a dream like this before. Not even when Adam had been...*alive*...

All of the heat of the dream was gone within a fraction of a second. Suddenly, I felt dizzy.

Dead, the voice in my head echoed. *Dead*.

I felt the blood drain from my head and numbness take command of my body. My heart, on the other hand, screamed silently in pain as if some terrible unseen knife were slicing it into a million pieces. A pale haze blinded me, and I reached out reflexively for something to grab onto. My fingers curled desperately around something soft.

"Are you alright?" a frightened voice asked. It was Lydia. I was hanging on to her.

I tried to nod. I had to be strong. I would not be some labile creature so easily destroyed by, by... by what? I didn't know. I had promised myself to be strong, and I had failed. *Again*, the voice in my head added, and the frequency of its appearance in my thoughts should have alarmed me, but I had more immediate problems.

I couldn't see, and the sound of my blood was a roar in my ears. My legs had turned to pudding. Everything was blurry, and the noise of my blood rushing through my body was so loud that I could hardly distinguish the sounds coming from outside my body. A cool hand pressing down on my face helped me refocus. I directed my eyes toward the face behind it and continued staring until I finally made out the outline of a familiar face.

From a distance, I could hear someone saying. "Claire! Claire! Are you okay?"

I was silent for a moment, unable to process either the question or a reply.

"Sit down," the voice commanded and pressed me down until I landed in a hard chair, which supported my weight willingly but didn't make me any more comfortable. I felt a wave of nausea and then, in a split second, it was over.

I was sitting in an empty classroom, and Greg and Lydia were crouched protectively around me. My right hand was still clenched on Lydia's sweatshirt. I forced my hand away from her.

"I'm sorry," I breathed out weakly. "Don't know what happened there—"

I looked away so I wouldn't have to explain myself for the hundredth time because, for the hundredth time, I wouldn't have a new reason—it was always the same.

"It's okay," Greg said. "Just stay quiet for a minute."

Only then did I notice Jaden. My guardian angel, but not with me. As far away as he could stand without leaving the room. Instead of showing alarm or concern or any intention to take action, his beautiful face was crumpled in agony. He made not the slightest move. Greg was speaking again.

"Can you stand up?" Greg's voice claimed my attention. He looked concerned when I did so. "Do you think you can walk?"

I pondered his question for a moment. "I think so—" I answered truthfully.

"Thanks," I said and set one foot after the other carefully.

Together, my friends ushered me to the door and watched with parental care as I ventured out into the traffic flow. I must have convinced them of my recovery because, by the time I turned into the next corridor, they were gone, and it was Jaden keeping pace with me. A sideways glance at him showed me that he was still wearing the same expression.

"What's happening, Jaden?" I asked in a low murmur, but he didn't answer. The look of anguish he had been wearing smoothed into a guarded mask, and then he vanished.

He didn't show up for any of our other morning classes, and it seemed like an eternity until lunch. Instead of paying attention in class, I spent my time puzzling over why he hadn't come to my aid. It was so not the Jaden that I knew. But then, did I really know him? Did he feel incapacitated by the presence of the other students? Or was he getting tired of saving me? Did he start to find my pathetic existence ridiculous? I couldn't blame him if he did.

When I sat down opposite Lydia and Greg with my bowl of Thai soup, I spotted Amber and Jaden at the other end of the room. Jaden was looking at her intensely like he was trying to decipher something. His face was strained.

Amber looked beautiful as always. I wondered how long it would take before Jaden finally forgot that he had come here to protect me. Maybe what had happened in the morning were the first signs of him changing his mind. I could already see him with Amber, hand in hand, a perfectly happy couple; both extraordinary, both beautiful. Once he recognized this truth, he was going to leave me to my fate.

I ate my soup in silence and waited for the others to finish.

"What are you doing this weekend?" Greg asked cheerily as we got to our feet and headed for the next class.

"I'm invited to the Walters'," Lydia hooted, all happy as she beamed at us. "Richard's parents wanted to have us both over for the weekend."

Greg rolled his eyes at me. I warned him off with a meaningful squint. At least one of us was happy. It was great for Lydia that her relationship with Richard was growing into something serious. Ian, Richard's brother was my sister's boyfriend. I knew Ian quite well, and if Richard was half as sweet to Lydia as Ian was to Sophie, Lydia was one of the luckiest women in the world.

"And you?" Greg asked me.

"Nothing special," I shrugged, "Sophie is leaving for her internship tomorrow," I quickly explained to them that my sister was going to Indianapolis for a while. "I guess I'll read a bit, catch up with homework, study, whatever..."

"You could come over and have lunch with my family on Sunday if you'd like," Greg offered with obvious hope in his blue eyes.

"Umm—thanks," I pursed my lips for a second, searching for an excuse, "—but I'm already meeting somebody this Sunday."

Greg eyed me suspiciously. "A friend of yours?" His casual tone was completely forced.

"Almost—" I countered, "—my boss." This was a lie. And then I realized that maybe this wasn't too bad an idea. I knew that I needed to talk to Mr. Baker anyway if I wanted to know more about what he knew. Time was rushing by, and I needed to learn everything he knew as quickly as possible.

Greg watched me think and finally shrugged. "Another time then," he said and led the way through the desks as we reached the classroom.

I came home from school early. When I opened the door and stepped into the house, Sophie's things lay strewn across the stairs and living room.

"Sophie?" I called before I even took off my shoes, tensing for a fight.

I slowly walked toward the kitchen to look for her. When I was halfway there, I heard her.

"Up here!" her voice came from her room upstairs.

I hurried back and up the staircase just to find Sophie in the middle of more clothes, kneeling on the floor next to an open trunk.

"I honestly don't know what I should pack and what I shouldn't," she said when I poked my head into her room.

I walked to the corner of the room and started picking up things she had dropped there. When my hands were full, I carried the pile of clothes to her bed and folded them neatly, wordless.

"You don't need to help," Sophie commented on my activities.

I ignored it. It was our last evening together. I wanted to be around for a while, I wanted her to see that I was alright on my own, that she could leave without a guilty conscience nagging her.

"It's alright," I said and handed her the small pile of folded shirts, "I'm glad to help." I sat down right above the trunk at the end of Sophie's bed. The trunk was half full.

"Do you need any of the things from downstairs?" I asked.

Sophie looked at me for a while. "Are you sure it's okay that I leave?" Her face was worried, and her young features looked old with the burden of taking care of me. I hated to see her like this. It made me feel like she would give up everything for me—if I needed her here.

"I'll be fine," I nudged her shoulder and gave her a reassuring look. "Don't you always worry about me. You've got a life of your own you need to take care of."

Sophie straightened up and hugged me quickly. "I'm gonna miss you, little sister," she said as she squeezed me for a moment. "Just promise me that you won't do anything stupid while I'm gone, will you?"

I nodded into her shoulder and pulled free of her arms. "Don't worry," I repeated, "I'll be alright. Nothing's going to happen to me. I've got Ja—" I stopped mid-word and coughed to disguise my mistake, "—Amber," I corrected quickly, "and Lydia and Greg. They are there for me if I need something." I searched her face, looking for signs that she had taken notice of my error.

"Of course," she answered with a smile. It made me relax. "You have a bunch of great people as friends." She bent back down to her trunk and put the pile of shirts I had handed her on top of the other things in there before she looked up again. "Tell them I said they should take good care of you while I'm away." She smiled at me and winked, and I nodded at her, not at all intending to forward her request to anybody.

9.
Coffee

The alarm clock rang aggressively on the bedside table. "Shut up," I groaned from somewhere between the pillows and curled more deeply into the blanket, but the noise didn't stop. So I reluctantly unfolded myself out of the pillows and killed the alarm with one hand.

It was Sunday morning. Sophie had left for her internship in Indianapolis the night before with Ian, and I was alone in our house. Sophie was going to be gone for twelve weeks—if nobody died this time.

To be honest, I was glad that I had the house to myself. I needed the time and the space to do some research.

As I had told Jaden, Jenna, and Chris, I was determined to help find out what I could about demons until I found something that would help us fight them. Naturally, Jaden had tried to talk me out of it after I had decided to fight with them. It had been exhausting. He had his points, that knowing too much would make me an even more attractive target to them and that whatever I found out, I would still be human and they would still be supernatural, strong and terrible and dangerous.

Still—I was the one to choose what I wanted to do with my life, and I was decided. I was going to fight.

I slid out of bed and got myself cleaned up and dressed at record speed. Today was the first day of my research, and I wanted to use it as entirely as possible.

I rushed to the kitchen and grabbed an apple, tucked it between my teeth while I zipped up my jacket, and ate it on my way out of the house. Pale sunlight greeted me from behind the houses. My car was standing in the driveway where I had parked it the day before.

I hurried through the cold March morning, the apple still between my teeth. I let them sever the flesh of the fruit and chewed while one hand fumbled for the keys in my bag. I slid into the car, put the key in the ignition, and continued eating. As I turned the apple to take another bite, my eyes fell on my wrist. A thin silver bracelet with a small purple stone woven into several layers of shiny silver was wound around it. It was Adam's birthday present. He had given it to me on my nineteenth birthday, and I hadn't taken it off since the day he had died. It made the memory of him somehow tangible. The purple stone glimmered in the morning sun. It looked so pretty that I couldn't take my eyes off it for a while, losing track of time, lost in memories. It was only when my cell phone rang that I could tear my gaze off it.

A text message from Sophie.

Hi! Everything is fine here. Call me when you can. Sophie

I stared at the display for a second and decided to call her later. First, I would meet Mr. Baker and do my homework on demonology. I was determined to be of use in the little pact with the Gallagers.

I finished my apple and turned the key to start for the city. I heard a low gurgle, and the engine fell silent.

"Oh, come on," I said to the car. I turned the key again. Another gurgling noise before the engine fell silent again. "Not now, please."

The car didn't respond. Neither to my attempts to start the engine nor to my pleas. So, I got back out, my bag tucked under my arm, and slammed the door shut behind me. Luckily, my destination wasn't too far, and I started walking down the street.

The curtains in the windows of the houses I passed were all drawn closed. It was too early on Sunday morning for anyone to bother getting out of bed. I didn't see many cars on the street before I reached the crossing into the main road five minutes later. It was quarter to ten. I was late.

When I hurried across the street, I already saw him standing in front of Noel's, the small coffee shop across the parking lot behind Aurora High School. He looked taller against the sunlight than he actually was. His old back bent a little, and his trench coat swung around his knees with every tiny step he was taking as he walked up and down in front of the window, waiting for me.

I hurried up even more and half-jogged along the sidewalk toward the old man.

"So sorry I'm late, Mr. Baker," I called as I was close enough for him to hear me. I had called him Friday evening and asked him to meet me. Knowing he would get part of my story, he had agreed to meet me to talk today. I had blocked the entire day for him so we would have time to talk about the details of our knowledge.

He lifted a hand and dropped it back to his side as if to say *it's alright, never you mind, girl*, but he didn't say a word until I stood in front of him.

"Good morning, Claire," he said in a rough voice. It sounded like he had a bad cold.

"Oh my God, Mr. Baker, you sound sick," I uttered.

He held a handkerchief in his hand and continued coughing into the checkered fabric.

"I'm fine, girl, I'm fine," he reassured me and blew his nose. "Let's get inside. It's still winter out here."

He shuffled toward the entrance door of Noel's and pushed it open with his free hand.

I hurried to help him hold it open while he entered the small shop.

"Good morning," a voice greeted us from behind the counter. It wasn't old Noel like I had expected. A girl my age was standing next to the coffee maker, a glass in one hand, a dishtowel in the other.

"Good morning," Mr. Baker croaked at her and walked past the counter toward the window where he sank into the nearest armchair.

I followed him quickly, shooting the waitress an uneasy smile for a greeting, and sat down at the table, across from the old man. He peeled himself out of his coat with some difficulty.

"Are you sure you're alright?" I voiced my worries. He looked older than usual, and the way he continued to cough made me start to think there was something seriously wrong with him. Maybe I shouldn't have called him and asked him to meet me today. If I had known how sick he was—

"Fine, Claire," he repeated. "Just get me some tea, and I'll be perfect." He smiled at me as he spoke. The way his eyes twinkled reminded me of the gleeful expression he'd had the last time we had talked; when he had thought I was an angel. What on earth had made him think that I was?

The waitress came over to get our orders. She reminded me of a younger version of Sophie. She was pretty, and her reddish-brown hair danced around her face as she moved toward us.

"What can I get you?" she asked in a girlish voice. She couldn't be much older than me.

"I'll have tea, and could you bring us some of those great chocolate cookies, my dear?" Mr. Baker said kindly.

The girl grinned and nodded. "Sure," she said.

I was positive that she wasn't used to seeing many old people around here.

"Hot chocolate for me, please," I quickly said and turned to Mr. Baker while the girl turned and moved back toward the counter where she started handling several pots and jars.

"Thank you for coming today, Mr. Baker," I said to him with still split thoughts. I didn't want to keep him out for too long when he was obviously sick, but I needed every bit of what he knew about our enemies, and I needed it fast. That part of my head, the one greedy for information, won over the commiserative one and I felt the first questions welling up in my throat.

I bit my tongue hard so I wouldn't drown him in questions right away. I had also promised to tell him what I knew and how I happened to know so much about angels and demons; I had to save some room for his questions, too.

My eyes crossed the room while I was thinking of a proper way to ask him if he knew how to help an angel get back his wings. We weren't the only customers in the cafe. At a bigger table, across the room, three women and a boy of maybe two years were sipping hot chocolate and coffee. The boy was playing with his spoon noisily. He looked perfectly happy, considering the way he smiled at me with his perfect rosy lips as he splattered his chocolate all over the table. It was the smile of a child who had nothing to fear, who was wanted and loved—not alone.

I noticed Mr. Baker watching me when I turned back to him.

"Perfectly happy, isn't he?" the old man asked, obviously not expecting an answer. "When was the last time we could feel that safe?" The tone he used made me think he didn't want an answer to that one either; and his eyes made me think that it had been a long, long time for him.

I shuddered as I thought of the reason why we were sitting here; not a fancy Sunday morning coffee but more serious matters; things we had to talk through to size up our chance of surviving; and Mr. Baker had no idea how very real this was for me.

"So, how come a young woman like you asks an old man out for coffee on a pretty Sunday morning like this?" Mr. Baker asked, his eyes twinkling at me, intrigued by the topic he was looking forward to discussing.

When I had called him, I told him it was important that I talked to him—somewhere the supernatural wouldn't expect us to be. I had been surprised that he had accepted my idea to meet at Noel's little coffee shop.

"I haven't been here in a while," Mr. Baker said. "Nothing has changed."

He watched the waitress set two cups down on the table between us. I waited until she vanished back behind the counter and then leaned forward.

Mr. Baker mirrored my movement. He took a sip of tea, coughed once as he inhaled the steaming air above the hot liquid, and set the cup back on the table.

I watched him for a minute as he warmed his hands on the heated surface of the cup before I decided that it was best to come straight out with what I needed.

"Mr. Baker," I started, "what do you know about angels that have lost their powers?"

My words hung in the air between us, their meaning hidden to the rest of the room by the sound of the child's spoon hitting the china of the cup over and over again.

Mr. Baker looked at me with wise eyes for a moment before he opened his mouth to answer.

"I've read many pages, and I've heard many stories about why they lose their wings," he said.

I leaned closer so I wouldn't miss a word.

"All of them begin with a demon murdering their mark."

The air in my lungs froze solid. The openness of the way he spoke took me by surprise.

"It's sort of a depression, I think. The angel becomes unable to use its powers because it cannot feel the connection to the marked person anymore... like they lose the connection to a part of themselves..."

His words made me think for a moment. Did that mean Chris would never get his abilities back—his wings and his powers?

"That's also why they try to use the marked people to apply pressure to gain control over the related angel," he continued when I didn't speak. "Angels would do anything to protect their marks from the shadows of the dark—" he looked into his tea, "—even leave them forever... or so I've heard."

I swallowed down the frozen air in one aching gulp and inhaled greedily. All of the pain I had so willingly fought over the last days took control of me; the way Adam had left me a few months ago—to protect me as he had said. It had felt like he had tortured me purposely. I felt hot liquid searching its way out of my eyes and closed them briefly to hide my moment of weakness.

This first time hadn't been the worst, I thought to myself. The worst, the unbearable, had been the second time. The time he hadn't left me on purpose. The time he had been murdered in front of my eyes and fallen off the edge of a roof, out of my sight and out of my life—forever.

Frank Sinatra's voice kept my inner torment at bay. It sang a tune too happy for my mood, too happy for my life.

"I've always known that the time might come for me to get involved in this never-ending story between good and bad," Mr. Baker said into the oddity of the bizarre discrepancy between my mood and the melody tootling perpetually in the background. I looked at the child. He had stopped hitting the cup and settled down to sip what of the content was left.

"But I've stopped believing that it would really happen. It's so exciting to meet another believer..." Mr. Baker finished his sentence. He looked far less sick when his eyes were all lit up like that. It was like he was in tune with the music. Happy that all of the mysterious stories, all of the things he had heard and dreamed of, had finally come to life for him.

"Believe me," I snorted without any appreciation for his enthusiasm, "it's everything but exciting to be in the middle of the story." I instantly bit my tongue, hoping to chew the words back. I wanted to fill him in on parts of the story, but it had to be done carefully and slowly. Mr. Baker was an old man, and I couldn't be sure how he would take the news that the ominous war between good and bad was going on right under his nose.

"Please, tell me about it," he asked, his face reflecting his fascination.

The coffee machine sizzled loudly while the waitress worked on fresh coffee for some new customers. I hadn't noticed them come in.

To avoid the wrong ears overhearing our conversation, I stood up and walked around the table to sit down in the armchair right next to Mr. Baker. He looked at me expectantly. For a moment, I hesitated, unsure whether I really wanted to draw this kind, old man into the depths of my misery.

"I haven't had a single day of peace since I found out they exist," I finally brought myself to speak openly, my words heavy with the weight of my knowledge. "Remember the girl who died in your library last year?" I asked in a hushed voice, afraid to bring up the topic.

Mr. Baker nodded earnestly.

I had known the girl, Colina, from school. She had walked into the library one day, and a few minutes later, she had dropped dead behind the shelves.

"It was no accident—*They* killed her." My voice was so low that it was almost swallowed by the background noise.

It had been demons—Jaden had told me so, and I had seen the shadows.

The old man's eyes widened as I spoke. And then he nodded like he had been expecting exactly what he had just learned from me.

"Knowledge can be a burden, girl," he said, his eyes full of wisdom. An expression I had never before appreciated. "... but you're not alone. There are so many people who believe that *they*," he emphasized the word and then coughed, "... exist. The good as well as the bad. They just don't call them angels or demons because they don't know for sure what it is that they feel around them."

"Doesn't it bother you at all that it was no accident?" I said a bit too loud and the heads of a tea-sipping couple at a table near the counter turned in our direction. I shrank into my armchair self-consciously and grabbed the cup in front of me to hide my face behind it while I watched the couple staring at me. Mr. Baker blew his nose. Frank Sinatra continued singing happy tunes that didn't nearly fit the topic of our conversation.

The woman looked away when she noticed me staring back. I wondered if she had overheard us.

I lowered my eyes into my chocolate and waited.

For a while, neither of us dared to mention topics more serious than the weather, my progress at school, or today's TV program. It was only when the couple finally paid and left that our conversation became a little more relaxed.

Mr. Baker cleared his throat beside me, and I took a deep breath and glanced sideways at him. He looked right back at me, his eyes mirroring my relief.

We watched them leave the coffee shop and vanish around the corner before we returned to the core of our meeting.

"Mr. Baker...," I half-whispered, too afraid to attract attention with what I was about to say.

"Please, call me Lucas," he interrupted, "we've known each other for quite a while now, and we share secrets that are beyond calling somebody by their last name." He looked like a kind grandpa to me when he smiled at me like that.

"Lucas," I said, feeling weird as I addressed my boss by his first name for the first time, "demons killed the girl at the library. They killed my cat, and they murdered my boyfriend. And I think I'm going to be next." I watched his horrified expression. He wanted to know and I had to tell him. It was fair—my knowledge for his. "I promised I would share my knowledge, but I need your help first. I need to know what I can do to help an angel get back its powers—it's crucial."

Lucas Baker looked at me with frightened eyes. "I never knew he was murdered, too..." His voice was hoarse, even more than it had already been from his cold. "I thought it was..."

"Suicide," I stole the word from his mouth. "Adam would have never—" I forced myself to stay calm, "... never."

Embarrassed silence spread between us for a minute.

Lucas took my hand into his wrinkled fingers and squeezed. "I'm sorry. I know you loved him."

My facade had grown strong over the last weeks but not that strong. I felt it disintegrate and reveal the mess I was behind it. It took all of my effort to hold back my tears.

"He was one," I breathed.

Lucas sucked in a breath, which led into another cough. "Angel."

I nodded reflexively at his whisper and pulled my hand out of his grip to lean back into my armchair.

"So you've known one—" Lucas mused, his eyes looking into the distance as if he was seeing something there.

I nodded again, unable to speak, incapacitated by my own bleeding heart.

Lucas' eyes were like two stars of excitement. "I've got so many questions..."

I had to calm down. It was essential to find out how to help Chris. If Lucas knew anything, I had to find out.

"Lucas, please, I need your help," I tried once more, "I know it's fascinating to you, but I really need to know what I can do to help an angel get its abilities back." My voice sounded desperate, and that was how I felt.

"Sorry, Claire," he apologized, "I'm... I just can't believe..." And then he scrutinized my face, comprehension gleaming in his eyes. "You need to know what you can do to help an angel get its powers back—does that mean you know there is an angel who needs your help...a real one?"

My chin sank against my chest in a single, unintended nod. It was like I had set off a firework with this one, simple gesture. Lucas Baker looked at me like a little boy at Christmas, his eyes all expectant and his hands clawing into each other with elation.

You have to be more careful, the voice in my head warned me, and I knew it was right. I couldn't give away the Gallagers' secret. I had to be way more cautious with what I did and especially what I didn't tell Lucas.

"Could you introduce us?" Lucas asked in a childlike voice. All of the grayness was gone from his skin. He looked almost healthy with the way he shifted in his green armchair, exuberant with joy.

"I don't know," I answered, unsure whether I could promise him anything right now. All I wanted was his help, but I had the feeling that now that he had sniffed out how real the angel-world around him was, he wouldn't settle for less. "Lucas, please... do you know anything about how to help him—" I bit my tongue. Now he knew that the angel was male. Very nice. In my mind, I extracted a club and let it crash onto my head virtually for my own stupidity.

"Of course—I'm sorry," he apologized again.

"Please, what can I do? What do your stories say?"

"I'm sorry, girl, there isn't a thing you can do," Lucas said with concern in his eyes. "Either he finds a way to regain control over his broken soul, or he..." His voice was suddenly dark and sad. It made a surge of unease run through my body.

"Or what?"

Silence.

"Lucas, what?" I urged, panic surfacing in my voice.

"You know that angels usually have the power of age-shifting?" he began his explanation, and I had the subtle idea that I knew where this was leading.

Lucas stared at me, obviously waiting for a sign of comprehension.

"I do," I whispered, my voice shaky.

"When an angel loses its mark, it can lose its powers. This includes the power of age-shifting.

"Whatever assumed age the angel has when its mark dies, the angel will return to its factual age, and if this is above a plausible human span of life..."

"...it dies, too..." I finished his sentence, my head full of pictures of Jaden, decayed to the bones. If his mark died, would he lose his powers, too? He had never told me anything about his marked person and what had happened to them. But they had to be dead. I couldn't imagine otherwise. Jaden was almost a thousand years old.

"Yes," Lucas nodded and took a sip of his tea. "Your angel is obviously still alive, or you wouldn't be sitting here with me, asking questions. So I guess he can't be that old."

"Umm—" He was right. Chris was still alive. Chris had spread his wings for the first time with Adam. He couldn't have shifted his age too much. He looked exactly around forty-five—the age he should be with a child at the age of twenty-one.

Lucas gave me some time to process the new information. His eyes lingered on my face, and he started humming to the music which was still tootling happily in the background.

"If he doesn't find a way, he's going to die like any other human being," he said after a minute or two, I couldn't tell; time had notched out of my perception. "It will be like he never was anything more than human."

I thought of the last times I had seen Chris. He had been a wreck. Lackluster and unable to spread his wings, but he had been able to sense my emotions. He couldn't be a hopeless case. He still had forty years ahead of him where he could get his abilities back. He didn't have to die. And part of his powers were still there, so there was a good chance he would soon get his wings back.

For the first time in months, I felt something like a moment of hope in this mess of pain and despair around me.

The sun was setting, and the downtown buildings were glowing red, accented here and there with windows that seemed to flash and burn with brilliant golden light. I felt better. Lucas had shared a lot of his knowledge with me, and I had grown to appreciate the old librarian as a person worthy of trust.

After seeing him struggle with that cough and runny nose, I wanted to be sure he would get home alright, so even though my house lay in the opposite direction, we crossed the bridge together and headed toward a modern apartment complex that looked out of place in its old neighborhood.

We talked about angels all the way to his flat, and he asked me questions about the exact consistency of the feathers on their wings, the color of the light when their eyes gleam, and if it was true that they could vanish and pop up miles away. I answered all his questions willingly, trying not to give him too many specifics that could endanger the Gallagers' secrecy—and Jaden's.

"Well, I'm home," he said as we walked up to the entryway. He paused to fish his keys out of his coat pocket with stiff fingers. "Thank you for walking me. Now, you'd better scoot; it's getting dark." He coughed again, this time a little more heavily than before. As I had feared, the walk in the cold air hadn't done him any good.

"Are you sure there isn't anything I can get you?" I asked, concerned. "The drugstore will still be open." But the old man just shook his head.

"I'm fine," he said and smiled. "You did enough for me by telling me about the angels."

"Okay, goodbye, then," I said. "Call me if you need anything."

I headed back down the walk, turning around at the sidewalk to wave at him and make sure he got into the building. The door was already closing behind him. I hoped he would go right to bed. At his age, he needed to be careful.

I began to retrace my steps, headed on the long walk home. I could feel the temperature dropping as night came on, and I pulled my coat collar up to my ears. By the time I re-crossed the bridge and left downtown behind, part of my mind was wishing I had thought to put some gloves in my pockets, but another part was noticing how very silent it seemed among the big, leafless maples and close-set houses of the old neighborhood. There were no cars, no pedestrians. Only a few children hurried around the corner away from a park I was passing.

It was Sunday night—people had school and work in the morning, and with the sun fully set, Mother Nature was offering no further inducements to linger outside. But still, I felt uneasy. An unseen dog barked—a big dog from the baritone sound of it—from a shadowy side yard, and I hoped there was a fence between us.

I was stepping carefully over a broken patch of sidewalk when I heard it. A low, rumbling, crashing sound, not far behind me. A most peculiar sound that I could not identify—similar to the noise of a garbage can falling to the ground but much, much lower. I paused and looked behind me to examine the darkening street. There was nothing.

A porch light snapped on at a house across the street, but no one came out. Maybe their garbage can, I thought with hope, but turned and sped up nonetheless. After a while, my heart was drumming, and I was breathing harder with this faster pace but I didn't let up. I had just crossed Woodley Avenue when a thought struck me. I stopped and thought for a second. From here, I was closer to the Gallagers' house than my own. I hesitated. I felt insecure, unsafe out there alone. It was cold, and I didn't know if I had really just imagined the sound. I felt paranoid, but I preferred being paranoid one time too many to being dead one single time. I whipped around and recrossed the street but at an angle this time, headed up Woodley toward the familiar long driveway that spelled safety to me.

Crash. I hadn't gone more than five steps when the noise sounded behind me again. Clearly, not a garbage can. I turned my head without stopping, fighting back panic, but there was nothing to see aside from the empty intersection lit by a dim streetlight.

I hurried up the street only to see a shape that was indistinct in the darkness but seemingly human. It was distorted as if made up of several layers of shadows, and it was waiting for me ahead.

I turned around in alarm and began to run back to the intersection but very nearly collided with the shape, which was now in front of me. At these close quarters, I could make out arms and legs billowing weirdly in the night air.

Too frightened to look up at the face, I retreated a few steps then turned and bolted back up Woodley, my only thought being to reach the Gallagers' driveway even though it was plain the creature could overtake me with ease.

Crash. Crash. The noise seemed deafening, but for some reason, the creature held back. I was being chased, sadistically, while my tormentor enjoyed my fear. My situation seemed hopeless, but the desire to survive kept me sprinting, digging now into the gravel of the driveway, feeling only the pressure of my pounding heart and the overwhelming need to reach the front door.

My numb fingers curled around my bag, which I was clasping against my body with all of my strength. My legs were getting weaker with every step, and my feet became slow and clumsy. I heard the sound behind me again and forced my feet to not give in to the exhaustion.

They carried me on, steadily enough to see the house come closer with each step. I saw a light in the windows to the left of the front door. They looked so appealing to me, so safe, that I forced another burst of energy into my lower extremities.

Where was Jaden? Couldn't he feel that I needed his help? Didn't he sense that I was in danger?

Keep going, keep going, my brain screamed like some insane cheerleader in my head. Just a little bit more, and I'd be at the door. Just another few steps, and I would yell.

With the loudest *crash* of all, the shadowy shape planted itself in my path, and a fearful whooshing sound above my head made me stop, confused and cringing and completely out of ideas about what to do next. Above my head, a vaguely human-like shadow swooped in tight circles, dropping lower and lower as the creature in front of me floated slowly closer and closer. There was something familiar about the figure in the air, but I had no time to figure it out. I was positive there wasn't a way to escape.

The shadow in front of me moved forward, floating above the ground. It was too quick for me to even think about running. I saw the gleam of a well-remembered medallion at the throat of the creature before me. Demon. It was reaching out for me.

And then, just when I looked up for what I expected to be the last time, I felt a tremendous blow from behind.

I hit the gravel face-down and immediately tasted blood. A great weight pressed my entire body down into the tiny stones below me. My bag was squeezed somewhere between my stomach and the ground. I was sure it would break my ribs if the weight on my back pushed down just a tiny bit harder.

Then, there was a brief flash of light—entirely blinding—that enveloped me. And a loud, rough scream. Suddenly, the weight was gone.

I didn't dare to lift my head and look around. Uncertain, I stayed motionless on the gravel. There was no sound, none at all.

When I finally lifted my face from the ground, my eyes looked into darkness.

10.
Artist

There I was, flattened on the gravel drive in the cold, not quite at the door of the refuge I had been so desperate to reach just a moment ago, and completely alone.

Gingerly, I rolled to one side, wincing. Every part of my body was hurting. The front, where the weight on my back had pressed me into the stones beneath, and my back and neck where the weight had slammed me into the ground.

I began to shiver as the freezing air worked its way through my clothes. It was cold, but also, I felt like I might be going into shock. I needed to act while I could—had to get inside, away from the demons in case they decided to return. I had known all along they would come for me sooner or later. Just because I had somehow escaped this time did not mean they wouldn't be back.

Carefully, clumsily, using both arms, I pushed myself into a sitting position and sat for a moment, catching my breath and trying to reconstruct the attack.

The demon with the amulet around his neck had clearly been the creature chasing me on the street, toying with me until he chose to kill me at the Gallagers' front door. But the one in the air, that was new. I squeezed my eyes shut to call back its image. I could only conjure up billowing shadows that somehow evoked a human form. It was a troublesome memory.

I gave up on analyzing and returned to my most immediate need—to get out of the cold and away from demons. I levered myself gracelessly into a standing position, remembering to pick my bag up as I did so, knowing it wouldn't be easy to get back down again.

I stood for a few seconds, taking deep breaths and checking my balance, then stumbled up the rest of the driveway as fast as I could, nearly tripping on the stairs and literally smashing into the heavy door, my fists already banging on the old wood urgently.

"Jenna!" I screamed. "Chris!"

The house remained silent.

"Jenna!" I tried again, "Help!"

Nothing. What if no one was home?

I glanced fearfully over my shoulder, looking for demons and trying to think of a Plan B if this didn't work. I kept on pounding.

"Geoffrey, are you there?"

My fists opened up in despair until my hand eventually fell flat against the wood.

"Ben!" I finally called. "Ben... help!"

My hopes were sinking. Even if Ben was at home, what reason did he have to help me? He had not once given me a kind word or a friendly look. All he had ever done was ignore me at the best. Even if he hated me for causing his brother's death, would he turn me away under the circumstances? "Ben... please..."

"Coming," someone said from inside. The voice sounded so sweet in my ears that it was impossible to ignore when my heart twisted in pain. It sounded so much like *him*—

Adam is dead, the voice in my head sprang to life once more.

I nodded to myself in answer to the voice.

"Please hurry," I begged, but I dropped my arms and waited for the door to open.

On my side of the door, there was night, panic, fear, and near hysteria. On the other side, the calm, orderly household of the wealthy Gallagers. No door in the history of doors had ever opened so slowly.

I pushed against it, unable to hold back, and then I looked into a face that made my heart hurt.

"Hello, Claire," Ben said.

My heart twisted again. It was so difficult to face him. How was I going to explain this frantic nighttime visit?

"Ben," I gasped.

He could barely tolerate the sight of me, I was sure, but I was in trouble and didn't have time to worry about that.

"Ben, I have to come in," I said and, with an aggressiveness born of desperation, pushed past him into the warm, softly-lighted hallway. There! I was in. Next, I would have to figure out an explanation for why, but at least I was in.

"Is there a problem, Master Benedict?" It was Geoffrey, materializing from the kitchen.

"Miss Gabriel has honored us with a visit, Geoffrey," he said, keeping a wary eye on me. "I believe we will have some tea in the parlor."

Geoffrey bowed slightly, opening his hands for my jacket, which he took with just a flicker of curiosity, then headed back for the kitchen.

I wondered if there was blood on it. Ben eyed my scratched and bleeding hands and my disheveled hair and clothing, but all he said was, "Perhaps you'd like to freshen up in the powder room."

He led the way to a door at the opposite end of the entrance hall and opened it, inclining his body to indicate I should go in.

"Okay," I said reluctantly.

That wasn't my priority, but normal people would certainly think that was the right thing to do. I washed my hands with soap and splashed some water on my face. After a preemptory rake-through of my hair, I brushed my sweater and pants. Tiny bits of gravel pinged on the marble floor, and I stared at them in horror. Who would be cleaning this bathroom, and what would they think?

It crossed my mind that I should wipe the floor and destroy evidence, but my head was already spinning, and I just wanted to get back to the parlor and the tea. And Ben—

Ben was waiting for me in the hall, leaning against the parlor door, his face surprisingly neutral and his eyes not really warm but not cold, either.

We entered the parlor without a word, and I took a seat on the sofa. Ben sat nearby on a chair. The tea was already on the table.

I glanced at the Gallagers' remaining son for a second and directed my eyes back to my knees when I was caught looking. My head didn't supply me with great ideas of what to say—it was blank while I was still filled with panic, adrenaline, and the feeling of being observed. The weight of Ben's stare was heavy. It made me want to say something. Just a few words to break the silence.

"So—umm—" I croaked. The sound of my voice startled me. "I'm sorry I made a fuss."

Ben didn't react. He just continued to stare at me. I didn't need to look up to know he did. "I was walking home, and I tripped and fell, and then I realized your house..."

"You should have some tea," Ben interrupted solicitously, apparently not in need of any explanations. I wondered why. With a rustle of his beautiful, lavender, plaid shirt, he leaned forward and neatly poured two cups then settled back in his chair. I had no idea what else to say, and I was always tongue-tied around Ben anyway, so I picked up the cup and sipped, grateful to be preoccupied.

Ben stared into his cup. I felt myself relax a little. It was warm and safe in the parlor; the events of a few minutes ago already seemed unreal, and now the once cold and distant Ben was quietly sipping tea with me.

I ventured a look at him. He was certainly Adam's brother. Maybe not quite so tall and perhaps a little more muscular. But with the same beauty and grace. Longing for Adam crept over me along with the first glimmer of hope that perhaps Ben was getting over the tragedy and would help me just as his mother and father would if things ever got really bad.

As though feeling my eyes on him, Ben looked over at me. He set his cup down and crossed his arms over his broad chest, causing the shirt to rustle again. Something about the sound was disturbing, and his steel-blue gaze was more than I could manage. I looked into my lap.

He did not take his eyes off of me, and a long minute passed while the scratches on my hands reminded me they were still there with a pulsing pain.

At last, he said, in a voice tight with some kind of emotion, "Claire, can I have a word with you?"

I flashed him a quick look of surprise. The request hardly seemed necessary to ask since we were already seated within a few feet of each other, alone in the big room in the big house. But he was struggling to convey something, and I was open to it. Ben had always been a mystery to me.

"Of course," I replied, but he merely fell silent again, staring at me with undecided eyes.

I shifted in my seat uncomfortably, unsure of whether or not I was supposed to be here. I was very aware of the fact that Ben had never before been eager to talk to me—ever. He had just been the cold, emotionless shadow in the Gallager family. He was so different now, though, seeming fragile almost, compared to the appearance of stony coldness he normally was.

I couldn't put my finger on what it was that made him look so vulnerable; maybe the way he held his fingers clenched around his knees or the way his forehead creased over his eyes. Maybe it was the way his voice had shaken with his words or how he seemed to be so unable to get out what he wanted to say.

My hands reached out for the cup in front of me and lifted it to my lips. I took another sip, waiting expectantly, while outside, the moon was reappearing from behind the clouds, throwing long shadows onto the ground. I watched them stretching on the grass and vanish as the next cloud shoved itself before the pale disk of the moon.

When my cup was empty and Ben hadn't spoken a word, my nerves cracked, and I couldn't keep myself from getting upset.

"You know, you could have spared us both this uncomfortable silence if you hadn't told me you needed to talk to me."

I was surprised by how smoothly my accusation left my mouth. As I listened to myself, I wondered what it meant. Ben hadn't asked me to come here. It had been me who had needed shelter, and I should have been grateful that he hadn't kicked me out.

Curious or not, in need of help or not, I decided I couldn't wait much longer for Ben to find his voice. I had to go home. I had hit the wall. It was late, and I was tired—and not in the mood for Ben's games. I had spent the whole day, talking about angels with Mr. Baker and been nearly killed by demons at nightfall.

I wasn't just going to sit here and make a fool of myself… The room was thick with an uncomfortable silence, and I couldn't bear another second of it.

Knowing it would be a mistake to leave the house, I exhaled sharply, a wordless rejection of Ben, and pushed up suddenly from the sofa.

Ben raised his head in alarm, his fingers unclenching from his knees. His face was torn in an unreadable expression.

My swift stride should have carried me to the door well before he could even get out of his deep chair, but in the hallway, I was surprised by a soft touch on my shoulder.

"Please, don't go," he said softly, pleading. His voice sank to a whisper. "I just can't talk here—I don't want to be disturbed by someone walking in," he whispered.

I frowned, puzzled, and looked around even though I felt sure that Geoffrey was somewhere else deep in the house and Chris and Jenna did not seem to be at home. They would have come to my aid if they had been.

I wondered if he was thinking straight, but it was tempting to stay in the safe, warm house a while longer, and I really was intrigued by seeing this new side of Ben.

"Will you come upstairs with me?" The words were still just a whisper. He waited for me to turn around—and after a few seconds of considering, I did. I was positive that whatever he wanted to talk about, it couldn't be worse than the hostile silence we had been sharing so far.

"Lead the way." I gave him an encouraging look, wanting to follow this new thread in our relationship and unable to bring myself to leave the house right now.

Ben headed for the stairs with a quick stride. He seemed to have reached some decision and was in a big hurry to carry it out. I had to scurry to keep pace with him, up the stairs and down the long hallway, until we were almost at a door that made me close my eyes in pain. Adam's door.

I wanted to break away from Ben and just tear open that door and find Adam in there, waiting for me as if nothing had ever happened. I wanted my old life back, and only Adam could give it to me. But I knew I could spare myself the disappointment—the room would be empty. And my soul—torn in two parts—would continue to painfully miss the part I had shared with Adam, and I would never be whole again.

Only the Gallagers were left to me now, and there I was with his half-brother, who was gesturing me into another doorway.

"Please, come in."

I tore my eyes away from the wooden portal to my memories of happiness, trying to steel myself against the upwelling of pain, and stepped over the threshold. He closed the door behind us.

When I felt I had regained control over my mind and emotions, I refocused on my surroundings. I looked around. The room was very long and narrow, compared to the dimensions of the rest of the house. Green brocade curtains were hanging from the ceiling, draped to the wall on both sides, parting the room in two. A simple wooden desk was standing on the left side under a window. In the far right corner of the room, a bed with carved wooden bedposts was standing against the wall. Next to it, a face looking very much like my own was staring at me from a white sheet of paper clipped to an easel. The lines of the face were drawn with charcoal. Beneath the face was another drawing—my face in profile. I stared at the picture for a moment, and then I looked at Ben, stunned.

"Is that—" I couldn't finish my question, for my words faded into a faint breath as I took in the whole scene around me. There were several easels spread across the room, all of them holding drawings and paintings of my face and my body. I recognized the cocktail dress Adam had given me a few months ago in one painting—the color was almost perfect.

"Did *you*—?"

I intended to ask if it had been him who had drawn and painted those pictures, but my question got stuck in my throat as I looked into Ben's eyes. Had I ever believed his gaze was cold and full of hatred? Right now, it was filled with anxiety, confusion, hope, and pleading.

"But—" I opened my mouth to speak and closed it again. I couldn't find any suitable words.

Since the moment I had first met Ben, I felt he disliked me and wished me gone from Adam's life. He had been angry and rude to me all the time. And Adam had warned me it would be so. But what was I to make of *this*? To be suddenly thrust into what seemed like a lair of obsession, with myself as the object, stunned me into silence.

I turned to look again at the display, evaluating if perhaps I was in danger from this new Ben or not. I needed information, for him to speak, to explain himself, this room, these drawings.

"What is all this?" I finally said, faltering.

I turned back to look at him, but he was rooted to the spot, just looking helplessly at me. It wasn't a frightening expression. He seemed to be pondering whether or not to honor me with a statement about his unusual collection of art.

After a few moments of watching him struggling with his dilemma, I decided to have a closer look at the artwork. I stepped farther into the room, past the green brocade drapery, and up onto the raised platform that held the bed and an easel. As I brushed past the soft and heavy fabric that somehow evoked a long family history, I discovered there was another easel tucked behind it, facing toward the bed. Another charcoal drawing of my face, but more this time. An entire body. An entire body that was also entirely naked. My heart began to pound in alarm.

I coughed involuntarily. This was going downhill and fast. I needed more than pleading gazes from steel blue eyes. I needed to understand.

Taking a deep breath, I wheeled around to face him where I thought he would be still frozen in confusion. Instead, he was standing very close behind me, his face flushed and his hands raised, palms out, in a gesture of apology and defenselessness.

Anger and adrenaline flamed up in me, making me feel stronger than I had in weeks. I had accepted that Adam was dead. I had accepted that demons would soon kill me, too. I had accepted that my world was strange and perilous and I was an innocent in it without protection. But I would not accept that I might also be in danger from a Gallager who disdained me to my face and drew nudes of me in private.

Ben took a slow step toward me. I backed a step away at the same moment, not wanting the distance between us to decrease even an inch.

"You need to talk to me, Ben—now," I demanded.

Ben had his hands still up, defensively. He dropped his head and said reluctantly, "I like to draw—"

The air left my lungs in a hiss as I shook my head at his unsatisfying answer. A big question-mark was floating in the room halfway between him and me. What did he think he was doing? How could he take me to this room? He must have been well aware that I would be more than a little irritated by the decoration there?

"Explain yourself," I demanded and folded my arms across my chest.

"As I said—I like drawing," said Ben.

"How come you are working only on one subject?" I threw at him with heavy sarcasm surfacing in my voice.

No answer.

I tapped my foot against the wood of the floor impatiently, boring my eyes into his, hoping to find a hint of what he would have said if he had been honest right now.

"You know, I'm not joking." It sounded almost as unfriendly as I had intended it to. I would get his confession, and then I would be gone. Whether or not Chris and Jenna could help me after that, I didn't know, but I was going to solve this particular problem right now.

"Tell me now, Ben," I said with a force that surprised even me. "Tell me now, or—" I realized I had no threat to offer. I knew nothing about Ben or what would motivate him. We were standing in his bedroom, surrounded by these drawings, but I actually knew nothing.

Then, to my relief, I saw that my bluff was going to be good enough.

Ben moved a step away, rubbed a hand once over his face, and began, "Claire, I know I gave you the impression that I hated you, and, believe me, I hate myself for doing that." His voice was soft, almost velvety, and so much like his brother's—his *dead* brother's.

Pang, the pain flared up in my chest like iron needles shooting through my heart. I felt my knees turn into pudding under my weight.

"Are you alright?"

Ben was at my side in a second. He had his hand at my back, ready to catch me if I couldn't support my weight by myself anymore.

I nodded, working hard on maintaining my vision.

"I don't believe you," said Ben. "You look like you're going to black out any second."

I shook my head, fighting against the needles in my chest. They slowly swallowed the control I had on my limbs, washing over me with a force they had never had before.

"Hey—you need to sit down." Ben was already pushing me toward his bed where he pressed me down into the soft mattress.

"I'm fine, Ben." I fought against his hands.

"You don't *look* fine," he told me coldly, not lifting his hands from my shoulders.

I inhaled deeply and shut the images of Adam away into the back of my head. That cleared my mind a little. I was wondering how he could still have such a hold on me, how he could still affect me so much—even now that he was dead, even with my split soul. I didn't know which part of this insanity was worse; that I couldn't walk anywhere without the memories of him tearing me apart all over again or the part of being unable to control the attacks of pain and horror I felt every time I was reminded of him. I had to get a grip on myself if I ever wanted to coherently interact with people again.

Another deep breath, and I felt stable enough to face Ben and the weird collection of portraits behind him.

"I don't know what's going on," I found myself saying. "With me or with you." I hadn't meant to sound so vulnerable.

Ben stiffened slightly beside me, the weight of his hands still on my shoulders.

I waited for a moment, counting to five in my head, preparing myself to stand up and leave if I didn't get an answer. At four, the pressure left my shoulders, and at five, Ben crouched in front of me, fixing me with sad eyes.

I couldn't bring myself to move even an inch. I was locked in place by those eyes, those usually so cold gray eyes, which were molten steel now, and all my anger just floated away.

"I don't hate you, Claire." Ben spoke the words slowly—more to himself.

Once more, I was shocked by how close the sound of his voice came to the sound of Adam's voice. I balled my hands into fists, digging my nails into the palms. The physical pain distracted me for a second, preventing me from falling into the dark hole of the misery in my soul. I was surprised at the effect and dug deeper until all I could feel was the physical pain.

"On the contrary, Claire—I think you are the most adorable girl I've ever had the honor to meet." Ben's eyelids fluttered, and he averted his gaze. "I think you are the most beautiful creature in the world—and the most pitiful thing I've ever met."

I felt my fingernails sever my skin. What was he telling me? Adorable—no way. Beautiful—I couldn't agree with that. Pitiful—definitely. Warm blood flowed from the cuts in my hands and leaked through my fingers. The flesh I was boring into felt warm under my fingernails. The warmth spread as the blood slowly oozed down my hands, hiding the tiny cuts from where I had been pushed down to the gravel, and dribbled from my wrists. I watched in amazement. I was totally awed by this new way of suppressing the much worse type of pain—the pain in my soul. I knew I would be willing to trade it for any kind of physical suffering in the future. Anything to get away from the inescapable memories that kept nagging at my mind, the incompleteness that was slowly driving me insane. At least, physical wounds healed after a while—something I couldn't say about my damaged heart. I was a hundred percent sure *that* would never be fine again.

"Claire?"

I had been so absorbed in my thoughts and the newfound power of physical pain that I had stopped listening to Ben. I nodded to myself, not unclenching my fists, and returned my attention to the boy who was crouching on the floor in front of me, his eyes wide open, a horrified expression on his face.

His hands darted out and grabbed my arms. He pulled my fists toward him, eying the blood with suspicious eyes.

"What are you doing?"

I tried to pull my hands back—without success. Ben held them in an iron grasp.

"Let go of me!" I half-shrieked at him. I knew that he was just trying to help—but help was exactly what I did *not* want. I wanted to be left alone until I was myself again, until I had regained at least some control over the part that was so intangibly distorted by the constant pain and finality of my angel's absence. The pain and instability were much worse in Ben's presence. He looked so much like his older brother when he was all worried like that.

I managed to pull one arm free of Ben's grip. His hand bounced back and grabbed the fist on the arm he was still holding. I couldn't fight the power of his grip opening my fist. As my hand opened, blood ran down my forearm.

"Open your other fist," Ben commanded. I knew if I didn't do it by myself, he would force it open like the first one. So, I decided it was better to follow his command than continue fighting.

I was sitting on Ben's bed, a picture of misery. Blood was dribbling down my forearms, soaking the sleeves of my shirt, and I was trying with every fiber in my body to keep my hysteria at bay.

Ben stared down at the palms of my hands. They were smeared with blood, and three cuts gaped on each palm where the fingernails had sliced the skin open. The tiny cuts from the gravel were almost invisible beside the fresh ones.

"Are you insane?" Ben asked with concern furrowing his brows.

I nodded at his question, fully aware that confessing my insanity wouldn't help the situation at all, but it was true all the same.

He let go of me for a second and reached for tissues, which he pressed into my palms forcefully. I flinched.

"You should have considered that a little earlier," he commented on my movement.

"Hrmpf..."

I watched him nurse my wounds in silence for a while. Red blood was soaking through the tissues between our hands. I liked the color and the smell of it, and the way it seemed to not want to stop flowing. It reminded me that I was alive—still.

"What were you thinking?" He asked with a kind of fear in his voice I had never heard before. His eyes were scrutinizing my face.

I shook my head at him. What should I say?

Ben eyed me for a moment then looked down at my bloodied hands. "It's him—" he whispered—not a question.

I choked at the name that sprang to my mind, and my fingertips snapped back into my palms, searching for the cuts to dig in once more. My body had learned fast how to avoid the pain in my soul—but they were hindered by the tissues and Ben's fingers, which covered the wounded flesh.

I didn't have to give him a verbal answer—the response of my body had told him he was right.

"It's going to be okay," he said with a rueful smile. "We are both struggling." His gaze was calm and comforting, and I fell into it with relief. It felt good to think we were in this together.

There was still this roomful of unexplained pictures, and I wanted to know more. Excluding the fact that it irritated me that I was the only subject in his sketches, I had to admit, they were pretty good.

"So, you are an artist," I ventured, sounding for all the world like a stranger making small talk at a party. Ben gave a small, awkward smile.

"I don't usually show my pictures to anyone."

"Except for me," I joked, trying to keep some easiness in my voice.

"I didn't think about them when I brought you up here. I forgot I hadn't stored them away." It wasn't a convincing line, and he lowered his eyes as he said it. "Otherwise, I wouldn't have chosen this room to talk to you in—it's—embarrassing—"

He gave a short sigh and changed the subject. "He's dead, Claire—you can't weep for him forever." Ben looked up at me with eyes of piercing steel. They told me that he was hurt and that he was determined, like a soldier in battle. I couldn't tell why, but I knew he was, and I had a vague idea it was me he was determined to fight for. Maybe it was the way his eyes grew all soft and warm the moment mine locked on them. Maybe it was the way he straightened up on his knees a few inches, automatically, so he was closer to my face. Or maybe it was just the way his room was filled with pictures of me.

"It's only been a few weeks—" I found my voice again. "—and you're already talking about forever—" As if my love for Adam was ever going to change, dead or alive. He had taken a part of my soul, and without a doubt, it was his forever. Nothing was going to change that. Even if I healed enough—someday in the far, far future—to see another man for what he really was—a man—it would never be so potent, so intoxicating, so perfect—the way it had been with Adam.

My hands were balling up into fists again, but I couldn't feel the pressure of my fingernails on my skin—they were digging into the back of Ben's hands.

"Ouch!" Ben exclaimed sharply, and my fingers opened reflexively.

"I'm sorry," I apologized. I looked back down at our hands. They were dirty with my blood, and the tissues between them were completely soaked.

"No—it's nice to eventually find out you don't hate me the way I always thought you did." I grimaced and looked around the room while I spoke, wondering about the perfection of his drawings. "These are really good." I nodded at the easel nearest to us. "Where did you learn to draw like that?"

Ben's face lit up for a moment. "You really think they are good?"

I nodded to encourage him, deciding that I had to somehow get along with him if I wanted to still be welcome in the Gallagers' house.

"I thought you might never talk to me again... not that we've talked that much before..." Ben's face was full of guilt.

I pulled my hands out of his grip and got to my feet. He watched me with cautious eyes as I started walking between the easels. I felt his eyes on my shoulders as soon as I turned around to look at the pictures. It made me feel observed, like I was some kind of wild animal locked up in a new enclosure. Was he expecting me to lose it again any moment? I felt him move behind me, close enough to prevent me from doing something stupid. I didn't know if he realized I was through it—for the moment.

My eyes rested on one of the drawings. It was my face like I hadn't seen it for quite a while, smiling and happy. I tried to imitate the image I was seeing without much success. Except for a little twitch at the corners of my mouth, my face stayed the same composed mask I wore so many hours these days, as if my lips had forgotten how to form this natural upward-curve and my eyes how to twinkle.

It was amazing how perfect Ben had put my features down on paper, considering he had drawn this from a memory. I turned around to look at him in amazement.

The spot where I had expected him to stand was empty. Instead, he was sitting on a couch at the other end of the room, close to the door, following my movements with his eyes.

"Where did you learn to draw like that?" I repeated my question.

Ben just shrugged his shoulders.

"You have a good memory," I tried to get him to talk.

But again, he shrugged. This time, he even lifted his hands a little defensively. They were still red with my blood. Reflexively, I looked down at my own hands, which were curling around the tissues in their palms. The blood had stopped flowing, and I started to wonder what had made me cut my own skin. A small voice in the back of my head chuckled darkly and mocked my ability to so quickly shove aside the bad things. I felt a slight twitch in my body, like I had gotten an electric shock, and recalled what had made me hurt myself. The voice laughed even darker as I shied away from the memories that threatened to well up inside my head.

My inner conversation might have taken half a minute. I couldn't tell.

"Are you alright?" a voice asked too close beside my ear.

I jumped and turned in the direction of it. Ben was standing at my shoulder with one of his dirty hands outstretched, but he wasn't touching me.

"Yeesh, Ben!"

I took a quick step away from him and inhaled deeply.

"Sorry." Ben stepped back at the same moment. He made an apologetic gesture, but there was something in his eyes that didn't seem sorry at all. It was a low shimmer in the steely blue depths.

I told myself that my eyes were betraying me. I told myself that I was dreaming—where else did those things happen? It couldn't be true. No...

I closed my eyes for a brief moment before I looked at Ben more closely. Another breath. There was no shimmer, nothing but worry. I must have been wrong.

"Maybe I should bandage your hands while we talk," Ben suggested.

"Umm—thanks," I nodded.

"I'll be back in a minute," Ben told me, and then he vanished through the door so quickly I had to blink several times to be sure he had been standing next to me only seconds ago. *No*, I thought again and instantly knew that the upcoming conversation would be important. I definitely had to talk to Ben, but even more than that, I had to listen.

Ben returned a few moments later with his hands washed and full of bandages and salves. He gestured me to the sofa.

I sat down willingly while he knelt in front of me, took one of my hands in his, and started cleaning it with pads and something that stung.

I was positive I wouldn't get a second offer like that, so I didn't complain. I bit my lower lip and endured. After all, I wanted to know what was going on here, and I was determined to bring a little structure back to my life. I couldn't go on existing like that—always in danger of snapping, always full of unleashed emotion and pain and this never-ending, aching longing in my heart that reminded me that I would never be complete again.

If only I could clear out some of the weirdness in my life, I might someday be able to exist without being a constantly ticking time bomb. *Tick, tock*, the voice in the back of my head mocked and laughed darkly. *Great, I'm schizophrenic now*, I thought to myself and forced my attention back to Ben, who was gently winding fabric around my hands. His eyes were fixed on my face, though. They were still worried, but the steel of his irises had become solid once more.

"How long have you been drawing my face?" I asked after a few moments of silence.

Ben held my gaze. He opened his mouth to speak. "A while." He sounded nonchalant.

"Why my face?" I shifted uncomfortably before I continued speaking. "I mean—there are thousands of pretty girls out there... Why me?"

I stared into his eyes, trying to melt the steel again. I wanted to see the real him, for once at least, now that we were already talking...

"You are the only one that has ever mattered to me besides my family," said Ben plainly.

I heard myself suck in a gust of air. I should have known. Hadn't, I swallowed before I thought it, Adam told me that Ben felt a little attracted to me?

"Umm—" I didn't know what else to say in response. I wanted to somehow acknowledge his openness, but I was out of words for the moment.

"Please, don't get the wrong impression." Ben finally tore his eyes away, pretending to check the bandage on my left hand.

His young forehead creased a little as he fingered the fastening on the fabric. "It's just... You meant a lot to my brother—and my brother meant a lot to me."

"I understand." I didn't understand. Ben could have drawn Adam if he really missed his brother that much.

I watched Ben's fingers release my left hand. They hesitated for a moment before they moved over to take my right hand from my thigh.

"If I'm the *only thing that has ever mattered to you besides your family*, as you said, why on earth have you never talked to me? I would have loved to feel a little more at ease in your presence." I was spilling the words without thinking. "If you had given me even a small sign that you didn't *hate* me—"

"Shut up!" Ben interrupted the words flowing from my mouth. My lips fell shut in surprise, and I stared at Ben, my eyes widening with every second he didn't speak.

"How could I show any kindness to the person who was going to be the death of my brother?"

Ouch! I had no idea what he knew, but it was definite that he knew something. I was positive that Ben wasn't exactly what he had been pretending to be. There already was something more to him than the unfriendly, full of hatred, younger brother.

"What is that supposed to mean? How could you have known—?" I began to ask, began to unpack the meaning of his words, but Ben flipped me off with a, "That's a discussion for another day," and a shrug combined with a look that made it clear he wouldn't talk. Especially not if I pressured him.

"So what was it you wanted to talk to me about?" I asked, pretending it didn't bother me how much he seemed to be hiding. I didn't look him in the eyes, afraid that he would see my thoughts.

"Nothing special—" Ben answered nonchalantly. "I just wanted to ask you if we could go out for coffee sometime."

"What?" I couldn't believe what I had just heard. "You let me go through all this just to ask me out for coffee?" My mood swung over to angry again. "You know, it somehow seems like you might hate me still." My tone was firm; the anger wouldn't bring it to modulate more than usual. It didn't even tremble. Nothing but cold anger boiling under the surface.

I had thought this conversation would be important, clarifying some of the strangeness about Ben. But it was obvious I wouldn't get any more answers or solve any problems tonight. I was simply overwhelmed by my crazy day. I was weak. His every word could smash me from happy to angry, from high to death wish.

Ben was staring at me with probing eyes as I looked back at him. He didn't speak, obviously waiting for me to continue.

"Coffee—okay," I agreed wearily, "why not?" and instantly regretted it.

11.
Torn

I got to my feet with reluctance. The day, the long day of learning so many new things was over. I needed to get home. I felt a twinge of panic at the thought of the night outside and the demons that could be waiting, and the empty house without Sophie at the end of a long walk.

I silently cursed my car for breaking down. Walking home seemed like an even worse option than asking Ben for help.

"I really don't want to have to ask this of you..." I said as I slowly walked toward the door, "but, would you mind driving me home? My car broke down this morning..." I wasn't expecting anything from him. Ben and I were patching things up, but he was not my protector.

Ben's lavender shirt rustled behind me as he followed me.

"You know," his voice was gentle and uncertain, "you could stay here tonight if you want to." He sounded almost as scared as I felt.

I slowed and turned partway.

"I mean, it's awfully late... and you must be tired, and, well—you're going through a rough time right now."

If only he knew about the attack on his driveway, I thought. Nothing seemed more attractive to me than the opportunity to stay safe in the Gallagers' house for the night. But to avoid having to make the choice to go or stay, I merely said, "It's tough for all of us."

The way he kept looking at me made me feel x-rayed.

"Okay, then stay." He seized the moment. "And we'll have that coffee in the morning," he said decisively, slipping past me through the door.

I wasn't sure what that meant, but I didn't want to argue about it. My mind was nearly blank with fatigue, and my limbs felt as though I were wading through wet concrete.

I followed him mechanically out his bedroom door, surprised by the offer and grateful that I wouldn't have to go outside before dawn. He led me briskly down the hall and opened a door not far from his.

"You can have our guest room for tonight," he announced and switched on a lamp.

I peered past him and gaped at the room. It was enormous. A huge, carved, wooden bed was standing to the right of the door. It was covered with mother of pearl-colored sheets that made a beautiful contrast with the deep blue wall.

"You already know where the bathroom is," he stated matter-of-factly. It made me wonder how much he had observed of the nights I had spent in Adam's room. "If you need anything else, I'll be in my room." He turned and walked away.

"Wait," I called when he was a few steps away. He stopped and looked back over his shoulder with big, steely eyes.

"Thank you." I didn't know what else to say. I didn't know what made Ben offer for me to stay. I had no idea why he was doing this for me, but what I did know was that I wouldn't forget that he had helped me—not even if he returned to being the cold-hearted man that I used to know.

He just gave me a smile then turned and walked on.

I waited until I heard Ben's door click shut before closing my own. Ben had no reason to grant me an overnight stay—at least not the *old* Ben. The *new* Ben had come as a surprise. Someone I hadn't expected. My mind curled up in a knot as I tried to wrap my head around what had just happened, and ending up without success, I finally walked to the bed with cautious steps.

Even in my bleary-eyed weariness, I could appreciate the beauty of the room. I wished briefly that I could be a real guest of this lovely family, here for some happy reason and looking forward to a sunny tomorrow. Instead, I was a frightened refugee from demons, mourning the death of my beloved, burdened with the secrets of Chris and Jenna, and now confused and alarmed by what seemed to be Ben's secrets as well.

The last time I had slept at the Gallagers' place, it had been in that one room down the hall. A room full of his presence, full of his smell—Adam's room. It was from a different life.

I turned off the lamp and fell gratefully on the pearly sheets, intending to think through some of what had occurred in this house this evening. Before I could go into detail thinking about Adam, about his brother's strange behavior, and about what had driven me here in the first place, I drifted off into a restless sleep...

It was dark. A flash of silver light tore through the air between me and Adam. He spread his wings the second the flash hit his chest. I held my breath and gestured to him to hide before they could strike once more. He didn't take any notice of my hands waving, trying to summon him beside me. He looked at me with burning red eyes. Red eyes I had never seen before, red eyes like fire. They bore into mine, and my body was burning, every single fiber in my being screaming with pain. It wasn't Adam; it was the shadow from the street, the human shape made of billowing shadow. I couldn't see its face, but a pair of red eyes were burning in the darkness. They were fixed on me while the shadow around them glided closer. I wanted to run, but my body wouldn't respond to my desperate commands. It remained frozen, burning in agony. I fought the finality of what was written in those red eyes. Death was what they said. Death and agony. I screamed...

"Wake up," a voice spoke beside my ear.

I shuddered as the voice touched my ears. I looked around for the source of it, but there was nothing but the red-eyed demon.

"Claire," the voice demanded, a little louder this time.

I opened my eyes, unable to find the speaker in the darkness of my dream, and the pain left my system instantly as I found myself back in reality.

The room was dark, but something, perhaps moonlight through the windows, gave a soft glow. I looked to the side to find Ben's face beside mine. I stared at him in the half-light. His eyes were the molten steel they had been earlier.

"I heard you scream, so I thought I might check on you," he said, his tone full of worry. "Are you alright?" he asked.

I continued staring. I wasn't surprised by his presence; it felt almost natural that he was there. My eyelids dropped, blocking my eyes from his view for a second as I blinked. When I reopened them, he was still there, his features serious, his face so close that the heat of his breath was warming my cheek.

"Sorry, I didn't mean to startle you," he said when after another half a minute I was still motionless like a statue, doing nothing but stare.

"You didn't," I whispered into his breath. I felt a jolt in my stomach as Ben closed his eyes for a second. When he reopened them, they glowed silvery blue.

I jumped and slid away from him, only to hit my head on the bedpost.

"Ouch!" I said and felt my scalp to examine if I had cut the skin somewhere. There was nothing wet in my hair, so I just rubbed the spot where my skull had hit the wood.

My eyes snapped back to Ben. He was still leaning on the bed, but to my horror, his eyes were gleaming. What had I done? It seemed like I was about to catalyze the Gallagers' second son. I had done nothing in particular to cause a change in Ben, I told myself and tried to calm down, although internally I was freaking out. Could just being there make Ben's angel powers awaken? This couldn't be happening. It was a disaster. What if I became his mark, too? I couldn't. He couldn't. I had to leave.

I scrambled out of the bed and stood, still rubbing my head with my hand, then carefully stepped toward the door.

"Where do you think you're going?" Ben's voice came from the bed.

"Home," I mumbled into my hair, which was falling into my face as I continued rubbing my head while I slowly made my way in the half-light.

"I don't think so."

I fell to my knees, stumbling in surprise away from the voice that was right there in my ears. It hadn't been more than a few seconds. He hadn't made a sound—none at all.

My bandaged hands hit the floor as I buckled forward. I didn't dare turn around. Instead, I tried to push myself back to my unwilling feet. How could it have happened so fast? His eyes had just started to glow, and he already teleported? The moment I asked myself the question, it was answered by Ben's pale hand reaching out to help me up.

I shied away from his long, slender fingers. They shouldn't be there. *Ben* shouldn't be there. *I* shouldn't be there.

Yes, you should, the voice in my head mocked as it woke up in the back of my mind. I shook my head at both, Ben's hand and the voice, and got to my feet without help. My knees were like pudding, and my hands were shaky. I was in shock—a state I was used to by now.

When I had fully straightened up, my eyes snapped to Ben's gray shiny ones. They didn't glow anymore, I noticed, and it was like I was looking at a totally normal man. I felt stupid for running away. Ben standing in the Gallagers' guest room with his half-outstretched hand and perfectly normal eyes made him seem ordinary. Except that he was anything but ordinary. He was part-angel about to develop his powers, and there was nothing I wanted more than to get out of his sphere before he spread his wings for the first time. There was nothing less useful for me now than to become the mark of another angel and turn into a double-target for the demons that were already trying to kill me. I needed a safe space; somewhere I could go when I wanted to hide from the world and where I could think.

"Don't be afraid, Claire," Ben said after a while of looking into my eyes. I didn't know what he had found there that made him use this utterly gentle tone. His expression turned all warm and tender, and it was like a mask was crumbling from his face.

I searched his eyes for a sign of gleaming, but all I found was the reflection of the moonlight coming through the window.

"I think it's time I told you something," he began. I loved this new gentle voice, but I didn't like the words he was speaking. My head wandered from side to side on top of my spine in slow movements while I continued staring like I was a complete idiot.

"I have to," he said, but I continued to shake my head, stricken dumb by utter dread of what he had to say.

"Please, Claire," his voice became harsher. I didn't like it. "I need to show you. I don't care if you don't want to know. I think you—if anybody—have the right to know."

My mouth opened to tell him I didn't want to hear it, whatever it was. His soft eyes made me think I knew exactly what he wanted to tell me, and I couldn't stand to hear it said aloud. How could he think I could... I still was too deep in the mess Adam had left behind. I couldn't simply replace him. How could Ben think I would betray the memory of his brother?

Ben came closer. I couldn't stand the vision of him so near to me. My head rolled to one side so I wouldn't have to look directly into his face. He came even closer and his hand grabbed my chin, forcing my face back in his direction.

I closed my eyes to evade his stare. It was uncomfortably intense, and his breath was coming in too quick gusts.

"I can be for you what *he* was," Ben whispered.

I tried to shake my head in his iron grip but didn't get it to move even an inch.

"Don't think I can't," he mocked.

I threw him an ugly look before I opened my mouth to speak. "You can never replace him," I spat, my jaw fighting against his hand. "You are not Adam."

"But I'm from the same family," Ben replied without a second of delay.

"That doesn't give you the right to take his place," I said harshly. My insides knotted into a hard ball and reminded me in a painful way that nobody could.

"I can give you whatever he gave you…"

"I don't want it," I said coldly.

"Maybe more…"

I looked at him for a while with a probing gaze.

The way his eyes were beginning to gleam made me anxious. I wasn't sure anymore if what I was fearing would come was where he was actually headed.

His hand loosed its grip. Maybe he took my unresponsiveness as a sign that I accepted his offer.

I shook my head in a quick motion. "No." The word sounded freezing.

"I'm stronger, Claire," Ben said in a quiet voice, "No one is going to harm you when you're with me."

"I don't care how many tree trunks you can carry," I snapped, thinking of him in the parlor just hours before, arms folded over his shapely chest.

His brow furrowed, but his lips curved in frustrated amusement. "No, no, no, not that, Claire," he said. "I'm older than Adam, and I have a purer bloodline."

"What?" I choked out. "I thought Adam was the older one. What are you talking about?" My head swam with incomprehension while Ben kept looking at me like he was revealing the first prize to the lucky winner.

"I'm not talking about *that* age," he said with dark humor in his eyes, waiting for me to comprehend.

But all I could do was stare as I waited for him to fill me in.

"Do you really not understand?" he whispered. With the strangest look, he stepped backward and gestured at himself like he was trying to tell me that the prize he had been talking about all along was him.

"Understand what?" was all that could leave my mouth before my questions were answered with a burst of blinding white.

Reflexively, I shied away from Ben's expanding shape—the image of a Gallager son exploding in front of me felt like deja-vu. I remembered the first time I had seen Adam spread his wings. It had been the beginning of a lot of happiness but also a lot of pain and now sorrow. I was living deep in the fallout still.

"Ben, no," I whispered in dismay.

He was standing there, shirt torn and hanging askew from his broad shoulders, revealing his muscled chest framed by a beautiful pair of shining, white wings. He was magnificent.

Hot tears sprang up without warning and stung my eyes.

"Oh my God, Ben—I'm so sorry." My voice was so low it was almost inaudible. So, I had sealed the Gallagers' second son's fate, too. Just as I had with Adam, I had triggered Ben's wings, and now I was marked by him. Could things get any more complicated? *Great*, the voice in my head came to life once more, *now you've got both of them on your conscience— murderer*. "Shut up," I responded aloud but only so loud that I could hear it, or so I hoped. A deep sadness spread inside of me. I *was* a murderer. I hadn't lifted as much as a finger against them, but still, I was responsible for Adam's death, and I would certainly be responsible for Ben's, too, unless some miracle delivered us both.

"I don't think God needs you to be sorry," Ben said much too casually for what I thought was the high drama of the moment.

His tone shifted me away from my own problems to consider what it was he might be saying. Why would he be so calm? Wasn't he afraid?

"You can stop blaming yourself now," he said, and his eyes locked on mine with a seriousness I had never ever seen on his face before.

"What—?"

"No, you're not marked," he said evenly, "You're not a target because of me, and you didn't trigger my wings."

My mouth fell open at what he was saying. Could it be that this boy knew everything? How long had he been like this? I didn't want to think about the future for this heavenly winged creature. He was too young to be exposed to this war. And still, he seemed so confident, the way he was standing with his angelic wings. He looked as if they had been part of him all his life.

"Ben, I—" I was at a loss for words.

His eyes started to gleam in a steely blue that looked even more alien than Adam's light green or Jaden's gold.

"Don't worry about me," he said reassuringly, his voice strong and confident.

I must have looked like a complete idiot because Ben suddenly launched into laughter. Pride and strength shone out from him.

"I'll be fine," he laughed, "I've learned to handle it."

"Ben—" I started once more, "how can you not be afraid? After what happened to your brother... As long as you use your powers, they might track you down, won't they?"

Ben just looked at me with his eyes glowing and the most beautiful smile on his perfect lips.

"How have you managed to stay undetected? I thought the demons could locate new angels when they spread wings for the first time." My voice trailed off as Ben just stood there smiling at me. I had more questions.

"How did you learn what was happening that first time? Adam told me how hard it was for him in the beginning—"

The mention of Adam seemed to cool his joy in revealing his powerful angel-self to me. His smile faded, and he looked down pensively as if mesmerized by the elaborate parquet floor of the room.

"He told me about the fear... and the changes in the physical abilities... and it was so hard for him to learn to control it..." I stepped back and sat down on the bed, my heart heavy with memories and my head bursting with thoughts I couldn't channel into one simple sentence. Instead of voicing what was going on inside of me, I fell silent and stared at the blanket.

The floor made a creaking noise as Ben moved, the soles of his feet brushing the wood as he walked slowly in my direction.

Everybody was supernatural around me. All of them were extraordinary, strong, had superhero powers, were beautiful, and, to name that part that weighed most heavily on me, immortal.

They wouldn't die. Unless somehow the forces of darkness could exploit a weakness, they would live forever—Ben, Chris, Jenna, Jaden... Adam should have lived forever, too, but I had been the weakness the demons used to destroy him.

A wave of guilt tried to choke me. I swallowed it bravely and turned my eyes back to what was left of my world. I had to think about the present. Ben sat down on the bed beside me.

"You don't need to worry about me," he repeated. "I've been like this for over five years. Not even my parents know what I am."

I held my breath. Not true! His parents knew very well but were keeping that from him to protect him. But if *he* didn't know that, it was one more burden for me to carry, another secret in this supernatural world I found myself in.

"I have learned control without any help—it all came naturally. It is as if I had always been like this—wings and torch eyes and aging at will." Full of charm and brio, he looked eagerly into my face. "It's not even hard to hide that I am so strong."

My heart filled with sadness as he spoke. I could only picture Adam and wondered why it couldn't have been that easy for him. Would he still be alive?

"And you are too beautiful to be sad," Ben whispered. His eyes lingered on my face as if he was sinking into my soul. They looked lost, searching for an anchor.

I turned my head to evade his eyes.

"Ben, I'm—" *lost, too. Caught in misery. I need someone to make it alright again.* Could I tell him this? I could barely acknowledge it myself.

"I know," he simply said. His hand reached out and stroked my cheek with the tip of one finger.

My cheek warmed under his touch. It was the closest to comfort I could imagine right now, the way he touched my face. I felt my defenses weaken, so welcome was the combination of place and person in my hungry heart. I could see the similarity between Adam and Ben more clearly than ever. They looked so similar when their faces were lit up by the glow of their eyes—except Adam's eyes would never again shine, ever. My heart sped up as I searched Ben's face for an answer to what was happening to me. He looked at me, victorious. Instead of giving me the answer I was searching for, he bent closer and breathed a kiss onto my cheek.

"I know, I'll never replace him..." he whispered, and his wings rustled behind his back as he moved toward me, "but I can try. At least—I'm alive."

I felt as though a knife had been stabbed into my guts. This fabulous creature so sweetly taking me over was so much like Adam. The way he smelled, his beautiful face, his tender concern. And he was right—he was alive. Alive, and immortal, too. While Adam, who should have been immortal, was dead, and that was because of me. My heart was split in two halves, torn down the middle.

I had half a heart that was in mourning for my true love and half a heart that yearned traitorously for the comfort and protection his brother could give me. Where the edges of my broken heart collided against each other, there was terrible pain and guilt. Pain and guilt that Ben was slowly, and apparently with my permission, pushing into the background.

What can you lose? the voice in my head asked. And it was right. There was hardly a thing I could lose now. What was left of my family was safe in Indianapolis, far, far away from everything that was going on here in Aurora. And the Gallagers were supernaturals—all of them.

I was the weak link in the chain, and the best I could do was surround myself with forces of the good. It would increase my chances of survival. But I couldn't replace Adam; not the way Ben meant. My heart was full of Adam's memory. There was little space to fit anyone else in.

12.
Replacement

The fog that was slowly lifting from the streets of Aurora was similar to the haze that was coiling in my head. I had the strong intuition that whatever I had been denying was going to reveal itself to me soon. Almost like I was sure that the fog outside the window was going to retreat upward and form into a soft, white cloud, which would be blown away by the fresh spring breeze. I also had the feeling that whatever I was going to find would, by no means, resemble the clear blue sky that usually follows when the clouds disappear. I was more expecting a darkened plane that would threaten to crash down on me. I could already feel it.

Several days had passed since the night at the Gallagers'. I'd had a lot to think about. These days, not many things in my life were able to penetrate my thoughts concerning my dilemma with Benedict Gallager. I hadn't felt as safe in weeks as I had felt with him. I hadn't even had the opportunity to feel guilty for enjoying this new feeling of being protected, not alone, the way I had felt before. Ben, Jenna, and Chris were a part of Adam, and somehow that made me feel better. It helped me drown out this sense of emptiness I had gotten used to. I actually, after all this time of pain, started to feel a little bit healed.

Sophie was still in Indianapolis. She had called the night before to let me know that Ian was going to come pick up some of her things today before lunchtime. He wanted to visit her—again. I wondered how he could be so blindly in love with my dear sister. Yes, she was pretty. Yes, she was bright. And yes, she had a brilliant sense of humor—sometimes. But she treated him without much respect. She had cheated on him once some time ago. Now that they were a couple again, I was waiting for her to make the same mistake. I found myself unable to understand how somebody could do such a thing. If one truly loved the other, there wouldn't be a reason. It was none of my business, of course, but it was a distraction to keep me from thinking about my own troublesome life all the time. I remembered the excuse she had used last time. She hadn't been entirely sure if Ian was what she wanted. She had felt physically attracted to the other man, and once the chance presented itself, she followed her instinct.

I wondered how it was possible to even think about it. I could never have betrayed Adam. Apart from the fact that he would have known the moment I came near him. He would have sensed that there was something wrong. The shame, the fear to be caught—

The doorbell jerked me to my feet, and I headed down the stairs to open it. Instead of Ian, whom I had been expecting,

Ben was standing on the other side. He looked at me with narrowed eyes.

"Can I come in?" he asked, simultaneously grabbing me by the shoulders and nearly lifting me back into the house.

"Whoa, what's up?" I asked, startled by his urgency.

"Just a second," he whispered and pressed his finger to his lips. He walked a few steps then stood in the doorway to the living room for half a minute, unmoving. I watched him freeze into place and turned around when after another five seconds, he was still stone-like. The door was still standing open. I grabbed the handle and started to push it closed when Ian appeared on the doorstep.

"Hi, Claire," he smiled. "How are you doing?" I eyed him critically for a moment then pulled the door back open.

"Come in, please," I said mechanically, still unsettled by Ben's behavior.

Ian stepped over the threshold in slow strides.

"Sophie told me to pick up her..."

"They are upstairs. I packed everything into the black leather bag," I told Ian without looking at him, my eyes back on Ben, who still hadn't moved.

"Have you got a minute so I can introduce you?" I asked Ben with the faintest undertone of sarcasm.

Ian noticed Ben for the first time.

"Oh, hi—"

"Ben—Ian, Ian—Ben," I gestured at both of them in turns, introducing my sister's boyfriend to the brother of my dead boyfriend.

"Sorry," Ben finally unfroze and turned around, reacting to my tense tone, "I was in thought..."

Sometimes Ben's phraseology was downright quaint, something I had noticed with all of the angels in my life.

He held out his hand to Ian politely, and his face grew into a warm mask that didn't resemble that alarmed, almost anxious look he had worn a minute ago anymore.

"Nice to meet you, Ben," Ian said and shook Ben's hand. Then he turned back to me. "Look, I'll just grab Sophie's things, and I'll be off. I have to drive all the way down to Indianapolis, and I want to see your sister as soon as possible." He winked at me and headed for the stairs.

"Okay." I exhaled quietly. I was glad that Ian hadn't found Ben's behavior fishy. The last thing I needed was somebody asking questions I couldn't answer because I was still waiting for an answer myself.

I waited until Ian was out of earshot and then turned back to Ben.

"What's wrong, Ben?" I whispered as I saw that his face was back to alarmed. "Tell me." I danced from foot to foot, feeling insecure and getting myself ready to run. The way the alarmed mask lingered on his face made me think that I might have a reason for running.

"I just thought I saw something," he told me.

"What?" I asked, uncomprehending, getting more nervous. Ben shook his head.

"How can you see something?"

Ben averted his gaze.

"Ben, look at me," I demanded.

A door was closed upstairs, and Ian's shoes tapping down the stairs in quick step announced that he was back within earshot.

"Anything else I should bring her?" he asked on his way to the front door. "Except for your warm regards?" Ian grinned boyishly. He was too good for this world. If Sophie would ask him to jump down from Indianapolis Hospital's roof, he would probably do it.

"No," I smiled at him, hoping that he wouldn't notice Ben's glare or my silly shifting from side to side. "That's all."

"See you, then," he said and he walked out the door, still grinning, obviously in a good mood.

"Tell her I am fine," I called after him. And I saw him nod while he turned his head to one side, looking at me over his shoulder.

I waved at him with one nervously shaking hand, and then I closed the door behind him.

"You are going to tell me what's going on, Mister," I said and darted toward Ben in a quick stride, my index finger pointing at his chest. "Why are you seeing things in my house?"

Ben's eyes narrowed, and he opened his mouth defensively. "I was in the area, and I thought I might drop by and say hello..." he said very unconvincingly.

"And then?" I demanded.

Ben looked afraid of me. His face blushed slightly, and his shoulders sank half an inch, just enough to notice.

"I saw—I felt that something dark was around, and I feared that the demons had decided to strike once more."

"And—?" I tapped my foot against the floor impatiently, feeling angry from the lack of proper information, my finger still poking into his chest.

"And I rang the bell, and you opened the door?" he offered, obviously hoping that being cute would get him off the hook.

I shook my head to deny the answer and frowned at him.

"And—?" he repeated, waiting for me to complete the question.

"And—*is* there anything dark around?" I demanded like a stern teacher getting to the bottom of some misbehavior.

"Actually, I guess maybe not," Ben said, abashed. He looked at me to check my reaction.

Well, here's a role reversal, I thought to myself. The big, strong angel in trouble with the ordinary human girl.

"What I mean is, whatever it was, it's not here anymore," he explained, his expression all open and attentive now. The new Ben-face I still had to get used to. It was too friendly, too human, too—

I looked away. It made him look so much like Adam, and I just couldn't bear that. His half-brother was dead, and we were standing there together with something unresolved between us. I couldn't even think about it.

"Why are you really here?" I asked quietly, my eyes on the floor.

Silence spread between us. I knew that there was an answer to that question, one that differed from what Ben had told me; but I wasn't entirely sure if I wanted to know. Something drove me to ask, anyway.

"Ben—" I persisted, lifting my finger from his chest, "—why?"

For the first time in my life, I felt like I could read a person's emotions the way Adam had always described it. *I perceive what they feel and somehow know their reasons.* I didn't know the reason, but I could tell that Ben had come here for me. Not just to drop by but to take care of me. I felt that strange pull between us. My hands shook, and my stomach was a bit nauseous. It was exactly what I didn't want to feel; I didn't want to know.

I let my head sink and looked away, turning to the side and walking toward the couch where I sat down.

"I—" Ben started.

"Yeah, it's alright," I said like I was speaking to the table in front of me, "you were around, running errands in the area..."

Ben shifted his weight and took a step toward me, slowly. "I was here because I..."

"Because you had stuff to do," I finished his sentence, not leaving any space for him to say what he was thinking. "Thank you for dropping by. As you can see, I'm safe. Nothing to worry about."

"And I fixed your car," he added.

"Thanks," I simply said.

I looked at him for a second, and as he blinked, too slowly to be a subconscious gesture, I looked back at the table awkwardly. The wood had several scratches on the surface where my sister and I had placed dishes or bottles or other things I couldn't remember. I followed the progress of a minor scratch which twisted into one of the corners in a sharp angle. Observing how badly we had taken care of this particular piece of furniture, I almost managed to ignore Ben's expectant silence.

"Claire," Ben said from closer in front of me than I had expected.

My head snapped up in the direction his voice was coming from.

"What?" I asked in a whisper, almost unable to bear the thought of getting an answer and wanting to hear it at the same time. My stomach clenched with tension.

Before I could even look at him, Ben reached for my hand and cradled it in both of his, softly, carefully.

"Claire..." he began. He looked into my eyes. "You know I have feelings for you..."

My heart leaped, and my head began to pound. Those were the words I had hoped to hear since that night at the Gallagher's, and those were also the words I could not bear to hear. I felt like a monster. I had led him on, encouraged him to speak, and for what... just to invoke Adam's memory and send Ben on his way.

"Ben," I panted, transfixed by his stare. "I can't."

Ben looked away for a long second, and when he looked back at me, his eyes had changed. No longer the blue of sunny skies, they were the color of solid steel. "I am sorry I made you uncomfortable," Ben said in the strangely formal way he sometimes had and quickly let go of my hand like he had burned his fingers.

My heart was wracked with pity, but I had no way to express it. I was glad he had understood that this was not the time for what was on his mind. But I didn't dare to look into his eyes again for fear I would change my mind.

"I think it is best if I leave now," he said quietly and stepped toward the door he had entered just a few minutes earlier with such anticipation.

It was only then that another thought occurred to me. What if my rejection on one level made him leave me on another? What if my not being able to love Adam's brother would kill our friendship, too? I would lose his protection. I would be more vulnerable again. I shuddered slightly as I turned my head to watch Ben walk out the front door.

"Hey," I called out very softly. I wanted him to feel my regret and affection.

He turned and paused, looking straight through me with his steely eyes. I hesitated, aware that my motives were selfish and unworthy of him.

"When will I see you again?" I asked.

He raised his eyebrows and compressed his lips, a disappointed man. "Oh, now you're worried," he said. "Well, don't be. I'll always be there for you when you need a protector." And with that, he was gone.

I didn't know if I was only imagining it, but the room was still filled with the echo of Ben's hurt voice, and it wasn't long before my guilt was filling the gaps in between.

I needed to get out of the house for a while. I needed some space and air to breathe. I had spent so much time in fear of what was hunting me that I had forgotten to live. The fact that I had Jenna, Chris, and Ben to protect me helped me stay calm enough to get through the days, and the knowledge that Jaden was never too far away let me sleep more or less restful. Jaden was around at school also, although there, he kept a good distance and spent a lot of time with Amber, who was thrilled by every word he spoke and couldn't take her eyes off him for even a second if her attention wasn't forcefully directed elsewhere. It still bothered me that Jaden gave her so much attention. But then, maybe it was for the best. Maybe all of this was what gave me enough freedom to move at school with enough space so nobody would notice I was being shadowed by Jaden Abelton.

As I headed for the front door, I grabbed my jacket from the hook and swirled it around my shoulders in a swift movement. Outside, the fog had cleared a little whereas the wafts of mist had grown thicker inside my head. I pounded down the porch stairs and headed toward downtown without any real destination. Something about this whole situation wasn't right, and I couldn't put my finger on it. I simply couldn't find an easy explanation. Was it me and my endless worries? Was it the pressure from the constant danger that was just sufficiently below the threshold to not drive me crazy with actual fear?

I was beginning to wear out. My strength was coming to an end, and I could name plenty of causes why. I tried to line them up in logical order. First, the constant fear of demons that underlay every moment of every day. Then, the grief over Adam's death. My new and troubled relationship with Ben. Chris's struggle to regain his wings. The pressure to stay in school and do well so that my future—if I ever got to have one—could be a good one. Sophie's safety. Hanging on to the few friends I had at Aurora High. I had avoided evil as well as possible, I had endured being stared at, being made fun of, being an outsider, a stranger in a group of people I thought I knew. The sun was beginning to timidly appear overhead, but thanks to my list of troubles, my day seemed darker than ever.

It wasn't just that I had all these worries and that I couldn't see an end to them. I couldn't even see where to start fixing them.

I was deep into a supernatural world, and I was not strong enough to thrive there. I had no one to turn to except the Gallagers. The Gallagers—I should at least be grateful for them. Chris, Jenna, and Ben. A stalwart little army of goodness and angelic strength. And Jaden, my guardian angel—sometimes there, sometimes not, but still my guardian. I was helpless without them.

My footfalls were unnaturally loud on the sidewalk, I noticed, as I returned from the mist in my head to the less hazy reality around me.

It took me a while before I recognized where my feet were carrying me. I hadn't talked to Mr. Baker in a while. He hadn't been there on my last workday. The boy who worked at the library usually had Mr. Baker's keys to close up in the evenings. I wondered if the old man would be there now. Eager to talk to someone who knew enough so I didn't have to pretend, but not enough to bother me with unwelcome questions about my role in this whole mess, I walked a little faster until the library building became visible at the end of the street.

The building looked the same as usual. What was abnormal was the cluster of people squeezing between ambulance cars and a police cruiser. The blue light was painting repetitive patterns on the faded colors of the facades of the buildings and on the people who were rushing in and out the entrance door.

Instinctively, I picked up my pace. What was going on? My feet were carrying me unnaturally fast toward the scene. As I was close enough to recognize faces, I saw Lydia at the very back of the crowd, Richard standing close beside her, holding her hand in both of his.

For a second, I felt relief. Whatever had happened, at least one of my best friends wasn't involved. Lydia was safe. And Richard. Not that he had been much of a friend to me, but he was Lyd's boyfriend, and that meant that I was happy he was okay.

Amber. Greg. My mind flashed to images of my other friends.

"Claire," Lydia called as she noticed me hurrying toward them.

"What happened?" I asked, still a few steps away from them. I almost bumped into them, so eager to get an answer.

"I don't know." It was Richard who spoke these unsatisfying words. "We just arrived a few minutes ago."

"I heard people mention that someone collapsed inside the library." Lydia gave what information she had.

"What are the police doing here?"

The moment the words had left my mouth, I heard a low murmur go through the crowd. People were standing on their tiptoes to get a better view of the paramedics and the body they were carrying down the stairs from the entrance. The body was covered with a white sheet from face to feet. I didn't see much besides that. Just a glimpse of gray hair, which was exposed at the top of the covered figure's head.

"Mr. Baker," I gasped.

A wave of sadness and fear washed over me and my ears began to buzz. I must have started to lose my balance because someone steadied me.

"Are you okay?" I heard a voice beside me. I couldn't even tell who it was.

Mr. Baker—dead. My breath rasped in my chest.

I caught myself looking around hysterically. Where was Jaden when I needed him?

A firm hand pushed me back into the crowd.

"Please stand back, folks," a tall and lean policeman was saying, "Let the paramedics through here."

Shaken awake by his voice, I jumped to the side.

"Officer, what happened?" someone in the crowd called out.

"Just a medical emergency," the policeman said, all business and plainly not going to share anything else. "We'll take it from here. You should all move on now."

One of the bystanders, a hunched old lady with disheveled hair, who was one of the library regulars, spotted me. She was a chatty character, and I usually tried to keep my conversations with her short, but today I was glad to see her.

"I heard one of those detective fellows say it wasn't anything violent," she offered, nodding toward a figure in a tan trench coat that matched his sparse hair.

The man was standing with two younger men who appeared very solemn.

"I guess it was just old age," the woman rattled on. "Too bad, he was nice. Guess we're going to need a new librarian now. I hope that doesn't mean they are going to change the reading room around too much. I like it the way it is. Two years ago when they..."

Lydia, perceptive as always, took my arm and said, "Come on, we've got to go."

I allowed her to steer me away but not before I noticed that the man in the trench coat was now standing alone on the bottom step as if waiting for the emergency vehicles to clear out one by one.

Lydia kept our arms linked, and along with Richard, we started walking. They were talking, but I wasn't listening. My brain was running laps, trying to collect any details I could remember that would help me understand.

Our destination turned out to be Noel's coffee shop, and with a shock, I thought of the last time I had been here. It had been with Mr. Baker, and he had been fighting a bad cold. Could that have been it? Perhaps he had developed pneumonia? Should I have insisted on going to the store that evening to get him medicine?

An image of dark billowing shadows passed before me, and I suddenly felt certain it wasn't pneumonia. Mr. Baker had known too much. It was *them*. A cold shiver went up my spine. And I could be next. Even more than poor old Mr. Baker, I knew too much.

"I wonder what will happen to the library now," Richard speculated, looking at me over his coffee.

I shook my head in reply, not really listening. I was watching Noel shuffling around, clearing the tables. He looked so sad. Did he know? Had he already heard about Mr. Baker's death? I fought the impulse to walk over and speak to him. I had never spoken to him before, and I didn't want to be weird. But somehow, my heart went out to him.

"... impact on your job?" Richard was asking me a question.

"Um," I said, trying to figure out what the first part of the sentence would have been. "I have not a clue."

I hoped that would satisfy Richard, but I caught his train of thought. What if the new administration had no use for part-time high school students? The job didn't pay very much, but still, I was putting all my paychecks into my college fund, a fund that seemed to promise the nice, normal future that I wanted instead of the perilous present. My heart gave a sad flutter. No matter how hard I tried, I might never get to that future.

Lydia was leaning on Richard's shoulder, her face grim. How much I was longing for a shoulder to lean on. Where was Jaden when I needed him? Did he know what was going on right now? Maybe if I were alone, he might show up...

Mr. Baker's funeral was short and simple. What he would have wanted, I felt sure. It had been hard for me to go into the cemetery, though. Adam was buried there, the little plot out of sight from us this morning but, in actuality, hardly more than a few steps away. I was standing in line with maybe fifty others who wanted to pay their respect to the town librarian. Jaden wasn't among them. Despite the little clique of mourners, I felt alone and vulnerable, surrounded by painful memories and a burden of sadness that went far beyond my regret for Mr. Baker.

The past days before the funeral had been full of doubts. The police had announced that it had been a natural death. Something with his heart that wasn't obvious at first. I doubted it.

First of all, Mr. Baker had been a protector of the angels' knowledge and was well-informed about the existence of demons. This alone had made him a target. And then, he had shared his knowledge with me, which had made him a liability. Angels would never attack Mr. Baker. But demons?

I looked at the black-clothed crowd around me and shuddered. It should have been me. Not him. I knew too much, too. Or even more than too much.

I had to fight to keep my eyes on the little funeral before me and not seek out the spot where Adam lay in the earth, his grave now spangled with the tiny red blossoms of the maple overhead. And with Adam dead, I might as well be, too. It would be an act of mercy if they did kill me, and sooner rather than later. Not that they even knew the concept of mercy.

Someone squeezed my hand, and I turned abruptly to find Ben beside me, a sympathetic smile on his beautiful lips.

"Thanks for coming," I whispered at him as we turned to leave.

We filed in behind the rest of the people and slowly made our way toward the gate.

Once outside the gates, I found James, who also worked at the library, waiting for me.

"Have you heard anything yet?" he asked, his face pale and full of worry. "About reopening?"

"No, nothing," I shook my head at him. "How about you?"

"No... Although I did hear that the new librarian won't cut our jobs. That's good, at least." He looked up from the ground.

"Oh, wow, for sure." That was a relief. "So I guess we just wait."

"Yep," James said, and gave a brief wave as he headed to his car.

I turned to Ben. He was frowning into the distance.

"What is it?" I tried to get his attention.

His mouth twitched ever so slightly, and he turned toward me.

"Don't worry about it." He shook his head.

That, of course, made me worry.

"What, Ben?" I tried again. This time, I got a stronger reaction out of him.

"I don't like the thought of you going back there. It's too dangerous."

He was obviously talking about the library.

"There is something about that place that makes it more dangerous than others."

I nodded in agreement. First the shadow, the first time Jaden had shown up. Then Colina. I swallowed. Then Mr. Baker.

Of course, the ancient book about angels and demons, the one without title, might play a part in this. It had made the library a place where mythical creatures seemed to walk in and out every other day.

"Jaden is always looking out for me, Ben," I tried to reassure him. "I'll be fine." But my heart rate went up, knowing that I probably wouldn't. Not much longer. And, of course, Ben would feel my anxiety. He put his hand on my shoulder.

We walked to my car in silence. Just when we reached it, something caught my eye. Ahead, a vague but familiar shape was standing under the spreading trees. It was no more than a shadow, but my heart did a quick flip flop. *Adam*, my subconscious spoke immediately. *Not possible*, my brain responded after a long second. Adam was dead. I had watched them bury him right here, in this graveyard. I shook my head at myself. My dreams, my nightmares had probably started following me through my days. I blinked hard and looked again, but the shape was gone.

I glanced at Ben, but if he had seen or sensed anything, he gave no clue. He just politely opened the door for me, and I slid into the driver's seat. I took a deep breath and exhaled.

"You coming?" I asked Ben, wondering what the plan was.

"I'll be right behind you." He closed the door and walked away.

I pulled into my driveway just ahead of Ben, thinking about my most recent conversation with Sophie.

Another funeral? Sophie had asked. And she was right. It seemed like I was attending more funerals than anything else these days. I was grateful that Sophie was out of town for now. Having her in danger because of me was inexcusable.

Ben walked me to the door. Had it been only three days since he had walked out, hurt and angry, and I had gone on that aimless walk to clear my mind? The walk that ended abruptly at the scene at the library?

"Do you want me to stay?" he asked.

I looked searchingly at him. I couldn't read his thoughts, but I could feel how much he wanted me to say yes. I smiled at him the way old friends can smile when they are on familiar territory together.

"Do *you* want to stay?" I countered.

He dipped his head. "We need to have another talk."

"Then, okay," I said, still smiling but on the alert for what might be coming next. I put the key in the lock. "Come on in."

He followed me in and shrugged out of his jacket, aiming it at the hallway chair before following me into the kitchen.

Dishes and old mail were still on the table. Ben sat down and began artfully piling the china into a tower.

I reached over and took the dishes from him, wondering if, as wealthy as the Gallagers were, Ben had ever learned to wash dishes. For a moment, I imagined him as a husband and father, helping some graceful young woman with the housework, maybe playing with the baby. It was a pretty picture. Ben was eyeing me as if trying to read my thoughts, and I was glad angels could not do that.

"Coffee?" I asked and quickly turned away, grabbing two coffee mugs from the cabinet. I needed for him not to see my eyes.

"Why didn't you tell me?" he started.

My hands stopped mid-air.

"Tell you what?" I held my breath, waiting for his answer.

"That you know so much about Chris and Jenna and—the rest of us."

Ahhh. Of course. Sooner or later, all of those angels living under the same roof would have had to discover all of the many truths about each other.

And he would wonder, at some point, how much I really knew. That meant he would know that his angel-powers must come from somewhere. A genetic predisposition inherited from one of the parents. Or in his case—both.

"Hmmpf." I set the mugs down and waited for the coffee machine to do its magic. "I guess, it wasn't my place to tell. When did you find out?" I asked.

"Just this week." His voice was dark.

"Did they tell you?" I poured the coffee and set the two mugs on the table in front of him before I sat on a chair next to him.

His face was unreadable. I could only imagine what emotions must be washing over him at that moment.

He looked into his cup like he was searching for answers there. "After Mr. Baker's death—"

I eyed him for one brief second and took a deep breath. Lucas Baker had known everything about angels. And he probably had died to protect the knowledge. To protect the Gallagers. Ben owed him as much as I did.

"—my parents decided it was time to warn me. They told me how you had let them know about Mr. Baker and about how the demons were drawing closer and I was in danger because of my strong angel heritage." He gave a grin somewhere between mischievous and triumphant. "You can imagine their faces when I told them I knew, that it had already happened for me. They couldn't believe I had handled it all by myself. Oh, and they were really relieved when they found out I hadn't marked anyone when I spread my wings."

A shiver ran down my spine. Ben was lucky enough not to have marked anyone. The same as Jenna. At least, neither one carried that burden. But that didn't make their lives any less dangerous.

"I have two part-angels as parents. That makes my lineage stronger than most. I developed earlier because of that." Ben looked up at me. "I wonder how they were able to keep it a secret for so long... At least, they had each other to confide in. If I were to love someone the way they love each other, I wouldn't ever keep a secret from them."

"That is quite impressive," I commented on Jenna and Chris, ignoring the last sentence he had spoken.

Ben's eyes became molten steel. "I just want you to know that you have three Gallager angels left. We can't ever replace Adam for you, and... well, to be honest, you can't ever replace Adam for us. But we are all bound to one another now through him. You carry part of his soul, and that makes you part of our family. Nothing is more important to us than to keep you safe in our love."

I leaned back wordlessly, staring at Ben with widened eyes. I had never looked at it that way. His soul was alive, tied to mine. Even if it was just a fraction of his beautiful soul. The thought ripped through my dark mood like a ray of sunshine.

It was an hour later when Ben finally left. I was still sitting in the kitchen, sipping my cold coffee.

The conversation had left me hopeful in different ways.

All the secrets were gone. The Gallagers all knew about each other now, and I didn't have to watch my words and actions the way I had before. They all knew, and they all understood. It made me feel a little bit better.

With a small smile, I grabbed an envelope from the mail pile and opened it. It was the paycheck from the library. And tucked in between the check and the envelope was a small piece of paper with Lucas' scribbling on it that said: *Trust Liz!*

I was staring at the words, trying to figure out their meaning. *Trust Liz!* Who was Liz?

This was obviously Lucas Baker's last message to me. He must have known they were coming for him. He had made sure I got this message even if he wasn't alive to deliver it.

13.
The Guard

It was Thursday. Almost a week had passed since Lucas' funeral. And the conversation with Ben.

I was glad all the secrets between the Gallagers were finally gone. It had felt wrong, knowing more than the trusted and loved ones around me.

It felt like all of us knowing made us stronger than ever. A unit of supernatural—plus me, the weak human. But I was still determined.

This afternoon was dedicated to going through the nameless book yet again.

I had studied it from cover to cover. It had chapters that were definitely of use to us. But there were no specifics. No instructions on how to help Chris get his wings back. It just said that he might. It gave me hope, but it made me feel inadequate in my position as the researcher of our group.

Jaden had started wandering off by himself in the afternoons, doing research of his own. He was determined to find out as much as possible about the group of demons around Volpert. I shuddered at the name. His absence left me under the protection of the Gallagers.

It had been a long school day, and it was going to be a long afternoon. Jaden would again be off to try and unearth what he could about Volpert. And so I found myself walking up to the library entrance, my hands sweaty and pulse elevated.

Ben would be somewhere nearby—just in case.

Thinking of Ben risking his life to make sure I was safe made me uneasy. Not because I didn't trust him. His art collection had made me see him in a different light.

I was anxious for Ben. I already had one of the Gallagers' sons on my conscience. I couldn't live with myself if anything happened to Ben.

The door made a low squeaky sound when I pulled it open. I was half-expecting to find Lucas Baker behind the counter. *He's dead. The same as Adam. The same as everyone who gets close to you*, the voice in my head woke up. I knew it was the truth.

"Claire Gabriel," a rich female voice greeted me from between the shelves. I turned in the direction it had come from and found myself looking at a woman in a trim, chestnut-colored suit with gleaming black hair and lively eyes.

"My name is Elizabeth Martinez." She hurried over, stylish boots clicking on the floor.

I looked at her, not knowing what to expect.

"The new librarian," the woman clarified.

She finally came to a halt in front of me and held out her hand.

"Pleased to meet you, Mrs. Martinez," I managed to croak and shook her hand. I had gotten a note to come in today. But I hadn't been informed about the new librarian.

"Mrs. Martinez was my mother," she laughed and exposed her pearly white teeth. "Call me Liz."

Something clicked into place in my mind.

The library was empty except for us. James must have left early.

"Lucas told me so much about you." Liz smiled.

We slowly walked up to the counter together, her firm footfalls a testimony to her womanly confidence.

"Coffee?" She held up a cup for me.

I took it from her hands. "Thank you."

The hot beverage smelled good. Not the cheap drip coffee from the staff room but strong, Italian coffee, the way you got it at Noel's.

"You knew Mr. Baker...Umm...Lucas?" I was curious. It couldn't be a coincidence. She must be the Liz from Lucas Baker's note. *Trust Liz!*

"I did." She looked down for a moment. "He absolutely adored you. Almost like a granddaughter. And when I look at you, I can see why."

Another smile spread on her face. It made the faint lines around her eyes and mouth more prominent. I assumed she must be in her mid-forties.

Liz lifted her own cup to her lips and took a small sip. She had style and energy to spare, and she fixed me with her dark eyes.

"Lucas wouldn't stop talking about you, Claire... I can call you Claire, right?"

I nodded, still a little taken aback by how straightforward this person was.

"Fine then," she set down her cup. "I was thinking about rearranging the library a little bit. I think I see where we can create a Young Adult department by moving some shelves and furniture. They're such great readers."

I listened to her, trying to figure out if she could be the *Liz*. She had known Lucas Baker. He had talked to her about me. It must be her.

"... and maybe a reading club. What do you think...?"

What had she just asked? My head was empty. I looked at her.

"Excuse me, I didn't catch that last part."

Liz smiled. "We should talk about those ideas soon. I'd really like your input."

I nodded, unable to come up with a coherent comment.

"Anyway," she added, "I need to head out. I've got a date." She winked at me and finished her coffee.

"Okay," I managed.

"I'll see you later." Liz swung her designer handbag over her shoulder. "Oh—and be prepared to work late tonight."

I watched her stride away from the counter on her high heels then swing confidently through the door. What had just happened?

After the whirlwind of Liz Martinez, the afternoon slowed to a crawl. I checked in the small pile of returned books and tried to think of something else to keep my mind off Mr. Baker. He should have been there, and I might never know how much I had contributed to the fact that he wasn't. I clicked into the catalog with the thought that this new librarian might approve of a shelf of New Releases. There were quite a few titles that would qualify. Rather fancying myself in the role of library innovator, I delved deep into the project, accompanied only by the soft tick and occasional chime of the library's famous old clock.

I looked up only when the door opened to another creature of high energy. It was Ben.

"Hey," he grinned at me like his day had just gotten better.

"Hi, Ben."

I walked around the counter and up to him. He closed the distance in a few quick strides and pulled me into a hug.

"You seem happy," I noticed.

"I am always happy when I see you, Claire." Ben turned to the side and walked me toward the window.

I let him, but wondered what he was seeing there.

"See?" he pointed at the half-busy street outside.

I shook my head, not sure what he was referring to. There were a few people walking. Cars were driving at moderate speed, but nothing stood out.

"Exactly." He nodded. "Nothing is going on out there today."

So far, the voice in my head added.

I curled out of his arm and walked back to stand behind the counter. Ben followed.

"So, how come you can spend so much time babysitting me?" I asked, encouraged by his high spirits to venture into the subject of our personal relationship.

Ben's cheerful expression turned serious.

"Claire, my family and I agreed to protect you from the demons. We all lost someone we love. We cannot afford to lose anyone else." He stared into my eyes as if to emphasize the meaning.

I looked at the floor awkwardly. It was very clear that, besides protecting me, Ben was following his own agenda.

When I looked up, he was still staring.

"Can I get you something to drink?" I changed the subject, uncomfortably shifting behind the counter.

"Sure."

I was glad to escape his gaze and walked around the stacks to the staff room in the back.

"Water, soda...coffee?" I called while roaming the fridge.

"Coffee," Ben's voice came from right behind me.

I jumped and stumbled into the open fridge.

Ben's hand caught me before I could hit the vegetable shelf.

I coughed, embarrassed, and closed the fridge behind me.

"Milk and sugar?" I breathed without even looking at the coffee machine. My voice came out as a hoarse conglomerate of syllables.

Ben's hand was still holding me by my shoulder, and his eyes bore into mine.

He nodded at my question.

I took a deep breath, unsure how to react. He made me feel insecure and safe at the same time. But there was something else lingering in the air between us—anticipation.

I felt my pulse accelerate as Ben let his fingers slide down along my arm and came to rest on my hand.

There was one thing I was sure about at that moment. There was something inside of me that wanted to be close to Ben.

I blinked at him without comprehension and pulled up my hand.

Ben, I thought, *Ben, don't let go.* And his fingers were wrapping themselves around mine, just as if he had read my mind. But it was probably more than that. He must feel what I was feeling. And what I was feeling was potent.

We stood there for a moment, looking at each other, each of us waiting for the other to make a move. But nothing happened.

After an eternity, he finally withdrew his hand.

"Just black, no milk, no sugar," he said and turned to the side.

I turned to the coffee machine, hiding my embarrassed face. But Ben was totally at ease. He walked around and grabbed his cup as soon as it was filled.

"Dinner at my place tonight," he informed me, smiling over the rim of the cup as if nothing had happened.

I couldn't help it and returned his smile as we were walking back into the main area of the library.

There was something about Ben that made me feel free and almost safe.

Ever since he had dropped the facade of anger and rejection, the beauty of his personality shone as brightly as his physical beauty. Almost as if he had forgiven me for Adam's death.

My stomach twisted, and I had to steady myself on one of the bookshelves.

"Are you alright?" Ben turned to me with a worried expression.

I nodded at him, and he nodded back, both of us one-hundred percent aware that I wasn't.

I didn't have time to put on my brave face when Liz appeared in the front door, her purse on her arm, tossing her raven hair out of her face.

Ben automatically took a step back from me.

"Hi," Liz greeted.

I blushed and waved. Ben nodded at her.

"Who's your friend?"

"Liz—Ben." I gestured at both of them with my hand while pulling a smile from the bottom of my psyche.

"Pleasure to meet you, Ben," Liz laughed and pulled her scarf from under her black mane of hair.

"Nice to meet you, Liz," Ben returned a smile and shook her hand before he turned to me.

"Actually, I need to get going. I'll pick you up at five."

"Make it seven," Liz interjected.

I eyed her for a second.

"I told you; prepare to work late tonight," she explained with a grin.

"Okay." I didn't know whom I was responding to. To Ben that it was okay if he picked me up, or Liz, that I would stay late.

"See you," Ben nudged my arm gently and walked away.

Liz and I both watched him disappear through the entrance door.

"Boyfriend?" Liz asked when Ben was out of sight.

"Ex-boyfriend's brother." I didn't look up.

"Cute," she observed after a minute of silence.

I grimaced.

Liz laughed at my expression knowingly and started walking.

"Let's get to work." Her shoes clicked past the counter to the back of the room. "Lock the door, will you?"

I did as she told me, mildly confused, and pulled the keys from my pocket on the way to the door, turned the sign to *closed*, and rushed after her with a squeamish stomach.

She was already standing at the counter with a fresh cup of coffee in her hand and an expectant smile on her face.

Every step I took made me feel more uneasy than the one before.

Trust Liz! I thought to myself. Was she *the* Liz I was supposed to trust?

"Sit," Liz patted one of the chairs.

I stepped toward it slowly, the uneasiness becoming more pronounced. Would Ben be around in case I needed him?

"Don't be silly," Liz commented on my hesitation, "I won't bite." She laughed again. "I am not the enemy here."

The moment I sat, Liz took a seat next to me. She put her cup down in front of her and turned to me with a serious face.

"Okay," she started. "I need to know everything that's going on."

I eyed her for a moment, deciding whether or not to take Lucas Baker's advice.

"Trust me," Liz said. "I am a guard. I can help."

"What?"

Liz's face spread into a laugh again as she took in my confused expression.

"A few weeks ago, Lucas got in touch and asked for my help."

I eyed her for a moment.

"Help with what?"

"Help with lost powers." Liz's expression was suddenly serious and wistful.

My stomach twisted. She must be *the* Liz.

"Lucas told me everything you told him. He was well-aware that you were in trouble."

"What type of help did he ask for?"

"The type of help only guards can give."

"What is a *guard*?"

Liz took a deep breath before she spoke.

"The Guard. An ancient organization entrusted with this world's most sacred secrets."

I gave her a disbelieving look. "What?"

"You know—angels and demons."

Liz smiled at my gaping face with honest amusement.

"You are part of a secret organization," I repeated.

"—a secret organization which protects the secrets of angels and demons."

"Angels *and* demons?" I asked with a hint of distrust.

The impressive Latina simply nodded.

"There is a natural balance in this world. Good and evil are two sides of the same coin."

Before I could think about this statement, Liz continued.

"The Guard is a secret organization. It is designed to protect the knowledge about angels and demons and keep it alive in case it is ever needed.

"We are positioned in strategic locations around the globe, always ready to come to angels' aid when they have problems starting off after transforming. Most angels have their families to pass on that knowledge, but every now and then, there is one who is all by themselves.

"We are there when angels have lost knowledge of their own kind's history over generations."

My mind was trying to keep up with what she was telling me.

"How many angels are there?" I wondered.

She looked at me intensely, measuring my expression for a moment.

"More than you could imagine, less than in the generation before us," Liz answered with concern.

I pondered her statement for a while. Lucas had said he had never met an angel even though there had been several right under his nose. Maybe Liz had a similar experience.

"Lucas said he never met one in person. How can you know the numbers? Angels don't register, do they?"

"They don't." She laughed. "There are other ways to know."

"We have a lot to talk about." She got to her feet. "More coffee?"

"Please."

A few minutes later, we were sitting with two mugs of steaming coffee, brooding over the recent events.

"Lucas was guarding one of the most important locations in the U.S.—Aurora, IL," she continued. "Lucas told you the story about the history of Aurora? Not the version from the history books?"

I nodded in wonder, remembering Lucas Baker's story about Aurora's special bookkeeper, the winged monster, and the first alliance between angel and human in order to bring the demon down. Liz was opening my eyes to how strong the network of believers and guardians of knowledge was.

"Then you also know about the importance of the book the bookkeeper left behind."

My head bounced again.

"Good." Liz smiled. Then she fell silent for a moment.

I waited for her to continue, anxious for what was about to come. I was excited to have someone to talk to, who was finally willing to give me information. Time was running out, and Chris and I were none the wiser about how to get his powers back. And he more than needed them in this supernatural minefield around us.

"I know about the Gallagers." Liz's face was suddenly serious.

It made me even more anxious.

"What exactly do you know?" I asked cautiously.

"Christian, Jenna, Adam, and Benedict." She eyed me carefully as she spoke each of the names. "They are all angels."

My heart picked up pace.

"How do you know?"

"Let's say we have our sources." She put on a knowing expression. "Four in a town like Aurora, that's quite a lot."

"Except for one of them is dead," I corrected.

"Tragic," Liz commented. "How exactly did it happen?"

I hesitated.

"You know I already know he was your boyfriend. And you know you can trust me."

The way she spoke about him was too nonchalant for how it made me feel.

"He was more than that."

"I know."

I gave Liz a summary of my time with Adam. Her face showed more and more concern as I mentioned the demons. Alabaster, who was dead. And Volpert, I shuddered, who was still out there biding his time until he would strike.

The last thing I mentioned was Chris's problem.

"No matter what he does and how hard he tries, they just won't show."

Liz watched the bubbles on her coffee swirl with the movement as she tilted her cup slightly to the side.

"Lucas mentioned that. I did some research before I came here, and there might be a way."

Her words were the best news I had heard in a while.

"How—"

"Meditation." Liz's answer was as difficult as simple.

"Meditation?"

"Exactly. You are Adam's mark; that means you carry part of his soul even though he is dead." Her voice was strictly business. No space for pity. "You will meditate with him. You will guide him in the meditation until he reconnects with the part of Adam's soul within himself."

Liz explained the whole process to me in detail. I sat, amazed by the depth of her knowledge and grateful for any hint that could help Chris.

We were so deep in conversation that I didn't realize how late it had gotten, when my phone buzzed.

Waiting outside. Dinner is waiting.

It was Ben's number.

"Go," Liz instructed. "We'll continue another time."

Coming.

I texted back.

"Thank you so much, Liz." I couldn't put into words what it would mean to all of us if her plan worked. "I'll try to convince Chris to start right away."

Liz laughed. "Let me know how it goes."

She turned and grabbed a small leather book from inside her purse.

"Next Thursday?" I asked.

"Yes. I'll need you for library duties."

"See you next week." I waved over my shoulder on my way out.

Ben was standing with his back facing the building, looking at the mostly empty street.

"Hey," I called as I made my way down the stairs.

He was beside me within a heartbeat.

"Hello, Claire."

"You know you didn't have to pick me up."

"I know."

"Jaden could have come."

"I know."

We walked to my car, avoiding each others' eyes. Our encounter from this afternoon was still thickening the air between us.

"Are Jenna and Chris joining us for dinner?" I asked when I climbed into the car, dreading more alone time with Ben. I wasn't sure I could trust myself anymore. Whatever it was I felt for Adam's brother, things were getting complicated. I needed to figure this out before anything happened and our newly-found friendship was ruined.

"They will." Ben grinned. He naturally would know how I was feeling. It didn't seem to bother him.

"Don't worry," he added as if he could read my thoughts, too, holding out his and for the car key.

I extracted it from my bag and handed it over, glad that he wanted to drive. Anything that kept him focused and from reading my emotions was good.

His fingers brushed mine as he took the keys, send an electric current down my spine.

Ben chuckled and opened the passenger door for me.

"I'm sorry," I mumbled as Ben climbed in on the other side. Why again was I apologizing?

Ben's chuckle turned into a wide-spread smile and he sped the car into the evening traffic.

It was a quiet ride. I was busy sorting my feelings and thoughts, and Ben was gentleman enough not to comment on what he perceived from me.

It wasn't until we turned the corner to the Gallagers' house that I spoke again.

"I have news regarding Chris's problem."

I saw Ben's face light up from the corner of my eye.

Jenna was waiting at the door. She pulled me into a hug the moment we entered the house.

Ever since she had shared her story with me, I saw her in a completely new light. She was the strong heart of the family. A loving, wise person. It was a little bit like having a mother again.

"Hi, Mom." Ben slid past us. "Claire has good news. Where's Dad?"

Chris was coming down the stairs just when Ben mentioned him. Antonio was at his heels, wagging his tail at the sight of us.

"Wonderful. Shall we get to the dining room? Geoffrey promised Italian," Jenna suggested and led the way.

"Great." Ben bounced after his father. "Claire has something to share we all want to hear."

"Is that so?" Chris asked curiously. His eyes showed a little more life than the past few times I had seen him.

The table was beautifully set with a draped tablecloth and flowers spreading from the center to each end in a line of orange and red. I had been at wedding banquets that were less beautifully decorated than this family dinner. A person who knew them mainly as warm, caring, supportive friends could so easily forget how exorbitantly rich the Gallagers were.

I sat down after everyone else was settled. A slight shift forward of my chair startled me when I sat.

"Excuse me, Miss Gabriel," Geoffrey's voice came from behind me.

I smiled at him over my shoulder. He was the family butler. Who knows how long he had been with the Gallagers. I was wondering how much he knew...

"So, what's the news?" Chris asked the moment Geoffrey had vanished through the door.

All three remaining Gallagers were giving me an expectant look.

There was something oddly satisfying about the fact that this time, I was the one bringing new and valuable information.

"Okay. I found out how Chris can get his powers back."

Before I could say anything else, Jenna was at my side, hugging me.

"That's wonderful."

Chris nodded, and something similar to a smile formed on his lips.

"It is. I only wish Jaden was here. He should hear this, too." I said the words without thinking. A second later, Jaden was standing at my shoulder.

"You called?" He practically chortled when he saw my reaction. I clapped a hand over my face.

"You need to stop doing this, Jaden," I muttered.

Jaden ignored that and said breezily, "Now that we are all here, what's so important I need to hear it right away?"

Ben laughed and pulled out a chair for Jaden.

"Claire knows how Chris can get his powers back."

"That's great!" Jaden's enthusiasm seemed real. "How?"

I took a deep breath.

"Meditation."

I waited for them to laugh. It had made sense when it had been Liz's words, but coming from my mouth, it suddenly sounded trivial—ridiculous.

No one laughed. Three Gallagers and my guardian angel were all sitting there, staring at me as if I had just enlightened them.

14.
Temptation

"Details, Claire." Jaden was the first to react.

"You all know how I still carry Adam's mark—a fragment of his soul."

The four angels nodded in unison.

"Well, apparently that's the key."

"How?" It was Chris this time.

"You marked Adam when you spread your wings for the first time. When a person is marked, they transfer part of their soul to the angel. There is a part of him in you, too."

"We all know that," Ben stated impatiently.

"Yes, you do." Jenna gave him a warning look. "Now, let Claire continue."

"When the marked person dies in a wrongful way, the soul of the angel is unhinged. And when the angel loses touch with the fragment of the mark that's still with them, they lose their powers.

"We need to reconnect you with Adam's soul, Chris." I looked at him mildly victorious. "And I have the best odds of guiding you in the right direction because part of his soul is in me, too."

"Of course," Jaden leaned forward and thoughtfully fingered a crimson flower.

"This sounds almost too easy," Chris doubted.

"Is it really possible?" Ben asked, his eyes on Jaden.

Jaden nodded.

"Chris is lucky Adam marked Claire." Jaden pulled the flower from the arrangement. "It's an old technique. It rarely works if the angel works by themselves. But with having another part of Adam's soul within Claire, the odds are in our favor." He plucked another flower and laid the pair in front of him. "You should really give it a shot, Chris."

Jenna had a tear in her eye. "You'll be fine."

Ben watched us for a moment. It was impossible to read his expression.

Geoffrey entered with a tray of breadsticks elaborately wrapped with thin slices of prosciutto and cut melon. I raised an eyebrow appreciatively. I couldn't help thinking this was never how Sophie and I started dinners in our modest kitchen in our little house on our time-worn street.

Between biting a slice of melon and lifting a breadstick, Jaden nudged my arm discretely.

"Can I talk to you in private?" he demanded and got to his feet.

His face was the opposite of enthusiastic. There was concern written all over it.

"Excuse us for a moment," he said politely and gestured me to come with him.

I did as he asked and followed him to the large living room across the hallway.

"What?" I eyed him suspiciously.

"Your theories about recovering Chris's powers—" His face became dark. "Where did you get them?"

I was surprised by his distrust.

"Liz."

"Who is Liz?"

"The new librarian," I answered childishly. I felt uncomfortable with the way he interrogated me.

"How does she know about those techniques?" Jaden's voice was slightly alarmed now.

"I thought you always knew everything. How come you don't know about Liz?"

"Claire, I am serious. How does she know?"

I took a deep breath.

"She's a Guard."

I waited for Jaden to react, but he just stared at me.

"Jaden?"

When he eventually unfroze, the alarm in his eyes was gone, but the concern was still there.

"You know, after Lucas Baker was murdered, she took over the library. She says she is here to help. That Lucas reached out to her before his death."

Jaden waited for me to continue.

"You have heard of The Guard, right?" I asked, now worried myself.

"Of course I have."

Of course, he must have come across them in his millennium-long life.

"Jaden, is everything okay?"

He nodded.

"I need to check a few facts about this Liz. She must be part of the inner circle in order to have access to such knowledge. I can't believe I didn't think of it myself."

"She said The Guard is there to help angels. That's true, isn't it?" I was suddenly worried I might have given away too much.

"They are. If any human can be trusted with information, it's them."

That relieved me a little bit.

"How much does she know?" Jaden bore his golden stare into me.

"Everything—about the Gallagers. Your name didn't come up." I tried to withstand his eyes. "She knew about the Gallagers before. I didn't tell her. I just filled the gaps in the story. Shouldn't I have told her? Lucas' last instruction to me was to trust Liz, and I trusted him, so I thought..."

"No, that's fine," Jaden interrupted. "Let's go back. We're being rude."

When we were seated at the table again, Ben gave me a questioning look.

"Everything okay?" he asked over the flowers.

"Everything's fine." I guessed that was the truth.

My eyes widened as Geoffrey placed a steaming platter on the table. Ben winked at the butler and said, obviously for my benefit, "Geoffrey's saltimbocca would be world-famous if he ever decided to share the recipe." It was clear from the smiles around the table that there would never be any encouragement for that. Geoffrey bowed slightly and left the room where silence reigned for a while as we all turned our attention to dinner.

When we reached the stage of second helpings, Jenna took up the conversation again.

"When shall we start?" she asked, her eyes wandering between Chris and me, her expression showing anxiety and urgency.

"Umm—I am ready when you are, Chris."

He hesitated a moment. "This upcoming Saturday."

Our eyes met, and I saw commitment in his.

"Let's get your wings back."

It was late at night when we were finished talking. We had lingered over the dinner table long past dessert and through several coffees. I wondered how they all stayed so fit and healthy with Geoffrey in their kitchen every day, but perhaps it was one of the angelic powers. I'd have to ask when I had the chance. The three Gallagers and Jaden had made a schedule for *Claire-duty*, making sure I was never unprotected. Jaden would take day-shifts at school, Ben and Jenna after school and weekends. Most of the night shifts belonged to Jaden, but every now and then, I would stay at the Gallagers' overnight. It underlined my helplessness as an ordinary mortal, but it also threw the spotlight on Chris's situation as he was unable to protect me or his family or even himself. It was good we were starting to work on it soon.

"Ready?" Ben asked with his hands reaching out to me.

I nodded.

"Let's get this over with."

The group consensus was that I should spend the rest of the week at their house. It would be easiest to protect me there, and the others wouldn't have to divert forces.

It was Ben's honorable job to teleport me to my house to pack my things. Jaden had taken off to find out more about the demons. He had mentioned a trail, and that made me worry even more.

I knew it was only a matter of time 'til they would come and take us apart, one by one. I shuddered.

Ben grabbed my shoulders, and I felt like I was being pulled through ice-cold water for a second as everything went black. I lost track of time and orientation. Then my feet hit the floor in my living room.

I pulled away from him and rushed up the stairs. It was still awkward to be alone with him.

Three nights. One school day. I needed to put together a bag that would last me that long.

"Do you need any help?" Ben called after me. His footsteps were light and effortless as he was jogging up to my bedroom.

"I think I have it under control."

I dove into my dresser drawers and pulled out random shirts.

Ben was waiting right behind me, ready to catch whatever was flying toward the bed. He placed them neatly with my jeans and toiletries on the *to-pack* pile.

"Are you sure you need all of these?" He pointed at the shirts.

"Positive. These and something else." I had to grin. "Turn around."

Ben raised his eyebrows.

"Why?"

I pointed at a drawer.

"The moment I open this, I want your eyes facing the other direction. Observe whatever you find interesting on the opposite wall."

"You are embarrassed," he noticed, reading my emotions.

"Of course I am," I admitted. "My underwear drawer is really none of your business."

Ben laughed and turned away.

It took me less than a minute to put together everything I needed and stuff my things into a bag.

"Done?" he asked and peeked over his shoulder.

"Done."

I dropped the bag on the bed and turned toward the door.

"I'll be back in a moment. Just need to get something to drink quickly."

I rushed down the stairs and to the kitchen. The fridge was almost empty. I was rarely home, and the fridge was a mirror of my absence.

I found a soda between an expired yogurt and a bottle of soy sauce and opened it.

"Do you want anything?" I asked. I didn't bother yelling. Ben would hear me with his supernatural senses.

"No thanks." The answer came from right behind me.

I jumped.

"Good. Because even if you had said yes, unless you enjoy drinking soy sauce, there is nothing I can offer."

Ben chuckled. It was a strangely compelling sound. It made me want to smile.

I turned around and felt my lips twitch.

Ben stood still. He was fairly close. Just a step away. The atmosphere in the room had changed completely.

"We should go," he said, unmoving.

I nodded and gulped down the soda before I set down the open can on the counter with an outstretched arm.

Ben watched me and waited for me to turn back to him. His smile was still in place.

"Shall we?" He held out his hand.

"My bag." My eyes wandered up to the ceiling as if they could see my room through joists and flooring.

Ben reached for my hand with his fingers and gently pulled me toward the stairs.

We walked up side by side. There was a familiar tension between us.

"My bag is over there," I pointed to my bed without thinking.

Ben stopped me in the doorway. He disappeared for a heartbeat and popped up in front of me, my carry-on strapped over his shoulder.

"Now we are ready." His words didn't mirror in his eyes. They were searching mine. I didn't know what he found there, but whatever it was made him lower his gaze.

I tried to read them, but they were hidden under his lashes.

"Claire—" he took my hands.

"Ben—" I tried to stop him from saying it.

At the sound of his name, his eyes connected with mine, liquid steel.

Ben knew how I felt. Even if he couldn't read my mind, my emotions were an open book to his angel senses. Besides which he could probably hear my heart beating as loud as any drum.

He gave me a brief smile, as if asking for permission he knew he didn't really need, and moved closer.

His breath came as a quiet sigh before his lips brushed mine ever so slightly.

It was a warm and soft touch. Controlled. Somehow, I could tell that he was holding back, and I could understand.

This was an experiment. For him as much as for me. I was one-hundred percent sure he could never be for me what Adam had been; but couldn't he be right for me, all the same? Just for now? Did I have to make a choice?

Ben's hands were still holding mine, their touch so light I couldn't be sure I wasn't just imagining it. It felt nice. Familiar somehow.

Like Adam's touch, the voice mocked. *Nothing like Adam*, I snapped back at it. The voice and I were both right, and I flinched away from the thought. Straight into Ben's kiss.

Eagerly, he responded by trapping my hands against his chest and pulling me in tight with his free arm. His lips pressed mine urgently. It was a mistaken response, but I felt a flood of heat anyway.

What can you lose? the voice in my head murmured temptingly, and for once, I just stopped thinking, giving myself over entirely to merely feeling.

Ben moved his lips away from mine, trailing them thrillingly along my jaw and down the side of my neck. He sank his hands into my hair and played with it down my back.

"You don't have to do this," Ben breathed onto my skin, "I can understand if you're not ready."

My breath was becoming uneven. I hadn't planned for this. With everything that had happened, I couldn't have seen this coming, that kissing another boy would feel right to me—if only for a minute.

"No, I want to." My fingers moved up his arms and behind his neck to prove I meant it.

Ben caught them before they reached his hairline.

"You sure?" he asked, a hint of doubt written in his features.

I nodded, not trusting my voice.

He kissed me again. Carefully this time. Like he was waiting for me to change my mind.

I wanted to be close to him. He made me feel better. *But how will you feel when you wake up tomorrow and you know you made a mistake?* The voice in my head started just in time to make me hesitate. I knew I would hate myself tomorrow if I continued now. I would feel bad—guilty. I already did.

Ben felt the difference. He had seen it coming, and he pulled back immediately.

"I'm sorry." I looked at the wall, not daring to meet his gaze. I didn't want to see the disappointment I had caused.

Ben let me go and stepped away.

"I've got time," he whispered. "Let me know when you change your mind again."

When I looked up, there was the hint of a smile on his lips.

But I knew I wouldn't. My heart and soul were Adam's. Even if he was dead. I couldn't help it, my heart beat for him—every single beat in remembrance of his existence.

"Can we go, please?" I was embarrassed. Ben must have felt everything. He must know exactly how there was no way this would work.

"Sure."

He took my hand and pulled me toward him. The next thing I saw was the familiar guest room.

Jenna was pulling back the sheets. She didn't seem startled by our sudden appearance, like she had been waiting for us.

"Everything is ready," she walked over and took my bag from Ben's shoulder, eyeing the two of us carefully.

I was wondering what she saw there in his and my emotions. Right now, I couldn't even tell myself how I felt.

"Good night, Ben," I said when he turned to leave. "And thank you."

He paused and gave me a smile before he disappeared through the door.

The sound of a zipper being opened called my attention.

"Everything alright?" Jenna asked with motherly worry in her voice.

"Sure." I shrugged and walked over to sit on the bed.

Jenna sat beside me.

"He means well."

I pondered that for a moment.

"You must understand; all his life he has been in the shadow of his older brother. And even now that Adam is dead, he loses against him."

Did I understand her right? Was Ben chasing me just to prove he could get something his brother had?

"Don't get me wrong. He loved his brother—he still does. And he suffers a lot. Adam was his idol. He is trying to figure out what man he wants to become." Jenna's face was between proud and worried.

"What type of man do you think he is?" I wondered aloud.

Jenna took my hand.

"He is a boy. He is still undecided. But one thing I have seen when I look at the two of you together. His feelings for you are real."

I gulped. "What should I do?"

"Give it time." She smiled. "What you and Adam had was special. I doubt there is a person in the world who can replace him—"

"That's exactly how I feel," I interrupted.

"—but maybe replacing him is the wrong approach. Maybe you'll find room in your heart for a new person without replacing your love for Adam."

"I don't understand."

"Adam is dead. He didn't leave you; he didn't betray you. What he left behind is pure."

She was right. Not to forget that a part of my soul died with him.

"Hold on to that pureness. Don't let anyone rush you. One day, you may be healed enough to let someone new in."

Jenna stood up.

"Sleep well, Claire." She left the room without a sound other than the rustling of fabric rubbing against each other when she moved.

"Good night."

15.
Meditation

"Breathe—" I instructed.

I was sitting on the floor of the Gallagers' library, cross-legged and surrounded by hundreds of books. Chris was sitting across the room, near the window. He looked slightly uncomfortable.

"Why again do we have to do this on the floor?" Chris asked with a crease in his forehead.

"Liz said it is the best way." I shrugged and took a deep breath myself.

Chris's shoulders were tense. I didn't need to be able to read his emotions to know he'd rather be anywhere but here.

"Come on, Chris," I encouraged him. "You can do this."

The talk with Liz had given me new hope that Chris would get his wings back. We had sat in the library for a long time after closing hours. She had seen a lot. Her knowledge was vast, and she had been very willing to help.

I had talked to Jaden about it more. The secret organization Liz was part of, The Guard, was a collective of humans who were believers and had been passing on the knowledge about angels and demons from generation to generation. Lucas had inherited the book without title from one of them. He had reached out to Liz after I had told him an angel needed help.

"So what exactly did she say I should do?" Chris sighed.

"Breathe deeply several times to calm your pulse," I instructed again.

Chris inhaled deeply. I watched his chest rise and fall.

"Close your eyes," I closed my own eyes with Chris. A little break from the outside world would do both of us good.

"Then, focus on your fingertips." I felt my blood pulsing under my skin lightly. It was still a fast pulse. Nothing like the slow heart rate Liz had spoken of.

I blinked quickly to check if Chris was still with me. He was. His shape remained motionless except for the slow movement of his chest. He looked almost peaceful.

"Guide your attention up into your palms," I said and felt my hands lay heavy on my knees. "Up to your forearms, your elbows..."

While I was describing the path we were routing our attention, my thoughts were wandering off.

I saw Adam before my inner eye. His eyes were looking directly at me like he was trying to burn me with his gaze. He was standing in a cloud of light which slowly vanished into him as if he was a dark void.

It hurt for a second, and I blinked my eyes open.

Chris was kneeling beside me, his hands on my shoulders.

"Are you alright, Claire?" he asked with a worried expression on his face.

I nodded, ignoring the memory of the pain and the image that had caused it.

"What happened? You were in pain..."

I took a deep breath.

"I thought of—him," I explained, avoiding speaking his name.

Chris sat down on his legs and measured my expression for a minute.

I was back to focusing on my pulse. It was getting slower with every breath.

"Shall we continue?" I asked and saw him get into position next to me.

"Go," he said.

Once more, I guided our attention through our bodies until we reached the heart.

I felt my heart beat evenly. Chris's breathing beside me sped up a little. My eyes opened to check if he was okay.

He looked relaxed, his features calm and his hands resting on his knees. What was different was his skin. There was just a hint of light on it. I couldn't be sure it was coming from within him. It could have been the afternoon sun playing a trick on my eyes.

"Okay, now try to identify the piece of your soul that doesn't belong to you."

Liz had explained how it works, but the gist was to find the piece of the mark's soul and re-bond with it. The death of a mark unhinges the soul of the angel to a degree that they can lose access to it. It sounded easy: Focus on the piece, and move it toward your own soul.

We were sitting in silence for a while with Chris's breath fast and slightly strained. It sounded like heavy work—not like the meditation it was supposed to be.

His mouth began to twitch slightly, and his skin now looked mildly luminescent. It reminded me of the way Adam's skin had looked when he had spread his wings for the first time.

A rush of energy ran through my spine. I closed my eyes and took a deep breath. It felt like an electric current was running through me, making my every cell vibrate with life. I had never felt like this before.

An image of Adam flashed through my mind. His features victorious and terrible. Not the Adam I had known. Why was my mind showing me this dark vision of him?

There was a knock on the door.

My eyes snapped open just in time to see Chris jump to his feet.

"Come in," he called.

"Excuse me, Sir," Geoffrey addressed Chris with a quiet step into the room. "Dinner is ready."

He shifted from foot to foot for a moment as if he was uncomfortable to be there.

"Mrs. Gallager asked me to come inform you. I am sorry if I disturbed you."

"It's fine, Geoffrey," Chris assured the butler. "We'll be down in a minute."

Geoffrey bowed slightly and withdrew from the room.

"Well, that went well," Chris turned to me after the door closed.

I smiled. *In more than one way*, I thought.

"Same time tomorrow?" Chris asked as we were walking down the stairs.

I nodded. We were on the right track. I could sense it. Chris already looked better after this one session. If we continued, this could be a breakthrough.

The whole weekend had been an experiment to help Chris. Today was Monday. A normal school day. I went through classes, thinking mainly about ways to support Chris even better. And what intrigued me more about the meditation was that I had seen Adam again. There was a connection that had survived his death. He was with me—always.

Maybe if I practiced, I would learn control over my feelings. Maybe I would be able to visualize him as he was. Beautiful and immortal. Maybe it wouldn't hurt so much anymore.

I watched the teacher scribble notes on the blackboard without interest, desperately waiting for the day to be over.

Jaden was sitting in the row in front of me. His head was perfectly aligned with his straight back in an unnaturally upright way of sitting.

Amber was watching him from two seats away. I shook my head. When would she let it go?

It wasn't long until the bell rang. I jumped up and rushed out of the building. I wanted to try meditating again. I needed to find out if this could be my way to heal.

When I got to the parking lot, Jaden was already waiting for me, leaning against my car.

"Hi there," he greeted me and turned to the side, one hand reaching down to the handle of the door.

"I thought I didn't know you when we are at school," I snapped at him.

He stared at me for a brief second then shrugged.

"I guess, after Amber introduced us, it's alright if we talk in public."

I couldn't follow his logic. He had been the one who was all secretive about us knowing each other. Nobody would even think twice if they saw us talking. We were in the same classes.

"Can I ride with you today?" he asked.

"Umm—okay." He took me by surprise.

Amber and Greg were hurrying to their cars. Greg waved. His face displayed concern. He nudged Amber in the side.

Her glare left no guessing that she was unhappy Jaden was showing me some attention. I waved at her and watched them disappear behind a row of cars.

My eyes got caught there. Just behind the cars, there was a row of trees on one side. Under one of those trees, a shadow was moving slowly toward the tree trunk.

I shuddered. *No*, I told myself. *No, he is dead. Stop hallucinating.*

Was my wish to see Adam, if only as a vision in my meditation, again playing tricks on my mind?

You really are going insane, the voice mocked.

"Are you alright?" Jaden's voice tore me from my thoughts.

I shoved the idea of Adam aside. It could have been anyone. It hurt. I wanted it so badly to be true—that he was out there. Looking out for me. The thought alone was comforting. But it was a lie, and I wouldn't lie to myself just to be hurting even more when I finally admitted to myself that it wasn't true. I was damaged enough as it was.

"Yes," I nodded at Jaden and got into the car. "Let's go."

The ride to my house was quick. At the final traffic light before home, I had to stop.

"Are you enjoying your high school experience?" I asked into the silence. Jaden hadn't spoken, and I was beginning to wonder why he had wanted to come with me in the first place.

"It is interesting," he commented without enthusiasm.

I gave him a wary look.

"But, at least, I can make sure that you are safe."

"You always have," I looked at him for a brief second.

Jaden averted his face. "Not like before."

"What do you mean?"

"I can't protect you the same way I used to."

I gave him a questioning look. "I don't understand."

"My assignment has ended," he stated.

The traffic light turned green, and I pushed down the gas pedal gently while looking at Jaden from the corner of my eye.

"Still don't understand."

He shook his head.

"Claire, I am not officially guarding you any longer. I failed. They decided that it is time for me to move on."

I swallowed.

"Why?"

Jaden stared into the traffic for a while. The tension made my skin itch.

"Were you assigned to someone new?"

Still no answer.

"Someone who needs you more than I do?" Someone who still has something to lose, I added in my mind.

The golden orbs turned toward me the moment my heart exploded with pain. He looked at me for a second, full of concern. Then he turned back to face the car in front of us.

"Will there be a replacement?" I tried another angle. If Jaden was assigned to watch over someone else, what would that mean for my own situation? Whoever it was he was protecting now, they were insanely lucky and didn't even know it.

"It's not that easy." Jaden's voice was strained like he was trying to suppress emotions he didn't want me to see.

"All I can say is I went back to school to be able to have a close eye on your safety."

We were almost at the Gallagers' when I felt like asking one final question.

"Will you give me all the answers someday?"

A low chuckle escaped Jaden's otherwise serious face.

"I will."

Chris was waiting at the door, ready to pick up where we had left off. Jaden disappeared without another word. He didn't say when or if he would return. That made focusing even more difficult than my lack of energy.

I spent most of that day's session worrying whether I had lost Jaden, too. Chris didn't notice. He had become so absorbed in the meditation. Ever since he had felt a tingle in his left palm, he was pro meditation.

My presence helped. The more of Adam's soul we could get in one room, the higher Chris's chances of success.

I was happy to help. To be able to contribute somehow. If I didn't have any supernatural powers to share, at least my presence was useful to help Chris regain his.

"Jenna and I will be out doing some research later," Chris mentioned after a long session.

I was hungry and tired, so I made my way down to the kitchen, hoping to find Geoffrey and found Ben instead.

He was handling various ingredients with an intense expression on his face.

When he noticed me in the doorway, he dropped a sandwich onto a plate and rushed over.

"I've been preparing dinner for you."

"That's very kind of you." I looked at the mess on the counter. "Where is Geoffrey?"

"He has his day off."

We both nodded, acknowledging what that meant.

"I am making grilled cheese," Ben offered. "It's almost edible."

I laughed involuntarily.

He carried our plates to the dining area and beckoned me to sit.

"So, how's everything?" he asked as I bit into my sandwich.

I chewed, picking my brain for an answer.

"School is stressful; I am being hunted by demons, and on top of it all I need to eat this—" I gestured at my plate and laughed.

Ben's face lit up when he saw me smile.

"It's been a while since I've seen you joke and laugh," he noted.

"Don't get used to it," I reigned in his enthusiasm. The dark cloud was still hanging there in my skies, ready to rain down on me any moment without warning. Jaden's news was living proof.

Ben watched me eat in silence and go back to a pensive mood before he started to clear the table.

"Dinner was great," I called after him before he disappeared around the corner to the kitchen.

Only two minutes later, Ben popped up beside me in the dining area.

"Grilled cheese and salad? Please," he mocked his own cooking achievement.

"Honestly, I enjoyed it."

"The best part was the company." Ben's eyes were a little too serious.

We were alone in the big house, except for Antonio, who was sleeping peacefully on his pillow in the corner of the room.

I watched the chocolate brown dog's chest rise and fall. When had I last had a peaceful sleep like that?

"Are you tired?" Ben guessed as he saw the look on my face.

I nodded. I was. School finals were coming up. All of the meditation with Chris, the fear of the demons, the dreams about Adam—it was more than any normal human being could handle at the same time.

"Jaden was supposed to stay with me for the night," I informed Ben.

Ben's face fell a little at my words.

"Okay then." He looked disappointed. "I thought you would stay here tonight."

"I might after all." Who knew if I could still count on Jaden after what he had shared earlier. He might be busy saving his new fosterling.

"Your things are still here," Ben encouraged me.

It wasn't much later when I fell into bed in the guest room.

Sleep came upon me the second I closed my eyes. School and helping Chris with meditation had drained the last drops of energy I had left.

The light fell through the door in a strange angle and tinted the room in a surreal color spectrum. I lifted my hand and observed my skin as it turned translucent where it touched the beam of light.

As I shook my head in wonder, a shape at the other end of the room, where the light couldn't reach, moved in the darkness.

"Hello?" my voice carried through the space between us effortlessly. The shape turned, and his face became visible.

My heart skipped a beat. It was the most beautiful face in the world. His eyes as light green as ever, his lips curved into the half-smile I loved so much. But there was something off about his appearance. Something was very different from the Adam I had known.

My legs carried me toward him before I could think. A few quick strides, and I was close enough to touch him.

"Adam," my voice came without my permission. I felt my lips returning his smile.

He radiated from inside. Not the way I remembered it when he was spreading his wings. White and bright and beautiful. There was something dark about the way he reflected. It was as if the light wasn't his. It was stolen.

After a while staring into each other's eyes, Adam reached out his hand and wrapped it around my translucent fingers. The second our skin touched, a wave of heat seared through my body. It kicked in like a stimulant. Like adrenaline. My heart started racing, and I was suddenly very aware of everything surrounding me. Including the body lying behind Adam. It was limp and facing downward.

The bedroom was dark when I woke drenched in sweat. My hands were shaking.

A silhouette was sitting on the side of my bed. It took me a moment to calm down and take a closer look.

"Sorry I didn't come earlier," Jaden's soothing voice touched my ears. "Bad dream?"

I wasn't sure what to say. I was still upset that he hadn't shared more information with me earlier. That he hadn't told me if I could still count on him.

So, I sat quietly and waited for the adrenaline to leave my system.

"Do you still want answers?" he asked into the darkness.

His hand reached out to stroke my face.

"Yes."

"What exactly do you want to know?"

I fidgeted with my blanket. *Everything*.

"Let's start with, how long have you been unassigned from me?"

"Since the day I nearly lost you to the demons. The day Adam died." Jaden's voice was cautious.

"But, that's an eternity." At least, it felt like it. Every day was an eternity of pain without Adam.

Jaden moved closer when he heard the alarm in my voice.

"Calm down, Claire." He took my hand and pulled me into his arms. "I've been there whenever you've needed me. I always will be."

He kissed my forehead and pulled me even closer into his embrace. His presence alone made me relax.

We were sitting in the darkness while I was trying to make sense of his behavior. What was going on in this ancient mind of his?

After what felt like a long time, Jaden shifted.

"I'm surprised how much you are like her." His voice sounded bittersweet. The tone of it took me by surprise as well as the meaning of his words.

"What do you mean?" I asked into his chest, cautiously. "Like who?"

The only answer I got was a low chuckle, and then he was gone from my bed. I couldn't tell if he was honestly amused or if it was the blackest of sarcasm.

I had never heard such a laugh from Jaden. It was disturbing. There was something wrong.

"Where are you, Jaden?" I turned to the side, following the sound of his laugh. "Don't play games with me."

The laugh vanished, and I heard a soft *whoosh* rising beside me.

"Come on, Jaden—please." I was starting to get nervous. I got out of bed and stood in the darkness for a minute, trying to make out Jaden's location.

"Jaden. This is not funny." I spoke into the blackness around me.

"Oh, I think it is," Jaden's voice said from closer behind me than I had expected. It was a low, cold breath on my neck. I shrieked quietly and wanted to turn around as I felt a hand pressing down on my shoulder, preventing me from turning.

"It's ironic."

Panicking completely, I flung my hands up and tried to free myself.

A second hand slung around my waist, pulling my body back toward his.

Unable to move in his grip, I opened my mouth and bit into his fingers with all force.

"Ouch!" Jaden gasped into my hair.

I had never experienced Jaden like this. He was like a different person. Like someone had switched off all of his self-control.

He freed me from his arms and pushed me to the floor with a hard hit on my back. My wrists hit the hard wood as I tried to catch my weight so I wouldn't fall onto my face. But before I could feel the full weight of my body resting on my arms, two hands grabbed my shoulders and turned me around.

"Jaden!" I hissed at him. "What's wrong with you?"

I struggled, trying to free my feet; but the more I fought, the harder his force became.

He was kneeling over me, pinning me down against the floor with one hand at my throat, the other one holding down one of my arms.

I used the chance and hit him in the face with my free hand.

"Jaden. Get. Off. Me." I coughed as the air started to get stuck in my throat.

The impact of my fist seemed to get his attention. He stopped for a few seconds—enough for me to free my second arm and remove his hand from my throat.

I gasped for air.

"Jaden, what is wrong with you?" I choked.

"Wrong," he repeated the word as if musing. "How long have I been waiting—" His eyes started to glow over me; two golden orbs in the darkness.

"Waiting for what?" I panted, unclear of how much danger I was in.

"I should just kill you myself," he whispered.

"What?" I wasn't sure if I could trust my senses.

Ben would hear us. He would come and help.

"It would be an easy death compared to what the demons have in store for. It would be a mercy." His words were harsh, but his tone full of doubt, full or desperation.

"I can't protect you, and maybe I should stop trying." He laughed darkly.

"I don't understand." I felt as if lightning had just struck me in the head.

"There is no point in protecting you now." The hardness in his voice emphasized the meaning of what he was telling me.

"Jaden—what are you talking about?" I tried to sit up and crawl out from under him.

Where was Ben when I needed him?

"I am lost as are you." His voice was dull and hopeless.

I blinked, uncomprehending.

"Jaden—" My voice was shaky.

"You are Agnes Hall's granddaughter," he stated the simple fact with an unreadable expression on his face and got to his feet, suddenly letting go of me.

The clouds outside drifted away and revealed Jaden's face with a beam of pale light. He looked undecided, his eyes fixed on me, his body frozen in place.

I didn't move, too surprised by what was happening.

After a long pause, Jaden finally moved.

"I made a bargain, Claire," Jaden said, his face unreadable. "You are my last chance."

He offered a hand to help me up. I didn't take it, not trusting the situation.

"But—I—" I struggled for the right words. "How? What?" I pushed myself up and straightened until I was standing beside him.

"You are my last chance to redeem myself."

He looked away. His face was nothing like before. He seemed embarrassed and a little bit in pain.

I studied him frantically, not sure whether to be afraid or not.

He turned back to me, staring with a familiar intensity. It was the same look I had seen so many times in his eyes. Burning. Caring. The way the Jaden I knew had always looked at me.

"You are my last chance to redeem myself, Claire," he repeated.

"Jaden—" I tried. "Would you please explain?" My fear evaporated, and I allowed myself to sink into his gaze.

"I made a mistake in 1947," Jaden started. "Everything began with my assignment to a new fosterling. The last one had died of old age after a full and happy life. He'd had a beautiful, loving wife, two sons, and two granddaughters, and he was ready to go." Jaden smiled at the memory of a peaceful ending.

"I got my next assignment right away. A little girl had been born—too early to survive healthily. I rushed to her aid immediately.

"Her mother was exhausted from giving birth, and the girl was barely alive…," he mused into the silence. "But there was something about her that made it clear she wanted to live. She was tough. Her tiny lungs barely capable of breathing, her heart beating weakly, but her will as strong as iron, even then.

"I had to save her. I didn't think—I just did it." Jaden paused for a moment, watching my expression.

"The baby girl grew into a smart kid, always curious about the world around her and more perceptive to the invisible forces of good and evil than any human I had ever seen before.

"She grew into a young woman. Beautiful and courageous. She had a mind of her own and didn't abide by any rules society dictated back then." He marveled at the memory. "She was a free spirit."

I watched him gaze into the distance for a few moments before he continued.

"It was the first time I caught myself having feelings for a mortal. The type of feelings that are forbidden to us." He lowered his head, shame in his features.

"I didn't mean to. She just was so overwhelmingly beautiful. Inside and out. She had the purest soul I had ever seen. And I was her guardian angel. I had excuses to be near her, to check in on her.

"I didn't realize what was happening until it was too late. One night, she almost died. She got caught in the current of the river."

I was listening to his words, waiting for the point where he would explain why he thought it would make sense to kill me.

"I revealed myself. After saving her from the water, I stayed with her to make sure she would be fine. She saw me. She realized who I was, and she asked me to stay with her.

"And I did. I couldn't deny her anything. She was the center of my universe. And I was craving her attention, for her acknowledgment, just like a teenage boy, and I wanted to be with her. I loved her."

Jaden's eyes glowed ever so slightly.

"Her name was Agnes," he smiled a pained smile. "Agnes Hall."

I gasped.

"You were in love with my grandmother?" I coughed. I couldn't believe it.

"Agnes liked me. Not the way I liked her—loved her—but enough to want me around. And I stayed. As long as she wanted me."

Jaden made a long pause. I was beginning to wonder if I would hear the rest of the story when he took a deep breath and continued.

"Remember Jenna said she had seen me argue with Agnes?"

I nodded, vividly recalling Jenna's coldness when I had introduced Jaden. She had witnessed an argument between my grandmother and my guardian angel.

"That was the day I tried my luck. I kissed her." He touched his lips with his fingertips absently.

"I stole one single kiss. And that's all. I knew it wasn't right. That I shouldn't be in love with a human. But I couldn't help it. And she suffered from my mistake."

His voice grew darker.

"I put her in danger with my selfishness. All I wanted was to experience love once. I had felt love—but only second-hand through my fosterlings. I had watched countless times when they had fallen in love. I wanted to feel it and understand it. And it was my turn—Agnes was my chance."

He fell silent.

"What happened, Jaden?" I asked. "Why did you fight?"

He measured my expression for a moment and sighed.

"I was replaced."

I didn't understand.

"What do you mean—replaced?"

"I was assigned to a new fosterling. Someone who needed my full attention." Jaden had leaned against the wall. He looked at me, his golden eyes full of pain.

"Agnes got a new guardian angel. The fight happened when I told her I was leaving. My wish to experience love, to feel human, had hurt her, and there was nothing I could do about it."

I swallowed, tasting the bitterness in his words.

"Why would you want to kill me?" My voice was toneless.

He looked up at me, his face unreadable. But his mouth didn't open to speak.

"Jaden?" I tried.

He sighed and his head dropped down.

"Since your grandmother, I haven't managed to protect one single fosterling."

I gave him a questioning look.

"All of them died an untimely and unnatural death," he explained. "It is as if I am cursed."

He looked desperate.

"What good does it do, trying to protect you, Claire? I'm going to fail you anyway. You will get killed because I can't protect you. And I won't redeem myself—again."

"Redeem yourself?" I wanted to know.

He smiled a half-smile.

"I broke the rules, Claire. As a guardian angel, the top rules are to never reveal yourself to a mortal unless it is an emergency, and never fall in love. And the odds are not in my favor when you look at my history." He gave me a meaningful look.

"We need to stay neutral in order to see the fosterling's path. To know when their time has come and to be able to let go."

I was listening quietly, not daring to interrupt his words out of fear they would cease if I threw in one of the many questions that were taking shape inside my head.

"When I almost lost you, I was called in to be reassigned to someone else. They didn't trust me after all that had happened. But I couldn't bring myself to leave you. I couldn't hand you over to someone new.

"Claire, I haven't been neutral since the day your grandmother looked at me and saw me for what I am. It's like a curse. And I need to protect you—guide you through your life until your time has come. I owe it to Agnes." Jaden's face was apologetic. Pleading, almost.

"So I made a bargain. I can keep protecting you, but in return, I lose all my guardian angel privileges. I can't feel you like before. I need to be close to you in order to know how you are."

His hand balled into a fist, and he shook his head in frustration.

"There is more, isn't there?" I finally spoke. I could see it in his eyes. In the pained expression his features were holding.

"Jaden, what is it?" I pushed.

"I had to give up *all* of my guardian angel privileges." He repeated. This time, his words had a new meaning.

"If I fail, I can't ever return home."

"Home?" I asked.

"Home—" He nodded. "Home, the light, heaven, whatever you want to call it."

My heart sank.

"Jaden, what have you done?"

He merely smiled.

"I did the right thing. You are Agnes's granddaughter. It is a gift that I am allowed to protect you. It's worth any punishment if I fail."

He stepped toward me with outstretched arms and pulled me into his embrace.

"But you are more than that to me," he breathed into my hair.

I waited for more to come, but he remained silent. I wrapped my arms around him, wanting to comfort him. If I'd had any idea how much he had suffered, what he had risked to be here with me...

Jaden let go of me.

"Now you know everything."

16.
Wounds

When I got out of the car, my eyes fell on a small purple flower that had nudged its way out of the soil.

Mom's favorite flower had been the crocus, I remembered with a pang. She used to say that when the crocuses appeared, we could be certain of spring. Spring and hope, I thought, although I wasn't sure there was any hope for me. But, at least, I could hope for Jenna, Chris, and Ben. That their lives would get better after the demons eventually eliminated me.

I bent down and picked the flower from the still brownish-green lawn. It would look nice on Adam's grave. I hadn't been there since the funeral. It was time I confronted myself with it.

With a sigh, I straightened up and carried the purple blossom into the house.

I would stop by the graveyard on the way to the Gallagers' later, I promised myself, while I placed it in a small glass of water and headed up to my room.

I let myself drop to the floor the minute I entered my bedroom.

My heart was racing in my chest from sprinting up the stairs. I took a deep breath to calm down and closed my eyes.

My hands felt heavy as they were resting on my knees, palms facing upward.

Relax, I commanded, but my body wouldn't listen. The chance of seeing Adam's face—to feel him, if only in my imagination—made me fussy.

I tried counting backward from a hundred. That did the trick. By the time I reached seventy, I was breathing evenly, and when I reached sixty, my mind felt able to focus.

When I reached forty, my palms started getting warm. I directed my attention there, trying to understand what was happening.

The skin beneath my fingers felt different. It felt as if I was touching a warm body. The warmth was getting more intense as I focused on my left hand.

The warmth grew into a heat. It was slowly spreading along my forearm, up my upper arm, and then across my chest.

It felt like pure energy was consuming my quiet meditation.

Just a minute later, Adam's light green eyes were staring at me from inside my head.

They were as perfect and beautiful as always, but they were ice-cold.

I shuddered. It had worked. I had successfully conjured up Adam's image. It was an image of him that was far from how I remembered him. There was no sign of love in his eyes, no caring in his features.

Just a second later, he was gone. I opened my eyes and waited for my head to clear.

The heat in my chest disappeared within a few moments, almost as fast as it had appeared.

What was going on? I had to ask Jaden about this. And Liz.

A glance at my alarm clock told me it was time to get to the Gallagers'. I unfolded from the floor and slowly got to my feet, feeling slightly dizzy as I was straightening into an upright position.

Ben would pick me up. He had volunteered last night.

I still wasn't sure what to make of Ben, Ben's behavior, and my reaction to Ben's behavior. Maybe it was just self-preservation speaking, but I felt better when I was with him.

All of the hostility, the coldness he had shown toward me the first few times I met him, had been a sophisticated mask.

He had seen me for who I really was—Adam's downfall. He had known I would be the reason his brother would get killed, and he didn't particularly like me for that. Which was still better than the way I felt about it—I despised myself for being weak. I had been weak when I had insisted on being with Adam, on going to that cursed pool hall where he got killed, and I was being weak again, allowing myself to enjoy Ben's company.

If anything, I deserved to be miserable for the rest of my life.

Ben saw that a little differently. He had forgiven me. Despite the role I had played in his brother's death, he had developed feelings for me. The selfish part of me kept encouraging his attempts. But the Claire who knew better kept reminding me that I was a monster. I had basically killed Adam. If things were to continue the way they were, Ben would be next.

I was a magnet for disaster. My hands flapped over my face as I wiped away a tear.

It wouldn't be long now, and I didn't want Ben to find me a mess.

If he felt how I was feeling, he would be in pain. And I couldn't inflict more aches on the second Gallager son than I already had.

The doorbell tore me from my thoughts. It was time to put on another show, to appear okay, sane, happy.

I slowly made my way downstairs to let Ben in.

But it wasn't Ben who was waiting on the other side of the door with a charming smile playing on his face.

Jaden took a quick step across the threshold, leaving his smile outside the door.

"You look terrible," he commented and pulled me into a hug.

His arms were like a remedy to my pain. Within a second, my heart was lighter, and I felt at ease.

"Will it ever get better?" I asked into his chest.

A long silence followed my question with Jaden pulling me tighter being the only sign that he had heard me.

I knew it was a no. It wouldn't. Ever. And I was okay with it. I had come to terms with the emptiness and the craving to fill it. It had become part of who I was now.

After a while, Jaden let go of me and closed the door behind him.

"Are you ready?" he wanted to know.

I tilted my head. "Ben was supposed to pick me up."

"Ben is home," Jaden explained.

"Why?"

"Change of plans," Jaden said without giving further details. "We will take your car."

"Okay—" I was waiting to see if there was more coming, but it was all he would share for now.

Jaden grabbed my coat and held it out for me.

"Thanks." I slid into the warm fabric and turned to get the little flower from the kitchen.

"Can we stop by the graveyard?" I asked as I returned with the fragile, purple blossom.

Jaden looked at me for a moment.

"I haven't visited Adam's grave," I explained.

Jaden nodded, his eyes full of pity and a second emotion I couldn't identify.

"But only for a few minutes. As I said, there was a change of plans."

Now I gave him a questioning look.

"I have information to share."

"Anything you want to share now?" I tried.

"I recently came across a piece of information which I want to share with all of you." He sounded serious.

"I will share when we are all together at the Gallagers'." He put on a knowing expression and led the way to my car.

I followed, holding the flower securely in my hands.

I didn't push him to tell me more. Ever since that night at the Gallagers', I saw him in a completely different light. He had given up everything just for the chance to protect me. It was personal for him. He wouldn't let anyone else take on that responsibility.

Jaden was already in the driver's seat when I got to the car.

"I guess you'll drive," I muttered while climbing into the passenger seat.

Jaden eyed me for a moment before he started the engine.

"Graveyard," I reminded him as we were rolling into the traffic.

He nodded. Something in his expression screamed *worry*.

"Is there anything wrong?" I tried.

Jaden looked straight ahead, his eyes unblinking.

A car cut into the street right in front of us.

My body slammed into the safety belt as Jaden hit the break. His hand flung itself onto my chest, holding me in place as he cursed under his breath.

I coughed, and my pulse climbed to a flutter more than a steady beat.

Dangerous scenes in traffic did this to me, ever since my parents' car accident.

"Are you alright?" He turned to me and measured my expression while slowly accelerating the car to normal speed.

My hands were clutching the little flower violently. They had mangled it to a point where it wouldn't stay straight.

I didn't answer. Instead, I let my head sink and hid in my scarf until Jaden pulled up at the cemetery.

"Ready?" Jaden asked, his face cautious and a little bit sympathetic.

It took me a minute before I could speak.

"Yes."

I opened the door with shaking fingers. My legs were slow and heavy as I set them on the ground. The rest of my body seemed similarly reluctant to face the proof of Adam's death.

His gravestone was all that was left of him in this physical world. The gravestone and the pain in my chest.

Jaden was at my side within a heartbeat.

"Shall we?" he asked, and I nodded in return.

We were walking along the gravel path, side by side. The Fox River had just come into view behind the trees when Jaden turned to me.

"I'll give you a minute."

"Thank you," I mumbled and glanced at the reflections on the river in the distance. I was anything but ready. He didn't have to see this. "I won't be long."

"I'll be waiting at the gate." He touched my arm once in encouragement and walked back.

Without knowing how my feet had carried me there, I found myself standing in the center of the graveyard, under the willow. Its branches were the strange green-gold color of early spring. A new season was being put into place by Mother Nature. I knew it hadn't touched me yet. All I felt was the cold emptiness that hadn't left me since the day Adam had died.

It had become bearable; through all my friends it had become endurable, but the cuts in my soul had never really healed, and the barbed wired hadn't stopped tearing through my insides on a regular basis. I was incapable of love. I couldn't just move on and fall in love again, the way I was supposed to. I was incapacitated by the loss, and a month or two or even three wouldn't change that. Maybe not even an entire lifetime would be enough to make me forgive myself and to make me forget about the unique thing Adam and I'd had.

I looked around. A light breeze made the branches of the willow wave around me quietly. The stone angel was standing, as always, in silent beauty. I felt oppressed by it. I wasn't in the mood for quiet peace. I was in the mood to scream, to fight, to hurt. I was in the mood for self-destruction. My inner pain was peaking inside me, and I felt incapable of forcing myself to calm down once more. I was sick of all of this artificial sedateness. I wanted to let all the feelings rush through me— over and over again. I wanted to be sure Adam hadn't been a dream. I wanted to feel, at least, what little of him remained with me. The wounds in my heart were bleeding anyway, every second of every day. There was no way I would force myself to ignore them—not even with my friends around me. Not even with other angels trying to keep the worst at bay.

A hand on my shoulder made me jump.

"Jaden!" I flinched from his touch.

His blond hair waved in the breeze above his young face like the branches of the willow. His eyes were normal—not glowing in any way.

"I felt something. I don't think it's safe for you to be here."

I shook my head at him, indicating that I was unwilling to turn around now that I had finally made it to the graveyard.

His face showed a little warmth as he stepped to my side, putting one arm around my shoulders. "Then, at least, let me stay with you." He pulled me close to his side. The touch of his hand didn't take the pain away.

"Do you see anything dangerous nearby?"

He held his breath for a second, and I felt him tense beside me. "Yes."

I couldn't help but mirror his tension.

"What is it?" I asked in little more than a whisper.

Jaden remained silent for another endlessly stretching second before he turned to me and bent down to whisper in my ear.

"It's them."

I froze in place. So, they had finally decided to come back for me. I had known this was inevitable, that it would come sooner or later; but as much as I had been aware of the danger, I still wasn't prepared to face them, nonetheless. I wasn't prepared, but I had to face them. I wanted to. I needed to. It probably was my one and only chance to look Adam's murderers in the eyes.

"I'll take us away." Jaden put his other arm around my shoulders.

"No!" I almost shouted.

"But I can't protect you here," Jaden protested.

"I don't want protection." My mind was settled. I knew what I wanted. No life rather than the continuous pain from my wounded heart and soul.

Jaden didn't get the chance to teleport us away when the first dark shapes stepped out of the shadows of the trees. They were too far away for me to recognize them. I heard Jaden inhale in shock. His eyes were wide open and focusing on one of the silhouettes.

"No," he hissed, his face turning all dark with anger.

"What is it?" I whispered, trying to see what he saw, but my human eyes were too weak to follow his gaze to where he was looking.

Jaden took a quick step forward, planting himself in front of me. I couldn't see past him.

"Jaden." I tore at his sleeve like a little girl. "Jaden, what the hell's wrong?"

"Hell pretty much describes what's up," he said to me over his shoulder in a low voice.

"Good evening, Jaden, Claire," a deadly cold voice sounded from the far end of the graveyard. I knew the sound of it. It was perfectly smooth, emotionless. My mind instantly drew up pictures of a man dressed in black with a blond ponytail.

"Volpert," I whispered into Jaden's back. His head moved an inch forward as if he was nodding to himself.

"The one and only," Volpert's voice carried toward me.

Of course, he could hear me across the graveyard. I shouldn't be surprised by things like that anymore.

"Step aside, Jaden," he continued, and I heard footsteps on the gravel path, moving closer to where we were standing under the willow. "We honestly don't have any intention of hurting you…unless—"

Jaden snorted lowly. His shoulder blades moved with the sound like they had a mind of their own.

"I give you ten seconds," Volpert informed us.

One. I knew he wouldn't mind taking Jaden down first—two—if he gave him a reason. Three. I couldn't let him die. Four. Adam had died—five—because of me—six—not this good person—seven—this angel—eight—this man, too. Nine—

I took a quick step to the side and several strides forward, positioning myself slightly closer to the demon than Jaden was.

He looked exactly as I remembered him. His ponytail was quivering with the movements of his head, which followed my movements. His body was wrapped in a stylish black suit, too clean and sterile for the scene.

"So you value your guardian angel's life more than your own?" An icy laugh accompanied the words as they escaped Volpert's mouth.

"Claire, no!" Jaden didn't whisper. His voice was both shocked and determined, his face still angry with worry creasing his forehead.

"I won't let you get yourself killed," I explained to him.

"I won't let you sacrifice yourself," he replied coldly.

"If you will honor me with your attention for a while..." Volpert interrupted our discussion with surreal politeness.

I looked to the ground, evading Jaden's accusing eyes.

Volpert turned back, gesturing to one of the shadows behind him. "Come to me, my son." He lifted one arm, virtually embracing the person moving toward him with hesitating steps. "It's time for your revenge."

The shadow moved closer, making practically no noise on the gravel. I watched him gliding to Volpert's side in elegant strides.

"Take your time, son," Volpert encouraged the black-dressed shadow.

It seemed like time was starting to move backward, and I couldn't watch him coming closer anymore. I knew that my time had come, that my last minute had begun, that I could start counting down the seconds until he would kill me. I looked back down to the ground, examining the gravel to distract myself, to keep Jaden from sensing my hysteria, and started counting.

When I was down to eighteen, and I was still standing, I finally decided to look up again. I wanted to face the person who would kill me, I wanted to know who would be the one bringing death to me. My eyes glided up, and I froze, rooted to the spot, unable to move, to think, to breathe, to...

A pair of light green eyes was staring back at me, piercing and cold. I couldn't blink to break the connection, however hard I tried. My heart was racing at a critical pace—I was positive it was about to break from the strain.

The black-dressed man took a few more steps toward me, his eyes never releasing mine.

"Finally," he said in a voice I almost didn't recognize—so much time had passed since I had last heard it; so many times had I imagined the sound of it speaking to me; how much I had longed for the sound of it.

"I've waited a long time to see you." The voice was so cold it sent shivers down my spine and made my hair stand up on my neck.

My mouth was hanging open, and I had no control over my body right now—I was caught in this moment of shock, petrified by the simple fact that I saw a dead person standing in front of me. I had seen him die. I had seen him being buried. I had suffered through all of the loss, all of the grief—and yet, he was standing there, obviously alive, fixing me with his green eyes, his perfect features dead and cold, his handsome face expressionless, his gorgeous body tense and flexing for the strike.

Breathe, I told myself. I had to be hallucinating. Facing death was supposed to do such things to people.

I blinked several times, but he didn't vanish. On the contrary—every time I reopened my eyes, he seemed to have moved closer. I could see his features clearly now. They were set in hard lines, determined.

Jaden shifted behind me. I heard the gravel crunch under his feet as he moved.

"Tell your little pet-angel goodbye." Adam's voice penetrated my mind, my thoughts, my heart like a dagger piercing through all the layers of myself. Before I could grasp the meaning of his words, he had closed the space between us in a few strides too fast for my eyes to see him move.

I stumbled back as he appeared right in front of me, his eyes unfocused like he was looking through me. I had seen this gaze only once before—the evening he had died, before we had left the house, when he had told me he could see my soul. He'd had an edge of greed in his eyes I had never seen before.

The way he was looking through me now was more intense. The greed wasn't only an edge—it was dangerously pronounced; it was potent.

Adam lifted a hand to the height of my heart, the palm directed at me. "Goodbye, Claire." He almost whispered icily with a cruel half-smile on his lips, his eyes refocusing on mine for a second.

"No!" Jaden screamed from behind me. A second later, he was behind Adam, his arms at his throat.

Adam struggled in Jaden's grip, growling wildly.

"Let go of him, angel, or I will kill you," Volpert called from somewhere behind them.

"No," I found my voice. "Please, don't... Don't kill him," I said, without knowing whom I meant—Volpert kill Jaden or Jaden kill Adam.

I took a step back and inhaled deeply to steady myself. "Let him go, Jaden. He won't hurt me."

Jaden snorted darkly, tightening his grip on Adam, whose eyes were unfocused, still looking through me, vicious. "He will suck your soul out."

"He won't." I shuddered as I recognized the unlikeliness of my words.

Jaden eyed me for a second as if he was probing if I was being serious. I was.

But this single small second was enough for Volpert to sneak up on him and detach him from Adam. Now, Jaden was struggling in Volpert's grip. His face was angry, the fury directed at me.

"How can you be so naive?" he said flatly.

Volpert sneered at me over Jaden's shoulder, talking to Jaden. "You know, first, I wanted to kill you, but now, I'm pretty sure I want to see you suffer a little before you die, and the best way to ensure your suffering is making her suffer—" He nodded at me. "—to let her die slowly, painfully. How many of your fosterlings have you lost by now?" The demon stroked through Jaden's blond hair as if to comfort him. "Such an unlucky guardian you are—never been able to protect the ones you should." He shook his head while gloom played in his face. "One more or less won't matter, will it?"

All the while he talked, Volpert never took his eyes off me like he was enjoying how I was standing there, petrified with fear.

"Go ahead, son," Volpert said, directing his attention back to Adam, encouraging him, as he pulled the struggling angel in his grip further back, restraining him from any attempt to help me.

I saw Adam's hand move up again. It came to a halt a few inches from my chest.

I didn't know why he was standing there, alive. I had no clue how he could be with the demons, how he could have become one of those from the dark side, but there was no doubt he was determined to kill me—to suck out my soul. I had to do something. I had to try, at least. If this really *was* Adam, the old Adam—my Adam—had to be somewhere in there, buried under layers of black, of dark, but still there somewhere.

I looked at his face. He looked like my Adam. His eyes were unfocused, and the greedy expression in them was frightening. I felt something stab into my heart as I waited for him to refocus, to finally recognize it was me, his Claire, whom he was going to kill.

"Adam—" I whispered.

No reaction. The pain in my chest grew stronger. I felt like strings were being pulled from the center of my heart—strings which usually kept me together.

"It's me—Claire."

The strings were now curling around my whole heart, ripping it out slowly. I looked down, moaning in pain, expecting to see blood streaming from my chest and my heart in Adam's outstretched hand, but my heart seemed to have remained inside my body. The pain had to be coming from another source. Not my heart—my soul. He *was* sucking my soul from my body.

"Adam," I panted in pain. My limbs started to shake from the strain, and cold sweat was forming on my neck and forehead. "Adam—you're hurting me."

I heard Volpert's evil laugh and Jaden's gasp as they heard my hoarse, strained voice. The only one lacking a reaction was Adam, who was focusing on the strings he seemed to pull out of my body, straight through my heart, inflicting torturing pain on me. Instead of diminishing the ache, he was intensifying the hold on my soul.

My insides burned as the strings tore through them, further and further into the boundary areas of my body—so far it felt like they were piercing my skin from inside.

I screamed through clenched teeth as the pain reached my head.

"Adam," I heard Jaden's voice. It was velvety. "Do you remember; you were good once. You had wings—strong, white wings just like me."

"Don't listen to him, Adam." Volpert's voice lured from somewhere outside my head. I couldn't tell exactly; with every second, my vision became more blurry and darker.

The strings were continuously ripping deep wounds into my already mangled heart. I couldn't fight against it—I was too weak.

"Adam, listen to me—" Jaden again. "There was a time before you became this dark creature. You loved a girl back then, remember?"

"I don't know love," Adam said in a humorless tone.

"Yes, you do." Jaden didn't give up. "You loved a girl—" My body sank to the ground. I heard the noise of it hitting the gravel, but I couldn't feel it over the pain that was racing through my system. I gasped for air, unable to breathe evenly. My lungs seemed to be tied up with the strings, being pulled against my ribs from inside. "—a beautiful girl." Jaden's voice was cautious. "Her name was Claire."

I knew I wouldn't be able to stand the pain much longer. My entire body screamed for me to give in and drift into the blackness that lay behind the agony. I couldn't believe that the man I loved so much, whom I had lost so many times, and once forever, was the one who would end my life—my miserable life since he had died. So, did it really matter it was him who brought death to me, that I would die at his hand? I still loved him more than anything. And I felt more than blessed that I had seen him again. He had been my angel in life, and he now would be my angel of death. Agony was the least thing I could pay for all the happy moments I'd had with him, for the perfection of our love.

"You .... don't h-have ..... to t-take ... my ... soul"—I coughed between shivers and cold sweat, tears wetting my face—"it has a-always ... been ... yours." I panted the words in a mere whisper, feeling the energy leave my body. The pain had spread through all of the layers of my system, the strings tearing at my muscles, my veins, my bones, my nerves... My arms were bracing me against the cold that came more from the inside than the outside, but they weren't strong enough to hold me together—I was slowly falling apart. I knew I was about to slip away—it couldn't be long now.

"I love you, Adam—" It was little more than a breath.

The black had almost enveloped me as I felt the pull on the strings fade a little. I gasped for air, unable to open my eyes or move my limbs. All I could do was lie there on the gravel like a puppet whose strings had been cut.

And then, suddenly, the pain ceased a little, too, and it felt like the strings were starting to flick back into place. They raced back through my heart, my bones, my flesh, until they reached my skin.

It hurt as if they were tearing through fresh wounds, making my insides burn with pain all over again.

I heard myself moan. It was an unnatural sound—too far away to be real—and the touch of a hand on my forehead.

"What are you doing?" a voice screamed. "You are supposed to kill her."

I heard a smashing sound and then another scream. All of it didn't really matter to me. I sucked in fresh air in rhythmical gasps, trying to endure until the pain ceased or the black took away what was remaining of my consciousness.

I couldn't tell how long it had been when I heard another loud smashing sound and then silence.

The hand was still on my forehead. It was wiping the sweat away with a light movement. The fingers were warm and tender. I was quite sure that I would look into Jaden's golden eyes if I were able to reopen mine. How many times had he crouched beside my body, trying to take my pain away, comforting me with his touch?

I coughed in distress. If it was Jaden's hand—where was Adam? Had Jaden killed him? Had this made him stop tearing my soul out?

"Jaden?" I pressed his name out between two coughs shaking my body. I was feeling hysteria creeping up in my system.

The weight of the hand vanished from my forehead, leaving space for new droplets of sweat. I blinked, searching for the familiar shape of my guardian angel, but I couldn't see. My vision was almost blackened. The dark veil lifted so slowly; it was a long while before I could make out shapes against the night sky.

The first thing I saw was a shadow hovering over me. It was the shape of a man crouching beside me and bending over my face.

"Jaden," I whispered, relieved.

"No," the shadow whispered back.

I blinked again, trying to regain control over my eyesight. After a few more seconds, I was able to see some brighter specks in the sky and a blurry, pale yellow disk. I was finally able to make out a mane of black against pale skin, a pair of tightened light eyes, a line of white behind slightly parted lips.

The face staring down on me was torn. His eyebrows were pulling together in a frown. His eyes were focused on mine, but the greed was obviously still there in the light green of his irises, which were looking a lot more gray than green in the shadow of the night.

"Adam," I breathed.

His eyes widened, and I could see the recognition spread on his face.

"Claire."

The whisper came from his mouth in a gust, fervent, his eyes burning into mine, all of the evil, all of the greed gone from them within a fraction of a second. He was so close that the air from his lips touched my face in a warm breeze.

I inhaled greedily, shuddering as I tasted his scent. It was like no time had passed at all. I could feel my body respond to him without hesitation, without logic, without reason. Every inch of me was screaming for him, ignoring the ache he had caused me a minute ago. It was against nature to love somebody so irrationally, so entirely, so unconditionally.

He was alive—for some reason I didn't understand, he was alive, crouching over me, his face only inches away. He just had to sense what I was feeling; it was so potently streaming through me, setting me on fire. I was sure Jaden would feel it even when he was much farther away—wasn't he?

I tore my eyes away from Adam, reluctantly, searching my surroundings for the person I had gotten so used to in the past months, the one who had kept me alive over and over again, the one who had protected my sanity.

A bunch of golden hair was visible too far away, the face under it turned to the ground.

"Jaden!" Cold panic returned to my body. I turned my head to get a better view of the scenery.

Jaden was lying on the ground, motionless. The way he lay there made me want to run and help him. He looked vulnerable—the strong guardian, who now needed my help for once. But I also wanted to stay in the spot, soaking up what time I had before Adam vanished from my life again.

Before I could consciously decide what part of me should win, I turned back to Adam. I found myself staring into transparent air. The space that had been filled with his flesh and bones a second ago was empty now.

My head snapped back to Jaden, fearing he would have vanished, too, but he was still lying there, unchanged in his position.

I managed to get to my feet and look around. Volpert was gone, too. We were alone again. Jaden and I.

My feet automatically moved toward my guardian angel. The way his body was still on the ground made me anticipate the worst.

"Jaden," I tried.

No answer.

I slowly made my way toward him, my legs shaking and unstable.

"Please wake up." I let myself sink to the ground next to his head, ignoring the gravel biting into my knees. My hand reached out to touch his hair. It moved slightly in the wind, and I could see Jaden's face.

There was a streak of blood running from his hairline down to his chin. The skin beneath it seemed to have sealed back together, leaving the red line as the only sign of the cut.

I brushed my fingers over his cheek. "Jaden." It was a whisper.

His eyelids fluttered for a second and then revealed the golden orbs I had become so used to looking at.

"Are you okay?" I asked, my eyes wandering up and down his shape to check for unnatural angles of his limbs. Everything looked fine.

"Give me a moment," Jaden rasped.

I watched him close and reopen his eyes several times. Then he lifted his head, making a face as his hands pushed against the gravel.

"Are you in pain? How bad is it?" I watched him, feeling helpless. "Should I get help?" I was aware that any doctor would have noticed instantly there was something wrong with the way this man was healing. What a stupid thing to ask.

"I am fine," he breathed, "just give me a minute."

I sat back on my feet, relieved, and focused on my heart rate.

Not more than a few seconds had passed when Jaden finally propped himself up with his arms and rolled to the side. He looked up at my face, his expression grim.

"Claire, I am so sorry." His eyes were apologetic. "I should have known. I should have anticipated..."

"It's not your fault." What had he done wrong? I had wanted to come to the graveyard. I had persuaded him that it was safe. That I needed to come here to stay sane.

We looked at each other for a brief moment.

"What just happened, Jaden?" I could feel moist warmth on my cheeks. "How can he be alive?" I couldn't speak the name.

Jaden shook his head. "I have never seen anything like it." His expression became hard. "No angel has ever survived a killing strike of a demon..."

"I was there," I interrupted. "We buried him, Jaden. I was there at the funeral." What had just happened was beyond comprehension.

"I know." Jaden sat up and wrapped one arm around me. "I don't know what it means. Was it even Adam...?"

My heart sank at his words. It was Adam. It had to be. How else could there have been the recognition in his eyes? How else could I have felt the way I had the moment he had spoken my name?

"We need to get away from here," Jaden urged. His face all compassionate with worry creasing his forehead. His second hand reached around me and pulled me to him. A second later, the ground under my legs vanished.

17.
Dark Half

I was lying on the Gallagers' couch, head on the armrest. Jenna was sitting on the floor beside me. Her lovely face showed concern.

After the first shock had vanished, my body had begun to feel sore all over. Each little part that had been touched in the process of ripping my soul from me was hurting now. It was the best pain I had felt in ages. It meant that I at least still had a soul. A soul, which was very much attached to Adam. A soul, which was throwing tiny flashes of hope at me.

"Even if it was him…" Chris started for the hundredth time.

"But how is it possible?" Jaden asked again.

They were both sitting in armchairs, staring at the fireplace. The low orange light made everything even more surreal.

"He was in that coffin, at the funeral," Jenna said, her eyes not leaving my face. "I saw it. I was there when they closed it."

I shuddered. The old wound in my heart claimed my attention at once. I could smell the rain and the wet earth at the thought of the funeral.

"Demons can't shape-shift, can they?" It was Ben. He had joined us as soon as he had heard Jaden's voice at the front door.

Jaden shook his head. "I have never heard of it. And I have nine hundred years of experience."

"So, assuming it was really him...," Ben started.

"It *was* him." I yanked myself up to a sitting position, anger rising up in my throat. "It was him." This time it sounded a little calmer.

"I agree," Jaden supported my outburst. "Just different."

All heads turned toward him.

"He didn't have a heartbeat, for instance."

Of course, he would have noticed something like that.

"Demons don't have a heartbeat," he continued. "At least, the real ones don't—the pure lines. Half-demons do. They are like half-angels. One of their parents is human."

I gaped at him. What was he saying exactly?

"They can't resurrect the dead," Jenna threw into the guessing.

"But how is it possible?" Chris stood up and walked around to stand beside Jenna. He looked down on my face. I wondered what he found there. "How can he have become one of them?"

Jaden looked at each one of us for a second—one after the other. Eventually, his gaze fell on Chris. "Unless he's bound by an evil spell... I need some time." He looked at the Gallagers. "Make sure Claire is safe. Don't let her out of sight for even a second."

Then he turned to me.

"I'll be gone for a short while. Don't do anything stupid."

Without another word, Jaden disappeared into thin air, leaving the rest of us wondering.

Chris slowly sank into an armchair. Jenna paced in front of the window, lost in thought.

I leaned back on the couch and found Ben looking at me from the chair beside me. His features had questions written all over them. None of them I had the answer to.

I closed my eyes and shut out the world. I knew what I had seen. It had been Adam. My Adam. Even though he had been hurting me, there had been a moment of clarity where he had seemed to have recognized me. The only real question I had was why I wasn't with him right now.

He tried to kill you, the voice in my head commented. Right.

My head was killing me. I took a deep breath and got to my feet. I needed to get away from everything.

"Where do you think you're going?" Jenna was at my side in an instant.

"I need some fresh air." My head was spinning from the events.

She put her arm around my waist and helped me to the door.

"Let's go out back."

Jenna led me somewhere I had never been at the Gallagers', the back garden.

When she opened the heavy wooden door, the evening light painted colorful patterns through the ornate glass inlays. We stepped outside, and a view of peace spread before us.

My eyes skimmed the perfectly-cut hedge that was surrounding geometrically arranged flowerbeds. They stopped at a bush with little red blossoms sticking out in every direction. It was an untamed element in an environment of perfect domestication. It was like an impurity to a world of perfection. I could relate to the shrewd branches and the fragile flower petals.

I let myself sink onto a carved bench and stretched my legs into the short grass.

Antonio trotted toward us from the other end of the garden and curled up at my feet. I patted his head absently.

"This must be extremely difficult for you, Jenna."

She gave me a meaningful look.

"But it's worse for Chris. I can't even imagine how he must be feeling."

"Why don't you go check on him?" I suggested. "I'm sure he needs you more than I do."

Jenna hesitated.

"I'll send Ben so you're not alone."

I nodded, not really caring whether or not anyone was there with me. My brain was already working on ideas on how to find Adam.

"Claire?" Ben sat down beside me, not more than a second after Jenna disappeared.

"How can he be alive, Ben?" I asked. "How can he be alive and not come to find me?"

Ben didn't respond.

"It was as if he had never known me. The Adam I knew would have never hurt me—ever. He must be under their influence. It's impossible that he did this out of free will. If I could see him. If I could talk to him…"

My reasoning sounded desperate, but Ben didn't comment on it. Instead, he wrapped an arm around me.

"I am sorry."

We sat there in silence for a while and watched the garden fall into twilight until the deep red of the flowers was the only color left.

I woke up to the sound of bird songs and the smell of flowers. Sunlight was tickling my cheeks. I opened my eyes to a gentle voice whispering my name and looked at the wall of the Gallagers' guest room.

"Claire."

It sounded so much like Adam.

I jumped at the thought and looked around.

Ben was sitting on the edge of the bed, his hands folded in his lap, looking down at me.

I blinked twice. Ben—not Adam.

I waited for the pain to set in at the thought of Adam's name, but it didn't.

Instead, hundreds of images washed up in my mind.

It had been a long night. After hours of discussing Adam's resurrection with the Gallagers after dinner, I had fallen asleep on the couch in their living room.

Ben must have carried me upstairs and laid me down in bed. I was wrapped in the covers but fully dressed underneath.

I slowly let the knowledge settle in and went from ecstatic to depressed several times, remembering that Adam was alive—and that he had tried to kill me.

Ben was eyeing me cautiously. Of course, he could feel what I felt.

"What time is it?" I turned to him as the expression on his face became worried.

"Almost noon," he answered without moving.

"I've got school today." I almost fell over as I jumped out of bed.

"Relax..." Ben got to his feet and caught me by my shoulders. "Jenna called the school this morning to let them know you are not feeling well and won't be coming in today."

"Thank God," I exhaled, focusing. "I can't afford another unexcused absence."

Ben grinned for a moment before he led me to the bathroom door.

"Get ready," he gently pushed me over the threshold. "We have tons to discuss."

Jenna was playing with the seam of her dress when we entered the dining room. She looked up, her expression a mixture of relief and worry.

Ben sat down next to Jenna while I took a seat on the other side of the table.

"Where is Chris?" I asked into the silence.

"He is meditating in the library," Jenna said and took a sip of coffee.

"Again," I wondered. "Has he made any progress?"

"Well, nothing substantial, he says. Just a tickle between the shoulder blades."

I was surprised. After Liz's suggestions, Chris had started to meditate regularly. He hadn't felt anything until recently—a tickle in his palms. A tickle between his shoulder blades would mean huge progress.

"That's great news," I let her know how I felt about it.

"I think so, too." She smiled her motherly smile at me.

"Do you think it has anything to do with yesterday?" Ben joined our conversation.

I held my breath.

"It is possible," Jenna replied. "Knowing that his son is alive has given Chris new hope."

I understood. Knowing Adam still existed out there gave me hope, too. None of us had been able to fully process the meaning of his reappearance.

How could he be alive? Why didn't he remember me? Why was he running with Volpert? Was he a demon?

"One thing—" Jenna said. "If they attack openly like this, we need to be stronger than ever." She looked at me intensely. "Chris needs to get his powers back. We need him. And he needs you."

Ben watched her with a worried face.

"Don't you think it's a little much after yesterday—?"

I could see Jenna struggle. She wanted what was best for Chris and she wanted what was best for me. This time, those two were conflicting each other.

"I'll join him now." I took the decision away from either of them.

Jenna nodded gratefully, and Ben jumped up from his chair when I stood up to leave for the library.

"Call if you need anything," he offered helplessly.

"Thanks." I was on my way before it could get any more awkward.

I could see in Ben's eyes that he was suffering. He knew that all of his chances had disappeared the second I had laid eyes on Adam.

I found Chris on the library floor, cross-legged. He opened his eyes when he heard me come in. His face was hopeful.

"If he's alive, that means we both could heal."

His words made sense. I wanted it to be true, but there was something cautioning me not to believe. Adam had hurt me. He had tried to kill me. If he was alive, it was a very different version of the Adam I had fallen in love with.

"Shall we?"

We both closed our eyes and started breathing deeply. My presence meant more of Adam's soul in one room, and that meant a higher chance for Chris to succeed.

Knowing I would help by my mere presence, I focused on my own agenda. It had worked before—meditating to conjure up a vision of Adam—but today was an instant flash of his face.

His pale green eyes were staring at me. They weren't set in the evil mask I had seen in the graveyard. They were lost. Confused.

Adam, I willed my mind to speak.

The eyes blinked.

I felt my pulse accelerate. Had the vision just reacted to me?

You have gone crazy before, the voice in my head commented.

I focused on Adam's face. His expression had changed. He looked like he was searching for something.

Adam, I tried again.

Before I could see a reaction, something brushed my face. It felt familiar.

"Claire," I heard Chris's voice from a distance. "Claire, wake up."

My eyes opened to a vision of white. Chris was radiating light from within, and he was framed by wings.

"You did it," I cheered weakly. He looked impressive. Beautiful. He had actually done it.

"We did it." Chris's face was gleeful. I hadn't seen him that happy since before Adam's death.

"We need to tell the others." They would be ecstatic.

"No need," Jenna's voice came from the door. Ben was standing right behind her, both of them smiling.

"Now we can take them on together, Dad." Ben stepped forward. He slipped out of his shirt and walked to stand next to his father.

A second later, a pair of wings was bouncing left and right of his shoulders. Even though I had seen him this way once before, I couldn't get used to the way he looked with that pair of feathery white wings. It was a breathtaking vision.

Jenna was leaning in the doorway, observing the scene. She winked at me when she saw me gaping at Ben.

"Put your clothes on, Ben," she instructed with a grin. "Chris, I'll get you a new shirt." She pointed at the torn fabric on the floor.

He laughed. It was a joyous sound. Almost surreal with all of the pain we had been enduring.

I leaned back and watched them for a while. They were talking. Obviously exchanging information and experiences related to their powers. I wondered if they had ever talked like this before. It was a whole new aspect of their relationship.

I had never fully appreciated the similarities between Ben and Chris. The way his chest was built. The hair and eyes. The way they lifted their chins slightly when they laughed.

This was a moment of victory for all of us. Then, why did it feel like something was wrong?

I slowly got to my feet and crept out of the room.

Jenna had left to get Chris a fresh shirt, and the others didn't notice that I was leaving.

I made my way down the hallway to the guest room. It felt as if I had moved in permanently; I was spending so much time at the Gallagers' now.

My limbs were heavy from the strain my body had gone through in the past days. It made me want to lay down and rest.

On the way over to the bed, my eyes fell on my phone. The display was lit up from an incoming text message.

I glanced down at the screen and gasped at the words I read.

I need to see you. Adam

All tiredness was gone in a heartbeat. Was it possible? Was this message really from Adam? My Adam.

This could be a trap, the voice in the back of my mind intercepted my thought process.

Yes, it could be. But it could also be Adam, wanting to see me.

I sat on the bed, conflicted over what to do, before my curiosity got the best of me.

When? Where?

I typed the two words carefully as if I could embed another message in them. The message I really wanted to send. *Adam, I love you. Adam, I miss you.*

My hands were shaking when I hit send.

I stared at the screen intensely, waiting for a reply. It didn't come. Instead, my phone buzzed from a call. I almost dropped it, jumpy from tension and anticipation.

It was Sophie.

"Hey, little sister," she hooted into the phone when I answered.

"Hi, Sophie," was all I managed.

She was wondering if she should come home over the next weekend.

"Honestly, I feel guilty for leaving you alone all the time," she admitted.

Having Sophie around was the exact opposite of what I needed at the moment. Things were getting more dangerous by the day, and the last thing I wanted was Sophie in the cross-fire of Volpert's feud.

So, I put on my lighthearted voice—as well as I could.

"You wouldn't see me at all. Even if you were here." I almost sounded convincing. "The Gallagers have practically adopted me. I am there all the time."

Sophie's voice was relieved. "That's good to know. I need to call Jenna and say thank you. It is crazy here. We don't get much sleep..." She was going into detailed descriptions of her days at the hospital.

My mind drifted back to Adam. He wanted to see me. This meant there was some part of him that remembered me. *Or it's a trap*, the voice in my head repeated my concern to me.

It could be. It was likely. But if there was even the slightest chance I might get to see Adam, to talk to him, to understand what was going on, I would take it.

Even if that would cost you your life? the voice asked.

It won't come to that, I answered and ignored the mild complaining in the back of my mind.

"Are you sure Ian shouldn't drop by to check in?" Sophie's voice pushed my thoughts into the background.

"I'm fine, Sophie," I reassured her again. "Really, don't worry."

I wouldn't put her at risk.

"Just make sure you learn all you can. I want a good doctor as a sister. Not one of those who mix up a liver with a kidney."

Sophie laughed. It was a good sound to hear.

"I need to go," I excused myself. "Talk to you soon."

"Talk soon."

I put the phone down and got to my feet, still waiting nervously for Adam's reply, but the phone remained silent.

Instead, there was a knock on the door. Ben popped his head in.

"Jaden is back."

When we arrived in the living room, Jaden was sitting on the couch. He jumped to his feet and disappeared for a second just to reappear right in front of me half a second later.

"You are here," he noted. "Everyone is here."

Jenna and Chris were standing by the window, their faces expectant.

Ben walked around the room in a slow circle while Jaden led me back to the couch and made sure I was comfortable.

"Excuse my short absence," he started. "I had to check a theory."

He had my attention.

"What theory?"

"Well, let's approach this logically." Jaden looked at all of us and sighed, obviously conflicted over how to break the news. "My research has confirmed there are only two ways Adam can be alive. Either he never died, or he never really died."

My mind stumbled over his logic. "Jaden, this is really just one option."

"Correct. There is only one slight difference." Jaden gave me a wistful look. "If he never died, he wasn't killed by the demons; he might have been petrified. In a temporary, death-like state.

"If he never *really* died, the demons *did* kill him, but only part of him." He looked at all of us, taking in our confusion.

"Jaden, I was there. I saw him die," I reminded him.

"Yes, you were there," he agreed. "But what did you see—or *really* see?"

I didn't get him.

Jenna and Chris exchanged a look, and Ben started walking around the room in slow circles.

"Tell us again," Jaden encouraged.

I took a deep breath.

"He was hit by the demons' lightning. Two at the same time. Right into the heart." I conjured the painful memories.

"What happened next?" he pushed.

The images were flashing before my inner eye as if it was happening right now. With the memories, there came pain.

"Is this really necessary?" Jenna's voice came from beside me. "Can't you see she is suffering?"

"We need to know what we are dealing with." Jaden's response was business-like.

"What happened next, Claire?" Jaden had turned to me and was standing right in front of me. "I need to know."

"He fell," I finally forced out after a long pause.

"Did he say anything after he was hit? Did he move?" Jaden pressed for even more details.

"Jaden, I can't—" This was torture.

He took my hand. "Please, Claire. You are the only one who was there. What you saw may make all the difference."

I closed my eyes, focusing on this darkest hour in my existence.

"He looked at me. And then his eyes rolled back before he fell."

"Before or after he was hit?"

"After."

Jaden squeezed my hand. "Thank you. I know this is hard for you."

It was hard for all of us. Every single person in the room could feel what I felt. They all suffered with me. I wasn't alone. Not this time.

Jaden let go of my hand and took a step back before he continued.

"This was the missing piece of information." He took a long pause and looked at each of us for a moment. "Adam died, but he never *really* died."

My head couldn't comprehend what Jaden was deducing so logically from my story.

"Adam was part-angel, part-human, right?" Jaden stated common knowledge. "When the demons hit him, they killed his angel-half and his human-half."

I watched Chris and Jenna stare at each other in horror.

"That's impossible," Chris shook his head. "I would have noticed."

"Think about it," Jenna said as if suddenly everything made sense. "It's the only way."

"He never *really* died," Ben joined the conversation. "It wasn't halves—it was thirds. There was a third part that survived."

"Or was awakened through the death of his human death and angel death," Jaden finished.

I suddenly felt left out. Everyone seemed to be comprehending. What was I missing?

"Would someone please explain to me what is going on?" I burst out.

All four of them looked at me as if they were just remembering I was still there.

It was Jenna who found her voice first.

"If both parts of Adam are dead—angel and human—but he is still alive, this means there must have been a third part hidden somewhere inside of him. Too weak to show itself while the other two were still alive—"

"Adam must have had demonic heritage," Jaden finished the thought.

I felt my jaw drop.

Ben was watching his father from the corner of the room where he had stopped pacing.

"What we need to know now is which parent he got it from."

All faces turned to Chris.

"And you are everything but a demon," Jenna reassured Chris.

Jaden nodded. "Chris, I feel nothing dark when I am next to you. Not even the slightest hint. It's impossible he got it from you."

I watched Chris's face go from horror to relief and back to horror.

"But Abigail was mortal," he reasoned. "She was mortal. She died giving birth to Adam."

Abigail, Adam's biological mother, I remembered. She had died giving birth to Adam, just seconds before Chris had spread his wings for the first time when he had held tiny, newborn Adam in his hands.

"I know this is hard for you to wrap your head around, Chris," Jaden looked at him intensely, "But think about it. Abigail died young. Even if she hadn't developed demon powers, the demon-gene could have been dormant. Having the gene alone doesn't make a demon. There are many factors. She might have never turned bad."

"I guess we'll never know," Chris said in a strained tone. He sat down in an armchair and buried his face in his hands.

Jenna was watching him with a weary expression.

I couldn't even begin to imagine what the two of them were going through right now. And Ben.

He was still standing in the corner, lost in thought.

I let the new information sink in for a few minutes.

So, the theory was that Adam was alive. That was good news. The bad news was that he wasn't anything like before. The parts of him that had been human or angel were gone. This gave me a lot to think about.

Jaden was watching me from the corner of his eye as I yawned widely. I was physically tired from processing everything.

"Time for you to lay down and rest," he commented. "We still have a lot to figure out. All we have for now is a theory."

"And a very good one," Ben threw in.

"We need to make a decision soon." Chris looked up.

"What do you mean?" I wondered.

"Adam is alive. Even if all that's left of him is a demon—he is still my son."

Jenna gave him a pitying look.

He was right. And I agreed with every fiber in my body. Even if he was a demon, and we weren't one-hundred percent certain that's what he was, he was still Adam.

I needed to see him soon. I needed to see for myself what he was—or wasn't.

"So, I have a demon brother," Ben said, his voice surprisingly light. "Should we stake him out and capture him?"

All eyes were on him now. Some filled with shock, some with admiration for how lightly he was taking the news.

"I just mean—maybe there is some spark of good left in him."

It was Sunday morning. I was staring at the message as if I could force more information out of it by pure willpower.

Jaden's theory changed everything. I needed to get a chance to talk to Adam alone before the demons attacked the next time. But would it make a difference if I did? If he was truly evil now—

It had been quiet after Adam's death. We hadn't heard or seen much of the demons. They had tried to get me twice. Ben had saved me once. Jaden the other time.

I wasn't sure if anyone would be able to help this time—trap or not. So, I had decided not to tell the Gallagers or Jaden about the messages.

Lucas Baker was eliminated. Who knew if they knew about Liz. I didn't know if they knew about all of the Gallagers. And I couldn't risk them finding out.

But did it really matter? Volpert was still upset that I had gotten away that night, and he would stop at nothing to take revenge.

It was certain revenge would come and that it would be painful; the only thing uncertain was what it would look like.

Whatever it will be, you deserve it, the voice in my head came to life. I quickly shut it up and tried to focus.

Another thing I could be sure about was that I wouldn't endanger any of the Gallagers this time.

I was just rolling over and forcing my brain to shut up when my phone buzzed.

My hand reached for the rectangle and held the screen before my eyes. I froze.

Tonight. Where it all began.

18.
Ice-Cold

The pencil scratched over the paper as I scribbled the note.

Gone to see Adam. I just had to go.
Sorry. Claire

I folded the paper in half and placed it on the bed.

It was getting dark outside. Jenna and Chris were busy in the library. Ben had checked in on me just a few minutes ago, and Jaden was out somewhere, trying to learn more about angel-demon hybrids. We had decided together that we had to get Adam back somehow. And this demanded information. If I was quick, I would be back before anyone could notice.

After all the Gallagers had done for me—and Jaden—I wouldn't risk any of them just to satisfy my childish and very dangerous need to see Adam.

With a quick look into the hallway, I made sure the coast was clear before I tiptoed downstairs and out the front door.

My car was waiting for me at the side of the building. I jumped in and started the engine.

No one came to stop me. They were all busy. So, I slowly drove away from the house and into the evening traffic.

Every few blocks, I checked the mirror for a familiar car and the street around me for familiar shapes, but there was nothing. It seemed my plan had worked.

I instantly felt guilty for running away like this. But I knew, if I had told any of the Gallagers about Adam's message, they would have never let me go. Let alone Jaden. He depended on my safety more than anyone.

Adam, the voice in the back of my head said. It was all I needed to hear to let go of all guilt. I needed to see him. I needed to know if it was true. If all that was left of him was an evil shell.

Where it all began, Adam's message had said. It was only a few minutes later when I parked at the graveyard. The street was empty.

I opened the old iron gate ever so slightly and slipped in. No sense letting the gate stand wide open for nighttime dog-walkers to use or a passing police cruiser to notice. My heart was racing in anxious anticipation. I didn't know what to expect. Would he come alone? Would he recognize me? Would he remember me?

"I see you got his message." It wasn't Adam's voice, but it was a familiar voice.

I instinctively turned toward the sound and found a dark, slender silhouette under a nearby tree.

When she stepped out of the shadows, I froze. Her face I would recognize any time, any place.

"Maureen." Adam's ex-girlfriend.

Maureen tilted her head, and her jacket shifted to expose a silver amulet around her neck.

She was part of this. I had suspected a connection with the demons after I noticed the pendant on her necklace at Adam's funeral—the same one the demons wore—but I couldn't be sure until now. Was she a demon?

A trap after all, the voice in my head warned me. Of course it was. But even knowing the odds of this being a trap, if there was the slightest chance of seeing Adam, I would gladly risk it.

"How nice of you to come," she said in a sweet and false voice.

"What do you want?" I felt stupid for coming alone. With his reduced powers, Jaden wouldn't know if I needed his help, and the Gallagers were all busy. I was on my own—I had planned it that way.

"Well—there is a small thing I need you to do," she started.

I glared at her, unwilling to give her whatever she would be asking.

"You need to stop thinking about him."

Definitely not that. If anything, Adam's image was the only thing left that I had. I wouldn't give it up—never. Especially not now that I knew he was alive.

I shook my head at Maureen. She could go ask someone else to forget the love of their life.

Ready to admit it had been a mistake to come here, I turned and started walking away.

What she was asking of me was impossible. It was ridiculous. I was ashamed that I had so easily fallen for the deceit, but she had dangled the one bait guaranteed to bring me running. That Adam wanted to see me. There was nothing I wanted more than for it to be true.

The voice in my head chuckled at me darkly at my discomfiture. I ignored it.

If I was fast, I would make it back in time so nobody would notice my absence. I could simply climb into bed and pretend I had never left. Destroy the note and forget my naivety.

I had just taken a step or two when a second voice spoke.

"You came." This time it was the voice I had been craving to hear.

I looked around to see where he had spoken from, but I couldn't make him out in the dark surroundings.

"Adam, where are you?"

"It doesn't matter where he is," Maureen's vicious melody touched my ears.

"The only thing that matters is that you came. You are making it so much easier for all of us."

I paused for a second, weighing my options. There could be more than two here. What if Maureen's petty request wasn't the only reason she had lured me here?

Trap, I was reminded harshly.

If I ran now, Maureen and whatever else was lurking in the shadows would probably not touch me. But then I wouldn't get the chance to see him. I needed to see Adam.

If I was honest, there was only one option, really—no matter the outcome.

My feet stopped before I had made the conscious decision, and my eyes were searching the darkness.

A movement to my right claimed my attention. There he was, hidden in the shadows. It was like when I had seen the shadow in the school parking lot. The same ghostly motions, the same outline. The same person.

"Adam," I whispered.

The dark outline stepped forward until I could make out his face. His mouth was a thin line, and his eyes were full of anger.

"Are you alright, Adam?" I addressed him directly, hoping he would respond.

"Don't bother talking to him," Maureen mocked.

She walked over swiftly, her dark mane fanning out behind her, until she stopped right at my shoulder.

My instinct was to run. But knowing that Adam was here, just a few feet away, I still couldn't bring myself to leave.

You have a death-wish, the voice in my head narrated. I nodded at it.

"You destroyed everything," Maureen whispered into my ear.

I shuddered.

"You took him from me. You made him into your pet-angel." Her voice was full of hatred.

"Maureen, I didn't make him anything," I defended myself, well aware that anything I said could set her off. "I didn't make him love me."

She laughed sweetly. The sound combined with her cold and cruel mask made the scene bizarre.

"Whatever you did or didn't do doesn't matter now, does it?" She placed her hand on my shoulder as if she wanted to comfort me.

I shrank away from her touch.

"He doesn't remember any of it. Your great, epic love. It was for nothing."

Her words stabbed right into my heart. I lifted my arms to brace myself against her attack. Even if it was just verbal.

For now, the voice commented.

It was right. I had no idea if Maureen had any powers—and if she did, would she use them to destroy me?

"I want you to know that there is nothing left of the Adam you knew." She let one pointy finger slide down my arm until it rested on my hand.

"He is all mine." Her lips puckered a little, making it look like she was feeling sorry for me. The next moment, her face was back to icy as was her voice. "His love is mine."

The way she said it brought back a memory of what Adam had said about Maureen. He'd had the emotional vision of me when he had still been with her. Even if her *love* was more lust and possession than real feelings, I *had* taken him away. This thought gave me strength.

"You don't know love." I knocked her hand off my shoulder. "Love is the one thing that survives the darkest times."

Maureen was surprised by my reaction. What had she expected? That I would let her put me down, insult me and my love for Adam, and expect me to walk away without a word in return?

"You make me sick." After one long look at my face, she walked away and disappeared into the trees.

"She's all yours," I heard her icy voice one more time before the darkness swallowed her completely.

Adam finally walked toward me. His hand was lifted the same way it had been at our last encounter.

"Adam, what are you doing?"

He didn't react to my words. He didn't speak to me at all. His stare was the only sign he had heard me.

Instead, he came closer and placed his hand in front of my chest. I felt the strings in my heart pull toward his fingers painfully.

He was doing it again. He was trying to suck out my soul. He was killing me.

Run! the voice in my head instructed.

I jumped as it tore me from my petrified state and ran.

Adam probably hadn't expected this. I was surprised that he didn't stop me right away when his footfalls came closer at a steady pace.

I slipped on the loose gravel and cut my knees and hands, stumbling over my own feet. I wanted to run, but I also wanted to reason with Adam.

Time for reasoning is over, the voice redirected my focus.

I picked myself up and continued running.

Whenever Adam came close enough, the strings on my heart began to tear and hurt again, but he never actually incapacitated me. It was like he was playing a game. One I wasn't sure he wanted me to lose. I needed to get away. I hoped that someone had found my note in the Gallagers' guest room. I had gotten myself in trouble for the chance of verifying I hadn't dreamt that Adam still existed. Now I knew. And the truth hurt almost as much as not knowing.

"Let her go," I heard Maureen's voice calling behind me when I had made it to the gate.

Of course, she had stayed to watch me suffer.

My sore legs hardly carried me to my car. I didn't look back. I was surprised I made it and drove out of the parking lot without looking. My right hand was searching my pockets for my phone.

I tried Ben's number first. It went straight to voicemail.

"Ben, I need help. I am on my way back to your house. I think I am being followed."

Chris's number was next. He didn't answer. Neither did Jenna.

When I saw a shadow running behind my car, I pulled into the next street. I *was* being followed.

My only option now was a distraction. Get rid of the car and hide.

The library was just a few blocks away from here. I checked the mirrors for the shadow—nothing—and quickly parked the car. Then I slid out and ducked behind a row of parked vehicles until I saw the crossing that led to the library before I finally broke into a run.

The library was dark when I entered. In my mind, I thanked Liz for the extra key she had given me a week earlier. *In case you ever need access to a certain read*, she had said and handed it to me.

The lock clicked, and the door opened slowly at the touch of my sweating hand. The shelves were all hidden in darkness.

There was no sound except for my panting when I rushed in and disappeared between the furniture, hoping to have lost my tail.

I was now cowering behind one of the large bookshelves. My knees were bloody from where they had hit the gravel each time I had fallen down, from the countless times they had slithered across the tiny stones.

The blood on my face was almost dry. My hands had drawn large traces on my too fair skin where they had touched it to wipe away the tears of anger and betrayal.

My fingers were clutching my ankles, holding my feet in place, and my head was resting against a spot on the bookshelf which was empty.

I had seen angels and demons in the last few months, I had seen them and remained brave however often they had interfered with my life. I had accepted that they were part of my existence, almost as much as my frequent walks to the graveyard were. But this time was one time too many.

My breathing was still too fast, and it rushed in and out of my lungs uncontrollably. The physical pain was not what bothered me. It was just a humming in the background. I had become almost immune to the constant ache in my limbs. I had suffered too much from it in the last weeks. I was almost as used to it as I was to the fact that Adam wasn't part of my life anymore. My heart continued pounding, no matter what hardship life presented me with. I was a survivor. It wouldn't even stop at my own command. But there were things I couldn't take—not now.

Adam appearing to be a bad guy was one of them. He was the one person I had thought I could rely on—another irony as it turned out he wasn't. He had betrayed me so easily; the one man I had once trusted with all of my life and my soul. The man I still loved.

I was positive there wasn't a place in this world where I was safe now. I was sure he would find me where ever I went—so I might as well stay right here.

There was just one thing that broke through my wall of fear and through my concerns; if Adam wanted me dead, he would have had countless opportunities to get rid of me easily; just let me die on the roof instead of stepping in. He wouldn't even have had to get his hands dirty.

I felt unearthly lucky that I was still breathing—considering that, measured by common means, I wouldn't stand a chance against his supernatural powers.

The door clicked open somewhere behind my back. I shrank against the hard front of the shelf like I had been whipped in the face.

It was Sunday night. The library was supposed to be closed—at least, the sign on the door told it explicitly to everyone who came close enough to read it. I hadn't locked the door behind me. One simple lock was nothing that would hold back the ones chasing me—neither of them. Most likely, they would pop up right in front of me and wouldn't lift more than a finger to produce the deadly strike.

My breath had reduced to little more than a thin line of air. The water was beginning to dry from my eyes, but I didn't dare blink. I was paralyzed by how much I was at the mercy of the shadow, which was drawing nearer in slow steps.

Within a few more steps he was close enough for me to measure his face. He was standing between the door and me, looking exactly the same as always, except that he wasn't looking the same at all. For a minute, I searched for what made him look so different. His face was perfectly calm with a hint of strain making his forehead crumple. The collar of his shirt was sprinkled with dirt, the traces of it reaching down to his knees. He looked as if he had laid on the wet ground.

The madness in his eyes was gone. I could tell as I leaned toward him without thinking.

Adam didn't move nor show any other sign he had the intention of attacking me any second. He looked as innocent, as angelic as ever.

I shuddered involuntarily at the thought of how quickly he would be able to knock me out if he wanted to; it would be so fast.

The way he kept looking at me, unmoving, made me feel tied to the spot with just his eyes. His features were perfectly calm, but the light-green mirrors between his eyelids began to show first signs of distress. They followed the motion of my breath, and I noticed how the air from my lungs came more heavily every time I exhaled under his stare.

I shrank back into the shelf, hoping that there would be more space behind my back, and hit my spine on the wooden boards. New tears shot into my reddened eyes. There was a silhouette moving beyond the veil of wet. I blinked to clear my view, and when I could see clearly again, the silhouette was filling my entire field of vision.

"Adam," I croaked, unable to put out the scream I felt like throwing at him.

To my surprise, he flinched at the tone of my voice. I was surprised myself—that I had been able to speak at all.

"Why are you so scared?" he asked, velvet. It reminded me a lot of the Adam I used to know, the Adam I trusted. I cringed away from him instead of letting him reassure me. *Treacherous piece of shit!* The voice inside my head and I were in accord for once.

"Do it!" the scream finally escaped my lips. It carried all the betrayal that was settling inside of me. "Do it if you have to," I looked him straight in the eye. "But don't play with me like a wolf does with a wounded doe!" I took a deep breath and sat straight, ignoring my body screaming as I forced it to straighten. I would die with my head high, eye to eye with my fate.

Adam lifted his hand slowly enough for my weak eyes to track the movement. It was just a moment though until it lay at my throat, near my collarbone.

My skin felt cold where he touched it. I shuddered and shrank back into the wooden boards behind me once more, hurting my sore back even worse.

"What's wrong, Claire?" he murmured into the silence of the library. "Why are you so afraid?"

His hand pressed against my skin harder, pinning me to the spot, and my entire body protested. I felt like vomiting from all the pain and fear I had been going through.

"It's me, Adam," he lured, his eyes glowing softly as he spoke. They didn't look loving or comforting to me anymore— they looked like a predator's, and I was the crushed prey, the weak animal that was cowering under who it recognized would be its death.

Once again, he opened his mouth to speak. His hand at my throat loosened its weight, giving me more space to breathe.

"What happened to you that makes you so afraid of me?" He knelt down beside me and his hand glided down from my throat along my arm to find my hand at the end of it. He squeezed it lightly.

"I'm sorry I was gone so long," he apologized. "I should have taken better care of you," he blamed himself for how I was reacting to him right now; and it *was* his fault. If he hadn't tried to kill me half an hour ago—again—I might not be afraid at all. I shuddered and let the sensation extend to my hands, hoping to shake out of his grip.

"What's wrong, Claire?" he reacted. "What happened?"

"Are you honestly asking me this?" I threw at him coldly. I tried to force him back with just the stare of my eyes, fury raging inside me.

He looked at me defensively, and his hand left my skin.

I shied away to one side, toward the end of the shelf.

"What have I done to you that you are afraid of me?" Adam's voice was the one panicked now, his eyes alarmed and the glowing gone.

What did he want from me? Why did he torture me by letting me live? Wouldn't it be a sign of mercy, of the love we had once shared, if he just finished me off?

He watched me slide farther away from him wordlessly, and then when I had brought some welcome space between us, he popped up right in front of me.

"You are going to tell me what's wrong!" he demanded, shouting now. His lips were trembling at the force of the emotions that were filling the room. He looked at me, desperate and full of fear himself.

"Why don't you just do it?" I shouted back at him.

"Do what?" He didn't stop shouting; he screamed right into my face, shaking my shoulders so hard that my head hit the board behind me again.

"Kill me! Get on with it, and do it!" My words hung heavy in the air between us for a moment, and then Adam was gone. The spot he had been kneeling in was empty, and I was staring into the half-light of the library.

"Kill you—" he said from a few feet away.

I turned my head to look at him. He looked at me with his mouth gaping, eyes uncomprehending, until after an endless couple of seconds, he blinked and moved his lips.

"Why would I do that?" His voice sounded truthful, and his face looked almost innocent, taken aback by my accusation.

"You already tried earlier today, remember?" I asked coldly, dreading the moment he would. It was almost schizophrenic the way he had forgotten within minutes that he had intended to kill me. I stared at him, ambivalent as to whether or not I wanted an answer.

Adam was frozen for a minute, and then he jumped to his feet so quickly that I couldn't follow the movement.

"Oh no!" He took a step as if he was intending to pace the room and then he was right in front of me, too quick for my eyes to see. "Damn!" The next moment he was at the other end of the shelf. He kicked the air with one of his feet.

He hissed and swirled around until he was facing me.

His eyes were dark with comprehension, and his features were formed into a bitter mask.

He cursed as he walked back down toward me, moving forward slowly enough for me to suspect he was trying to stretch the time until he had to tell me what was going on as long as possible.

I had expected anything but this reaction. It made my fear slowly fade into curiosity.

"What is it, Adam?" I asked before I could swallow back the words.

Adam took another step and a deep breath before he came to a halt in front of me.

"I can't kill you," he stated.

I looked at him, still scared, while waiting for more. He looked back at me, his face set into the same mask, his hands balling into fists, but nothing came for a long minute.

"I must kill you," he murmured then.

"What?" I spluttered out before I could help it.

My heart jumped into my throat and hammered violently.

I was surprised as Adam let himself sink to the floor in front of me, cross-legged, and opened his mouth.

"I must kill you," he said slowly like he was speaking from a different time, a different world, his eyes growing distant, almost like he was just beginning to comprehend. "They said I must."

"Who?" my voice raced out of my mouth.

"The others."

"Adam, I don't understand." His family was trying to protect me. They would never… "Who are you talking about?"

"Volpert, Maureen, Blackbird—my family."

"Demons," I gasped.

"If that's what they are…," he shrugged.

"Adam, you have a different family. A father, a brother."

"If I do, I can't remember." His face was indifferent.

There was something about his behavior that made me think his family wasn't the only thing he couldn't remember.

"Do you remember who I am?" I asked, fearing the answer.

"It doesn't matter." He shook his head without giving a real answer. "I don't have a choice." His eyes were sad. He almost looked like the Adam I had fallen in love with, the Adam I had trusted, the Adam I still loved.

I stared at him, processing what he had just said.

"Why?" It was a mere breath. I felt that he was struggling. If I could only get him to tell me who was pressuring him.

His eyes bore into mine, and I lost track of time. There was no hint of the angelic glow they used to hold. They were empty.

"What happened to you?" Whatever it was that made him do this, it wasn't him alone. Even if he couldn't remember any of his past, he would never hurt me. There was something more to this. More than was visible. More than he would tell.

If I could only buy some time, maybe Jaden or Ben would come to help. If they had found the note.

I had to give it a try.

"It's me, Claire… your Claire…" My voice sounded surreal as I was listening to my own words, hoping they would trigger his memory.

A simple nod was all I got in return. It wasn't a nod of agreement or a nod of understanding. It was a nod of determination. I could see what was about to come. And it was inevitable. I stood no chance against him. Not if his mind was set.

19.
Captive

I was staring at my fate. Wide-eyed. Adam was beautiful; even now, I couldn't deny the fact.

His face was determined, but his eyes showed hesitation. It made me believe there was still something in him that cared about me.

I didn't have time to ponder that. The room suddenly brightened up. Four sources of light were framing Adam. Each of them had a pair of strong, white wings.

Before I could make out their faces, Adam's hand reached out to touch me. It was only a fraction of a second, and he was pinned to the floor by three of the four angels. The fourth had taken a stand in front of me. He was holding out his arms protectively, shielding me from Adam—and blocking the view.

I recognized the shape. It was Ben.

"Are you alright?" he asked, alarmed.

I nodded and tried to see around him. What were they doing to Adam?

Ben stepped aside, and my eyes found Adam crouching on the floor with tied-up hands and feet. Chris and Jaden were holding him at each arm. He wasn't fighting them. Jenna stood beside them, ready to jump in any second.

"Get her out of here," Jenna instructed Ben.

A moment later, I found myself in the Gallagers' library. I didn't even get the chance to object.

I wanted to be there. I needed to be there. Frustration got the best of me, and I considered yelling at Ben, well aware that I had brought this upon myself. Instead, I decided for calm cooperation.

"Where are they taking him?" I requested.

"They'll be here any second." Ben stared at me accusingly. "How could you do this to me?"

Naturally, he was referring to my solo initiative. He was right. There was no excuse.

"I was on duty tonight, and you slipped out right under my nose." He sounded upset. "And I didn't notice." He shook his head at himself.

There was more to it than just his anger with me. He was upset with himself for having missed my intentions. Had he paid better attention, he might have read the coming betrayal in my emotions. But he hadn't. He had trusted me.

Ben's disappointment stung like a thorn in my side.

Are you happy now? the voice mocked, taking advantage of my moment of clarity.

"Ben, I am sorry."

"No, Claire," he fumed. "Sorry is not good enough—"

He turned away and took a deep breath.

His wings were folded on his back, rising gently with the movement of his chest. When he exhaled, they quivered slightly.

I stared in awe.

"Do you have any idea what it was like to find your note with you gone?"

My head sank in guilt.

"Or the voicemail." He turned back, and his expression hadn't changed. "Thank God, I heard that one in time. Who knows what would have happened if we had shown up a minute later."

A minute, the voice in the back of my head joined the conversation. *You mean a second.*

Disappointment was still obvious in Ben's features, but there was something else I had never seen there before... And he was so anxiously trying to hide it.

"Ben, I am so sorry." I took a step toward him. "I know I made a mistake. But I couldn't just let this chance to see him go."

Ben looked at me with liquid steel eyes.

"He would have killed you. If we hadn't shown up, you would be dead now." He took a step toward me, his eyes denying the possibility of my death being caused by his slip. "I wouldn't be able to live with that."

"Ben—"

I wanted to tell him it wasn't up to him what I decided to do with my life...

He caught me off guard, pulling me into a tight embrace, and placed a kiss on my cheek.

I blinked at him in surprise and pushed myself gently away from him. "Ben..."

"I can't lose you, Claire."

Ben tilted his head to the side and looked at me from under his eyelashes. Why again did he have to look so much like Adam when he did that? Looking at him hurt. It was a constant reminder of what had happened to Adam.

We stood there for a minute or longer. There was nothing more I could tell him, and he knew it.

Ben was hurting, and it was my fault.

I was waiting for guilt to consume me when four figures appeared out of thin air right next to us.

"Jaden," I squeaked at the first one I recognized.

He didn't look up. He was busy holding down the struggling bundle that was hidden behind him and Jenna.

"Adam—" My hands flapped over my mouth like they were trying to catch the word before it was out.

"Stand back," Jaden instructed.

Ben's arm reflexively slung around my shoulders and pulled me to his side, further away from the four of them.

I got to my toes, trying to see around them.

Adam was half-lying, half-sitting on the Gallagers' library floor, hands and legs tied up. His face was hidden in the shadow of his black mane. Jaden and Jenna were holding him down while Chris's hands were lying on Adam's shoulders.

The struggling got less intense by the second and finally ceased completely.

"Oh my God," I couldn't keep myself from speaking. "Is he alright?"

Ben let go of me and took a step toward his half-brother, who was now lying there, motionless.

"I think so," Jenna answered my question. She let go of Adam and sat down on the floor beside him, right next to Chris, who wouldn't let go of Adam's shoulders.

Jaden was the only one still on alert. He checked the rope on Adam's wrists and ankles.

I followed Ben's lead and stepped closer. Adam's face was now clearly visible in the low light. It looked pale and cold.

"Are you sure he is alright?" I tried again.

Jaden abandoned his inspection and gave me a warning look.

"He is knocked out," he explained. "He'll live."

He grabbed my arm. "How could you do this?"

I was startled by his harsh tone.

"If I had told you about Adam's message earlier, you wouldn't have let me go—" I excused my actions.

"Adam sent you a message?" Jaden exploded. I had never seen him this furious. "And you didn't bother telling me?"

"I needed to see him."

"Do you have any idea what we all went through after Ben found your note?"

I shrank with every word he spoke. He was right. It had been wrong.

"If I'd seen another way, do you really think I would have gone?"

"You are right; if it had been up to me, you would have never walked out that door." Jaden was standing only an inch away from me. He pulled me against his chest and whispered in my ear. "You know what happens to me if I fail to keep you safe. This isn't just about you anymore."

"We were so worried," Jenna's voice came from behind Jaden. "I wish you would have trusted us enough to tell us."

Her hurt tone was even worse than Jaden's fury.

"I am sorry." My eyes wandered back toward Adam's limp body.

"Can't anyone see the positive side of this?" Chris got to his feet. "Yes, we all were worried and had to put ourselves at unnecessary risk. But, on the other hand—look what we came home with."

He gestured at his son, who was still and pale and none of us knew what to expect once he woke up.

"True." Jaden stepped away from me and knelt down beside Adam. "Who would have thought that we would capture him this fast."

"What next?" Ben was looking down at his brother with a crease on his forehead.

"We get him to talk," Jaden answered.

Jenna frowned at him, full of disapproval. "We will find out what he knows. But nobody will hurt him."

"Do we know what he is capable of?" Ben asked.

"He has tried to kill Claire twice. Isn't that enough?" Jaden answered icily.

Ben was right. I had felt his powers on my own body, and it hadn't been a mind-easing experience. None of us knew the full extent of his demon-powers.

"How can we make sure he doesn't attack when he wakes up?"

"Enough," Chris stopped us all. "This is my son we are talking about."

His eyes were glowing. The others had made their wings disappear, but Chris's wings were still floating at his sides.

"How long will he be asleep?" I finally dared to ask.

"A couple of hours maybe," Jaden estimated. "At least, that's how long it lasts for humans. I have never actually sent a demon to sleep like this before."

He looked at the Gallagers. "We need to be prepared for him to wake up earlier."

They all nodded in unison.

The way Adam was lying on the floor made my heart break.

"Can we put him on a bed?" I suggested.

The others looked at me.

"Or at least, put a pillow under his head?"

"We can put him in his room," Jenna agreed that Adam deserved better.

She exchanged a meaningful look with Chris.

"We left everything the way it was." Chris lifted Adam from the floor gently and started walking.

We followed him along the hallway until Jenna opened the door to the memories of the happiest days of my life.

Adam's room was exactly how I remembered it. The couch was covered in books, and one of Adam's shirts was draped over the armrest. The wrought iron bed was covered in the same plain red sheets it had the last time I laid there with Adam.

Goosebumps rose on my neck. The last time I had been here was the night Adam was hit by the demons. We had kissed right here in this room.

Chris walked toward the bed slowly. His wings were floating behind him. It was an image like that from an old bible. Except for the ropes on Adam's wrists and ankles.

I could see the love of a father for his son in every step he took. How he carefully placed Adam's head on a pillow and slid the blanket over his legs.

Jenna sat down on the edge of the bed and placed her hands on Adam's.

"Welcome home," she said and placed a kiss on his forehead.

Ben was watching them from a few feet away. There was conflict visible in his features.

He caught me staring and smoothed his expression. I gave him a smile.

This was good. Adam was alive. He was with us.

"I'll stay with him until he wakes up," Ben offered.

"Me, too." I wouldn't leave his side until I knew what was going on inside his head. I needed to know what he had meant earlier. If there was any part of him that still loved me.

"I'm not going to leave his side," Chris positioned himself on the other side of the bed.

"I guess we are all staying," Jaden noted and settled down on the couch, pulling me down with him.

"You need to rest," he told me and pulled me against his side.

It seemed he had forgiven me, and I relaxed under his touch when he placed his hand on my head and sent me into a dreamless sleep.

"... if he attacks."

"Let's assume he does. It's not safe for her to be here."

"She'll be target number one."

Low murmurs woke me up. I couldn't tell what time it was, but it was still dark outside. I closed my eyes again and listened to the voices.

"Should we get her out of here?" I made out Ben's whisper.

"It would be the smartest option. But where? Who can we trust to protect her in case Volpert decides to go after her?" Jaden pointed out. "And trust me, he will."

They were discussing shipping me off. I couldn't let that happen. Not now that Adam was finally within reach.

"Do you think they have figured out yet that he is gone?"

"Well, it's likely. But we can't be certain. If Adam was by himself when they met, there is a good chance the demons have no clue—" It was Chris. "But we haven't taken the time to ask Claire what exactly happened. Maybe we should wake her up—"

"I'm awake," I claimed. "I'll tell you everything, but please don't make me leave. I need to be here."

"You are awake," Jaden noted.

"For a while," I let him know I had heard everything.

I turned to Chris. "To answer your question, it was a trap. Maureen was there."

"Maureen? Adam's ex?" Ben asked incredulously.

"Exactly." The hair on my neck stood up at the thought of her.

"She is a demon?" Jenna wanted to know.

"Not sure." I wondered myself. She hadn't used any powers herself. All she had done was insult and threaten me and order Adam to kill me.

"She must have made Adam send the message. She seemed to control him somehow."

"What did she want?"

"She seemed to have been on a revenge trip. She claimed I stole Adam from her—which I didn't—"

"That's not entirely true," Chris interrupted.

What was he referring to? "I didn't even know Adam when they broke up."

"I remember the short period of time he was dating Maureen," Chris explained. "He was happy. And then, from one day to the next, he cut her out and started to fantasize about a *dream girl*."

That must have been the night he'd had the emotional vision of me. Adam hadn't known it was me then. He'd just been waiting to meet a face to match the vision. And he had been sure it wasn't Maureen.

Having experienced how painful it is to be rejected by Adam, even after all she had done to me, I felt sympathy for her.

"Anyway, Maureen had access to Adam. That means she must be connected to the demons somehow," I steered the topic away from my part in the jealousy drama. "She has a silver pendant just like Volpert."

"Can you draw it?" Jaden asked.

I wasn't much of an artist, but I could remember the pendant well enough to sketch it.

I nodded.

Jenna grabbed a piece of paper from the old davenport in the corner and handed it to me along with a pencil.

Jaden watched how I slowly guided the pencil over the white surface. When I was halfway through the curved pattern, he swiped the paper from under my hands and held it up.

"I recognize this—" he mused, holding it up in front of him. "It's a..."

A groan from the other part of the room claimed all our attention.

Adam was moving his head from side to side like he was having a bad dream.

"He is waking up." Chris teleported from the couch to the bed before he had even finished the sentence.

The others followed. I was the only one to walk at human speed.

I stood next to Jenna and Ben by the side of the bed, unable to move any closer.

Jaden and Chris were sitting on each side of Adam, both ready to react.

The tension was unbearable. I chewed my lower lip and waited.

When Adam's eyes fluttered, my teeth cut into my lip. I tasted blood, and my heart rate went up, my system all alert and prepared to run.

You have been waiting for this, the voice in my head came to life. *Are you really going to run?*

His eyes fell on Chris first.

"Welcome home, Adam," Chris spoke.

There was no hint of recognition in Adam's expression. His face remained a pale mask. He raised his arms and looked at the rope on his wrists.

Chris watched him with concern. Jaden was ready to do whatever was necessary.

Adam didn't try to free himself. Instead, he tried to sit up a little and realized his legs were also tied.

"I am so sorry, Adam," Jenna apologized when she helped him sit up so he could lean against the headboard. "This is a necessary precaution."

Adam looked back at the rope and then up at Ben, who had sat down on the bed next to Chris.

I watched the scene with growing concern. It seemed like he didn't recognize any of them.

He looked around the room for a while before he spotted me behind Jenna.

When he laid eyes on me, they were searching my face for something. Insufferable tension spread inside my chest. He saw me, but did he *see* me?

Adam blinked several times.

"Where am I?" he asked and closed his eyes.

His voice was low and rough like he had a dry throat. The sound matched his pale skin.

"You are home," Chris put his hand on Adam's shoulder lightly.

"This is not my home," Adam stated. Chris flinched.

"Where are the others?"

"Who is he talking about?" I heard Ben whisper at Jenna.

"My family," Adam answered Ben's question. "Volpert, Maureen, Blackbird—"

The three Gallagers turned almost as pale as Adam at the names he spoke.

"Adam, we are your family," Jenna finally spoke. "Chris, your father." She gestured at him. "Ben, your brother. And myself."

Adam took a long look at each of them before he finally turned to Chris.

"Can I go back to the others?"

Chris and Jenna exchanged one of their looks again. It was like a secret language only they understood.

"You look hungry, Adam," Chris finally said, evading Adam's request. "Why don't I get you something to eat?"

"I actually am hungry," he realized.

Jenna nodded.

"You got this?" Chris asked Jaden.

Jaden gave a thumbs up and moved closer.

"I'll get you something from the kitchen." Within a heartbeat, Chris was gone.

I was positive that he needed a moment alone to process things. It must be horrible for him. It certainly was for me, and I was only his—what was I?

Even though I still carried part of his soul inside of me, his angel-part was dead. He probably didn't even feel that he had marked me once.

I still didn't dare speak to him. I had been craving this moment that I could finally get answers. But now that it was here, I couldn't bring myself to speak.

It had been easier when he had been about to kill me. We had been alone. My disappointment had been mine and mine alone. Whatever Adam triggered now, everybody else in the room felt it as much as I did. Once more, I was transparent.

It was very quiet in the room. My heartbeat seemed to be the loudest sound. Jaden was sitting calmly, prepared to step in if necessary.

Adam had closed his eyes again. The way he was lying there stone-like, motionless, made my heart race in panic. It reminded me too much of a dead body.

Ben noticed my uneasiness and came closer, an arm outstretched to wrap it around me. I didn't object.

It was less than five minutes when Chris returned with a small, sandwich-loaded tray in his hands and Antonio at his heels.

Chris set the tray down on the bedside table while Antonio trotted up to the bed. His snout nudged Adam's arm lightly, and he gave a soft bark. The dog obviously recognized Adam. That was a good thing.

Adam reached out his bound hands slowly to touch the dog's head, and his fingertips brushed the soft, brown fur.

Jenna smiled at the gesture. I almost wanted to join her at the sign of recall, but my smile froze before it had a chance to spread on my face.

Antonio yelped and, within seconds, sagged to the floor. There was no sign of life left in him.

We all stared at the dog, horror-struck. What had just happened?

"Thank you," Adam broke the silence. "I do feel much better."

Jaden was the first to react. He seized Adam's hands at the wrists and jerked them out of reach of Jenna, who jumped off the bed.

Chris knelt down to check on Antonio and shook his head. The dog was dead.

I felt all the pain of the past months and all the bottled-up fear break free from my chest and shower down on Adam as I screamed at him in exasperation.

"You just killed your dog! Why on earth would you kill your dog?"

The Gallagers stared at me, alarmed and surprised by my reaction.

Adam's eyes locked on mine. They had more life than earlier tonight.

"He said he would get me something to eat." His tone was apologetic. "I thought the dog—"

Adam looked down at the dead body. Then his gaze fell on the bedside table, and it hit him.

"The sandwiches—" he muttered, apprehension written in his features, "—not the dog—"

For a second, I felt the urge to laugh at the absurdity of what had just happened. The next second, I grasped the meaning of it. Adam gained his energy from other creatures. He fed off souls like demons did.

Chris disappeared with the dead dog.

"Time for nice is over," Jaden announced. "We need to know what you know."

Adam eyed my guardian angel innocently.

"Let's start easy. What's your name?" Jaden demanded.

"Everybody calls me Adam," Adam replied, confusion surfacing in his features.

"Who are we?" Jaden pushed.

"I have never met any of you in my life." Adam's eyes wandered back to me. "Except for her."

"What do you know about her?" Jaden's tone was harsh. I was glad he was on my side.

"She is the target," Adam admitted. "Volpert said she needs to die."

We looked at each other for a moment. There was something about his gaze that told me there was more. It was the same thing he hadn't told me earlier. Whatever reason he had to kill me, it hadn't been him to put the target on my back.

As Maureen had mentioned, Adam was a tool.

"And yet, you didn't kill her," Jaden continued his interrogation. "You had the chance twice, and you didn't follow through."

"That's because I am weak." Adam lowered his gaze, embarrassed.

"That's because, deep down, you know there is more to this girl than whatever Volpert has told you," Ben reminded his brother.

"There is something familiar about her. Like I know her from a different life—"

It was unbearable to hear him speak about me in third-person when I was standing right there. My legs carried me toward the bed before I could stop them.

I sat down just out of his reach and folded my hands in my lap.

"But it's not just him who wants you dead," Adam finally spoke to me. "Maureen wants it, too."

"Why?" Jaden wanted to know.

"I don't know exactly." Adam looked lost. "They all keep talking about revenge—but I can't remember... anything."

Chris returned as Adam was speaking. He gave Jenna another look and came to stand beside me.

Adam looked up at Chris. "I am sorry about your dog."

Chris nodded.

"What's the first thing you *can* remember?" Jaden pushed, ignoring the moment.

If Adam could feel remorse, there must be a spark of good left in him.

"It's not far back. I woke up in the dark, and I had to dig myself out of the soil," Adam diverged into his oldest memory. "I was in a graveyard. It was raining."

Adam's eyes were gazing into the past as he sat up. Jaden moved closer, ready to act, but Adam stayed still.

"I ran—I ran until I realized I wouldn't get tired. I hid in the woods. And then they found me."

He was speaking of the demons again.

"I was alone and scared. I couldn't remember who I was. They took me in. They showed me how to feed. They explained to me how my powers work—they saved me." His eyes returned to the present. "They are the only family I have."

My heart sank with every sentence he spoke. He couldn't remember who he was or who he had been. That meant that he really didn't remember his family or me.

Chris sighed quietly beside me.

"If I had known, I would have stayed and waited for you to wake up," he promised. "I would have protected you. You are my son. I would have done anything to bring you home safely."

Adam eyed his father, his face guarded.

"Did Volpert tell you who you are?" Jaden went back to questioning Adam.

He shook his head. "I am a demon; that's all I know. I exist to punish those who hurt our cause."

I shuddered. The man who was sitting on the bed was nothing like the Adam I had known. He was like a fragment of a broken vase.

"You are more than that," Chris informed Adam. "You have angelic heritage. You died to protect Claire—" Chris gestured at me.

"Why would I protect her?"

Adam's words were like a dagger to my heart. His expression was suddenly cautious.

"Volpert warned me you would try to turn me. You would sweet-talk me, give me a reason to doubt that she deserves to die." Adam reached out his bound hands toward me.

"Enough," Jaden shot at him just before his skin could touch my arm. "You won't touch Claire." He looked ready to throttle Adam, who pulled back his hands immediately.

I could only imagine what was going on inside Jaden's head. He saw the threat right in front of him, and yet he couldn't get rid of Adam like he would have disposed of any other demon.

"Claire, move away from him," Jaden instructed.

"He won't hurt me," I insisted, but I slid back until I was next to Adam's feet, knowing better than to challenge Jaden. Adam's eyes didn't blink as he continued to look at me.

"That's enough for today," Chris finally decided.

Jaden agreed. "It's late at night. We all need some rest."

I watched Chris gently push Adam back into the pillows and Adam's eyes close at his touch. He was putting him to sleep the same way as he had earlier.

Jenna and Ben had watched everything quietly. I had almost forgotten they were there when Ben spoke.

"What are we going to do?"

Chris shook his head. "We need to find a way to bring back his memory."

"It's worse than I had expected," Jenna joined in. "He seems to be loyal to them. As long as he can't remember who he really is, this is going to be impossible to deal with."

"I hate to agree," Jaden spoke in a heavy voice. "But if we don't get him to remember, it might be too dangerous to keep him alive—"

"Don't even think that," I fired at him. "Don't you dare consider that. It is *not* an option."

He couldn't honestly believe that I would stand by and let him execute Adam.

"Chris," I looked to him for help.

Judging from the look on Chris's face, I knew I had an ally. Chris wouldn't let his son die, neither would Jenna or Ben.

"We need a way to control him, though," Jenna suggested. "You saw how fast he killed Antonio. We didn't even realize what he was doing until it was too late."

"We can't let our guard down," Chris agreed.

The Gallagers and Jaden watched Adam sleep for a minute or two before they decided who would take the first watch.

"You go to bed," Jenna instructed Ben and me and ushered us out the door.

Jenna, Chris, and Jaden stayed behind, discussing arrangements and potential scenarios.

"Doesn't look good," Ben commented as we were walking down the hall, side by side.

I wasn't sure what he meant. Not good for Adam, for me, for all of us? But I didn't bother asking. My head was full with the events of the evening.

"Good night, Ben."

I slouched down to the guest room, not even bothering to look where I was setting my stumbling feet, too tired to pay attention. All I could think of was that *he* was alive; in whatever obscure way he existed, all that mattered to me right now was *that* he existed.

It was a miracle how I had made it through the night without exploding.

My hand pulled back the sheets, and I climbed in, fully dressed, unable to think straight.

All of the bliss of that unbelievable moment when Adam had recognized that it was me, the moment he had reacted to me, was replaying in my mind, and all I could do was be the quiet observer; I had no chance of turning my brain off, of calming. I was caught in an endless loop. Adam was just a few rooms away. He was really there. It still felt like a dream.

My body was heavy as it finally hit the pillows. I felt as if I was sinking through the mattress into the ground.

Get a grip, I told myself and inhaled deeply and exhaled quietly and slowly, trying to calm down and process what had happened.

I was dead-exhausted, but the scene kept spinning in my mind, and Adam was the center of everything. His eyes, his hands, his face, his vicious glare as he had approached me.

I was sure he had recognized me. It had been obvious in his face. He had spoken my name.

Of course, he recognized you, the voice in my head mocked. *You are his target. He will end you.*

20.
Interconnected

It was 4:17 in the morning. Despite exhaustion, I hadn't slept at all. The fact that Adam was only a few rooms away was keeping me up.

I needed to find a way to confront him alone. At least, without the whole family watching. Something told me he would be more receptive to my words than to anyone else.

If I waited too long, I might not get the chance. And I couldn't sleep, so why prolong the wait?

My toes touched the wooden floor noiselessly. A few steps to the door. I would sneak out of the room like I had done the night before.

When I reached the hallway, there was a crack of light visible from the other end. The door to Adam's room wasn't shut completely. There was no sound to be heard except for my accelerated breath.

I rushed toward the seam of light, always careful to not fall over my own feet and wake up the entire house, and gently pushed the door open.

Adam was lying in the exact same position as he had been when I left. Jaden was sitting at his side. He looked up when he heard me tiptoe toward the bed.

"You are not supposed to be here," he whispered.

"I can't sleep," I justified my presence.

Jaden's face showed that he felt how much I needed to be here. He wouldn't throw me out.

"Is he still sleeping?" I crawled onto the bed beside Jaden and settled there.

He bobbed his head.

"Can I talk to him?"

"You can tell him anything you want," Jaden informed me. "But I doubt he will hear it. He is in deep sleep."

I wasn't sure if Jaden was right. He had erred once in assuming I wouldn't feel anything or hear anything when he had put me to sleep like he had Adam. At the demons' house, I had been aware of everything—it had just felt like a dream.

"Is it safe to touch his hands?" I asked Jaden's opinion.

"As long as he doesn't wake, he can't do you any harm."

I scooted closer and lay my hand on Adam's. The mere touch comforted me. It made Adam real.

"You have no idea how much I have missed you these past months," I whispered.

I refused to look at him as an evil creature. Even if the glorious angel had died, he was still Adam—to a certain extent.

My mind replayed his funeral for me in a vicious attempt to pull me back into the darkness and pain.

I didn't let it. Adam was alive. I was touching his precious hands in mine right now. I could feel his skin. He was alive.

My heart felt hot for a second. Just like the broken part was sealing itself back together.

Jaden was examining me from the side as I slowly bent over and placed a kiss on Adam's forehead.

He was taking in every input he could possibly get, reading my emotions, just so he would be prepared to react in case he needed to.

However prepared he was, he wasn't ready to handle what happened the moment my lips brushed Adam's skin.

Adam freed his arms and legs in a swift movement; he tore the ropes by simply pulling his wrists and ankles apart.

He must have stayed bound by choice if it was this easy for him to free himself.

His hands grasped my shoulders within a fraction of a second.

I jerked back, surprised by his sudden action. He let me pull back half a foot before he locked me in place. Just far enough that I could see his eyes burst open.

Jaden moved at my side. I saw him reach for Adam's arm in an attempt to free me. Adam was faster. His hand released my arm for an indistinct moment, and Jaden crashed to the floor on the other side of the bed, out of sight.

"Is he dead?" my voice found its way out of my mouth.

Adam's eyes were staring at me unblinking. They weren't staring *at* me, they were staring right *into* me.

"Just knocked out." His voice was husky.

I took a deep breath, relieved that the hit hadn't been fatal. Knowing Jaden, he would be awake in no time.

Adam's expression claimed my attention. There was a hunger in his gaze I had seen before. He was craving my soul.

My heart was flying at an uncontrollable speed. I felt sweat on my neck. And then I felt a hollow echo around my stomach.

I had never experienced anything like it. It was like hunger, but not for food. I needed pure energy, and I could sense it in the air.

Adam was observing me with his pale-green eyes, his hands still clutching my arms.

Something inside of me urged me to run. I ignored that more sane part of me easily at the sight of Adam's face. I wasn't afraid.

My hands found their way onto Adam's chest by themselves. They were searching for something intangible. Something I wanted to rip from him. A new type of excitement surged inside of me.

Adam let go of me and pushed my hands aside.

The moment his touch disappeared, I sank back, my sensations back to normal. What had just happened? A wave of shame washed over me.

"Who are you?" he requested, watching every single one of my emotions cross my face.

"Claire," I used the easiest option.

I waited for him to attack me, but he didn't. Instead, he watched me with curiosity while I fidgeted nervously.

"I know that," Adam informed me. "Everybody keeps telling me, you are Claire—" He lifted a hand and pulled a strand of hair that had gotten caught on a button of my blouse back behind my shoulder.

This simple gesture was like a soothing balm. I wanted to lean into him and put my arms around him, but this time, I listened to the voice that was calling for caution.

"—but who is this Claire?" His eyes scarched mine. "Why do they want you dead? What did you do to upset them?"

It was difficult to hold his gaze. It was intense, almost burning. I couldn't answer right away.

"You won't believe me if I tell you," I challenged him, well-aware that I was at his mercy. He could kill me at any moment if he decided to. But there was something about the way he was looking at me for answers that made me confident I had a few more hours to live.

"I have no memories of my past, Claire." He gave me a look that induced pity. "But your face has been haunting my dreams."

I froze. He had been haunting my dreams.

"You keep showing up, and my dark dreams become bright and colorful. It's like you own the key to a different me. Someone I might have been but cannot find inside myself anymore.

"Help me figure out who I am by telling me who you are."

I sat there for a while, letting his words sink in. How much could I tell him? Would he believe me? I simply had to try. I didn't know how much time we had left before Jaden would wake up.

"Adam, it is not important who I am. What is important is who you were."

I drew up all the courage I could find and told Adam what he needed to hear.

"Adam, you were born a hybrid. One of your parents was part-angel the other one part-demon.

"Not too long ago, you were hit in a fight, and part of your hybrid-being died."

I tried to stick to the truth as much as I could without exposing anyone.

"That's when you lost your memory. And when you lost your memory of your angel-past, you lost all memory of me."

Adam was hanging on my every word.

"I was part of that angel-past." I swallowed at the images that were flaring up in my mind. "I used to be an important part of your life."

"How important?" he demanded.

"Very important," I said quietly.

"Most important," Adam mused.

The way he said it made me smile. It made him appear almost human.

"Why do they want to take revenge on you?" he asked after watching me with tightened eyes for a minute.

"I got away twice." What was the point in denying it? "The first time I got away, another demon was killed."

"You killed him?" Adam interrupted.

"No," I had to laugh. "I am not that strong. I was being held and tortured to get to you. Someone else made sure I got out safely and disposed of Alabaster on our way out." What had happened at the demons' house seemed like a different life to me now.

"The second time?" Adam wanted to know.

"You stepped in before they could kill me." The memory of the horrible night on the roof filled my head and I flinched. "I wish it had been me."

"That's how that other part of me died?"

I nodded, unable to speak.

Adam's hand was on my arm within a heartbeat and warmth spread through my body.

"You would have given your life for me?"

I nodded again, finding myself yet again incapable of denying him anything.

"Who are you, Claire?" he repeated his question.

The moment it was out, I knew I would give him an answer even if that would cost me my life.

"I was your soulmate."

Adam's face was serious. The hunger was back in his eyes. I felt it, too. It was spreading through my body like adrenaline.

Something on the side moved. I made out Jaden from the corner of my eye.

"Goodbye, Claire," Adam said and removed his hand from me.

Jaden leapt across the bed like an attacking predator, but all he hit was the empty spot beside me. Adam was gone.

"Are you alright?" Jaden asked as he rolled over and sat beside me. "Did he hurt you?"

If Jaden had experienced any of the scene that had been going on a minute earlier, he wouldn't ask. He would know that Adam wasn't going to hurt me—not if it was up to him.

I shrugged. He was the one we should be worried about as he was the one Adam had attacked.

"Are you?"

"Fine," he reassured me with a glance down his chest. "Where did he go?"

Both our eyes automatically searched the part of the bed previously filled with Adam and found empty sheets.

Naturally, none of the Gallagers were happy about Adam's disappearance. Chris was especially affected. He had been counting on having a little more time with his son.

"He has amnesia," I repeated for the third or fourth time. "I believe him. He can't remember who I am."

If there was any memory of us left in him, he wouldn't have left. He would be with me, holding me, kissing me. He wasn't.

Ben carried a plate of toast to the kitchen table while Jenna and Chris were placing cutlery between the dishes.

The Gallagers had decided it was time to send Geoffrey on vacation for a while. Too much was going on, and they couldn't risk that he found out about the family secret.

Thinking about the kind man, I couldn't imagine he was suspecting anything. It was right they had taken precautions to eliminate risk for him.

He would be visiting his nephew in Seattle for two weeks. Enough time for things to turn either direction.

"We need to get him back." It was Jenna.

Chris nodded.

While they were discussing ways to track Adam and bring him back, my thoughts took a different direction. I felt Adam's hands on my arms again, the way he had looked at me as if I had the answers to all of his questions.

"Something really strange happened when he was touching me," I remembered aloud. An image of Adam's hungry eyes and my own craving flared up in my head.

I gave a brief summary of what had happened, watching Jaden's mouth open in astonishment as I proceeded.

"This is unexpected," he commented on my revelation. "I have never heard about anything like it."

Ben gazed at me over a slice of toast. There was a heaviness to his look that made me want to hug him. It must be difficult for him to learn so much bad news about his brother.

I smiled at him in a pang of sympathy. Ben didn't return the smile. He speared the butter with his knife and spread it on his bread with his full attention.

By now, I had gotten used to being readable to everyone in the room. But the way my body had reacted to Adam's touch—like it had been mimicking his emotions, his sensations, and his desires. That was something entirely new to me.

"It is like a connection that surpasses death—considering Adam's angel-self is dead, and so is his human-self.

"Maybe it's time we bring in someone who has recently helped us," Jaden completed his thoughts with a serious look in my direction.

There was only one person who I could think of who this applied to—Liz.

When we filled in the others on the plan to involve Liz to find out more about this strange connection between Adam and me, I could already see it in their faces. They were hoping—whatever this connection was—that it would eventually lead us to Adam.

It wasn't much later that we were walking up the stairs to the library. The street behind us was busy with Monday morning traffic.

It was before opening hours. We would stop by briefly to get the facts we needed and then head off to school. I simply couldn't afford to miss any more days.

I pulled out the keys.

When we walked through the entrance door, Liz was standing behind the counter, typing on her phone while balancing a cup of coffee in one hand.

"Hi, Liz," I tore her from her activities.

"Good morning," she looked up, her expression full of pre-caffeine disapproval and post-weekend grogginess.

"It's Monday, Claire," Liz questioned my entrance. "What are you doing here?"

Her voice was concerned as she watched me approach the counter, but her bronze face lit up with a broad and knowing smile the second she noticed Jaden beside me.

He had turned into a fifty-something in the car on our way here.

Why? I had asked him.

To get the right answers even faster, he had informed me with an insightful expression.

I had refrained from asking further questions. I was sure he had a plan. He always did. If appearing as somebody who could be my father worked, then so be it.

"Good morning, Mrs. Martinez," Jaden fashioned one of his brightest smiles.

Liz lowered her coffee cup to the counter and straightened out her maroon sheath dress. Her black hair hid her face when she looked down to check the flowers on the narrow belt.

"Please, call me Liz."

"Very well, Liz. Jaden Ableton." Jaden shook her hand slowly.

I watched Liz stare at Jaden for a moment before I dared interrupt.

"Liz, do you have a minute?"

She tore her gaze away from Jaden and gave me her full attention. She probably saw the questions in my face.

"What's the matter, Claire?" Liz wanted to know. "Judging by your out-of-schedule appearance, there is something you need my help with. Am I right?" She was the bold Latina I remembered.

She leaned back against the counter and folded her arms, waiting to hear our request.

"Liz," Jaden took over. "We are so entirely grateful for your help with Chris Gallager." He thanked her.

"He knows?" Liz asked me without taking her eyes off Jaden, her face suddenly blank.

"He does." I was tired and wanted to get this over with, so I didn't care much for formalities. After all of the knowledge we had shared, I knew I could trust Liz with Jaden's secret.

"I know more than you can imagine," Jaden beat me to it. "Thank you for so effectively protecting our secrets and for guarding our history."

Liz's eyes widened in awe when she realized what his words meant. She dropped her head to her chest, bowing to Jaden.

"It's an honor, Mr. Ableton."

Jaden lay one finger under her chin and lifted up her head. "The honor is mine. Please know that your work and your loyalty to the The Guard are seen and appreciated."

Liz's cheeks blushed. I couldn't tell if she had ever met an angel before, but it was obvious how devoted she was to her job in the secret organization.

"Everything you told me about the meditation worked, Liz. Chris is fine." I let her know that she had helped us a great deal.

Liz turned to me and smiled the smile of a blind believer who had been rewarded with sight.

"What can I help you with?" She checked her watch. "We have forty minutes before business hours. Coffee?"

She still looked slightly dazed when she led us to the small kitchen in the back.

"Well, there is an issue we need your opinion on," Jaden started.

Liz listened to him while getting us a fresh cup of coffee.

"We recently got into a situation that requires knowledge about a particular type of hybrid. What do you know about angel-demon hybrids?"

She looked at our expectant faces and held out our cups. "I know all the literature by heart. You need to give me more context."

Jaden gave me an unreadable look.

"The second Gallager son returned from the dead," he filled Liz in. "We found out that he must have demonic heritage. He returned as one of them. To make things worse, he is suffering from amnesia.

"But there is one thing that is particularly disturbing about the situation—"

I flinched at his phrasing.

"—he has a connection to Claire we don't fully understand. When he touched her, she felt his hunger for her soul, and she got the same craving."

Liz was inhaling every word Jaden was speaking. The way her eyebrows were knitting together let me guess that she was searching her memory for related knowledge. What I couldn't guess was if she was finding anything.

"I've also seen him during meditation," I completed the information. "I've had dreams about him that seemed real."

She took a sip of coffee. "That's an interesting twist."

"You've heard about those connections?" Jaden's voice was hopeful.

"I have read about them." Liz's mind was still working hard to retrieve every piece that might help us. "Angel-demon hybrids. When their *good* half dies, their mark doesn't get lost. The connection transforms."

She sounded like she was reading from a book, her eyes going back and forth like rushing over lines.

"Part of the hybrid's soul remains in the mark. This part keeps looking for a way to heal. It feels the darkness its original owner dives into once the hybrid transforms into a demon.

"Claire, have you felt anything before Adam touched you?" She interrupted her lecture.

"I have." I nodded eagerly. "I have woken up from dreams on adrenaline rushes. I have felt exploding energy while seeing visions of him during meditation—"

"That's the type of thing I was looking for," Liz interrupted.

Jaden was leaning against the fridge, obviously amazed by how Liz's mind worked.

"Contextus Daemonicus," she chanted in amazement.

Question marks were floating from my eyes.

"Contextus Daemonicus. It's a theory. If a hybrid loses their angel-part, the connection stays intact but changes since with the angel-part's death, the soul dies.

"The theory says that the connection doesn't happen by choice but by a prior Contextus Angelicus, or the *mark* as you call it."

"What's the difference?" I voiced my confusion.

Jaden straightened up a little. He, too, seemed to have questions.

"Contextus Angelicus is a connection caused by the mutual exchange of a fraction of both sides' souls. It is triggered by the first wings-spreading of a newborn angel," Liz answered my question.

I remembered the moment Adam had marked me. The white light radiating from within him, the glowing eyes, bright-green, and the beautiful pair of white wings. My chest tightened. I would never see this glorious version of Adam ever again.

"The Contextus Angelicus is pure. It doesn't hurt either involved party. But there are drawbacks—you have experienced what it means when the mark is being abused to get hold of the corresponding angel." She looked me deep in the eye.

I raised an eyebrow and nodded my head. I did know. I had experienced it for myself when Alabaster and his subordinates had tortured me to get to Adam.

Jaden crossed the narrow kitchen in two quick strides and wrapped one consoling arm around me. Of course, he had read my emotions. If he put two and two together, he would know exactly where my mind was.

His hand squeezed my arm, and my head automatically dropped against his shoulder.

Liz eyed us for a moment. I wasn't sure what the scene looked like to her—

"The Contextus Angelicus binds both parties to each other, but it doesn't burden them. It makes them stronger," Liz picked up where she had interrupted her explanation.

"The Contextus Daemonicus, on the other hand, would be a residue of the Contextus Angelicus. It is an escalation of the former angel's—now demon—search to regain his missing other half. Of course, his own soul is gone, but there is a fraction still alive on this planet; it is preserved in the mark.

"The second the residual soul senses the existence of the former angel, it will reach out. It normally happens in dreams."

"Or meditations," Jaden interrupted.

Liz nodded. "It is the soul's ultimate call for reunion."

"This sounds good. I am waiting for the catch." I lifted my head from Jaden's shoulder and took a sip of coffee.

"Well, there is." Liz gave me a serious look.

I gulped the coffee down, preparing myself for whatever was about to come.

"The Contextus Daemonicus starts off as harmless dreams for both sides. When ignored, it can become daydreams or visions.

"The scary thing about it is that everything is real. Whatever the demon feels or does, there is an increasing chance, as time progresses, that the mark will feel everything."

"Makes sense," Jaden said, accepting Liz's explanation. "Whenever Adam was feeding, you were able to feel it. It is like a rush of energy. Or adrenaline. All the force of his demonic powers. You know, like at school when you almost fainted…"

The thought of that experience made my knees shaky. Jaden pulled me tighter to steady me.

I remembered the adrenaline rush, the energy—I was grateful he left the part about my steamy dreams out of the conversation. There had been so many times I had felt Adam. It had felt real. Now, if their theory was correct, it meant it was.

"Your souls are still interlaced. Even if the part of his soul that had remained in his body is dead, the part that lives inside of you is looking for a way home."

Liz nodded as Jaden continued her thoughts.

"You two are probably the only pair being connected like this. It is unique." Her eyes popped with excitement.

Now I felt more like a science project. But she seemed to have struck a chord with Jaden.

"I have seen that angels' marks suffer when their angels get killed. I have seen them go insane—"

Jaden looked at her then eyed me from the side, his gaze measuring my expression.

"—but a Contextus Daemonicus—I never thought it was possible. You seem to be healing and yet suffering. Your soul knows he's alive. But by every demonic action he is taking, he is weakening you."

"That explains how you have been feeling all those things," Jaden was satisfied with Liz's theory. "You get weak when he does. You are hungry when he is. You feel strong when he does."

I listened to them as they were explaining my mood swings. It made sense—kind of. After all, Adam and I were permanently linked through him marking me when he had spread his wings. But if he was dead—if his angel-self was truly dead—would he ever truly remember me? Would his memory return, and would he ever love me again? Right now, he saw a target when he looked at me. Nothing more, nothing less.

21.
Traces

Jaden was quiet on our way to school. The conversation with Liz had given us a lot to think about.

We will need to fill in the others tonight, he had said with a stern face.

He was right. Even though this part of Adam's resurrection concerned mainly me, the others needed to know. We needed to be prepared.

We were sitting in silence, each of us following our own train of thought.

Mine was going through all the times I had seen Adam in my dreams. Each emotion, each sensation... everything. A collage of memories.

The crease on Jaden's forehead slowly disappeared as he changed back to his teenage appearance the moment we hit the main street, but the pensive expression remained.

What was it like for him? He always knew things... And then with Chris's lost powers, and now with this weird connection...

My brain ran through the dialogue over and over again. Contextus Daemonicus.

The thought that Adam and I were still connected lightened my heart, but the nature of the connection made me slightly uncomfortable. Everything I had felt was real. Every energy rush, every dream…

My mind flashed back to the countless dreams of Adam. The first dream, where he had floated away from me. It had been shortly after the funeral.

I couldn't put together the full meaning of it then. It seemed, though, like that particular dream must have occurred when he had awoken as a demon. Following Liz's logic, this would be an explanation.

Or the heat waves a while ago in class, when I had felt Adam's touch—there must be some reason I drifted into that sensation for a minute. I envisioned Adam dreaming of me the same way. Would I ever find out if he had?

The energy-rush—Adam must have fed just before. My shoulders shook involuntarily as I shuddered at the thought of Adam feeding on another being's soul.

Jaden's eyes automatically found mine.

"Are you sure you are okay to go?" He made sure I was up to the challenge of a full day of classes.

His hand reached out to gently stroke my cheek.

Warmth momentarily spread through my system, and I leaned back and relaxed, drowning out all my thoughts until we stopped in front of the school building.

Going to school was a risk but a calculated one. We knew that Adam wasn't as dangerous to me as we had thought at first, and I desperately had to catch up with classes, otherwise—even if the demons never caught me—there wouldn't be a future to look forward to.

Jaden would be in every class with me. Jenna had agreed to stay on call for the morning, and Ben would pick me up after school and make sure I arrived at the Gallagers' safely.

Students were trickling in from all directions as we were walking up to the entrance.

It was like a second reality to my life. There was school, and then there were the Gallagers and Jaden and the constant fear of the demons.

The fact that Jaden would sit through this with me comforted me.

After all we'd been through, he was still at my side. He had risked everything to keep me safe. And yet, I had to treat him like any other student when we were at Aurora High.

"You can do this," he said when he opened the door for me. "Just focus. The day will be over in no time."

I gave him a wry smile.

For now, focus was what I needed. I had to make it through the finals. There was no alternative.

We headed to class with everyone else. Greg and Amber were sitting together when we walked through the door.

They both looked up. Amber's face didn't show any sign of dismay.

I exhaled in relief. Amber had not been happy when Jaden had started giving me more attention than her. I had been too caught up in my second reality to talk to her about it. But what would I have told her?

Obviously, she had gotten over it fast.

I noticed that Greg's hand was resting on her wrist. There was something different about the way they looked together. They looked *together*.

My mouth rolled into a smile at the sight of them, and Amber gave me a look that screamed *I need to talk to you!*

I want to know everything, I mouthed to her.

She giggled in return and Greg watched her with admiration.

It had finally happened. Amber and Greg. They were a beautiful couple. I was honestly happy for them.

I walked up to my usual desk and sat down, enveloped in a layer of gratitude. Gratitude that the first reality of my life still held pleasant surprises such as Amber and Greg.

Holding on to this positive emotion made it surprisingly easy to pay attention during classes. Plus, knowing that Adam was alive, that we still had a connection—that he had refrained from killing me when he'd had the chance—was like a secret talisman I was carrying in my heart.

It was a good feeling to be catching up on things, to feel a little bit of normality, and to take a step toward putting school behind me. I hadn't really decided what to do after high school.

College was still far away. I couldn't think about it with everything going on. Who knew how my story would end. If Adam never regained his memory…

After class, Jaden and I were walking toward the cafeteria when a hollow feeling hit my stomach. It wasn't hunger for the food that was presented in the displays and the dishes people were carrying on their trays.

It was the type of hunger I had felt when Adam had touched me. I was craving energy. Not the energy that was freed when sugar was burned in your system but pure life-energy. Souls. I stopped near a window outside the cafeteria, no longer sure I would be able to sit down and pretend like nothing was going on.

What was happening to me? Was Adam hungry? Would he be feeding—killing? Would I be able to control myself? Would I do the same?

I suddenly didn't trust myself anymore.

Jaden was right behind me. I turned toward him in a silent cry for help and looked into his alarmed face.

He grabbed my arm and locked me to his side.

"You need to focus, Claire," he told me as he pulled me toward the wall.

I heard him as though through a thick haze and dropped my chin to let him know I'd heard him.

I had felt Adam before, but this was so much more potent than any of the visions of him I'd had. It was like I was him. Like he had left his traces on me.

"What can I do?" Jaden asked, helpless. He was still clutching my arm, appearing indecisive about whether it was safe to let go.

The sensation was slowly creeping through my body, making it impossible to think straight.

Jaden's grasp tightened when he felt my increasing panic.

I didn't know how long we had been standing like this when relief washed through me in a slow wave, clearing every inch of my system.

The haze lifted, and I was able to think straight. Everything felt normal. Except for the knowledge of what the relief must mean—Adam had killed.

"Claire?" By the sound of Jaden's voice, my face must have been ashen.

The thought of what had just happened made me nauseous. I could feel the color leave my skin.

He grabbed my other arm under the elbow, making sure that I wouldn't stumble.

"Adam just fed." I put the past minute into words that made it sound more harmless than it actually was. My voice was almost casual.

An echo of the energy-rush I had experienced before flowed through my body. I could feel the blood return to my cheeks.

Jaden couldn't be fooled by words. He grasped the meaning before I had finished the last word. He saw my face change—ashen to pink. He felt how I was suddenly steady on my legs, and he perceived my energy-rush second-hand.

What worried me most was that the connection with Adam had become stronger since he had touched me. It wasn't just a faint vision; it was physical sensation.

"Don't leave me alone," I begged Jaden as fear crept up my spine. I would have to go through school days until the finals. I needed someone who would cover for me if I blacked out like this again.

It was dangerous to experiment with something we didn't fully understand in a public environment.

You could ditch school, a familiar voice in my head suggested.

It was an appealing thought. Easy. Just ignore this one reality and drift over into the other one completely.

Not quite yet, I silenced it. I needed to progress in normal reality. Independent of the supernatural roller coaster I was riding on a daily basis.

Jaden let go of my arms but stepped beside me like he was clarifying where he saw his place. He would be at my side. He knew exactly what I meant.

"Thank you." He would feel my gratitude, but it felt right to say it aloud anyway.

He smiled deliberately before he looked around. "Shall we?"

Nobody had noticed us standing there for a few minutes. We simply melted back into the stream of students and were off to the next class like nothing had happened.

I made it through the rest of the classes without another trace of Adam's powers or cravings.

It was easy to focus again—I had to. This simple fact was a motivator to get me through the day until Ben would pick me up.

Jaden had to disappear for a few hours this afternoon, but he didn't leave before he had delivered me safely to Ben, who was taking the afternoon shift.

He had been quiet since Adam's return from the dead. I wasn't sure where we were standing, and I wasn't looking forward to the alone-time with him.

The tension between us had never really eased. Even after our last encounter—I didn't really dare think of it—the kiss—I hadn't had time to set things straight.

Let me know when you change your mind again, he had said.

Foolish as I was, I hadn't told him, then and there, that there was no way it would be possible. I wouldn't change my mind—even with the undeniable attraction I had felt for Ben.

Ben drove silently, his eyes on the traffic like he was avoiding a conversation.

I wasn't certain how much I would suffer for the moment of weakness I'd had with Ben, but the torment would be just.

I would take his silence. I would even take it if he was angry at me. The only thing I wouldn't take was losing his friendship. Too much had happened, and I couldn't imagine walking into the Gallagers' house without being on good terms with Ben.

When the car stopped in front of the house, I looked up in surprise. I hadn't noticed we had arrived.

"Thanks for picking me up." I let Ben know how much I appreciated his effort.

He gave me the first smile of the day. His silent mood from the drive seemed to be gone the moment he opened the door for me.

"Did you learn something today?" His smile was still in place.

I couldn't help but return it. "As a matter of fact, I did."

Ever since the strange conversation with Adam, I felt better. It was easier to smile, easier to focus, easier to function. I guess I could call it hope. There was hope—hope that he would one day wake up and remember...

We walked up the stairs, side by side.

Ben stopped in front of the guest room, his features full of expectation.

I didn't understand at once what his intentions were, but then it hit me when he took my hand and ran his fingers over my palm.

Something inside of me rebelled.

"A lot has changed since the last time we've been alone like this." Ben looked at me, his eyes liquid steel.

They were echoing the hope I had felt moments before.

I couldn't do more than stare and watch him lean in. He was about to repeat what had happened before.

The rebelling part of me curled up and purred. What was going on? Did I want this?

I searched myself for answers but couldn't find one in time before Ben had reached his aim.

His lips brushed mine gently. It was just a brief moment, but it was enough to draw back in surprise when my heart took a tiny, joyous leap.

I found myself staring at the door, embarrassed and ashamed.

Every beat in remembrance of Adam's existence, I reminded myself.

"Ben—I can't—" My eyes remained glued on the door.

Ben wound his hands more tightly around mine, unwilling to let go.

I knew there was something there—something I couldn't ignore. A pool of affection for Ben had built up over the past weeks. It would be foolish to pretend there wasn't anything there.

Ben knew it, too, and he was brave enough to act on it.

If only my heart didn't belong to his older brother... I would have a chance at a fresh start. After all, the love of my life didn't even remember me.

But my heart knew better than that. My soul was Adam's.

Ben was waiting patiently for me to make a move.

I let him wait for a long moment, considering all of the recent events and findings. The answer I came up with remained the same. Angel or demon—I was Adam's. In darkness and in light.

"Knowing that Adam is alive…" I started. "Even if he can't remember me…" I couldn't look at Ben; I couldn't look at his face and into his eyes when I knew all I would see was a mask of pain. Or even the hostility he used to display around me. "… it changes things."

Ben's chest sank slowly as he exhaled.

"Even if he is trying to kill you," Ben said quietly.

"Even then."

It was silent except for the sound of our breaths. I listened to them for a while, waiting for Ben's reaction. Waiting for him to turn me away. Bracing myself for the rejection that was about to come.

"Claire—" It was a mere whisper.

"Ben—" I finally looked up.

Ben's eyes were molten steel. They showed pain and worry. His lips were curved upward on the sides into an angelic smile.

"—I know you love him. You always will. You don't have a choice." His smile became harder as if he was struggling to keep it in place. "But I know how you feel about me, Claire. I can feel it. Every second of every minute we spend together."

"Ben, don't—" I tried. But he was right. Over the past weeks, he had become more than my friend. I might have kissed him for the wrong reasons. But there was definitely something that was drawing me to him. Ben had left traces on me, too.

But what did this mean for our relationship?

"You know how I feel about you, Claire," he said, holding my eyes in place with his gaze, "Now it is up to you what you make of it."

A half-hearted smile was all I could give in return. I

escaped to the guest room, my heart once again affected by the encounter with Ben.

What was it about this boy? He was Adam's half-brother. His mother was part angel, the same as his father. He had the strongest lineage in the family. After all the hatred, the cold stares, we had finally made it to a place that could be called friendship. Only he had different feelings for me.

Even when my heart unconditionally belonged to Adam... I had gone too long trying to break free from this permanent hold Adam had on me. Too many weeks of denying myself to feel that way, because I had thought him dead.

This must have created fertile ground for Ben's attempts, and I had softened up toward him.

With my musing about Adam and Ben, the confusion of the past days resurfaced. Too many things had happened.

The world had gone from a dark, unwelcoming Adam-free hell to a thin ice of new-Adam-demon and all the consequences he came with.

Within a week, he had tried to kill me twice. He'd had the opportunity more often. But he didn't. There was no way of knowing how much I could trust my luck. Would he strike the next time our paths crossed? Or would he still see me as the key to finding his answers? Where was he now? Would he return?

I grimaced at the beginning of my panic and fought it back with pure willpower.

Now was not the time to lose it. Or to dwell on any of the Gallager boys. It was time to drown out my inner conflict by doing something that would inevitably catch up with me if I ignored it for one day longer.

I sat down on the bed and pulled out my textbooks.

22.
Visitor

Time had passed... maybe ten days. with no sign of Adam. We couldn't be sure if he had returned to Volpert's clan. There hadn't been any news regarding them either. The finals were still drawing closer with every day. There were moments when things were getting so intense I was wishing for Volpert to come get me so I wouldn't have to study much longer.

Maniac, the voice kicked me.

The twenty-four-seven supervision made it possible that I could get through the days. Jaden, with his never-ending patience, was dedicating most of his time to sitting through school with me. In the afternoon, he would rarely miss an hour of babysitting me, making sure I was up to the task of studying.

He wanted me to succeed. He made it his personal challenge to get me through the finals. And he was good at it.

When he thought I wasn't looking, every now and then, I would catch him with worry in his golden eyes.

Whether it was worry about my finals, my safety, or his own agenda, I couldn't tell.

After I had run away to see Adam, Jaden had become more cautious about leaving me to the Gallagers' supervision.

I still spent most nights at their house. Jenna and Chris needed my company as much as I needed theirs.

Long conversations over dinner always ended up in one question. Where was Adam?

My exclusive connection with their demon-son helped us all to believe it hadn't been a dream that Adam had been here not even two weeks ago. That and that Antonio was gone.

It was hard to believe that Adam had killed his pet without a second thought, but it was true. If he was capable of that, what else was he capable of?

Every now and then, I got an idea. The visions of Adam in my dreams hadn't disappeared. They had become more solid.

Within the past week alone, I had dreamed of him five times. He had always been alone when I saw him. There was no background image that would give away his whereabouts. Just his staring green eyes. Full of questions. Full of hunger.

The dream always ended the same way. I would reach out my hand to touch his face, he would withdraw before my fingers would reach his cheek, his eyes would brighten in color ever so slightly, and then he was gone.

I had no idea what it meant or if it was real. Was he searching for me in his sleep?

During the days, I was moderately energized and just motivated enough to make it through.

Amber and Greg rarely spoke to me anymore—they were busy being a newly in love couple—and I was glad they avoided me. Seeing them, however happy I was they had each other, made me yearn for Adam… my old Adam. The one who had loved me uncategorically.

But that Adam was gone. Maureen had illustrated it perfectly for me. He was a tool for Volpert. At his disposal. Or at Maureen's—I still hadn't figured out her exact position in the story.

I couldn't count on this new, dark Adam. His black heart had killed and fed off souls. He had inflicted pain on me—willingly or not. The old Adam would have never done that. He would have laid down his life for me.

My stomach twisted at the realization. The voice in my head laughed, humorless.

And then there was a part of me that longed for someone else. Someone good. Entirely and thoroughly good.

An image of Ben's face flashed through my thoughts without warning.

Ben had been avoiding having deep conversations with me recently. There was no doubt he was still hurt from my reaction. But he also knew that I wasn't indifferent toward him.

It was visible in the way he looked at me over his plate at dinner and in his gestures when he wordlessly teleported me back and forth to get stuff from my house when he walked me through the Gallagers' mansion to make sure I wouldn't sneak off again.

There was always a cautious enthusiasm about spending time with me, but he didn't allow himself the warmth and open-heartedness I had experienced in the past weeks. Almost like he was going back to hide behind his mask now that Adam was back.

It worried me, seeing the man I had gotten to know disappear. I liked that Ben. The Ben who spoke his thoughts and who never gave up on me—no matter how miserable I was.

However much I missed my old Adam and the new Ben, there was nothing I could really do about it. I'd rather have a world where Adam was a demon than no Adam at all. I loved him. If this meant that Ben would disapprove of me, that's what I would have to live with.

I fought back my unease to the darker regions of my mind and returned to my books, disgruntled.

"What's wrong?" Jaden asked. He was checking my history essay for errors.

It was almost comical, seeing a millennium-old creature checking an essay on history he had most likely experienced.

I shook my head at him. He knew what was wrong with me. We had discussed it at least a hundred times. There simply was not a legitimate reason to hash it out even one more time.

I had learned to cope with things on my own. Of course, I was glad to have the Gallagers and Jaden to talk to and voice my fears and concerns, but I didn't want to burden them more than necessary. It was enough strain as it was for them to feel my emotions whenever I was with them.

"I am fine."

Jaden smiled the way only an understanding guardian angel could. He knew how I felt. He knew me inside out. He had been watching over me my whole life, and he had risked everything for me. I had caused him enough trouble. Making his life easier was one thing I was determined to do from now on.

He watched me study from the corner of his eye while he was reading through the essay.

Today was one of the rare days I spent at my own house. Jaden had agreed that it was safe for me to study at home if he stayed with me.

It had been a quiet day so far. No incidents at school, no visions. Just Jaden, me, and my textbooks.

"This isn't bad," Jaden handed me back the essay with surprise written on his face.

He wasn't the only one surprised by this news.

"Dinner should arrive any second," he said, rubbing his hands like a starved teenage boy.

It was so easy to believe he was human—

Before I could finish my thoughts, the doorbell rang.

I raced down the stairs and bumped into Jaden, who had teleported.

"You stay here. Keep out of sight." He was super-cautious.

"I doubt demons deliver curry," I claimed, a little annoyed that I couldn't even open my own door in my own house.

Jaden ignored me and went to collect our dinner.

He had a point. It was risky to open the door to strangers when we had no idea whether Adam had informed the demons about the little kidnap.

They could come for us any day. Unexpected. Turn up out of nowhere. I wouldn't even be surprised…

"Keep the change," I heard Jaden dismiss the delivery boy without delay.

The smell of Indian food spread in the house immediately as we opened the boxes.

"No one dangerous?" I teased Jaden.

He handed me the curry with a sour face. "Not this time."

It was obvious that he was tense, always expecting the inevitable attack to finally hit.

Jaden watched me stir in the chickpeas with moderate enthusiasm.

"I need to take you back to the Gallagers' soon," he announced, speaking more to my curry than to me.

Of course he did. It was safer for all of us when we were together in the same place. Exceptions like today were a compromise for my personal benefit to be able to focus better. But eventually, the day would end, and I would lay down in the— by now too familiar—guest room and close my eyes to a night full of Adam's eyes, staring at me and questioning me silently.

I was fine with that. Most of today's work was done. I had successfully tackled the history essay. What was missing was a shower to wash away my troubles.

The hot water of the shower was soothing to my thoughts... for a moment. Then the weight of my imbroglio crushed down on me without mercy.

Why again did I have to love Adam against all better judgment? Oh, right—I didn't have a choice. I was marked, and he, even though his angel-self was dead, was still the person I was linked to. His joy was my joy and his pain was my pain. Contextus Daemonicus.

Everything would be so much easier if I could simply break free of the connection we shared.

This led me to a new question. If I died—now that he was a demon—would he suffer? Would he, by killing me, inflict pain on himself? Did his cold and darkened heart intuitively know? Was this the reason he'd been avoiding a deadly strike?

When I stepped out of the shower, my hair weighed at least triple its normal weight, soaked as it was; or was it my thoughts that made my head feel all heavy and useless?

I let the past few weeks replay in my head once more. Adam still being alive—in a different, much more different way than I could have ever imagined—had come as a shock, as a relief. Every fiber in my body was unspeakably grateful that he still existed somehow, even if this new version of him was craving for my soul.

All the pain, all the torment, my bleeding heart hadn't been in vain. It had all been worth going through just to see him again one single time.

Besides the visions and dreams, it appeared he had sought me out more than once. Those few times I had seen him in the shadows; they had been real.

All this time, I had been considering myself crazy, actually, I was pretty much sane.

Yeah—right, the voice came to life, insulting my newfound confidence. *Because you are* not dreaming of eating souls.

I scorned the voice with a dismissive gesture.

Besides my Adam-related episodes—the ones where I wished to suck people's energy—I *was* mentally sound.

The barbed wire that had frequently tormented me after Adam's death had disappeared almost completely.

How different Adam was now—a demon, creature of the darkness, rather than light, like he had been before—didn't really make a difference to the ceasing of the pain.

Probably my heart didn't care about what form Adam had returned in, as long as he *had* returned.

And then, there was the un-ignorable fact that Adam wasn't going for the kill. He had freed his hands so easily there on his bed. Like he was tearing a spider web rather than thick rope.

Even though he could have—anytime—he hadn't done it right away; he had waited until he'd had the chance to be alone with me.

Incapacitating Jaden rather than disposing of him completely, too, was proof that he couldn't be the cold-blooded demon we thought he was.

In fact, I was ninety-eight percent certain that Adam hadn't known what he was doing when he had inflicted that abominable pain on me in the graveyard. I wasn't certain, though, if he had been under some kind of spell, if the demons had bewitched him.

Despite the knowledge that all good had died in him on that God-forsaken roof, I couldn't tell what exactly had become of him. It was undeniably clear, though, that the angelic presence he used to be was far gone.

Pondering all of this, I got ready for the transfer to the Gallagers'. As ready as anyone could get with all of this going on around them. But ready as I may have felt, nothing could have prepared me for what was coming next.

When I stepped over the threshold to my bedroom, a shadow moved in the corner next to the window. I turned my head to look closer and froze in place where I was.

It was him. In all his glory and with his scary gaze.

There was the curiosity, the hunger, the fear I had seen before. There was confusion and hesitation written all over his features.

It was like an unstable mask, switching from channel to channel of emotion. I couldn't be sure which one would win this time. Last time, it had been the uncertainty. He had left—just like that. And it had broken my heart—to see him struggle and to experience him looking at me like a target.

And it was the same this time. His eyes were tying me to the spot. I couldn't escape his glare.

"Adam," I exhaled, finally able to get my thoughts together.

He didn't move but lowered his gaze to the floor, looking at something behind my bed.

My eyes searched the space where he was looking and found Jaden, still and pale like he was sleeping.

Was he sleeping? Or had he killed him this time? Had I been wrong to believe there was more to him than a creature of the night?

"Jaden," I asked. "Is he—" I couldn't even finish out of fear to get an answer I couldn't live with.

Adam shifted his weight and bent down to turn Jaden to the side.

"Incapacitated," he indifferently said, and I sighed with relief.

He had come back to find me, and he had come alone. He hadn't sold me out to the demons. Not yet. Would he?

"Where have you been?" the words shot out of me, uncontrollable. Seeing Adam in my room, no matter the circumstances, felt almost normal.

But it wasn't.

He didn't answer. Instead, he eventually looked up, his eyes burning with curiosity and hunger.

His stare took me back to the dream I'd had over and over again. The one that ended with Adam disappearing.

I was determined to not let that happen this time.

The room tasted of indecisiveness. I wasn't sure if it was his or mine. What I was sure about was that I had to get some information out of him. I needed answers, I needed to know what was going on. I needed them to keep my freshly-discovered sanity—because it felt to be becoming more diminished by the minute.

He was still staring at me with those pale-green eyes as he did in my dreams—our dreams.

"Why did you come here?" My words weren't more than a whisper, my breath shallow from the tension.

The tall, dark figure remained silent, his hands folding across his chest, the only sign he had heard me.

After a couple of breaths that seemed to not bring enough oxygen supply to my system, I couldn't stand to wait any longer.

I took a slow step toward him, his eyes always holding my gaze.

"Stop." He suddenly recoiled from me as if I were a threat.

I froze in place. "Why?"

There was something new in Adam's gaze, something I hadn't expected to see there. It was a spark that brightened his irises ever so slightly.

"I don't want to hurt you." The hunger was obvious in his face, and I felt it in my own system, too. The craving.

It took some effort to ignore it, but I'd practiced with Jaden the past couple of days. And it paid off.

It melted away from me like a layer of ice in the sun. My focus belonged to myself once more, and I directed it back at Adam.

"You won't," I reassured him—or threatened him—I couldn't tell—and took another step toward him.

This time, he didn't object. His shape floated away from my unconscious guardian angel and toward me. His feet seemed to not be touching the floor; that's how lightly he walked.

It was eerie and graceful at the same time—like a beautiful ghost.

My mind remembered a different type of craving as I was watching him move. It was an echo of how I had felt before, but it was a potent sensation. One I hadn't felt since my last day with Adam, the angel.

I shook my head at myself. He had given no indication why he had returned. How could I even believe for a second that there might be a way he had remembered… us?

A step away from me, within my arm's reach, Adam came to a halt. His eyes hadn't released mine, his intense stare beginning to make me dizzy.

"Who are you?" His question lingered between us for a brief moment before I could collect my thoughts.

Last time he had asked, I had answered, I'd been his soulmate. Apparently, that hadn't been good enough for him.

"Who are you?" he repeated when I didn't show any sign that I was going to answer. This time his voice was harsh.

Suddenly, he was intimidating, the stare cold, and he was lifting his hand in the air.

It was but the tiniest time-span until the pull on the strings through my heart began. The pain seared through me like hot iron strings, cutting through my flesh and bones, just to sling around my heart—no, my soul.

My knees buckled as I bent over in agony.

"Adam," I gasped, as I hit the floor.

He watched me for a minute, struggle distinct in his features.

"Why are you haunting my dreams?"

The moment he spoke, he lifted a finger, and the pull on the strings intensified.

I shrieked.

"I am your mark," I cried in pain.

Adam looked at me without comprehension and did nothing to end my agony.

The strings were pulling tighter and tighter around this intangible part of myself. I fought with every fiber in my body. I wouldn't give up my soul. I would find a way so he would stop. Listen.

"You haven't always been like this, Adam." I had to try. "You marked me... when you spread your angel wings..." I coughed the words out, unable to speak. "Part of your soul is in me... I am a part of you."

The moment the words were out, I realized what they meant. And that they were true.

The pain stopped, and Adam ghosted away from me until he was standing still in the farthest corner of the room. His features were unreadable.

"I am a part of you," I repeated, almost inaudibly. It was the undeniable truth. He was part of me. Part of me was him. We were connected. We were one. My heart would never forget that, and my soul couldn't ignore it.

I straightened up into a standing position, ignoring the screaming of my body.

"I love you, Adam." It had slipped out before I could coherently weigh the potential impact of what I was saying.

Adam sighed lowly at my words. His face told me that he couldn't follow me one-hundred percent.

Why couldn't he see that after all I had gone through—after all of the pain, the misery, the torture, the fear—after everything, I was still existentially in love with him?

I didn't care that he was the enemy or that I was supposed to be afraid of him. I didn't care that he had tried to kill me, that he was probably considering the thought at that very moment. And yet, here I was standing, vulnerable, presenting my human heart and soul to him.

He didn't evade my gaze when my eyes bore into his now, full of questions.

At first, it was a mild, tingly sensation. Almost ignorable. I wouldn't even have paid attention to it if it hadn't continued to grow stronger.

I stopped for a moment and took a deep breath. This couldn't be happening. Not now.

Adam was standing on the other side of the room. His arms were folded across his chest, his face reluctant. He was clearly uncomfortable. His eyes showed the hunger I had become so familiar with, but there was something different about his expression now. I couldn't put my finger on what exactly it was.

The tingle forced my attention back on my own body. My feet, my legs, my knees, they all were feeling the same as usual, but there was something different in my torso.

I closed my eyes for a moment as my head started spinning. *Not now!* I yelled at myself in my mind, willing myself to stay focused. I couldn't pass out. Not now. I needed to be clear in my head. I needed to look at him. I needed to make him understand...

Another glance toward the opposite wall reassured me that Adam hadn't moved. He was still following my every move with his gaze, the hunger more pronounced than ever.

The sensation began to roll up and down my back in slow waves, each one stronger than the one before. It made my hair stand on end. The tingle became a stinging that concentrated in my upper back. I arched my spine and shook my head to clear it.

Adam was all but a shadow in my peripheral vision now. I couldn't see clearly anymore. My hands flexed without my permission as I was trying to regain focus. Why was he doing this to me? And, what was it exactly that he was doing to me?

"Adam." It sounded weak. "Why?"

"What do you mean, why?" His voice was the only clear thing in my head, everything else was a blur.

"Why are you doing this to me?" My question came as a gust of air.

Adam's shape was coming closer with every onerous breath I took.

The waves became shorter and stronger. I could feel how they were rolling from shoulder blade to shoulder blade.

From the corner of my eye, I could make out Adam's lifted hand. It was reaching for me—not like before where it had clung to the strings that held my soul in place. It looked as if he was reaching out to grab for my hand.

"I am not doing anything, Claire," his voice assured me, making the waves come even faster.

He wasn't? Where was this coming from then? I forced my eyes to look at the man I so ill-fatedly loved.

He, himself, seemed to be shaking. The expression in his eyes, under his quivering black hair, I could finally name. It was regret.

It escaped my attention—what was left of it anyway—what he would be regretting.

"Adam, what is happening?" I was close to losing consciousness.

He continuously came closer until he was right beside me.

"Claire," his voice washed over me. The sound of it made me choke.

My head turned toward the open window, desperately searching for fresh air in an attempt to stay alert.

The incoming breeze brought temporary relief and the smell of grass.

I inhaled greedily, absorbing every last particle of oxygen in my lungs.

For a couple of deep breaths, I focused on suppressing the ache in my spine.

Why couldn't Jaden just wake up? I needed him.

Breathe through it, I told myself. I had to.

Adam was so close I could almost feel him shake. One more breath, and I would be strong enough to face him.

I turned and caught an eerie greenish reflection in the glass—a pair of clear, gleaming eyes were looking back at me.

The pain spiked for a long second, searing up my back and through my shoulders, making my hands ball into fists and my head snap back in agony.

And then it was gone.

The next time my lungs expanded, they weren't restricted by a solid fence of pain. They moved freely, pushing my ribs gently outward.

The smell of grass was still lingering in the air—just now, I could appreciate it differently. It filled my head, and my mind pulled up images of pale-green culms and blades.

It was the color of Adam's eyes; the eyes that were staring at me with a subdued glow.

They were unblinkingly piercing mine. I saw nothing but his eyes. They were hypnotic.

"Claire." His voice was calm and steady, claiming my attention.

"What just happened?" I asked automatically, unable to look away.

No answer.

Adam moved even closer. His hand was slowly moving up the way it had earlier.

I shrank into the wall, bracing myself against what was coming. The pain wouldn't surprise me this time. I forced my eyelids to drop, cutting his direct link to my emotions. The pale-green orbs disappeared behind a curtain of black, and I was ready.

Nothing happened.

Was he playing with me—an evil predator, toying with its prey?

Unwilling to give him the satisfaction of reading the fear in my eyes, I waited in silence. It couldn't be long now.

Still nothing.

His hand didn't pull on the strings, and the pain I was so warily expecting didn't set in.

"Claire," he spoke again, softly, as if he was hoping to gain my trust.

Hadn't I already told him I loved him? Wasn't that enough? What was he waiting for?

"Open your eyes, Claire," he asked, and my eyes obeyed.

The curtain rose, and I found myself looking at Adam's face, too close to make out details. It was a familiar closeness.

My better judgment told me to move away, but behind me, there was only the flat wall. Even if I had found the strength to try, it would have stopped me.

A movement in my peripheral vision caught my eye. Adam's hand was an inch away from my cheek.

I suddenly realized that he wasn't going to hurt me—

Was this even possible? It most certainly felt like it...

"Claire," he spoke my name for a third time. This time it was tender and emotional. "I remember."

My heart stuttered.

I blinked at him, not trusting my hearing, while he was gazing at me fiercely as if searching for a sign of comprehension.

I was far away from comprehending anything.

Another trap? the voice suggested. I shook my head at it. Not this time. It wouldn't take the moment away from me.

His sudden closeness made me want to drown in him, to block out all the past, the future, everything that was tainting the moment.

His fingers on my cheek tore me out of my momentary mental absence. They were tracing my cheekbone lightly, making my skin tingle under his touch.

"I remember," he repeated. And it sank in. "I remember you. I remember—everything."

23.
Memories

A slow wave of warmth made its way through my body when the knowledge settled in.

He remembered.

All of the hope I'd treasured in those past days, all of the suffering hadn't been in vain. He remembered.

"Adam—" I whispered into the palm of his hand. My fingers slowly lifted to touch the back of his hand, to seal it to my cheek.

I couldn't find words to voice my elation. Instead, my body found a way. My heart was flying, exhilarated and wide-open for him.

Adam carefully wound the fingers of his free hand around my other hand, gently pulling it up between our chests.

My skin burned with delight where he touched me. It was like my whole body was singing in joy. Adam's breath touched my face, that's how close he was. His lips touched mine—hesitantly at first—and my mouth dropped open, inhaling his breath, inhaling him.

His kiss was silky and soft. It brought me back to feeling like the Claire I had once been. It was like the healing of an old wound. I felt whole.

He lingered for a brief moment before he pulled away—too early for me to be ready to let go, but the urge to look at his face, see the recognition there again, was stronger than the urge to object.

"I am so terribly sorry." Adam pulled me against his chest, his arms enclosing me into a long embrace.

All I could feel was him—all I could smell. It was the most perfect moment. I snuggled against his shoulder and let my own arms sling around his waist.

He felt perfect—like I remembered. My hands clawed into the fabric of his shirt, intending to pull him even closer against me, and touched skin.

There was a tear across the back of his shirt, exposing his back. I let my fingers slowly search the smooth skin and hit something soft near his ribs.

It was a familiar feeling. Light and feathery.

In an impulse of curiosity, I opened my eyes and peeked over Adam's shoulder. They were looking at a thick black layer of feathers. It was flowing down along his back to where my fingers had touched it.

Are you happy now? the voice in my head wanted to know.

I was. I had known there must be something left in Adam that was part of his former self. The pair of black, feathery wings streaming down the back of his shape was proof I'd been right.

I am, I thought at the voice and silenced it forever.

With a smile, I closed my eyes again and went back to enjoying the moment.

I couldn't tell how long we had been standing like this; I had lost track of time and place. All that mattered were Adam's arms as reluctant to let me go as mine were to let go of him. But there was a rustling claiming our attention from the corner.

"Jaden," it shot from my mouth.

Adam moved, turning me toward the sound with him. When I reopened my eyes, Jaden was standing up behind the bed. He looked dazed.

"Jaden, are you okay?" I tore out of Adam's arms and rushed across the room.

By the time I made it there, Jaden had comprehended what was going on. He was skeptically looking at the new attachment to Adam's shoulders.

"I am fine," he reassured me, rubbing the back of his head with the palm of his hand. "What happened?"

Before I could open my mouth to speak, Adam gasped in pain. His hands flung to his shoulders.

Both Jaden and I reacted immediately, though our reactions were slightly different. While I felt heat creeping up between my shoulders while rushing back to Adam to find out what was going on, Jaden had disappeared and reappeared next to Adam. He had forced him down on the floor where Adam was now writhing under Jaden.

"Don't hurt him," I squealed at Jaden. My feet were not carrying me half as fast as I wanted to be there, the heat slowing me and making me slightly less coordinated than usual, but when I finally knelt down next to the two of them, Adam's motions had become weak.

Jaden was still pinning him down with both his hands, making sure Adam couldn't lift his arms or hands to attack.

Wonder was written in Jaden's features. He must be as surprised by Adam's wings as I was.

"Did he hurt you?" Jaden asked over his shoulder, checking on me for a brief second before turning back to Adam.

"He didn't." Of course he didn't. "Jaden," I put my hand on Jaden's shoulder, trying to calm him. "He remembers."

Adam's struggle had ceased under Jaden's constraint when Jaden finally let go, face blank.

"He does?"

I nodded. "He remembers who I am."

Jaden read my face for a minute, and without a doubt, he was reading my emotions. His features were mirroring my own feelings—the bliss, the fear, the confusion.

"What happened?" he asked, lifting his hands from Adam, and gestured at Adam's feathery attachment.

I looked down and was taken back to the short moment of happiness I'd just experienced.

"He didn't hurt me," I assured Jaden. "Quite the opposite... He kissed me—" I blushed and stopped mid-sentence.

Jaden eyed me with a mixture of amazement and disapproval. I knew I was going to get a lecture about blind trust later. But not now. My focus was on Adam.

"What did you do to him?" I asked my guardian angel, and we both looked down on Adam's motionless body. I wasn't sure about Jaden's thoughts, but he looked suspicious.

"I just held him down. I didn't do anything else. He passed out by himself." Jaden's eyes were following the line of black feathers on Adam's back.

He passed out—he was unconscious. My eyes followed Jaden's gaze until they were caught by a thin, crimson trickle that was sticking the feathers together.

Blood. Adam was hurt.

Jaden noticed the expression on my face. "I swear, this wasn't me."

He bent down to take a closer look.

"What's wrong with him?" My voice was impatient. An echo of how I was feeling on the inside.

"I can't see. It must be under the wings." Jaden looked confused.

I dug my fingers into the feathers carefully, separating them until I uncovered the area where the wings were growing out of Adam's back.

The pale skin was severed, blood leaking into the black fringe.

"I have never seen anything like this," Jaden whispered beside me. "We need to take care of this. Now."

My eyes wandered back and forth between the pooling blood and Jaden's concerned face before I could react.

"What do you need?" I unfroze. "I have a first aid kit in the bathroom."

I was on my feet.

"Water, clean towels, tourniquets," Jaden ordered.

"We need to locate exactly where the bleeding is coming from on this wing," his voice came from the bedroom.

I was slamming through the cabinets, snatching every towel I could find, and filled a small bowl with warm water.

"Correction—On both wings," Jaden informed me as I returned with my arms full of equipment.

Jaden grabbed a towel and started to clear the blood pool which was spreading around the roots of Adam's wings and in between his shoulder blades. The wings he had folded up in an awkward angle from his spine.

Jaden carefully dabbed the wound with towel after towel slowly turning red, until we finally laid eyes on Adam's ruptured skin. It seemed like the wings had literally torn through the fragile layer.

Jaden applied pressure to one side with a tourniquet and handed me another one.

"Do the same thing on your side," he directed.

I took it from his hand.

"Keep the pressure on until the bleeding stops."

My hands mechanically pushed down on the wound, which made me feel relieved that I could help.

After a long while, the endless stream of red ceased.

"I don't know what happened exactly," Jaden said over a heap of blood-drenched towels. "But this is not normal."

I looked at him, alarmed by his statement.

"What now?' I asked.

Jaden gathered up the bloody towels thoughtfully and then examined one of the wounds for a long moment. He gestured for me to be quiet and extended his hands an inch above the broken skin. Light emitted from his palms, shimmering from the gaps between his fingers.

The torn tissue knitted itself back together loosely. The deep clefts disappeared bit by bit, but the wounds didn't seal completely.

I watched the aggravatingly slow procedure, biting down on my lip nervously. It was almost impossible to stay patient, but I knew Jaden was doing what he could to make the situation better. I trusted him. And so I continued to observe until a blood-red pattern branching out across Adam's shoulder-blades and along his spine was all that remained.

"I did what I could. The rest needs to heal on its own." Jaden got to his feet, lifted the towels, and disappeared to the bathroom.

Relief spread through my system.

"We should bring him back to his family." The idea sounded logical to me. Chris and Jenna would want to know what had happened. And they would want to take care of him and be there for him—the same as I did.

"I agree." Jaden reappeared next to me. "I will need help teleporting him back to their house. I need to find Chris or Jenna."

He measured my expression. "Will you be alright if I leave you for just one minute?"

"I will." I would simply sit and watch over Adam—make sure the blood didn't start flowing again.

"I'll be back very soon." He put his hand on my head. "I will inform them what happened and get help."

"Jaden," I called when he pulled back his hand.

"Yes, Claire?"

"What if he wakes up?" I simultaneously hoped for and dreaded the moment, frightened that Adam's memory would be gone again.

"He needs to stay still so the wounds don't reopen." It wasn't an answer to the question I had asked, and I felt Jaden didn't know what to say. "I'll be back in no time."

He disappeared into thin air with a last golden look at me. His eyes were glowing gently.

Beside me, Adam stirred slightly. My hands dropped onto his arm as if to comfort him, and his breathing got deeper and steadier. He looked peaceful. Almost like he was just sleeping.

"I don't know if you can hear me," I said to him lowly. "When you wake up, please don't leave again. You have bad injuries that need to heal."

Adam remained still, the only sign he was alive being the steady rising and falling of his ribs and the dancing of the black feathers of his wings.

"Jaden is getting your Dad and Jenna to help bring you back home. Everything will be fine."

Would it? I wondered and stroked strands of dark hair out of Adam's face. Would he stay this time? Would he go back to the demons? Would his returned memory change anything?

"I love you, Adam." I wanted him to know again. Even if he didn't hear me. "I love you more than I can put into words…"

I stared at Adam's face, studying his features. They looked exactly like my Adam—no trace of darkness was visible there now. It was so easy to forget that he had seen me as a target just a few hours ago. When he woke up, would he still?

"You might be a demon, but there is good in you. I can see it when I look at you. I felt it in your embrace—in your kiss—"

My mind yearned to return to that memory, but I didn't let it. I needed to stay alert.

"—are your wings physical proof of that goodness? Can I hope—" I asked, not expecting an answer.

"There is always hope." Jenna's voice startled me.

Before I could get to my feet, she was kneeling beside me.

"Jaden came to tell us what happened," she explained. "Chris will be here any moment to help bring Adam back to our place."

"Does Ben know?" I asked, and Jenna nodded.

"He's preparing for our arrival."

We were both looking down at Adam.

"His back looks really bad," Jenna finally noted.

"Jaden says he's never seen anything like it." Jaden had improved the condition, but the red pattern on Adam's back was still reason to worry.

"Neither have I," Jenna agreed. "I wish I knew what it is so I could help. But then, there is probably no reference in history that would help us."

"What do you mean?" I tore away from the disturbing red lines and faced Jenna.

"You told us Liz said that the Contextus Daemonicus has been hypothetical so far. A theory. Until it was verified through Adam and you."

"True." I listened to her, curious as to where she was headed.

"But the theory ends with the connecting bond between demon and prior angel's mark. There is no mention of what happens when the demon remembers who he was."

"We will need Liz to verify, but I assume you are right." It was more than unlikely that anything like this was documented somewhere. And even if so—what would be the odds of finding it? After all, none of the angels around me had heard about Contextus Daemonicus—and this was only a continuation of that theory. None of us knew what would happen if the demon remembered who they were.

"Have you ever seen black wings before?" I asked Jenna, more to confirm my thought process.

She didn't disappoint. "Never."

My fingers automatically reached out to brush the closest part of Adam's wings. They were unspeakably soft.

"What do you think it means?"

"There might be more of the old Adam left in there than we had expected," Jenna guessed.

That moment, Jaden reappeared across from us on Adam's other side. Chris was right beside him, face set in a mask of suppressed hope.

"He's still unconscious. Moved slightly once, but apart from that, no changes," I informed Jaden of the development.

"Thank you," Jaden acknowledged my report.

It was a strange conversation, almost professional. I thought of my sister caring for sick people in her hospital far away. I was sure she would never have a case like this. I hoped she never would.

Jaden bent down to carefully lift Adam from the floor, supporting his torso with both arms. "Chris, take his legs," he instructed.

Chris had Adam by the waist at once, gently lifting the lower part.

Adam's wings were flowing down beside his ribs to the floor where they twisted in an unnatural angle.

Chris and Jaden looked at each other briefly before they disappeared with Adam in their arms.

"Our turn," Jenna pulled me to my feet with an outstretched arm.

Before I could blink, we were gone.

The next thing I saw was the Gallagers' living room.

Chris and Jaden were carefully laying Adam down on his stomach on the couch while Ben was arranging Adam's wings so they wouldn't touch the wound, and he folded one across the backrest while he let the other one spread on an armchair someone had pushed toward the sofa.

The fear for Adam was like a ghost hovering among us. Even Jaden, who owed Adam nothing—who had given everything just to make sure I was safe, for whose mission Adam was a constant threat—even he was anxious about his well-being.

"Will he wake up again?" I asked through clenched teeth, trying to hold back the slowly upcoming panic.

What if he didn't wake up again? What if his remembering had destroyed him—no space for good within bad or whatever someone might call it...

Ben creased his forehead as he examined Adam's back.

"This looks painful," he said with a voice that let me guess he was imagining his own wings damaging his body the way Adam's new wings had.

Jenna left my side for a minute and returned with a bowl of water and two sponges. "I'll clean the wounds again. Maybe the warmth helps—"

"Help me?" She handed me a sponge, and I was grateful she gave me a task to keep my hands busy and be close to Adam at the same time.

Some of the tears had reopened a bit, and fresh blood was leaking onto his pale skin.

I dabbed at the injury the way I had observed Jaden do it and reran the events in my head. Jenna was discussing the severity of Adam's wounds with the others. The common opinion was that we didn't know enough about them to understand if there would be permanent damage. All they knew was that there was no immediate danger for Adam—and that reassured me.

Nobody asked what had happened, and I was grateful. Knowing that Jaden had already shared with the others took away the awkward feeling of needing to explain myself. Also, it spared me from having to share details with Ben. I didn't want to hurt him—not if I could help it.

Long after we were finished, I was staring at the disturbing scarlet pattern on Adam's back.

"Maybe Liz knows something," I suggested absently.

"That's a great idea," Jenna confirmed. "She helped with Chris's wings. She knew about the Contextus Daemonicus—who knows what theory she'll come up with for this."

"We do need to get more information," Jaden agreed and turned toward me. "Maybe you should call her."

24.
Speculations

"Thank you for coming on such short notice." I hugged Liz and pulled her in over the threshold.

Nothing that had happened since we'd met led me to treat her as anything other than a trusted friend.

"The traffic was horrible," she excused herself. "I'd have been here sooner if it wasn't for that truck that drove like we are having ice and snow. Trust me, I did everything to speed them up—"

There was a hint of amusement in her voice, and I could imagine the woman gesturing at the truck driver wildly and yelling at him—she was the type.

"Anyway—" Liz tore out of my hug and eyed me skeptically. "What's so important that it can't wait until tomorrow morning? I don't dump a hot date for just anyone."

"I am so sorry, Liz." I blushed. If I had known she was on a date, I would have waited to call her. But this situation didn't allow for delays. I shifted from foot to foot, embarrassed that I had disturbed her evening plans.

She flashed her pearly teeth when she saw my expression.

"If you hadn't called, I'd have had to find a different excuse to bolt." She laughed a hearty laugh that didn't match with her outfit. "The guy was lame."

"Nice house." She dropped her clutch on the sideboard and walked further in. "Do you live here?"

It sometimes felt like it.

"No," I answered truthfully. "It belongs to Adam's parents—to his stepmother, to be precise."

I followed her to the foot of the stairs.

Liz turned gracefully in her ankle strappy heels. "So what's this emergency you called me for?"

I swallowed. How does one explain what had happened just a few hours earlier?

"Maybe it's best if I just show you—" I suggested.

"Okay," Liz shrugged. "Show me."

The others were waiting in the living room—positioned around Adam, so they could all react in case he woke up—when I pushed my nervous hands against the heavy wooden door.

Jenna and Chris were standing in front of the couch, blocking Adam from view.

"Liz, meet the Gallager family." I gestured at the room. "Everyone, this is Liz."

Liz's face became solemn when she stepped inside. Similar to the first time she had seen Jaden at the library.

"It's an honor to meet you," she bowed her head lightly.

Jenna's eyes widened in surprise when she saw Liz's reaction to the presence of four angels.

"Please," she said. "It's an honor to meet you."

Jenna walked toward Liz with an outstretched hand. "You saved my husband. We owe you so much. Please come in, take a seat."

"Such a pleasure to meet you, Liz," Chris greeted her and shook her hand. "My lovely wife is right. We owe you everything. If it wasn't for you, I would still be flightless." He chuckled. "Please meet our son, Ben," he added and gestured Ben to come forward.

Liz was taken aback by so much kindness and openness. She hesitated for a second before breaking into a smile. "Well, this is different."

"Hi, Liz," Jaden waved from the back of the room. "Nice to see you again. Thanks for coming."

Liz struggled for a moment, not realizing who she was talking to. Jaden had been in his early fifties the last time she had seen him. Today he was my age.

"Nice to see you, too, Jaden," Liz grinned as she recognized him.

Then her eyes fell on the black-winged shape in the center of the room. She froze.

"Who is that?" she asked, her smile wiped from her face.

I stepped to her side, pausing there for a moment. "That's the reason I called you," I admitted. "This—" I said as I continued toward the couch, "—is Adam."

Liz's jaw dropped as she took in the meaning of what I was saying.

"He's back."

"He is." It was Jaden. "And we need your help."

"Whatever it is you need," Liz stuttered. "I'll do everything I can to assist you. The code of The Guard demands it, and my heart verifies it."

She bowed her head again. Deeper this time. "My time to serve is now, and I am ready."

"And we honestly appreciate your assistance," Jaden reassured. "But first, let's sit."

Jenna gestured at an armchair near the fireplace, and Liz sat down without a word.

"I'll get something to drink," Chris announced and walked out the door—he didn't teleport, probably not wanting to startle Liz—and reappeared just a minute later with a tray of coffee, milk and sugar, and a bowl of cookies.

"It's going to be a long night," Jenna explained, apologetic.

As if I needed coffee to stay awake. Adam was here, in this very room. He had kissed me—my lips still tingled where his had touched them. He remembered me. And he was unconscious.

I wouldn't rest until he was fine again. And Liz was our best hope for unlocking the secret of his coal wings and his wounds.

My heart twisted at the sight of the crimson lines across his back.

Chris put the tray down on the table and poured a cup for Liz. "Milk and sugar?" he asked as if this was the most natural thing to do.

I had never seen him in the position to cater to anyone. After weeks at the Gallagers', I had become so used to the family butler taking care of everything. Only recently, since he had been sent on vacation—for his own safety—had I seen the Gallagers' various talents in culinary hospitality.

It seemed as surreal to Liz as it did to me. Her eyes widened in surprise, and she subconsciously shifted in her chair as if she was about to jump to her feet and take Chris's task from him. It was obvious how uncomfortable it made her, being served by one of those she had bowed to moments ago. One of those she had pledged to serve.

"Liz?" Chris repeated.

"Excuse me," she dove out of her moment. "Just milk."

Chris smiled at her bewildered expression. "We are normal people here in Aurora. Please don't treat us as anything different."

"I'll try," Liz answered with a face that gave away her reluctance.

She hadn't been half as intimidated when Jaden had shown up at the library with me. But then, he had been only one angel. Now there were four—and whatever Adam was.

I had become so used to the presence of the supernatural that I wasn't disturbed by it at all.

"It gets easier," I whispered at her, well-aware that all of them would hear me. All, except for Adam, who still was as motionless as he had been ever since Chris and Jaden had laid him down on the couch.

Ben grabbed a cookie and watched me while chewing slowly.

I had no idea what he was thinking. From his indifferent behavior, I assumed he was either hurt that I had turned him down or that he was giving me space to make up my mind.

"So," Liz asked over the rim of her cup. "How can I help?"

Everyone had sat down in comfortable positions, but for me, it was obvious that they were building a protective barrier between Adam, and Liz and me.

"Well, it's hard to overlook what happened to Adam." Jaden pointed at the dark wings that were spread over the furniture, his face mildly forlorn.

"What happened exactly?" Liz switched into business mode. Suddenly she was the confident Liz again.

"It's best if Claire tells the story," Jaden suggested. "After Adam knocked me out, she was the only one to witness."

All heads turned toward me. Jenna empathetic, Chris hopeful, Jaden disgruntled, Liz curious, and Ben—well, Ben.

I sighed, knowing that I would have to share a precious moment that I had just experienced, and I wasn't sure if sharing it would taint the memory. But then, all our safety and Adam's well-being depended on this, so I didn't give it another thought. This was what was best for all of us. Even if it would hurt Ben.

"The quick version—Jaden helped me study at my house. I took a shower before returning here, and when I came back to my room, Adam had knocked out Jaden." I glanced at Jaden, and he nodded, encouraging me to continue.

"Adam wasn't there to attack me. He asked me the same question he'd asked before. He wanted to know who I am and why there is a connection between us—apparently, he kept dreaming about me the same way I did about him."

I left out that Adam had used his powers to get me to speak. He had been tearing at my soul, without a doubt.

"I told him that he marked me when he spread his angel wings... that he hasn't always been like this, and that part of his soul is still with me... and that I love him." I added the last words almost inaudibly.

Ben shifted when my eyes searched his for signs of pain. They were solid steel when they stared back at me without emotion.

"What happened next?" Liz interrupted my distraction.

"Then I felt all strange, like I would pass out. At first, I thought Adam was doing it to me, but he wasn't. And when it became almost unbearable, it stopped. His eyes glowed, and he had his new wings. And he remembered everything."

Again, I edited out something—the fact that he had kissed me.

"He remembers *everything*?" Liz asked incredulously.

"That's a good question," Jaden answered for me. "One we have yet to answer. But it is very likely he does. At least he remembers Claire… or he wouldn't have kissed her."

Ben coughed lowly. I bit my lip, wishing that this could bring back Jaden's last sentence. By the time my eyes had made it to meet Ben's, his face was almost back to composed.

"He has wings," Liz stated the obvious.

"He does." Jaden smiled without humor. "And that's why we need your help.

"He has wings. Going by what you told us about the Contextus Daemonicus, Adam is a demon. And demons—"

"Demons don't have wings," Liz interrupted, intrigued by the riddle Jaden was presenting.

"Exactly," Jaden took back the word.

"That's the first thing we are wondering about," Chris threw in. "Why does he have wings? Does it mean there is some part of his angel-self alive in there?"

"Like it was in hibernation—" Ben suggested.

"And now that he remembers who he is, his body also remembers," Jenna finished the thought processes.

It was like the first time I had seen the Gallagers think like this. Like they were one mind rather than separate brains. It was overwhelming. And it made me feel left out.

"So, have you ever heard of anything like this? Or read about it? Even the wildest theory would help," Jaden closed the circle.

No one referred to the fact that Adam's wings were as black as the night.

"Does it mean anything that his wings are black?" I reminded them that I was still there.

"Very likely it does," Ben answered, his eyes on his brother. Jenna and Chris exchanged one of their looks, and for once, I wished I could read their emotions the way all of them could read mine.

"I wish I knew," Liz said, her eyes following Ben's. "Why is he injured?" she eventually asked the one question that needed an answer the most.

If we didn't find out why he was injured, how would we be able to keep it from happening again—if he ever woke up...

He had been out for too long. It was making me nervous. The only reason the Gallagers were still calm was that they had their extra sense. They knew that Adam was technically fine even though he was unconscious and wounded.

If there was the slightest chance he was slipping away, all of them would be on their feet, including my loyal guardian angel.

"We don't know exactly," Jaden answered.

"He collapsed in pain, and then we found the wounds. There was blood everywhere around the roots of his wings," I made sure Liz had all the information she needed. "His skin was ruptured like the wings just tore through it." The memory of the blood pool made my hair stand on end.

"I healed the wounds as much as I could, but the ruptures won't seal more than what you can see now."

"You tried *everything*?" Liz asked, piercing Jaden with her dark eyes.

She didn't seem surprised by what Jaden could do, but she seemed surprised by the limits of his powers when it came to this particular case.

"Everything," Jaden looked her in the eye, and she didn't question him again.

"So, can you help?" I asked before I broke from tension. I needed to know—we all needed to know—what was going on. If we could rely on him waking up and remembering what happened or if he would be a danger, if he would wake up at all.

Liz looked at me for a second before she stared at Adam for one long moment. Then she closed her eyes to browse through her brilliant mind. Everything she had ever read was stored there. A library under her thick, dark, wavy mane.

The atmosphere in the room became tangible with expectation. Five pairs of eyes—four of them smoldering in the evening light—were fixed on Liz's mouth, waiting for whatever would escape her lips that would enlighten us.

"There is nothing about Contextus Daemonicus that I haven't told you."

The disappointing flavor of her answer tasted bitter.

Before any of us could dwell on it, she continued.

"Let's look at the facts." Liz fashioned a serious expression. "Adam is an angel-demon-human hybrid. We don't know exactly how strong his demon-lineage is, but apparently, his angel-gene was stronger as it catalyzed first.

"His angel and human parts were destroyed by demons—or so we think," she added before anyone could object. "But his wings—black as they may be—are living proof that there is something more than a pure demon inside this boy."

"Demons don't have wings," Jaden repeated in a whisper.

All our eyes wandered over to Adam's shoulders. My heart took a tiny leap of joy that he was still there, and then it sank because he hadn't moved at all.

"The wounds, of course, are shocking and deserve all our concern. Personally, I believe this is a good sign. If I think of Adam's wings as something non-demonic, that would explain the wounds. His body wasn't prepared for it. When Adam died, his angel powers must have died with him. And when he woke up as a demon, his body must have forgotten that it has the ability to sprout wings," Liz continued her lecture.

What she was saying sounded logical to me. Even Jaden was hanging on her words like a child, making sure he wouldn't miss a thing.

Jaden was the oldest angel I knew. Nevertheless, he had limited experience when it came to anomalies. He had spent his entire existence guarding and protecting his fosterlings—not studying details of the history of demons the way Liz had.

"And when it did remember," Liz continued, "the tissue wasn't ready. The wings are an angel-debris in his demon-body."

"Will he heal?" Chris asked. He looked weary. Finding and losing his son twice within ten days must have been too much for him. It was too much for anyone in that room—and still, we all were there, coping with what we had been given.

Hope was the one straw we were clinging to.

"Of course, I can only guess. There is no written word about a winged demon. And I would know. I've spent more than half my life reading angel and demon history."

I could only imagine how full Liz's brain must be with written line after line. A memory like hers was rare, and I couldn't think of a better purpose to dedicate it to.

"Judging by what I see and by what I can make of it, all I can say is to give it time. If the wounds heal completely, he should be okay in a while. When he wakes up, make sure he rests.

"If his body still works like that of a demon, he will need to feed on something."

"Souls," Ben interrupted, his face showing mild disgust.

"Yes, souls. Energy. Whatever you want to call it. But he'll need to stay strong enough to heal. And he'll need plenty. So much about his physical condition. About his mental condition and his memory, we'll find out once he wakes up." Liz's words weren't exactly reassuring.

"Can he feed without killing anyone?" I asked, naive enough to entreat such a question. I was certain everyone else in the room already knew the answer.

"Animals, plants—it doesn't have to be souls," Jaden confirmed my suspicion. "He can feed on the energy of any living thing. Human souls are just the most nourishing source for demons."

"So he will eat plants—just differently from before?" I asked, sounding silly.

"Or animals like Antonio," Chris explained in a surprisingly calm voice, considering Adam had recently killed the family dog.

"But he will always see food when he looks at us, too," Ben commented. Jaden nodded absently.

I let that sink in. He would crave souls. I had felt the hunger myself. I knew what it would be like for him.

Would the connection still be the same now that his memory had returned?

"We'll make sure no one gets hurt. We'll find a way—that is if he wakes up before he starves." Jenna wiped Adam's hair off his face.

Liz eyed the scene with half-open eyes. Her finger was lifted in front of her chest, pointing at an invisible book she was reading in her mind.

"There is nothing written about a demon with wings...," she repeated. "But there is something else."

She fell silent again.

As her eyes kept flashing from left to right rapidly under her eyelids, I could see the change in all of the Gallagers. They were having a hard time waiting for her to come to her conclusion—as was I.

Jaden seemed to be the only one who didn't mind. He had the patience of a millennium.

"There is a scroll I've seen once," her attention returned to the room. "It is not history. It is more like a prophecy."

"A prophecy?" Jaden asked. "There have only been a few made. The documentation you shouldn't have access to." He looked upset. "Not even I know what's written inside. How did you get hold of that document?"

Liz looked at the floor, embarrassed to have upset the angel. "Believe me when I say I didn't ask to see it. I was asked to take a look at it, to verify if it was real.

"The man who brought it to me didn't tell where he got it. It doesn't matter where it came from," she dismissed the topic. "What matters is what it says."

"What does it say?" I couldn't refrain from asking.

"Yes, Liz, we'd like to know," Chris pushed.

Liz took a deep breath and went back into her perfect memory.

"*He, who fell and was reborn evil, will be awakened, and he will rise like a phoenix from the ashes. His shell will be black, but his heart will be golden, and his soul will be light.*" She quoted like she was holding the scroll in her hands right now.

"*The reborn's life will be eternal, and his power will be great, but his love will save us.*"

Liz's eyes fluttered open. "Could it be this is about him?" She nodded in Adam's direction hesitantly.

"It could be fake," Jaden pointed out.

"Or it could be real," Liz disagreed. "The man said the prophecy brought him back to Aurora. Why would he move around the globe for a scroll if it isn't real?"

Jaden scowled at Liz for a moment. It was obvious how hard it was for him, having to rely on someone else. It didn't matter how grateful he was for Liz's help—he was used to being the strong one.

"For the sake of pure speculation," Chris mused. "Let's assume the prophecy is a real thing."

"Let's," Jenna supported her husband.

"What would that mean?" he finished.

"*He, who fell and was reborn evil,*" Liz repeated.

"Adam fell off the roof," I noted. "Does that count?"

Jaden grimaced at me. "It does. This can mean *fall* like the literal act of falling or *fall* as in figurative falling. Like a fallen angel—"

"*...will be awakened,*" Liz continued. "His memory returned when he was with Claire. This could be the awakening."

"But *rise like a phoenix from the ashes*?" Ben questioned the theory. "He hasn't risen. Quite the opposite," he referred to Adam's flat position.

"It could indicate the return of his wings," Jenna suggested.

"And the *black shell* could refer to the color of his wings," I added. Jenna bobbed her head at the thought.

"*His heart will be golden, and his soul will be light*," Liz finished the first part of the quote.

"This would mean that he is good." Chris watched Adam's motionless body with glowing eyes. "He is good."

"He would have *eternal life* like any angel or demon," Jaden played along. "*Great power*—we have seen that."

"*But his love will save us*," Liz quoted again.

"He will be able to feel love," I spoke more to myself. If he was capable of love, that meant there was a chance that we would be together.

Everyone fell silent, letting the meaning of my words sink in.

Jenna and Chris exchanged a look again. This time, I knew what it meant. It was the same thing it meant for me. If he was capable of love, they would have their son back. Ben would have his brother back. They could be a family again.

"*His love will save us*. What does that mean? What from?" Ben asked into the quiet room.

Before he could get an answer, a green light flashed through the room and hit my eyes when Adam suddenly popped his eyes open. They were burning into mine with familiar intensity.

Everybody was on their feet in an instant.

Ben and Jaden were ready to spring at Adam's arms while Chris and Jenna were just an inch from each wing to hold them down in case he should move.

He didn't. All he did was stare at me.

I waited for the hunger to set in, for the strings to tear at me. They didn't. He stared at me, feeling hunger or not, wanting to kill me or not, I wouldn't be able to tell.

What I could tell was that he was in pain. His mouth was twisted and his forehead creased.

"Adam, can you hear me, my son?" Chris addressed him first.

"I can," Adam groaned.

"Don't move," Chris continued. "You were injured."

"I can feel that. My back hurts—like someone ripped my skin off." Adam flinched when he lifted his cheek from the couch. "What happened?"

My heart stopped. He didn't remember. How much didn't he remember? Was everything gone? All of his memory? Jaden gave me a warning look when he felt that I was becoming hysterical.

"Claire, calm down," he instructed while laying his hand on Adam's forearm.

He was right. I wasn't the priority. It didn't matter if he remembered me. It was more important that we got him to stay still so he could heal.

After a deep breath, I was ready. I tore away from Adam's green-glowing eyes and found Liz gaping next to the fireplace. The hysteria immediately disappeared. She must be completely overwhelmed by what was going on.

"Adam," I heard Jaden behind us. "When you spread your wings earlier, they tore through your skin. You need to stay still so the wounds don't reopen. Do you understand?"

"I understand." Adam wasn't fighting any of the Gallagers who had now placed their hands on him to make sure he wouldn't accidentally hurt himself.

"Claire," he called me. An instant wave of comfort rolled through me. His voice was beautiful even when it was distorted by pain. Especially when it was saying my name.

I turned around to face him, unthinking, and my feet had carried me to his side before I could even grasp what I was doing. I knelt down.

"Did I hurt you?" I saw my own disbelieving face reflected in Adam's eyes—the glowing had disappeared.

He was lying there on the couch, enduring pain and a group of people hovering over him, and he wasn't worried about himself. He wasn't trying to escape or fight. He was worried he had hurt me. If that wasn't a sign that there was good in him, then what was?

"I am fine," I took his hand in mine.

A smile spread on his tired face. "Ben, would you mind shifting my right wing a little bit? Something is blocking the blood flow and the tips are beginning to tingle like they are filled with ants."

25.
Bloodline

It was impossible to tell which emotion was more pronounced on Ben's face—shock or amusement.

Jenna and Chris shared a secret smile that told me everything was going to be alright. For the moment at least.

"I would move it myself," Adam pushed. "But I was forbidden to move."

A laugh won the fight over Ben's face. He reached down and gently lifted the wing in the joint at half-length before he pulled it toward Adam's legs—always careful to not touch the wounds—and laid it down there.

Adam's hand was still tightly wrapped in mine. He gave a low groan when Ben moved the feathery extension, and his hand twitched in mine.

Jaden was hovering next to me, making sure that Adam wouldn't hurt me, always at the ready to step in.

"How are you feeling?" Jaden asked.

"It hurts a lot," Adam answered. "How long have I been out?"

"A few hours," Jaden answered.

"Not as bad as I thought." Adam winked at me.

I felt my lips part and shape into a girlish grin. I couldn't believe he was here—alive, and with his memory back. It was almost too good to be true. Of course, there were the scarlet lines on his back that threatened to burst open with every movement. And the fear of him turning against us without any warning.

"Hi, Dad," Adam looked at Chris, recognizing his father. "You look tired."

If he'd had any idea what Chris had gone through since that terrible incident on the roof—I couldn't even think what we all had been burdened with. It was a miracle Adam was back. I could see it in all their eyes that they were feeling the same.

"Not anymore, son." Chris had tears in his eyes. They were exquisite tears of joy.

Jenna hugged Chris with one arm and stroked Adam's cheek with the other hand.

"Mom," Adam smiled up at her.

"Welcome home, Adam," she beamed back at him.

"Jaden," he creased his forehead. "I am sorry I had to knock you out so often—three times—" There was embarrassment in his voice and also a hint of pride. "No hard feelings?"

After all, he had surprised and overpowered Jaden at the graveyard, in his room, and at my house. And Jaden was the most powerful angel I knew. This had been only an appetizer of Adam's power. *The reborn's power will be great*, I remembered. Impossible as it may seem, the prophecy began to grow on me.

"I forgive you. But if you do it again…" Jaden grinned, but his eyes were serious. I didn't even want to imagine what he would threaten Adam with.

"I am sorry, but I don't recognize you," Adam noticed Liz, who was still standing near the fireplace. "Should I?"

Liz broke into a look of astonishment. "You shouldn't—I mean, you wouldn't. We've never met."

I empathized with her. After tearing her from her utterly normal evening plans, I'd thrown her into a room full of supernatural creatures—one of them appearing to potentially be the object of a prophecy. She must have been beyond distressed.

"That's a relief," Adam grimaced as he lifted his head to have a better view of the room. "I was worried this brain of mine missed out on recovering some things. Glad it didn't."

"Adam, that's Liz," I explained. "She's a friend who knows all about your family and you. We can trust her."

"Pleased to meet you, Liz," Adam smiled at her. "I'd be more polite and get up if they'd let me."

"Oh—please, not for me," Liz found her confidence at Adam's joking tone.

I heard Ben chuckle behind the couch.

"How long before I will be able to sit up?" Adam asked, serious this time.

"We don't know exactly how long it will take for the wounds to heal." Jaden repeated to Adam what we already knew. "None of us have ever seen anything like your injuries."

Adam nodded cautiously.

He was bound to stay still until it was safe for him to stand up. However, we couldn't predict the speed of the healing.

This made me think of a factor we hadn't addressed yet.

"Adam," I asked, disturbing the elation of his return. "Who knows you came to see me? Do the demons know? Maureen? Volpert?"

Liz's gasp was audible through the room, even for my weak human ears.

"Excellent point," Jaden cheered. "About time we discuss this."

Adam rested his head and looked at me with a gaze that made me feel like I was the center of his universe. His pale-green, glimmering eyes were the center of mine for sure for that moment before he spoke.

"After I bolted from this house a few days ago, I returned to Volpert's clan," he started. "They weren't happy with me. I'd failed to kill Claire for the second time."

His eyes didn't release mine while he was speaking to all of us.

"Maureen was especially unhappy about the development. She found it unsafe for me to go anywhere near Claire after that." He shuddered at her name. Did he remember his history with her?

"Maureen has been doing anything she can to prevent my memories from returning. It's one thing Volpert want's Claire dead—but Maureen, that's a whole different story.

"For her, it was pure revenge. She wanted to take revenge for my loving you—and if my memory hadn't returned, I would have eventually killed you and never even known how terrible a thing I'd done," he addressed me directly this time. I felt hot and cold at the same time. Hot because of his confession of love, cold because of Maureen's lack of scruples.

Everybody was hanging on Adam's words.

"Maureen suspected you would be the key to bringing back my memory. After she told Volpert her theory—and after my hesitation in the graveyard—he kept me on a tight leash. I only got away a few times to see you from a distance when I took detours while I was out feeding.

"If any of them had suspected that I had visions of you and I saw you in my dreams, they would probably have locked me up."

My heart revolted at the image of a locked-up Adam.

"Whenever I saw you from a distance, I knew I had to be closer. Something was drawing me toward you." Deep sadness filled his features. "Had I known back then that I'd been ordered to kill the love of my life, I'd have run earlier.

"But I couldn't just run. Maureen was the one who found me after I woke up. I didn't know who I was or where I belonged. She gave me a new family by introducing me to Volpert's clan. And with meeting her came the powers—"

"That's incredibly interesting," Liz interrupted Adam's story.

"What exactly?" Jaden wanted to know. His face gave away that he was already playing with theories of his own.

"Maureen—" she explained as if it was the most obvious thing in the world. "With her came the powers. She catalyzed his demon powers."

"I was thinking the same," Jaden agreed, intrigued. "But there is more. What you don't know is that Maureen was Adam's girlfriend for a short while before he met Claire."

Liz walked over to Jaden's side. Now we were shaped in a cluster around the couch. The tension in the atmosphere was gone. It was more like a family sitting together, discussing. Liz was as much part of it as anyone else. She knew everything, and I considered her a trusted friend. She knew more than my actual family—Sophie, the only person who was left.

"This gives an even more interesting twist. Who would have thought—" she stopped mid-sentence and looked at me with her big, brown eyes.

"What are you talking about?" The way she was looking at me made me uncomfortable.

"Maureen's a demon, Adam, right?" Liz asked without looking away.

"She is part of the clan."

"Chris," Liz turned to Adam's father who was curiously waiting for the explanation. "Have you told Adam about his mother?"

Chris swallowed. I could see how the thought made him uncomfortable. It was a sensitive topic even without the new aspect to it.

Still, there was no way around it now. We were unearthing the truth about Adam's death and resurrection, and he had the right to know.

"Your mother was part-demon, Adam," Chris rushed out the words. "She never catalyzed her darker side, but nevertheless, you have demon heritage."

Adam gawked at him. "I was born part-evil?"

"I said part-demon. Not part-evil," Chris corrected. "I believe that's a different thing—your mother was a good person. I would have never guessed. We just recently found out.

"The only way you could wake up after having died is if there was a hidden part of you that hadn't been awakened yet. And the demon part was hidden—until it was triggered by the demons when they killed your angel-human part."

Adam processed for a moment, deep in thoughts he didn't share, before he looked back at Liz with sad eyes. "So what's the theory?"

"Maybe the demons knew about your heritage—at least the demon part—and sent Maureen to try to trigger it."

Now I was gaping at her presentation. "How could they know?"

"Maybe they keep better track of their offspring than our side does—" her voice faded at the indirect accusation toward the celestial species she was serving. Her eyes snapped up at Jaden. "I am sorry."

He dismissed the apology immediately. "You have a point. We've lost track of where angelic blood runs in whose veins on this planet. It's an uncomfortable truth."

Liz smiled at Jaden's honesty.

"Continue the theory," Ben requested from his position behind the sofa. He had been quiet, but the new development seemed to intrigue him as well.

"His angel-side was catalyzed before Maureen got to finish her assignment. Volpert was unhappy that he lost a potential addition to his clan to our side," Liz finished her thought.

"And that's why he wants to take revenge," Ben concluded.

It sounded logical. But what did I know?

"Almost," Adam intercepted. "I agree with the plausibility of the first part. And the way Maureen hates Claire makes me believe there must be more to her grudge than just the fact that I left her before I had even met Claire. There is more to her dedication to getting rid of Claire than that.

"The second part—Volpert's revenge—is something a little different." He freed his hand to graze my cheek.

Heat rushed through my skin where he touched me. I wanted to reach up to hold his hand in place there on my cheek, but I was too aware of five pairs of eyes watching us intently. "Volpert wants revenge on the family that killed his father. He thinks Claire is the last descendant of James Albert Thompson."

I was the only one to look at him with a question mark in my eyes. Everyone else was fashioning an expression of horror I didn't quite understand.

"That's impossible," Jaden objected. "Absolutely impossible."

His icy tone scared me.

"Are you sure?" Jenna questioned one of the two statements. I wasn't exactly sure which one.

"Claire, what do you know about your ancestors?" Jaden asked.

I swallowed. "I don't own a family tree if that's what you mean—" I explained before I went into detail. "—my parents died so early; I never got much information about my family. My mother's side came from somewhere northwest. Seattle area. I never met her parents before they died.

"My father's side is from here. At least, my grandmother—but you already knew that."

"Agnes Hall," Jenna remembered.

"And my grandfather I never met. He was a foreigner who left her before my dad was born."

I glanced at Jaden, well-aware that the others didn't know about his affections for my grandmother. He flinched a little at the thought of Agnes being left. It was obvious nobody would be good enough in his eyes—even if my grandmother had loved my grandfather and had never fallen in love again after him. Jaden seemed to be blind when it came to her. Too much pain had written their story—at least his part of their story.

"He's right," Jenna confirmed what Adam had presented. "Agnes' grandmother was Constance Thompson."

I still didn't understand why this was so important.

"So he is right," Adam murmured.

"No!" Jaden was furious. His golden eyes were narrowed, and his golden-blonde hair was dancing angrily as he jumped to his feet. He almost broke the chair behind him with the force of his motion.

Chris watched him with concern as did Ben. All of them.

I sat in silence for a while, waiting for the mystery to unravel itself, but nobody spoke.

"Would someone please explain to me what's going on?" I lost my patience.

Four angels and one demon looked at me with wide, concerned eyes, their thoughts cloaked in silence.

It was Liz who followed my request.

"Do you remember your conversations with Lucas?" she asked with an expression as if my life depended on remembering.

I didn't have her perfect recall, but I did remember everything Lucas had told me.

"The unofficial history of Aurora," I answered blankly.

"What did he tell you?" she wanted to know.

The others were watching us in shock as I was uncovering the truth myself.

"The demons were haunting Aurora and killing innocent people," I put it together in a short version. "An angel was accused and hunted down before the bookkeeper was warned by his guardian angel that he was going to be next and that they had to kill the real demon."

"Yes," Liz encouraged. "What happened next?"

"One demon was killed; the other got away. The one with the ponytail—Volpert." I froze.

"What did that second one promise?" Liz pushed.

"He wouldn't rest until all of the bookkeeper's family was eradicated."

It hit me—like walking off a cliff.

Liz mirrored my horrified expression when I spoke the words aloud.

"The bookkeeper was James Albert Thompson."

Jaden pulled me to the side and threw his arms around me protectively like he was shielding me from physical danger. But there was no danger in this room. The danger was out there, they were coming for me. Not because of Adam or because I had gotten away before—they were coming for me because of my bloodline. Even if Adam had never existed, they would still be coming for me.

Jaden looked at me, his eyes fearful as he watched me process.

I fought his arms half-heartedly and without much success when another thought hit me.

"Lucas knew. That's why he died." He had shared the story with me shortly before he was killed. "He died because of me."

Jaden nodded, and Liz reached out her hands like she wanted to comfort me.

"He wanted to warn you. One of the last things he told me was to remind you of the importance of that myth." Her eyes were sympathetic. "I am so sorry, Claire."

On a list of the top five worst moments of my life, this was very high up the list. Not because I was in danger—I was used to that. It was because what we had just talked about was only part of the truth. There was something much worse connected to this new development.

I took a deep breath and stopped fighting Jaden. If this was all true, I would need him more than ever.

"—Sophie—"

The room froze when I spoke her name. I wasn't the only last descendant, and they all knew it. Sophie was my sister. The same blood was running in her veins. She was as much in danger as I was—the only difference was that she was oblivious to the menace that would be coming for her.

"I am so sorry, Claire," Adam demanded my attention. "If it wasn't for me, Volpert wouldn't even know—I put you on their radar."

I couldn't think straight. Did it really matter what happened to me if I couldn't protect my family?

"We need to make sure Sophie is safe," I told Jaden.

Jaden's arms were still restricting my movements subconsciously.

"We will," he reassured me.

"Who is we?" I demanded. Sophie was all the family I had left. I needed details. "You all can't risk your lives for us. There must be another way." The Gallagers were as much of a family as I would ever again have. I couldn't be responsible for endangering them. It was different when they were protecting me because we all thought I was in danger because of Adam. But this was different. Now there was a way to keep them safe by leaving them out of everything. For the first time, I understood why Adam had felt it was best if he left to protect me.

"Does she have a guardian angel like me? Can they be trusted? Are they experienced enough?" I asked, desperate for options that would keep Jenna, Chris, Ben, and Adam safe.

Adam—I had just gotten him back. I couldn't risk losing him again. Not even if that meant I had to stay away from him.

Jaden eyed me as I went from panic to anguish and then to vigilance. He seemed disturbed by the fact that I was worried about everyone else so much more than myself. His goals were diverging from mine to a degree that must make his head ache. After all, his mind was set on making sure I stayed alive.

My mind, however, was searching for ways to keep Sophie safe. Before any of them could answer my question, I had found a path that might lead to my sister's safety.

Thinking in that direction made me grateful she was out of town. It made me glad we hadn't been in touch much lately. It would make it easier for her when I would be gone.

"There is a way," I informed the others. Everyone looked at me. Four of them alarmed—they were feeling my determination. Two curious.

"If I give myself up willingly, they might spare Sophie."

"No!" This time it wasn't just Jaden who reacted strongly. It was everyone in the room—besides Adam. He was eying me with a thoughtful expression.

"It might work," he said.

"Absolutely not," Ben and Jaden hissed in unison.

"We haven't spent months protecting you just so you can walk right into their arms," Ben scolded me.

Jaden nodded heavily. I tore out of his grasp.

This wasn't about any of them anymore. It was about my sister. I had to do something.

"You think they would make a deal?" I asked Adam. He eyed me for a moment before he spoke.

"They might make a deal with you," Adam voiced his thoughts.

"She will not give herself up!" Ben insisted.

"Wait a second," Adam stopped Ben. "We could use this to take them down. Set a trap—"

"They don't know that you can remember who you are," I realized, "we could deceive them."

"I have been gone for half a day, that's not longer than an average hunting trip. If I return by myself, nobody will ever know.

"Claire can simply show up and declare her offer. I'll help persuade Volpert to take it. And then the rest of you step in and finish him."

"This sounds too easy," Jaden questioned Adam's plan. "How do we know we can trust you?"

Adam gave a dark laugh. "You can't. Unless you trust that I would have eradicated all of you by now if I'd wanted."

I shrank away from him instinctively. He was still a demon. Memory or not. We didn't know what was really going on inside his head.

"I haven't and I won't," Adam solemnly said. "I just got all of you back. I won't risk this by betraying you."

Jaden was listening, his face like stone. After a long pause, he sat down and spoke.

"This could be our only chance to get rid of Volpert forever."

I couldn't believe my ears. Was he actually supporting Adam's plan? This was a surprise.

"He has been causing this region too much pain. And now that he is after someone important to me—and someone who is important to this someone...," he smiled at me. "We need to make the plan one-hundred percent safe, though. Otherwise, Claire is not going anywhere near that devil. Am I clear?"

"We'll find a way," I jumped in. "If I get to keep Sophie safe without having to die in the process, that makes the plan all the better."

Ben flinched at my dark humor.

"We'll find a way," Adam agreed.

"One-hundred percent safe," Jaden reminded.

"First, I need to find a way to make my wings disappear without bleeding out," Adam said and shifted slightly.

The scarlet lines were fading slowly, but they were still visible around the roots of his wings. The injuries did look better, though.

"Are you still in pain?" Chris asked with probing eyes.

Adam moved his head, and then he propped his chest up on his arms. He held it up for a second before he slammed back on the couch, biting back a gasp of pain.

"Still does," he confirmed. "Not as bad as an hour ago, though."

Jenna laid her hand on his arm, comforting her stepson. "Maybe in a couple of hours, it will be gone completely—"

"Jaden," Liz addressed him with a sudden wave of spirit. "You tried healing the wounds with your powers, and it worked to a limited degree, right?"

"Correct," Jaden answered, surprised.

"What if you all combine your powers? Maybe together, you can overcome that limit."

Liz was right. She had a way of seeing ways where there seemed to be none.

"Why hadn't I thought of this?" Jaden shook his head at himself.

"It's worth a try," Jenna agreed. "Ben, Chris, shall we?"

Chris had his hands on Adam before she could finish her sentence. Ben was a little more reluctant.

"Is it safe?" he asked Liz.

She smiled at him. "There is no reason why it wouldn't be."

At her words, Ben and Jaden added their hands to Adam's back.

"Step back, Claire, Liz," Jaden instructed. "Adam, are you ready?"

Adam nodded.

"On three. One—two—three—"

A blinding light erupted when all of them directed their healing powers at Adam. Liz shielded her eyes, but I couldn't look away. I needed to see what was going on.

The eruption lasted for a moment. Then the room lay in half-light like before.

Adam was standing in front of the couch. I could see his outline after my eyes had adjusted to the darker lighting. His head was bent forward, but his back was upright, the silhouette of two black wings folded against his spine.

Four angels were standing around the winged demon, all expectant for his verdict.

"Adam?" I couldn't wait. "Are you okay?"

He rolled his head in my direction, and two pale-green orbs were glowing at me from his dazzling face.

"I am." He flapped his wings gently and flexed his arms, rolling his shoulders. "No pain."

My heart missed a beat. It had worked.

Within a fraction of a second, he was next to me, his arms wrapped around me. I rested my head against his chest and closed my eyes. It felt like coming home. It was the safest place for me to be—his arms. Only that it wasn't. Adam was a demon. He would be hungry for souls at some point—for life-energy at least. We couldn't rely on him to be the object of a prophecy we didn't even know was real. There was no way we could tell if he could be trusted or if all of this was just a clever mirage to get me to give myself up to Volpert.

I took a deep breath and shoved all thoughts aside. Adam was here, and I was in his embrace. It was all that mattered—for now.

A rustling sound tore me from my moment.

Jaden and Ben were at our sides, both scowling at us, when I reopened my eyes. They were both uncomfortable with the way Adam was monopolizing me—for different reasons.

There was distrust in Jaden's face that echoed my own doubts about trusting Adam. Ben, on the other hand, was jealous. It was plain on his face.

"Adam," Jaden controlled his agitation. "Please let Claire go."

Adam looked at me with questioning eyes. I didn't want him to let go. Playing safe seemed to be the right way to go, considering tonight's previous events. We wouldn't want to push our luck.

"It's okay," I reassured him. "For now, it's probably safer for all of us if we don't experiment."

My heart protested when Adam reluctantly let go of me and stepped back.

"When all this is over, I'll never let you go," he whispered a promise before his hands slid off my arms, leaving a tingly trail where he had touched me.

Jaden relaxed instantly when Adam moved away. Ben, however, held the disapproving look on his face.

I ignored him for the time being and focused on what lay ahead. Make sure Sophie is safe. That was the task I had.

"So, what's the plan? How do we get rid of Volpert?" I tried to get the tension out of the air with a nonchalant tone—and failed.

"Adam?" Jaden looked at the statue-like creature in front of him with a mixture of fascination and concern.

Adam flapped his wings, and with a soft rustle, they disappeared.

"That was easy," he commented, satisfied with what he had just done. "Volpert—we need to make him believe that Claire figured it out by herself. He can never know I have my memory back. If he finds out I betrayed him, we'll all be dead."

"Well, that's something to cheer us up," Ben murmured, his face cold.

"Ben, be nice," Jenna hissed. "We are family; we support each other."

Ben sat down on the couch where Adam had laid before and pursed his lips.

"How do we make him believe I figured it out on my own?" I asked, ignoring Ben's dark looks.

"Lucas Baker." Adam's answer brought back the feeling of guilt. Lucas was dead because of me.

"The demons don't know how much he shared with you before they got him—just that he knew and that he shared something with you," he continued.

If I pretended he'd told me everything, then Lucas' death wouldn't be in vain.

"Okay," I nodded. "How can I contact Volpert? I assume not through you, or he'll suspect something fishy..."

"The phone—" Jaden remembered. "Maureen contacted you from a cell. You could text that number."

Adam gave an approving smile while the others were watching us plan.

"You'll suggest for him to meet you in the graveyard. That's a place he's familiar with. He'll feel safe there."

"Okay," I had my phone out of my pocket within seconds, checking whether the number was still there—it was.

"I'll make sure Volpert comes alone to meet you. Of course I'll be there. He still has this obsession with me being the one to kill you."

I shuddered. Adam had had the chance numerous times, but his curiosity had kept him from taking action.

"The rest of you need to be ready to teleport in. You'll need to be close enough to hear the conversation but far enough away so that Volpert won't sense your energy." Adam grimaced, and his eyes flashed at me—but he was looking through me rather than at me—the hunger I'd seen there was back for a brief moment before he averted his gaze.

"You'll wait and make sure we are alone, and then you strike him down quick. He is extremely dangerous—ancient and stronger than any demon I've seen."

"If he's that strong—how are we going to defeat him?" Ben asked sullenly.

"The same way you healed Adam's wounds," Liz stepped forward. "You work together. Combine your powers, and you'll defeat him."

"All of us," Chris gave Ben a warning look.

The rest of the night was talk of details. Adam had left shortly after we had coordinated everything that was relevant to him. He had tried to make his wings appear and disappear—they did without leaving fresh injuries. That was good news.

The bad news was that Volpert had reacted to my message immediately, which didn't leave us as much time to prepare as we'd wanted.

Two hours. Come alone.

Jaden and I were staring at the display.

"I'll be just a blink of an eye away," he promised. "We all will."

Jenna, Chris, and Ben were nodding so as to support what Jaden was saying.

Jenna had teleported Liz back to her house with the instructions to call if anything unusual happened. Liz had assured us that she would be available anytime if we needed her again.

Now we were ready to leave for the graveyard. Tonight would make all the difference for the safety of my old family and my new. I had to play my role well, and I was determined.

Jenna had brought my car on the way back. Everything was prepared—as prepared as a two-hour timeframe would allow.

We had maybe fifteen minutes left before I would have to drive to the scene of Volpert's future destruction. My left foot had crossed the threshold behind Jenna, Chris, and Jaden when Ben caught me by my elbow and pulled me back roughly.

"Ouch—" I protested.

The others turned around, alarmed by my noisy objection.

"We'll be out in a minute," Ben called over my head and pulled me inside.

"What's wrong, Ben?" I hissed.

He was still holding my arm, hesitant to let go.

"You don't need to do this," he said. His eyes were soft steel, gentle and pleading.

"You know I don't really have a choice," I told him, expecting he would understand. After all, he had lost a brother—gotten him back, but lost him before.

"There is always a choice."

"What would that be? Bolt, leave the country?" I was a little upset with what he was asking. I wouldn't let any of them down. I wouldn't leave my families.

"I would come with you—"

I closed my eyes as my heart fought with itself. I was aware that Ben had feelings for me—deep feelings. But it was new to me that he would choose me over his family. However, I would never put him in the situation to choose. No matter how loudly that tiny piece of my heart was telling me that running with Ben was the best option.

He was waiting patiently while I was going through emotion after emotion. Reading me the way he could, he knew how I was feeling, and he knew how I would answer. I spared us both a moment of awkwardness and removed his hand from my arm gently.

"The others are waiting, Ben." I squeezed his hand and walked out the door. He followed closely.

26.
Sacrifice

The gravel crunched under my shoes as I walked up to the center of the graveyard.

It felt strange to return here after everything that had happened. All of those times I had come here to talk to the dead. And only a few times had been of real significance. The day I had met Adam, his funeral, the day he had returned from the dead—

Tonight was different. I was coming here to make a deal with the demons, knowing that it could be my last hour. I was coming here for Sophie, not for myself.

After all of the planning that had been possible within two short hours, I felt considerably prepared. Four strong angels had my back. They would be positioned around the graveyard, ready to step in.

And, of course, we had Adam, who was supposed to make sure Volpert came alone. If things went as planned, we would be safe within the hour.

However, we didn't know if Adam would stand by his word. He had just gotten his memory back. There was no way of telling if we could trust him. His word was all we had—and I had his kiss—as proof that he was on our side. Even if the prophecy was valid, we didn't know if Adam was the one it was referring to. We had taken a great risk.

The others had gotten out of the car at a safe distance. They would approach by foot and stay out of sight until I gave the signal to attack. By now, they would be close enough to see everything that happened but far enough not to draw attention.

I was sure that they were perceiving the mixed emotions that were flaring up inside of me. The fear for all of them. The worry about Adam. The hope to save my sister.

It was only a few steps to the willow now. The branches were moving in the breeze like slender ghosts.

I stopped and looked at the stone angel. How many times had I stood here and talked to my dead parents?

Sophie was all that was left of my old family. Of course, I had my new family—the Gallagers, who had all but adopted me—but Sophie and I had the same blood running in our veins. And she was innocent. We had to protect her.

"Mom, Dad, I hope you can forgive me for what I am going to do. You know it is for the best. I love you."

"How precious," a cold voice interrupted from behind me.

I turned and looked into Volpert's smiling face. It was an unnaturally sweet mask that had *dangerous* written all over it.

"I am sure they will forgive you for giving yourself up," he said in an equally sweet tone that made me shiver.

How did he know? I hadn't mentioned the nature of the deal in my message—just that I had a deal to propose.

Had Adam betrayed us that easily? My mind was refusing to believe it.

"It really wasn't that hard to guess," Volpert answered my unspoken question. "You have lost everything." His mask changed to an expression of fake compassion, which was even worse than his smile. "Your parents, your trusted friend Lucas, your angel—"

Anger was welling up inside my chest.

"The question is—will they forgive you if you give yourself up for nothing?"

I stared at him in disbelief.

"You didn't think I would spare your sister just because you came here willingly?" he mocked.

"You can't—" I stuttered. "We had a deal."

"We had nothing." Volpert's voice was back to icy. "I didn't agree to anything."

A lump was building in my throat.

"And now it's time for my revenge—James Albert Thompson's last descendants," he mused and gestured at the tree.

Adam stepped out of the shadows and noiselessly glided to Volpert's side.

I glanced at him. There was no sign that he recognized me, no sign of the promise he had made earlier tonight. His eyes were flat and lifeless. If it was an act, it was convincing, without a doubt.

"Such a shame, he doesn't even remember who you are— one would think a love as strong as the one you shared couldn't be forgotten," Volpert claimed my attention. "Isn't it ironic that you will die at the hand of the person you were once willing to die to protect? He will kill you and not even know what he lost."

Volpert motioned Adam to come closer and whispered at him.

Adam lifted a hand—the way he had before when he had sucked my soul—and the hunger returned to his eyes.

I took a deep breath and cleared my head.

The others were waiting for my signal to step in. Everything was set up. Volpert had brought Adam to kill me just like Adam had predicted, and they were alone. It was time.

I swallowed the lump in my throat. "You don't know what love is," I said in a clear voice, full of unexpected confidence. "And I still would die for him." I was ready. "Now!"

Before I could even think, Volpert was encircled by four white-winged shapes. A blinding light exploded around him, and I heard a scream.

I tried to see, but my sight was blocked by a pair of black wings.

Adam scooped me up in his arms and took off with me before I could make out what was going on.

"Where are we going?" I tried to look over his shoulder, but the darkness had already swallowed the scene below us.

"I am getting you to safety," Adam said curtly.

"Why?"

Adam was quiet. I waited for him to answer while he was moving forward with the rising and falling of his wings, carrying me through the night sky.

The plan had been to wait until the others attacked. Take down Volpert together, and then escape together. If Adam was bolting with me, something must have gone incredibly wrong.

"Adam?" I tried again.

"I really need to focus on flying, Claire," he spoke into my tousled hair. "I haven't done this in a while. I am out of practice."

He tightened his grip, and I snuggled into his arms as well as I could with all the rocking movement and buried my face in his shoulder.

After what seemed like a long time, we hit solid ground. Adam set me down on my feet, but his arm stayed around my waist. He seemed as reluctant to let go of me as I was reluctant to step out of his embrace. Tiny sparks seemed to fill the gap between our bodies.

I inhaled his scent, and his hand glided up my back, tracing up my neck into my hair. For a brief moment, there was only him and me—and then I returned to reality.

With a sigh, I tore away from him and looked around.

As far as my weak eyes could make out, there were long fields encircling us.

"Where are we?" I asked.

Adam's eyes glowed lightly when he reached out his hand to hold mine.

"We are safe here." He didn't answer my question.

"What happened?" I demanded. "Why didn't we stay with the others?"

"Everything went according to plan—"

"If everything went according to plan, why are we here—alone?" I interrupted.

"Let me finish," Adam slowly said, carefully choosing his words.

I pulled my hand out of his—it helped clear my head—and looked at him expectantly.

"Everything went well. Dad, Mom, Ben, and Jaden hit Volpert."

"That's good, I suppose." Why wasn't he looking like this was a good thing?

"Almost at the exact time my family teleported in, Maureen showed up. Volpert must have brought her in as a backup in case I would fail to kill you—again." Adam looked at me apologetically.

"But the others got Volpert," I tried to make sense of his serious face.

"Maureen directed a blow at you, that's why I took you away." Adam's face was sad.

"There is more—" I wanted to know. His expression made me uneasy.

"Ben took the hit."

"Oh my God—is he okay?" The small part of my heart that had admitted to having feelings for Ben was screaming at top volume, tuning everything else out. Ben had sacrificed himself for me. He was injured—and I didn't allow myself to think anything more than *injured*; anything worse was not an option—because of me. Guilt and frustration crept up my spine. If only I were stronger, I could protect myself, and no one would need to take any hit for me. I would be able to fend for myself and for the ones I loved. Ben wouldn't be—

Adam watched me with serious eyes as I was suppressing hysteria. "I honestly don't know."

"We need to go back," I reacted mechanically. "We need to help them."

"I can't take you back there right now—not before I know it is safe to go." He gave me a meaningful look. "I promised Jaden I would get you out of there and make sure you are okay—in case anything went wrong."

Of course, Jaden would ask something like that of Adam. My safety was his priority—independent of the fact that my safety was his ticket back home.

"How long before we'll know?"

Adam held my gaze as I was trying to read the answer in his eyes.

"They'll be in touch." He pulled a phone from his pocket. "They know how to reach me."

I watched him check the display with a disappointed look.

"When?"

"Soon."

How long could it take them to finish off Maureen?

"What if they don't?" It was a scenario I didn't want to consider, but it was one possible outcome. If Maureen hadn't been the only backup Volpert had brought without Adam's knowledge, it was highly probable that no one would be left to call.

"They will."

We looked at each other, not knowing what was going on in the other's head.

Adam's eyes were two green disks in the otherwise colorless landscape.

"What do we do now?" I asked, not knowing what else to say.

"We wait."

Adam flapped his wings, and they disappeared between his shoulders, leaving a torn shirt hanging on his torso.

"You must be tired," he assumed. "It's been a long day for you."

"For all of us," I corrected.

Adam shrugged out of his shirt, laid it out on the ground, and sat down beside it. "Please," he gestured at the makeshift blanket.

I dropped next to him and wrapped my arms around my knees. *Ben*, I thought.

That same moment, Adam's phone buzzed. He pulled it out in a movement so fast it blurred in my vision.

"Dad," Adam answered.

My body went stiff with apprehension. I could hear Chris's voice on the other end of the line, but I couldn't understand his words.

Adam was quietly listening, nodding to himself.

"I see," he said after a minute. "I am sorry."

Again, Chris's voice was audible but unintelligible. My fingers clawed into my pants and I nervously bit my lip. What was he sorry for? Was Chris bringing bad news? I couldn't even think—

"If I'd known, I would have warned you." Adam's voice was calm. No reason to jump to conclusions.

"Thanks, Dad. We'll be there within the hour." He hung up and pocketed the phone.

"And?" I couldn't hold back.

Adam's face relaxed in relief. "They're fine."

My heart jumped. I let myself fall back into the grass and smiled, sending a quick *Thank you* to the stars. They seemed to be smiling back.

"Ben's injuries are minor. He might need to spend a day or two in bed to fully recover."

What a relief.

"And the others?"

"Fine, too." He looked down at me and scrutinized my face. "Did he tell you what happened?"

"Not the full story. They'll share more when we return home."

He let himself sink onto his side next to me, head propped up with one arm. "You are beautiful."

My mouth twitched in a mixture between attraction and embarrassment. Could he still perceive my emotional climate, or had he lost the ability when he had become a demon?

Before I could elaborate on the question, he bent down to kiss me.

The sparks were back in place, making my skin tingle where he was close enough. His lips were soft and gentle—the way I remembered them.

My hands searched their way up his chest until they found his neck and disappeared in the shock of dark strands.

Adam's breath became heavier. The fingers of his free hand grabbed me around the waist, and he pulled me closer until the sparks all but melted us together. His hand wandered up my back and came to rest between my shoulder blades.

"Claire," he sighed. It wasn't a sigh of pleasure, it was a sound of exasperation.

He pulled away within the blink of an eye, and I dropped back into the grass. My head hurt a little where it hit the ground. I rubbed my scalp and looked up at Adam in surprise.

Behind the veil of night, Adam's hungry eyes were staring through me. I couldn't feel his hunger yet, but the expression on his face had become all too familiar. He was hungry for my soul.

"I am sorry," he apologized behind his obvious desire.

"It's okay."

The look on his face became pained.

"I am in control." He seemed to be speaking more to himself than to me.

As I watched him, one thing became crystal-clear to me. It didn't matter that Adam had his memories back. He would keep thirsting for my soul. The question was whether it was enough—would his memories be enough to keep him from harming me.

We both sat in the grass, staring at each other.

"We should get back to my parents' house," Adam said.

I nodded, resigned, even though I had tons I wanted to tell him. All of the past months of pain and fear—I wanted to tell him about how I had missed him, how every breath had been agony without him.

It would be too much, and I knew it. I wouldn't scare him off by sharing my torment. Or the intensity of my feelings for him now. Silence was golden. *I love you, Adam*, I plainly thought at him and staggered to my feet ungracefully.

Adam remained in the grass. He pursed his lips and eyed me with a distant look.

"Are you alright?" I asked.

"I will be." He laid his palms flat on the ground beside his body. "Step back, Claire," he asked. "I don't want to hurt you."

I automatically took a few steps away from him. As I watched him sit, the ground beneath his fingers began to softly glow. White streaks of light were pulling toward him, collecting in his hands.

The lines became longer and the radius of his reach wider. A spot right before my toes lit up, and I watched the source wander over the surface, leaving a trail of smoke behind, toward Adam's palms, which were all but radiating with bright light. It lingered there for a second or two, and then it disappeared into him.

Everything was dark again. The smell of burnt grass filled the air between us.

"What was that?" I wondered aloud.

Adam bounced upright, an image of youth and perfection.

"I ate." He hid his face in the shadows. "I am sorry if I scared you. This was the only way to make sure I won't be tempted on the way home."

I wasn't exactly scared—more curious how he had fed on grass and soil, but I didn't dare ask him.

"The others are waiting." Adam walked toward me, his eyes glowing to life and his wings exploding from his shoulders. He held his arms open as an invitation.

Without hesitation, I skipped into his embrace and put one arm around his neck.

"Ready?" he asked.

"As ready as I'll ever be."

He gave me a faint smile then lifted me against his chest and took off without another word.

My body was sore from the constant up and down when Adam set me down at the front door.

"Come in," Jenna ushered us in with nervous looks to the sides. "Are you sure nobody followed you?"

"I am," Adam said and slid past her into the living room.

He had circled the town and flown in from an angle that made the shortest distance to the Gallagers' house with the lowest risk of curious eyes spotting us in the night sky. Of course, my weak human eyes wouldn't be able to tell—

The door closed behind us, and Jenna seized my arm on the way in.

"Did he hurt you?" she asked without further warning.

I shook my head, knowing that all the others in the house would hear my spoken words.

Jenna blinked her eyes in acknowledgment and walked me into the living room.

I was relieved to see that Chris and Jaden were as unscathed as Jenna. They were both pacing, awaiting our return for different reasons. Jaden stopped mid-step and teleported to my side before I could even raise my hand to wave at him. Chris pulled Adam into a hug.

"I'll get you a fresh shirt," Jenna said to her stepson and disappeared.

"Where's Ben?" I asked Jaden quietly.

"He's resting." Jaden's eyes were focused on Adam.

"What happened?" he asked the exact same thing I had been about to ask.

"What do you mean?" I followed his gaze and found Adam watching me with a dazed expression.

"That," Jaden referred to Adam's staring.

My cheeks felt hot, the way they usually did when they were blushed with embarrassment.

"Is it that bad?" Jaden commented on my emotion.

"I'll tell you later."

"So, what happened after Adam got me out of there?" I asked, curious to hear the whole story and eager to change the subject. "Is Volpert gone for good?"

"We can't tell for sure," Jaden jumped onto the new topic, saving my little dilemma for later. "All four of us hit him, definitely. All four hits combined should have been critical, but before I had a chance to verify if he was dead, Maureen showed up.

"She must have hidden invisibly in the trees. She aimed at you when Adam didn't strike immediately. Volpert must have brought her as a backup," he mused.

"I thought the same thing," Adam agreed. "After all the times I've been too weak to kill Claire—I am sorry Claire, but that *was* my assignment when I was with the demons." He gave me an apologetic look. "He must have lost trust in me."

I bit my lip. Commenting on Adam's attempts to murder me wouldn't help any of us. After all, that had been before he had remembered who he was going after. Now that he remembered me, revenge and Volpert's orders didn't have any hold on him. The only thing that did was his own demon-nature—the hunger for energy, for souls. For my soul, specifically.

"If it hadn't been for Ben...," Jaden creased his forehead, and I recognized the tormented face he'd had when he had thought he'd lost me before. "He threw himself between you and Maureen. Her attack hit him."

Once again, I was drowning in guilt. All of them had risked their lives to help me protect Sophie. How could I ever repay any of them?

"He will be alright?" He had to be.

"Yes," Chris responded, and the look on his face didn't betray him.

"A few days of rest," Jaden added. "It's a wound inflicted by a demon—it can't be sealed as easily as normal wounds."

He gave me a serious look. "Ben was extremely lucky."

"I'd like to see him," I blurted. "—to say thank you, I mean."

"I'll let you know when he's awake." Chris smiled at me and then at Adam. "I am glad you both are safe."

"Adam saved me." I glanced at him and found him eyeing me with glowing green eyes.

The dawning day tinted everything in a pale light. The horrors of the night seemed less severe when they were lit up by the first rays of the rising sun.

"You should rest," Jaden reminded me how exhausted I was. The past twenty-four hours had been a roller coaster of fear and hope.

"Your bed is still made," Jenna said to me when she reappeared and put a shirt into Adam's hands. "Yours, too, Adam."

All eyes turned to Adam. Was he going to stay? We had never talked about what would happen to him if our plan worked.

Adam's gaze wandered back and forth between Jenna and Chris, from one to the other, finding the same hope on their faces.

"That is if you want to stay—" Jenna added.

Before he spoke, Adam gave me a long, questioning look, like he was asking my permission. I hesitated for a short second. He was a risk to all of us, but we loved him anyway. He was their family. And he was my fate.

"Stay," I quietly said. It was so low that I wasn't sure I had even spoken, but Adam broke into a smile that made it clear he had understood.

"I don't have anywhere else to be," Adam confirmed.

Jenna and Chris hugged him at the same time. It was a lovely image of a happy family. The only blemish, the insecurity concerning whether we could trust that he had changed enough to not harm any of us.

For a moment, I could see it all. The prophecy—Adam as the redeemed demon who was capable of love and good. It felt plausible—and that was good enough for now. Only time would tell if we were erring in bringing him back into our lives.

"Good night," I said, ignoring the break of day, and gave them some privacy.

"Sleep tight," Adam called after me when I had already turned around to leave. His words enveloped me like a soft cover that carried me into the land of dreams the moment I laid down in bed.

The sun was tickling my face when I opened my eyes.

Jaden was sitting motionlessly on the foot end of the bed, watching me wake with a tender smile.

"What time is it?" I asked into the bright light.

"It's mid-afternoon." He slid up to sit beside me. "The others are downstairs."

"Did I miss anything?" I sat up, ready to jump out of bed.

"Not really," he grinned at my sleepy movements. "It was a long day yesterday. You needed to rest."

I pondered his statement for a moment and figured it was okay if I stayed in bed for a few more minutes.

The day had been long, indeed. Many things to think about.

Would Adam stay for good? If he did, we would need to find a way for him to not draw attention—everyone thought he was dead.

Geoffrey would be returning soon. The Gallagers would need an explanation—or a new butler.

He wouldn't be able to simply pick up his life from before. There were too many factors that made it an impossibility.

Even if he was the subject of the prophecy and even if the prophecy was real—

"Do you think the prophecy is real?" I voiced my thought to Jaden.

His forehead creased, and he rested his back against the pillows.

"Would you stay away from Adam if I told you it's not?" he asked in return.

"Probably not."

"Then what difference does it make?" He looked up at the ceiling then closed his eyes as if he needed to rest them.

He was right. It didn't. Staying away from Adam was not an option anymore. I had seen him do good, even after he had turned bad. There was love in him—his love for his family and, even if it was just a memory, his love for me.

A knock on the door interrupted our conversation.

"Come in," Jaden called.

Chris's head appeared in the door, showing a happy face.

"Oh good, you're awake," he noted. "Ben just woke up and is ready to see you."

I almost fell out of bed—standing up without getting out of the covers first—and jumped into my clothes the second Chris disappeared.

Jaden turned to face the wall like a gentlemen.

Before I rushed out the door, I stopped and gave Jaden a hug.

"Thank you for everything. You deserve to return home—more than anyone. The fact that you are still here, dealing with me after all the mess I have made, proves it."

He blinked his eyes and smiled faintly. "Whether or not I will be allowed back is not for us to decide."

His arm wrapped around me for a second before he pulled out of the hug.

"You should go. Ben's probably waiting.

My heart pounded when I walked down the hallway to Ben's room.

"Come in," he said before I could even knock on the half-open door.

The room itself hadn't changed—the thick curtain was still draped to the sides in the middle of the long space. What was different was the decoration.

The countless drawings of my face had been replaced with drawings of wings. Some of them light, some of them dark.

There was only one portrait of me left. It wasn't any I had seen before. It was new, and I was wearing last night's clothes in it. The background was black as the night.

"Hi, Ben," I said as I slowly made my way up to him.

He was lying in bed, head propped up on a stack of pillows, a sheet of paper in one hand.

After a moment of hesitation, I eventually sat down on the edge of his bed.

He looked fine—a little pale maybe. I took a deep breath of relief.

"You're a hero," I said.

"Maybe," he grinned darkly. "But aren't heroes supposed to sacrifice themselves for others?"

I didn't quite understand what he was saying.

"Which is exactly what you did," I clarified my view on things.

"It's nice you think that highly of me," Ben put down the paper. "I didn't sacrifice myself for anyone else, though." He gave me an unreadable look. "I did it for myself."

"Ben, you took a hit for me. If that's not a noble thing to do—"

"It's a selfish thing," he interrupted. "I didn't do it to save you. I did it to save myself from a life without you."

I didn't know what to say and lowered my gaze, processing his words. He was aware that I loved his brother.

Of course, he felt that there was this tiny part of me that had feelings for him. He would never let it go until there was nothing for him to perceive.

Ben shifted under the cover, watching me think. He didn't seem disturbed by my silence. Instead, he gave me an understanding nod.

"I just wanted you to know the reason." He looked at me with his steely eyes, a hint of hope reflecting in his words.

"You're still a hero to me." I tried a lighthearted smile but got stuck in a grimace that felt like my lips were forming a crooked line.

"Maybe—" Ben's eyes were still holding mine in place. "You know how much I disapproved of you for being an ill-fated attachment to my brother," his words stung, "but I also hated myself for disliking you. And after Adam's death, I thought I could never forgive you," his eyes lit up with the tiniest glow, "but then, when I got to know you better, I found that my feelings for you are so much stronger than my dislike could ever be—"

When I thought back to the first few encounters we'd had—his cold, hateful glares—who would have believed we would end up here, where we were now... It felt like a different time. A time before living through the loss of Adam—for both of us.

"—I know Adam has returned," he continued. "And I know that you love him. Just don't forget that things have changed." His eyebrows knitted together, and his voice changed into a concerned whisper. "He has changed... Now Adam is the ill-fated attachment—" Ben paused and laid his hand onto mine. "You're pure. He is danger... I won't lose you."

My skin heated under his touch. This was a dangerous path for all of us. Adam wasn't dangerous just to me. And I already had my doubts about how things would work out for all of us—Ben's feelings were adding another layer of complexity that I simply couldn't allow.

With a conscientious twist, I slid my hand out from under Ben's and ran it through my hair as an excuse.

I was afraid of hurting Ben. Maybe also a little afraid of myself—that if I let him continue speaking, he would find those right words to change my mind—and I might let him.

"Are you in pain?" I changed the topic. He looked fine, but who knew.

"Nah—nothing that I can't handle," Ben made a dismissive gesture with his free hand. "I might even come downstairs for dinner."

He was acting strong. Or maybe he was stronger than I had given him credit for. He had surprised me with his warm, caring side he had hidden so well in the beginning.

"That's good to hear." It was. And I was grateful that he had recovered so well. However, an unexpected heaviness was weighing down my relief.

There and then, I knew that it didn't matter how I would decide—whether I would change my mind or not—I would always hurt one of them. And hurting them was hurting myself. Any joy I would find was bound to be tainted.

I got to my feet. "Rest if you can," I ordered with a forced smile, which Ben returned with a set face that made me suspect that he wasn't any more comfortable than I was.

When I turned to leave, Ben rolled to his side, and I caught a glance of the piece of paper in his hand.

It was a drawing of me—next to him, his wings framing us and his hand resting on my cheek.

He is an artist, I told myself and averted my gaze. Ben didn't show any sign he had noticed I had seen his artwork.

With a pounding heart and mixed emotions, I crossed the room and hurried out the door.

Jaden was waiting for me at the top of the stairs.

"You look like you could use some fresh air," he said with a crease in his forehead.

Fresh air was exactly what I needed—and to think.

He grabbed my elbow and guided me downstairs, across the hallway, and to the beautiful door with the ornate glass inlays.

The peaceful aura of the back garden was the perfect place to hide for a while and think.

Jaden led me to the wooden bench, and we sat down, side by side. For a moment, my mind was drifting back to Ben's picture. A wave of sympathy followed a moment of wonder before I ended up feeling admiration for his talent.

Jaden cleared his throat beside me and brought me back to the present.

"You still owe me an answer from last night," he ignored my current state of mind and state of emotion—for he, without a doubt, knew how I was feeling.

"What do you mean?" I replied absently. My head was still in cognitive overload.

Jaden bent forward and inclined his head so he faced me.

"What happened after Adam got you out of the graveyard?"

With all of the remaining energy I could find, I directed my attention to him.

"He carried me to a field. I can't tell where—"

"Did he hurt you?" he interrupted, his expression not as serene as I was used to.

"He didn't," I negated.

"What were you embarrassed about earlier?" he demanded, still not entirely convinced everything was alright.

The heat returned to my cheeks, and I could picture myself with a tomato replacing my head.

Jaden's eyes widened. "It can't be that bad…," he encouraged me.

"He kissed me," I admitted, my eyes on my hands. Why was I so embarrassed about it? Probably because of the nature of the kiss and what it had led to—

"He kissed you—that's all?" Jaden interrogated me for details. "You know that I need to know. I don't trust him—not yet."

My mind wandered back to the wasteland Adam had created with his hands while—it was hard to think of it as that—eating.

"You are uncomfortable," Jaden noted.

I was. There was no way around it. Jaden had a right to know. He had given up everything for me. It was only fair that I gave him the truth about how difficult his task might become in the future.

"There was a moment where he was hungry for my soul—" I started.

Jaden jumped to his feet in reflex, ready to shield me from any approaching danger.

"Sit down, Jaden." I pulled him back to the bench gently. "He got it under control all by himself—he didn't hurt me. Not even a little bit."

The way I phrased it made it sound more harmless than it had actually been. Jaden couldn't be fooled.

"He compensated, right?" he asked and eyed me accusingly.

I fidgeted. Alerting Jaden was the last thing I wanted to do. Luckily, I didn't need to answer.

"I did," Adam said from behind us.

Jaden froze next to me. "Who did you kill instead?"

Adam stepped forward and smiled.

"No one," he said and walked toward the wild bush in the center of the garden and laid his hand on top of the little red blossoms. "I found a way—let me show you."

Before Jaden could react, the branches of the bush turned gray while streaks of bright light were running toward them from the ground below and collecting in Adam's palms. Within the blink of an eye, he had absorbed the glowing layer under his fingers and smiled.

Jaden eyed him in disbelief. "You can live off plants?"

"I guess I can," Adam answered, hope lighting up his eyes. "This way, it's safe for me to be around all of you."

He didn't show any sign of the hunger for my soul—or any of the others'—at the moment, but I knew it was in there. Caged for now but in there anyway.

Jaden didn't object. I could see how hard he was trying to believe Adam was—and would stay—in control.

"Mom and Dad won't be happy about the bush," Adam winked at me—my stomach jolted with a million butterflies—and turned to walk back inside.

"You love him," Jaden said—a fact, not a question.

"More than is healthy," I sighed and leaned back on the bench.

"Despite the fact that he is a demon," again, not a question.

I just nodded.

Of course, it would be better for me to love someone whose instinct didn't tell them to drain my soul. Someone less demon, more angel—like the one who had sacrificed himself for me.

I didn't mention that against all rational thought, a segment of my heart had developed an attachment to Adam's little brother, too. That tiny part kept painstakingly screaming for my attention.

It would have to wait.

Even with the prospect of Volpert's defeat, there were plenty of challenges awaiting us in the near future—not all of them involving the supernatural.

My finals were around the corner. It was the one thing I couldn't procrastinate—and I shouldn't. Now that I had the hope of a future once more, I wanted to be prepared to live it.

And I wouldn't be the only one to expect that from me. Sophie would return from Indianapolis soon. She would want to see me graduate, and it was because of my wonderful new family that I could. They had made sure I was safe.

Volpert was gone—for now. Jaden had said, that even if he had survived the attack, he wouldn't be coming for us anytime soon, and his clan would be disorganized without him. His face hadn't been one-hundred percent convincing, but I chose to trust him—he had been right before.

"Do you think we should tell Sophie?" I asked him, my eyes on the dead circle of vegetation.

"We'll have to eventually. Even if Volpert is dead, there will be those seeking revenge for him. Demons are vindictive creatures..."

We had both been staring at the garden for a long while when Jaden pulled me against his side and kissed the top of my head. "I have somewhere I need to be."

He slid to his feet and smiled his angelic smile, his eyes soft-glowing orbs of liquid gold. "I'll be back soon."

And he was gone.

The sun was escaping the sky and vanishing behind the horizon when I sat down on the front porch. Jenna had dropped me off—in her very own angelic way, teleported me into my kitchen. I had cleaned the house just enough to make it look like I had been living there for the past few weeks.

My mind was still caught in the dilemma of the Gallager brothers. Both of them had declared their feelings for me. Hard as it was to admit, my heart was split and beat for both of them. One, I loved in a fated way, but an impending affection for the other was sneaking in.

No matter what would happen, Adam was part of me, and our love had survived death. There was a chance it would survive his instincts. He had demonstrated that he was capable of control, and there was a good chance he would do so again—and I would be at his side to help him get through it.

I wrapped my arms around my legs and rested my head on my knees. For the first time in weeks, I was alone. After our victory, it had been a group decision that permanent supervision had become temporarily obsolete, and I was free to walk more than three steps without a Gallager shadowing me.

It would take a day or two to get used to the regained freedom. By then, Sophie would have returned home, and I would have survived the finals. At least, that was the plan.

Of course, there were more things to consider than that. There would come a point when Sophie would need to learn about the threat she had escaped. I was planning on protecting her from the truth for as long as I could, but with Adam back in my life, it would have to be sooner rather than later. His resurrection, without a doubt, was going to raise questions.

And wasn't it better to be prepared if Volpert did return? We didn't know if or when his clan was going to avenge our attack on their leader. It was bound to happen—*not any time soon*, Jaden had said—but it was going to happen. And then, it would be an impossibility to keep Sophie out of it.

I watched the last rays of sun tint everything in beautiful orange light until my heart felt a little less heavy.

It was impossible to know what, exactly, would be coming for us—even though we knew that something would—but if the prophecy was right, we wouldn't need to fear as long as we had Adam's love, for it would save us all.

Epilogue

JADEN

Their eyes were following me with detestation, resentful glares watching every step I took up toward the front of the translucent hall.

Glistening light was filling every corner of the space. It didn't hurt my eyes the way it would hurt normal ones. My angel eyes were made of light, hidden behind golden irises, disguised as human eyes. Light didn't hurt my kind—I was light.

My feet carried me forward steadily, the familiar yearning to walk through the gigantic portal at the end of the room setting in without delay, but I was forbidden. I had made a decision. I had traded my right to return home. This hall, the gate to the eternal light, was as far as I would get. For now.

Knowing that Claire was safer because of me made it worth the risk of being denied entry forever. Being allowed to protect her made it even worth enduring their stares.

It wasn't how they would normally look at me. I was one of the older ones among them—an idol for some. In our hierarchy, this demanded respect.

It was also not how they should be looking at me. The celestials were supposed to be noble and forgiving ... tenderhearted. But centuries of serving in the realm of mortals had rubbed off on all of us. We weren't as dignified as we liked to think.

One pair of eyes didn't shun me. Compassion was welling, enclosed inside two perfectly round, violet disks, when I walked past the celestial who was sitting a little aside from the others.

Garreth nodded at me, and his chestnut braid moved on his shoulder as I passed him.

Thank you, I thought at him.

If anyone understood, it would be him. He had made the same mistake I had. He had fallen in love with his fosterling. The difference between him and me was that he had been able to let it go. He had moved on as instructed, and he hadn't failed to protect those who came after Constance.

When I looked into his eyes, I saw how he was different from the others ... the purer ones. Those who had never been intrigued by human emotions.

They were perfect in their roles. Functional protectors. A force of good keeping the balance in the world those humans had to live through before it was their time to move on.

Garreth and I were frontier runners. We both had conceived the thought of human love, and it had softened us over decades until we had finally allowed ourselves to dive into the emotion.

It had cost him the respect of the others, and it had cost me everything.

When I'd been assigned to Claire fifteen years ago, I'd thought of it as fate's cruel joke, seeing the smile of the love of my existence—all new and innocent—on Claire's lips. Seeing Agnes's graceful movements in Claire's every step.

I had gotten used to it—to Agnes's eyes looking back at me from Claire's face, staring at me in awe, in fear, in hope...

The tips of my wings' lowest feathers touched on the perimeter of the most elevated area in the hall as I was stepping up the stairs.

They were wide and flat and smooth under my bare feet. Brilliant, little rainbows were flickering across my white garment and up along the stairs, delivering my attention back to where I was headed.

The Council of Elders was throning on the platform, each of them radiant with light.

I shrank as the sight of perfection epitomized my own flaws.

All four of them sat in stoic stance. Nothing could touch their peaceful and righteous aura—or so it appeared as I watched them.

They only gave a sign that they had noticed me when I stopped at the foot of their seats.

"Welcome, brother," Jophiel greeted me in her breezy voice. Her presence trickled down my back in a whirl of elegance and delicacy as she turned her pate to face me, and her translucent hair cascaded in gentle waves, shining in soft shades of the entire color spectrum.

I lowered my gaze in awe from the most beautiful, most perfect of all Elders when her light-gray eyes met mine.

Beside her, Ameretat lifted a slender hand in greeting. Apart from that, her petite figure stayed motionless. Her dark skin was gleaming most exquisitely under strands of silky, black hair, but her equally black eyes remained focused on a distant point behind the present.

Azrael nodded at me, strands of purple hiding his perfect features.

"You have come for re-assessment," Michael finally spoke. The cloak of light flowed around his majestic figure when he stood up. It didn't fail to call for the same reaction I always had when confronted with him.

"I have." My voice was thick with the knowledge that I hadn't achieved what I had promised.

Displeasing the Elders was inexcusable—especially displeasing Michael.

Now it was time for me to defend my actions. I had wanted to keep Claire safe. Instead, I had agreed to a risky path by allowing Adam back into her life, putting her in danger every moment of her short existence. It was a step backward.

And worse than that, I had put her at risk by letting her go to Volpert.

Of course, she was safe and he was gone—for now—but I couldn't rely on the crisis to be over. Only after I'd seen Volpert's dead body would I believe he was gone for good. Until then, I wouldn't rest for even a second—insignificant as that timespan may seem to an old soul like me. I had made poor decisions ever since I had been watching over her—

My chances of ever seeing the other side of the portal were melting away.

"Your mortal fosterling is still alive," he recognized, curls bouncing around his face when he nodded at me, acknowledging the miracle that Claire was still breathing.

"She has been close several times. Fate has been knocking on her door more than once since we have agreed to this arrangement," Azrael noted, and he would know. After all, he was the one to help humans transition into what was awaiting them beyond their mortal lives.

I swallowed.

"What can you tell us about the demon?" Jophiel asked through my fear. She was intuitive and empathic—maybe the closest one to understanding my decision to bargain my right to return home. Love radiated from her like a solid wave. She *was* love. The same way that Ameretat *was* immortality. It wasn't something any mortal could understand.

"He has a conscience," I spoke the first thing that came to my mind.

Jophiel sighed an airy sigh and gazed into the distance.

She drew up the image of Adam from my memory for all of us. In this realm, we all had a shared consciousness we could tap into.

The demon was drifting within all of our minds, his black wings the only proof of his once angelic nature.

"He remembers everything," I defended my decision to allow him near Claire. "He remembers that he marked her. He remembers his family. He helped bring down a powerful demon."

Ameretat changed the vision of Adam to an image of Claire resting in Adam's arms, eyes closed, face full of trust.

"This is dangerous," she warned. "He is immortal. She is human. We don't know if his conscience will be enough to save her."

I saw the image through her eyes, and her angle became clear momentarily. I could feel the danger, the strength of his immortality, the misplaced trust, and Claire's breakable soul next to Adam's dark heart.

"He remembers he loved her," Jophiel shed her perspective onto the vision, and it changed in all our minds.

Suddenly, Claire's trust appeared like an investment. Her pulsing heart was pumping not only blood; it was pumping affection—love—through her entire body. And where her skin touched Adam's, the love would seep into him—crystal liquid disappearing between black stones.

I felt warmth and hope at the possible facet of what we were seeing, and the others could see it, too. There was something in Claire's fundamental being that could change everything. There was a chance.

Azrael turned his onyx eyes on me, presenting me with his slant on the scene. All warmth drained from me when I watched Claire turn cold beside Adam, her pale, trusting face becoming a reminder of my selfishness.

Four consciousnesses were lingering in mine, observing my hope being shredded to pieces as Claire's light disappeared within Adam until she was nothing more than a cold shape against him.

I sank to my knees under the weight of the possibility. "I won't let this happen."

The vision disappeared, and the gleaming light dazzled me after the image of darkness.

Michael's diamond eyes pierced into my mind, and he spoke without using his voice.

"She is still alive. And you still have time to right what you have wronged." He sat and held my gaze for a time span that human senses cannot comprehend before he dismissed me with an infinitesimal gesture of his fingers.

It felt like an absolution.

I bowed my head to the Council and got back on my feet.

All four of them were meeting my gaze before I turned to leave. Jophiel's light-gray irises were gleaming. She *was* love, and love was what she was anticipating.

Her vision of Claire and Adam carried me along the rows of spectators like a raft. All of them had seen what I had seen. They all knew my pain and my hope. But none of them understood—none but Garreth. His violet eyes still held the ancient grief of loss.

After one last longing look at the gate, I continued to the other end of the hall until I stood at the fringe of the realm.

Claire was my last chance to redeem myself. I would stay with her until her very last breath—even if this meant I would never return home.

About the Author

"Chocolate fanatic, milk-foam enthusiast and huge friend of the southern sting-ray. Writing is an unexpected career-path for me."

Angelina J. Steffort is an Austrian novelist, best known for her Wings Trilogy, a young adult paranormal romance series about the impossible love between a girl and an angel. The bestselling Wings Trilogy has been ranked among calibers such as the Twilight Saga by Stephenie Meyer, The Mortal Instruments by Cassandra Clare, and Lauren Kate's Fallen, and has been top listed among angel books for teens by bloggers and readers. Her young adult fantasy series Shattered Kingdom is already being compared to Sarah J. Maas's Throne of Glass series by readers and fans.

Angelina has multiple educational backgrounds including engineering, business, music, and acting, and lives in Vienna, Austria with her husband and her son.

Printed in Poland
by Amazon Fulfillment
Poland Sp. z o.o., Wrocław

35471766R00283